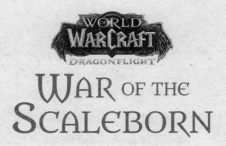

WAR OF THE SCALEBORN

Also available from Titan Books

WAR OF THE SCALEBORN

COURTNEY ALAMEDA

TITAN BOOKS

World of Warcraft: War of the Scaleborn
Print ISBN: 9781785655050
Ebook ISBN: 9781785655067

Published by Titan Books
A division of Titan Publishing Group Ltd
144 Southwark St, London SE1 0UP
www.titanbooks.com

First Titan edition: October 2023
10 9 8 7 6 5 4 3 2 1

A CIP catalogue record for this title is available
from the British Library.

Printed and bound by CPI Group (UK) Ltd, Croydon CR0 4YY

To Bo, who brought me to Azeroth,
And to champions past, present, and future—
We still have so many stories to tell one another.

THE BROODLANDS

THE
WAKING
SHORE

THE
EMERALD
PLAINS

WAR OF THE SCALEBORN

PART ONE

A Kingdom Born

CHAPTER ONE

WHAT HAVE YOU DONE, ALEXSTRASZA? VYRANOTH wondered as she soared over the rising spires of Valdrakken. *What is this place?*

In all her long years, Vyranoth had never seen dragonkind build such strange aeries. Alexstrasza—Vyranoth's oldest friend and the newly made Dragon Queen—had called Valdrakken a *city*. Vyranoth rolled the word over her tongue, thinking it tasted like titan magic. *City.* A foreign word befitted so foreign a place.

Vyranoth understood none of the sights below: Hand-wrought stone spires perched upon the mountains of Thaldraszus. Rivers ran through the sky on gilded spines. Floating islands nested in the clouds, their waterfalls tumbling into the open air. Young drakes chased one another, nipping at each other's tails and laughing. Dragons roosted on grand platforms, talking together and enjoying the beauty of the day.

Valdrakken. *City.* A place that seemed to radiate peace . . . and yet dark doubts crept into Vyranoth's heart. Every dragon in sight bore the mark of the keepers' Order magic, which had utterly transformed them, mind, body, and soul. Vyranoth did not recognize the ordered as dragons, though they were certainly dragon-*like*. On the ground, the ordered folded their wings against their backs like birds, whereas natural, primal dragons like Vyranoth relied upon their wings both on the ground and in the air. The ordered did not look like proper dragons; not anymore. By embracing this strange power, Alexstrasza and her followers had turned their backs on the very planet that had given them life.

As a primal dragon in Valdrakken, Vyranoth was an outsider among her own.

So many of you have chosen the keepers over your own kind, she thought. With a great flap of her wings, she crested one of the city's peaks. Even as she cruised along the city's outskirts, she counted hundreds of ordered dragons, their jewel-toned hides glittering in hues of blue, black, bronze, green, and red. Each color represented one of the five dragonflights led by an individual Dragon Aspect.

The five Aspects had been the first to be infused with the keepers' Order magic, to embark on a dangerous path, to turn their backs on the natural order of things. Now, they had convinced so many others to follow them into this folly.

Vyranoth checked her speed, then dived beneath an arch of ornamented stone. The shadows of her wings rippled over the city's jarring angles and sharp, golden edges. Below her, the titan-forged swarmed over the mountains like flies on a carcass, carving stone from the rocky flanks to build their spires and arches.

Even if the Aspects had dreamed up Valdrakken on their own, the city brimmed with their masters' power. Here, the keepers' influence was omnipresent, inescapable. Order imbued the very wind that filled Vyranoth's wings, nostrils, and lungs, sending a shudder across her scales. Had Vyranoth not made a promise to Alexstrasza, she would have turned tail and never looked back. Yet Vyranoth was a dragon of her word.

Today, the Dragon Queen and the red dragonflight would swear an oath to defend their world. *Azeroth,* Alexstrasza had called it, though it sounded like yet another titan word. Alexstrasza had personally invited Vyranoth to the ceremony; perhaps she hoped that Vyranoth could be convinced of the righteousness of the Aspects' cause. Vyranoth knew her old friend to be honorable and true. Alexstrasza would not have chosen this path without good reason. Still, Vyranoth's doubts remained. Why should dragons have to change themselves to fulfill the wishes of the keepers? To her mind, it made no sense.

A great trumpeting echoed off the city's spires. On instinct, Vyranoth banked toward the sound, sweeping past the hollow bones of a half-finished spire. A multitude of dragons took flight, their scales flashing in the sun. The thundering of their wings whipped up the wind and turned the clouds into a froth. Had Vyranoth not been so unsettled by the sight, she might have found it exhilarating. She climbed higher with ease, lofted by the air currents that swirled off a thousand wings.

"Vyranoth, my friend!" A red dragon glided into Vyranoth's airstream. Like all ordered dragons, the red had a sinuous, elongated neck and longer forelegs, which when on the ground would allow him to stand on four feet rather than two. The ordered had slim heads and lacked a primal dragon's thick, impenetrable armor on the skull and spine. This particular red had two heavy, twisting horns on the top of his head and frills over each eye.

The red was accompanied by a small contingent of other reds—four, to be exact. In the Dragonwilds, no one would have dared approach Vyranoth with such an easy manner, especially not in a pack. Had the keepers' magic made them forget the customs of their kind?

"I am Saristrasz," said the first red, performing an elegant roll in the air, as if in greeting. "Majordomo to the Dragon Queen. Alexstrasza has asked me to be your escort during your stay in Thaldraszus."

"I thank you, but that shall not be necessary," Vyranoth said, not wanting to offend. "I do not plan to stay in Valdrakken long."

"Alexstrasza thought you might say that," Saristrasz said with a laugh. "And she was right, you speak very well for one of your kind!"

Your kind? Vyranoth narrowed her eyes but said nothing.

"At the very least, allow me to show you where today's ceremonies are to be held," Saristrasz said. "You are our honored guest."

"Very well," Vyranoth replied, following the majordomo

as he banked right. The other reds followed them, close in pursuit.

As they came around the corner, the whole of Valdrakken opened to them. A white spire rose in the distance, scraping the clouds overhead. Rivers flowed around its base. Lush, purple-leafed trees clustered close along their banks. At its peak, there looked to be a landing platform of sorts.

"That is the Seat of the Aspects," Saristrasz said, his voice lilting with pride. "The tower is the soul of Valdrakken, where our honored Aspects conduct business on behalf of the five flights. But the Seat is not our destination today. Come, Vyranoth, and let me show you Tyrhold!"

"Tyrhold?" Vyranoth asked, suppressing a harsher tone. She recognized that name—Alexstrasza had spoken to her often of Keeper Tyr and his *interference* in the affairs of dragonkind. If she recalled correctly, Tyr had been the one to suggest the Aspects be ordered.

"Yes, a great edifice in the east," Saristrasz said, nodding to the stone rivers. "It is the source of the life-giving waters carried by aqueducts throughout the city."

"Aqueducts . . ." Vyranoth said, testing the word carefully, looking at the water shimmering below. "Tell me, why is it important to move the water from one place to another? Why must you remove it from its source, especially when it flows in such abundance throughout the Broodlands?"

"The water serves many purposes in Valdrakken," the majordomo said as they crested a hill. "It is easier to conduct the water via aqueducts than by any other method."

Vyranoth looked at Saristrasz from the corner of her eye, lifting a brow.

He chuckled. "I admit, Valdrakken was startling at first— the buildings, the aqueducts, the temples, the gardens. But I promise you, it will make more sense in time."

Buildings? Vyranoth thought. *Temples? What need does dragonkind have for such things?*

"Perhaps," she said, uneasy. Nothing about Valdrakken made sense to Vyranoth, and she wasn't certain she wanted that to change.

Her escort led her past a waterfall that splashed down a mountain's face. Cool mist dampened their wings. They swept over neatly tended emerald gardens that filled the air with the scent of sweet honey, then dipped past the scalding heat of the black dragonflight's forges.

There should have been a certain delight in following Saristrasz through the city, in swooping beneath its arches and scudding over the clouds, in listening to the joyous calls of the dragons as they headed for the ceremony. Yet everywhere Vyranoth looked, all she could see was what Valdrakken could have been without the titans' influence. How tall had that mountain stood before it had been whittled down into "buildings" by the titan-forged? Why had the gardens been pruned into an orderly perfection, rather than be allowed to flourish and grow in their own wild designs? And what of the noble, primal silhouette her brothers and sisters once had—the strong carriages, the majestic bearings—why had those, too, been carved away for order's sake?

Where the titans had found flaws, Vyranoth saw unbroken beauty. The world needed no improvements, no titans, no Order magic. Perhaps the world did not need *cities* and *buildings* and *Aspects* either.

Saristrasz and Vyranoth skirted the flank of a sharp cliff. A grand spire rose in the distance—no, Saristrasz had called it a *tower*—and its white marble walls gleamed in the sunlight. The tower pointed to the heavens, shooting a bright beam of light into the sky. Tall white stones encircled its base, reminding Vyranoth of outstretched wings. All the rivers in Valdrakken seemed to flow from its source.

Tyrhold, Vyranoth thought, her lip curling in upset.

Hundreds upon hundreds of dragons hovered around the tower, darkening the day with their wings. *So many of you,* Vyranoth thought, casting her gaze over the assembly. *How could so many of you have chosen this path? Easily rejected yourselves and everything you once were?*

"Welcome to Tyrhold," Saristrasz said. "Come! The Dragon Queen has requested your attendance on the main platform. You are to be in the presence of the Aspects themselves."

"What an honor," Vyranoth said flatly. If Saristrasz noticed her discomfort, he said nothing.

They alighted on the main platform. Great stone ribs rose high overhead. "Pillars," the majordomo said when he caught her looking at them. The peaks of Thaldraszus loomed on either side of the tower, proud and powerful. The keepers' presence was at its thickest here, creating a dull ache in the base of Vyranoth's skull. It hummed in her ears like the silence after a thunderclap and crawled under her scales like mites. Perhaps Order magic had made their influence easier to bear, but Vyranoth could hardly stand it even for an instant.

A crowd assembled on the platform. Vyranoth thought she recognized a few among them: That large, ancient red had to be Tyranastrasz, Alexstrasza's consort and confidant. His brown scales were now the warm, brilliant color of heart's blood. He turned his head as if he sensed Vyranoth's gaze, then gave her a nod in greeting.

Vyranoth returned the gesture, careful to keep her expression even. Inside, however, her heart was a maelstrom. To think that a dragon of his stature had accepted the keepers' shackles! Perhaps he had done it out of love for his mate. Or perhaps, in all his wisdom, Tyranastrasz saw something in Order magic that Vyranoth could not.

An unfamiliar shade crept into Vyranoth's heart. What wisdom was there in accepting power that fundamentally altered who you were? Were dragons not noble enough, not courageous enough, not *strong* enough without the keepers' magic?

Tyranastrasz wasn't the only one. As Vyranoth cast her gaze over the assembly, she did not see a single natural-born dragon. She barely recognized Malygos, now the blue Aspect, whose eyes glowed with arcane fire. Runes shimmered over his wings. His mate, Sindragosa, stood at his side, speaking to another blue. Sindragosa tossed her head and laughed at something the blue said.

Alexstrasza's sister, Ysera, had become the green Aspect. Her scales had deepened to the color of spring leaves, and a set of four great golden horns adorned her head; flowers sprouted beneath her talons. She stood surrounded by her flight, all dragons who Vyranoth could not name. Smaller creatures frolicked in the shade of their wings. Butterflies danced in the air around them. Even from this distance, Vyranoth could smell the verdant life emanating from the green dragonflight—budding grass and wet earth.

On the other side of the chamber, Nozdormu shifted his wings, sending up a cloud of shimmering bronze sand. Alexstrasza said he could now manipulate time itself. Nozdormu had been powerful before accepting the keepers' magic, but to be able to manipulate time itself? She could not fathom such an ability.

Finally, she turned her attention to Neltharion, the black Aspect. She knew of him from Alexstrasza's stories but had not been acquainted with him personally. He stood taller and broader than the other three Aspects; his scales were as black as char and as gleaming as obsidian. According to Alexstrasza, the keepers gave Neltharion dominion over the earth and its deep places.

Alexstrasza herself, however, was nowhere to be seen.

The Aspects were surrounded by members of the red dragonflight—and there were even more red dragons gliding in the skies above. The Aspects circled a white stone carved to resemble a dragon safeguarding a gemstone with its wings. A large, blood-red ruby was set into the spire's base. Even from where she stood, Vyranoth could sense the magic within the stone.

"What is that object?" Vyranoth asked, nodding to the carving.

"It is the Oathstone of the red dragonflight," Saristrasz replied. "Beautiful, is it not? Once empowered, it will become a symbol of our promise to defend Azeroth and all its denizens. The red dragonflight plans to house it at the Ruby Life Pools, once we have finished their construction."

Oathstone? Ruby Life Pools? Vyranoth wondered, cocking her head to look at the red. This was all so strange—the longer Vyranoth lingered in Valdrakken, the more unsettled she became. None of this seemed natural; how could Saristrasz follow the Aspects so fully and unquestioningly?

"Tell me, Saristrasz," Vyranoth asked, her throat dry, "why did you choose to be infused with Order magic?"

Saristrasz was silent a moment, considering her question. He made a humming noise in his throat, then said, "Galakrond changed things for our kind. He showed us—no, the *Aspects* showed us—that dragons are stronger when we work together."

"Could you not have supported Alexstrasza as you were?" she asked. "In your true state?"

"I suppose." He smiled and spread his wings, gesturing to the dragons who filled the space around them. "But I wanted to be a part of the red dragonflight. I wanted to be something *greater* than myself, to witness the heights the Aspects would help us reach. There is no higher calling in this world."

Vyranoth's stomach churned, but she made no reply. Before she could ask anything further, a roar reverberated through the crowd. Movement drew her gaze to the tower's base.

The doors of Tyrhold had been thrown open, and Alexstrasza stepped outside, her head high. Like the other Aspects, she was wholly changed: Sunlight glinted off her gold-tipped horns. Her scales shimmered vermillion. Alexstrasza now walked on four feet with her wings tucked against her back, her movements swift and sure.

Vyranoth could still see hints of her old friend under the ordered exterior: Alexstrasza had always emanated gentleness and kindness. Most dragons would find it difficult to match her grace and charisma. Her eyes glittered with a fierce, unyielding intelligence.

She was Alexstrasza . . . and yet she was not *Vyranoth's* Alexstrasza. She was the Life-Binder. The Dragon Queen. The red Aspect, leader of the red dragonflight.

The thought drove shards of ice into Vyranoth's heart.

A bipedal figure strode out with Alexstrasza, one who resembled the titan-forged creatures who scurried about the city. This one, however, stood taller than the rest of the titan-forged and wore garments of crimson and gold. One of his limbs gleamed silver in the light.

Ah, Vyranoth thought, recalling the tales Alexstrasza had told her of Galakrond, *that one is Keeper Tyr.* She suppressed a growl. Tyr had ordered the Aspects and charged them with the creation of the dragonflights; he had been the one to teach dragons about *cities* and *buildings.* No doubt Tyr had coerced Alexstrasza into this ceremony—why else would she need to make a public pledge to protect their world? Was her intention not enough? Were her *sacrifices* not enough?

Alexstrasza halted before the Oathstone, spreading her wings in welcome. "Greetings, my friends! Full glad am I to see you all assembled on such a momentous occasion!"

A great cheer resounded through the skies and shook the stones beneath Vyranoth's feet. It echoed off the peaks of Valdrakken in a rising chorus.

"I extend a hearty welcome to my fellow Aspects and their flights this day," Alexstrasza continued, "and I am thankful that our benefactor, Tyr, has joined us for this event."

More cheers. This time, Saristrasz lifted his head and added a bugling call to the celebrations.

"Today, the red dragonflight will be the first to make a sacred pledge," Alexstrasza said. "As we empower the Oathstone of our flight, we swear to protect and defend this world from harm, not just to Azeroth itself, but also to the keepers"—Alexstrasza nodded to Tyr—"and to one another. In the coming days, the dragons of the green, black, blue, and bronze flights will hold similar ceremonies and empower the Oathstones that their flights have created."

"This is madness," Vyranoth muttered under the dragons' joyful shouts. In her heart of hearts, she wanted to rush to Alexstrasza and beg her to reconsider her actions. She wanted to bristle her mane and chase Keeper Tyr out of the Broodlands. She wanted to call out to the assembly and have them rend Tyrhold from the mountainside.

But Vyranoth did none of these things. Alexstrasza had made her choice.

The Dragon Queen approached the red dragonflight's Oathstone with the keeper. "Now, let us begin," she said, spreading her wings wide. The dragons in the chamber fell silent.

"I, Alexstrasza the Life-Binder," she began solemnly, "Aspect of the red dragonflight, and queen of the five flights, do so swear to defend Azeroth this day."

The Oathstone shot a beam of ruby-red light into the heavens. The light tinged the skies as with sunset, scattering pink and orange hues across the clouds. Dragons gasped in wonder.

"I charge the red dragonflight to protect all life," Alexstrasza said, her scales reflecting the Oathstone's ruby glow. "Whether it be found in the Emerald Plains of the Broodlands or high atop the mountain peaks of Kalimdor, deep within the oceans, or in desert climes, we vow to maintain harmony and peace in this world."

The ruby light emanated out from the Oathstone, spreading among the assembly. Cries of glee and delight stole through the crowd as the Oathstone's magic touched the red dragons. When it drew close to Vyranoth, she backed away in fear. Beside her, Saristrasz sucked in a breath. Light danced across his scales, which flamed as red as a sun-kissed horizon.

"This magic," Saristrasz said under his breath, his eyes wide with wonder, "it is . . . it is so *warm*. I have never felt anything quite like this."

Vyranoth only growled, keeping low to the ground. The Oathstone's magic burned in her heart, beckoning to her. She snarled, pushing away its temptation.

"On this day," Alexstrasza continued, "each red dragon is granted a greater measure of courage, empathy, and resilience. May you show bravery in the face of danger, seek common ground with your enemies, and always have the strength to take to the skies in defense of our beloved home. So long as we draw breath, Azeroth shall not fall. By wing and by talon, we shall see it done.

"On behalf of the red dragonflight, this I swear upon our Oathstone," Alexstrasza concluded.

Keeper Tyr stepped forward next. "As an envoy of the titans, I accept your oaths this day"—Tyr extended his giant silver hand toward the Oathstone—"and seal them here, in stone. May this Oathstone stand as a reminder of the pledge the red dragonflight has made—not just to me, but to this world. Fly well and wisely, and may you fulfill the measure of your ordering."

A final, glittering burst of red light exploded from the Oathstone, so powerful that it rattled Vyranoth's teeth.

Another cheer rose, a chorus of voices that lifted high on the winds. As the other Aspects stepped forward to congratulate Alexstrasza, Vyranoth turned to Saristrasz, her stomach churning.

"Before I return to the wilds," she said, "I would like to have a private word with Alexstrasza, if I may?"

"But of course," Saristrasz said, his scales still aglow with the Oathstone's magic. "Wait here, and I will make the arrangements with the Dragon Queen."

...

A SHORT TIME LATER, Saristrasz led Vyranoth to a bright cavern within the Seat of the Aspects, though *cavern* wasn't quite the word for the place. Vyranoth paused at the threshold, lifted her gaze, then drew in a sharp, surprised breath. Never in her life had she seen such beauty: The chamber was lit with a soft, aquamarine light, as if filtered through warm southern seas. Two stone dragons reared before a stunning "stained-glass mural"—Saristrasz's words—that portrayed a dragon in flight. The glass glimmered in red, green, blue, bronze, and black, each color representing one of the five dragonflights.

"I must return to my duties, but Queen Alexstrasza will meet you here in the antechamber," Saristrasz said, almost by way of apology. "Keeper Tyr requested an impromptu audience with the Aspects after the ceremony, and they have only just arrived. I do not expect them to be long."

"Very well," Vyranoth replied, though she was anxious to quit the city.

Saristrasz dipped his head. "If there is anything else you need, the drakonid will assist you." With another bow of his head, the majordomo turned and exited the antechamber, leaving her alone.

Two red drakonid stood watch outside, giving Vyranoth her privacy. The antechamber's only egress point seemed to be its entrance, and the thought put Vyranoth on edge. The drakonid were more manifestations of the titans' stain— tarasek taken and twisted by Order magic. Were natural tarasek not enough for the keepers? Must they, too, be befouled by magic?

Vyranoth knew she need not be troubled. Alexstrasza's heart remained noble and true, and the Dragon Queen would not force Order magic upon anyone. Still, she could not ignore the doubt creeping into her mind. It mingled with a yearning, too, which left Vyranoth adrift on uncertain winds. While Vyranoth rejected the idea of submitting to the keepers' Order magic, she *liked* the idea of dragonkind living together in harmony. Like Alexstrasza, Vyranoth believed dragonkind could achieve greater things when they worked together. That perhaps they *needed* one another.

The Broodlands were home to many dragons, both ordered and primal, but the Aspects had clearly delineated territories in which their word was law: the Waking Shores, the Emerald Plains, the Azure Span, and Thaldraszus. The Broodlands were surrounded by the greater Dragonwilds, where most of the primal dragons had retreated after the Aspects began ordering new dragons.

Much as Vyranoth did not mind this arrangement in theory, trusting the keepers seemed like folly. Tyr had helped the Aspects destroy Galakrond, but beyond this, Vyranoth had no reason to trust his motives.

Minutes passed, stretching longer. The sun changed its slant. Just as Vyranoth considered taking her leave, an oblong-shaped light flared at the top of the staircase in the middle of the room. Vyranoth had seen the blue dragonflight creating similar magical rifts before—she believed they called them *portals*. Keeper Tyr emerged from the light, followed closely by Alexstrasza.

Paying Vyranoth no heed, Tyr said, "Think carefully upon my words, Alexstrasza. I only wish to see your dragonflights thrive."

Alexstrasza lifted her chin and narrowed her eyes, a subconscious gesture that had forever signaled her polite disagreement. To see her do it now, in her ordered form, was . . . *unsettling*.

"I will consider your counsel," Alexstrasza said.

The keeper nodded. "See that you do."

Alexstrasza's eyes narrowed further as the keeper turned away.

Vyranoth cocked her head, thinking. *So, the Dragon Queen appears to retain her free will, but the keepers still seek to exert control over her. What is it that Tyr wants Alexstrasza to do?*

"For now, I shall take my leave of Valdrakken," Tyr said, starting down the steps. "I will return when Neltharion and the black dragonflight are ready to empower their Oathstone."

"Very well," Alexstrasza said.

Keeper Tyr swept past Vyranoth, barely sparing her a glance.

As soon as he was gone, Alexstrasza shed her solemnity. "Vyranoth!" she cried, bounding down the stairs. She pressed her cheek to Vyranoth's. "Words cannot express how glad I am to see you, my friend. Thank you for coming."

The joy in her voice melted the ice in Vyranoth's heart.

"And I, you," Vyranoth said. Alexstrasza still *smelled* like herself, at least—though there was a new, underlying note that Vyranoth couldn't quite identify. To her palate, it seemed to be the scent of smoke and stardust, something not of their world.

"Tell me, was your journey a good one?" Alexstrasza asked. "Have you eaten?"

"The winds were calm. The Broodlands have blossomed under your care."

Alexstrasza beamed, her golden eyes glowing. "I would love to show you more—the gardens of Valdrakken, perhaps? Or perhaps the new construction on Neltharion's Obsidian Citadel? There are so many wonders to share. Give me but a moment to inform the other Aspects, and then we can take flight."

Before Vyranoth could muster an answer, Alexstrasza turned to the portal and started back up the stairs.

"That . . . will not be necessary," Vyranoth said, trying to take the cold bite out of her tone.

Alexstrasza pivoted back to face her friend. "Whatever do you mean? I was hoping we might at least spend the afternoon together."

"You know I treasure our friendship, Alexstrasza, but this . . ." Vyranoth trailed off, shaking her head.

"If you have something to say to me, please continue." Alexstrasza used a hint of that same diplomatic, queenly tone she had used with the keeper. "You have always been my most honest and straightforward of friends, Vyranoth. You know you can be true with me."

Vyranoth prided herself in her sincerity and forthrightness, but somehow, this issue felt more fraught than most. To criticize Order magic was to criticize Alexstrasza herself.

Vyranoth needed to choose her next words carefully. She no more wanted to hurt her friend than she wanted to bend to the keepers' will.

"You are following unknown winds, my friend, and I worry for you," Vyranoth said. "You are the most honorable of our kind, Alexstrasza. I loved you as you were, and it pains me to see you bow, to change yourself for another. From where I stand—admittedly, on the outside—I fear the keepers seek to exert control over you and your flights."

"My agency remains inviolate," Alexstrasza said. "Tyr offers what guidance he can, but my decisions are my own."

"What will you do if he asks you to force dragons to join your flights?" Vyranoth asked. "Will you disregard the desires of those who disagree with you?"

"No, never," Alexstrasza said with a shake of her head. "I have sworn that Order magic will always be a choice."

"Swear it to me, then," Vyranoth said. "Swear to me that you will never force a primal dragon to bow to the will of the keepers."

Alexstrasza looked Vyranoth square in the eye. "I swear it."

In all their long years of friendship, Vyranoth had never known Alexstrasza to lie. Deceit wasn't in her nature. And yet, the Alexstrasza standing before Vyranoth today was *not* the same dragon who Vyranoth had known through the long ages. The keepers' magic altered Alexstrasza's physical form; had it changed her integrity, too? Would she, like her keepers, do anything to achieve her goals . . . even lie to one of her oldest and dearest friends?

Vyranoth could not answer these questions. Only time could do that.

"I trust you, Alexstrasza," Vyranoth said, leaning forward and pressing her forehead to her friend's, "but I do not trust your keepers."

CHAPTER TWO

ALEXSTRASZA'S HEARTSTRINGS PULLED TAUT, MAKING it difficult to breathe. As Vyranoth walked away, Alexstrasza nearly cried out, *Can you not stay and listen, just for a moment more?* The Life-Binder held her tongue. She would not beg, especially when Vyranoth refused to see reason.

Of all the dragons in Azeroth, Alexstrasza thought Vyranoth would understand why the Aspects chose order over their primal natures. She and Vyranoth had ever been of one heart, one mind. Order magic made it *easier* to protect innocent lives, a goal that Alexstrasza and Vyranoth shared. How many dragon clutches had she helped Vyranoth save from Galakrond's hunger? Had she not fought with wing and talon in defense of Vyranoth's own brood? In defense of Vyranoth *herself*?

Vyranoth had always been headstrong—the same stubbornness that made her slow to accept change *also* made her a keen survivalist. Still, she had nothing to fear from

Order magic. Had she but stayed in Valdrakken, Alexstrasza could have shown her the wonders of its transformative powers—how these could be wielded as tools to achieve their shared desires. Instead, Vyranoth chose to close herself to Alexstrasza, to the Aspects, and to the future of dragonkind.

However, the Life-Binder knew Vyranoth better than any other; though her heart moved like a glacier, it would melt in time.

When Vyranoth disappeared, Alexstrasza sighed and turned back to her duties. She could not spend long wallowing in self-pity—the other four Aspects awaited her in the Seat's towering aerie.

The Seat of the Aspects was one of Alexstrasza's favorite places in Valdrakken. She teleported to the top in a flash of light. The tower soared high over the city, affording her an all-encompassing view of the Broodlands. On a clear day, she could see everything from the volcanic ridges of the Waking Shores to the rolling hills of the Emerald Plains. When the winds blew from the south, Alexstrasza could even smell the woody, earthen scents of the ancient redwood trees in the Azure Span. Today, dragons filled the skies over the city, celebrating the red flight's newly instated Oathstone. They dipped, danced, and dived through the air, basking in the magic it had bestowed upon them.

Alexstrasza wished her heart could know such peace, but Vyranoth's words left her unsettled . . . particularly in the wake of Tyr's request.

The dragonflights must grow more quickly, Alexstrasza, Tyr had said. *Take primal dragon eggs from the wilds and infuse them with Order magic. Your flights must be prepared to defend Azeroth when the time comes.*

Alexstrasza had balked at the idea, especially because it hadn't been phrased as a request.

Inside the upper chamber, Malygos lounged before his dragonflight's banner, tapping his blue-tinted talons on the floor and exuding an aura of boredom. Ysera sat to Alexstrasza's left, her emerald tail tucked around her toes. Alexstrasza's sister regarded her with kindness, and perhaps a little sympathy. They had all seen Vyranoth's departure, no doubt.

Neltharion stood to Alexstrasza's right, his face unreadable, his eyes closed. Thinking, as always. Nozdormu turned his head as Alexstrasza strode back into the Seat. Bronze sands danced around his wings, ever moving. Each Aspect stood before a banner representing their flight, and all were flanked by their various majordomos and guards.

"So," Neltharion said as Alexstrasza took her place before the red banner, "I take it Vyranoth did not appreciate today's ceremony?"

"She did not," Alexstrasza said. "But we have more pressing concerns at present—I would like to discuss Tyr's latest admonition with this council. Majordomos, guards, leave us. I wish to speak to my fellow Aspects alone."

The majordomos bowed their heads to the Life-Binder and exited the Seat, taking to the air and cruising around the tower out of earshot. One by one, the drakonid filed out, back to the lower chamber.

When they were alone, Alexstrasza returned to her business. "Tyr has asked us to take primal dragon eggs from the wilds and infuse them with Order magic, thus expanding our flights at a faster rate. I will not lie, the request—"

"You mean the *command*," Malygos said, interjecting. The blue Aspect rolled a bit of arcane fire through his talons, looking to the Life-Binder. "He did not give us a choice."

"We always have a choice," Alexstrasza said. "We may choose to follow his admonition, or to risk his displeasure and refuse. What say you all?"

Neltharion cocked his head, the light sliding over his oil-dark scales. "You have ever been adamant that Order magic should be an individual's choice, Alexstrasza. Why would you consider infusing eggs without their bloodline's permission, or their own?"

Alexstrasza sensed no malice from the black Aspect, nor defiance. Neltharion was always the first to question Alexstrasza—he liked to prompt discussion and examine issues from multiple angles. On occasion, he could be rather tactless about it, but his questions generated the desired results.

"You speak true, Neltharion, but we know little of the threats to our world, nor of the dark forces that the titans themselves shield us from knowing," Alexstrasza replied. "We have been entrusted with safeguarding the lives of all dragonkind, of all Azeroth. If infusing more eggs will improve our chances against future threats, perhaps we should consider it."

"You do not seem convinced, my queen." Malygos swirled his talons in the air, and the arcane flames twirled from his talons like ribbons. "Though I agree with Tyr—if we want the dragonflights to survive, it may be in our best interests to bolster our numbers."

"The flights are thriving, are they not?" Alexstrasza said.

"Yes, for now." The blue Aspect looked up, dousing the fire with a snap of his talons. He rose to his feet. "But opposition rises on swift wings. Your own cousin speaks against you."

"Fyrakk?" Alexstrasza replied with a scoff. "Fyrakk may be a firebrand, but he is no leader. Were he to incite a rebellion against us, he would spend as much time fighting his own allies as he would engaging our flights."

"Fyrakk is a warmonger and a zealot, and I do not think it wise to underestimate him," Neltharion said.

"You do not know him as I do." Alexstrasza paused, considering her next words. Fyrakk loved one thing, and one thing alone: fighting. He was an unmatched combatant in the air and on the ground, and he had taught Alexstrasza how to hunt and do battle. In recent centuries, however, the thrill of the fight had consumed Fyrakk, which was no doubt why he called for rebellion against Order magic.

"Yet I see the wisdom in your words," she continued. "Fyrakk was like a brother to me, but his actions have set him apart. He is different now. *Changed*."

Malygos inclined his head. "In more ways than one, it seems. Have you heard the rumors? It is said that Fyrakk has been imbued with elemental energies. How he did this, none can be sure—were they granted by a stronger ally? Drawn from the elemental plane? He claims his power rivals that of the Aspects. Primal dragons flock to his side."

"My scouts have said as much," Alexstraszza said. "They tell me Fyrakk has grown in size and strength, that living flames now dance across his scales. Still, I do not fear my cousin—he would decimate his own forces over a perceived insult. He may draw primal dragons to his cause with fiery words and impassioned spirit, but his reckless ways and impulsive nature will fail to keep them."

"While that may be true, I do not want to ignore the threat he poses," Malygos said. "If we discount Fyrakk and his rabble-rousing, he may do irreparable harm to our flights. What would happen if he were to convince other primal dragons to draw on the elements, as he has done?"

"We have no authority over Fyrakk," Alexstrasza said. "What would you have me do? Slay him? My own kin? That is not a course I am willing to entertain."

Malygos opened his mouth to respond, but Neltharion interrupted the blue Aspect with a deep, quaking rumble in his chest. "It is not Fyrakk who concerns me," the Earth-Warder said, his voice no more than a murmur, "but Iridikron."

The name Iridikron fell like a stone weight into the room, sending vibrations through the floor. Alexstrasza sensed the other Aspects' shock. Even Nozdormu, who looked as composed and stoic as ever, shuddered at the thought. Ysera whipped her tail, agitated. Malygos blinked, his shimmering runes flickering for a moment.

Reclusive and withdrawn, Alexstrasza had never even *seen* Iridikron. The Stonescaled tended to keep to his den in Harrowsdeep, far to the north in Kalimdor; but she knew he was nearly Neltharion's equal in strategy, cunning, and strength. Neltharion and Iridikron had long been rivals. Iridikron's tactical skill and considerable resources, along with Fyrakk's impetuosity, would indeed be a concern.

Malygos frowned, turning to Neltharion. "You did not tell me Fyrakk was pursuing Iridikron's support."

"No, I had word only this morning," Neltharion replied. "If Iridikron allies with Fyrakk, they will stir the winds of war."

"I cannot believe they would take things so far," Alexstrasza replied, shaking her head. "Dragon should not fight dragon."

"Our detractors do not see us as *dragons,* but as the keepers' conscripts," Neltharion replied. "They would raze Valdrakken to the ground, given the opportunity. I agree with Tyr. We should bolster our numbers. Every egg we claim from the wilds now is one less enemy we face in the future, and one more ally by our side."

"This is madness," Alexstrasza said, but she could sense the depth of the Earth-Warder's concern. "Do you support this plan, Malygos?"

The blue Aspect hesitated. "*Support* is a strong word, my queen, but Neltharion's reasoning is sound. If Iridikron the Stonescaled decides to join with Fyrakk and marshal the primal dragons, we will struggle to defend the Broodlands with our current numbers."

Alexstrasza shook her head. "I refuse to believe that dragonkind will be led to the brink of war over a difference of opinion."

"Is it a *difference of opinion?*" Neltharion asked. "Or a fight for our respective ways of life? For our bloodlines? Not everyone has chosen to join in this endeavor, and more than a few have sworn to stand against us. Their ranks will swell, just as ours will continue to do."

Alexstrasza released a soul-deep sigh. She trusted Neltharion's dedication to the cause more than that of any other, save perhaps Ysera. His flight had been charged with the protection of the Broodlands, so it came as no surprise that he would be agreeable to Tyr's admonition. Malygos, too, for he and Neltharion were often of like minds.

"It is prudent to prepare for all eventualities," Malygos said. "Would you not agree, Nozdormu?"

The bronze Aspect harrumphed, giving both his wings a precise shake and sending bronzed sands scattering across the floor. "I would not agree. This course of action may provoke the very conflict you wish to avoid."

"Which means?" Neltharion asked, lifting a brow.

" 'Tis impossible to say with any certainty," Nozdormu replied. "I see a *thousand* futures before our flights, but I could not tell you which way the sands of time will flow. Taking primal dragon eggs from the wilds may be a boon to our flights—it also may be the choice that ends them."

"The Highfather's gift has made you frustratingly cryptic, my friend," Malygos said, but he smirked at the bronze Aspect.

Nozdormu gave him an elegant shrug in reply.

"And what of you, sister?" Alexstrasza said, turning to Ysera. "You have been unusually quiet throughout this council." Ysera, knowing the full extent of Alexstrasza's gifts, exuded love and compassion for her sister, and for all dragonkind. Empathy, too, given the weight of the decision they faced.

Ysera tilted her head, considering Alexstrasza for a long moment. "I stand with Nozdormu on this matter," she said. "All things must grow in their own way and in their own time. I cannot condone the disruption of life's natural cycle, even if Order magic allows for a greater expression of its flow."

"Then it seems we are at an impasse," Alexstrasza said, feeling the full burden of her mantle. She had expected the role of Dragon Queen to be difficult, but she had *not* expected to have her deeply cherished principles at odds with the needs of the dragonflights. How could she make such a decision? How could she, a mother herself, take precious eggs, only to infuse them with Order magic? It was unconscionable, even if the eggs *were* abandoned and without protection in the wilds, for that was the condition to which she had agreed with Tyr.

And yet Neltharion and Malygos were right—Tyr had given them no choice. What would happen if the Aspects defied the will of the keepers? Would they be deprived of the blessings that had transformed their lives, forced to return to the unenlightened existences they had lived before? Or would their lights be snuffed out entirely, gnats before the might of gods?

Alexstrasza looked out at the dragons who filled the skies above Valdrakken. Their joy was so perfect, so pure. The heart of each burned like a star, so it seemed to her, as though galaxies circled around the Seat in hues of red, green, bronze, black, and blue. She was Dragon Queen, yes, but who was she to risk the health and happiness of the dragons who had chosen to follow her toward a new horizon? How could she place her own morality above their well-being? The individual could not come before the collective, not even when that individual was queen.

No, Alexstrasza would not risk turning the keepers against them, especially with Fyrakk raising a rebellion against the Broodlands. Were that terrible future to come to pass, the Aspects would need every ally they could call upon.

"I see great wisdom on both sides of the matter," Alexstrasza said, turning her attention back to the other Aspects. "While I personally may object to collecting primal dragon eggs from the wilds, we cannot risk losing the support of Tyr and the other keepers. Were we to deviate too far from their guidance, we cannot know if they would revoke our ordering."

Neltharion curled his lip at the idea but said nothing.

"Furthermore," Alexstrasza said, looking to her sister, "you and I both know the survival rate of primal dragons' eggs in the wilds is abysmally low. Only one in four whelplings might make it to drakehood there. Half the survivors might see five hundred years, or even a thousand. We must think of the lives we will save—those eggs will be better protected in the Broodlands. More whelplings will make it to adulthood under the care of the red dragonflight, and our augmented numbers will better defend the world we all love so well."

Alexstrasza paused; no one spoke.

"Therefore," Alexstrasza said, still unsure if the words she spoke were the right ones, and pushing the promise she had made to Vyranoth to the back of her mind, "I sanction the titan-forged to collect primal dragon eggs they find unguarded in the wilds."

Neltharion and Malygos shared a satisfied look, while Nozdormu simply dipped his head in agreement. Ysera leaned closer to her sister, bumping Alexstrasza's shoulder with her snout.

But no matter how hard Alexstrasza tried to justify the decision to herself, a shadow moved over her heart.

ALEXSTRASZA SPENT THE REST of her day meeting with various members of her flight, inspecting progress at the Ruby Life Pools, and instructing a larger force of red drakonid to care for the incoming eggs. Wherever she went, Neltharion's words haunted her: *Our detractors do not see us as dragons, but as the keepers' conscripts. They would raze Valdrakken to the ground, given the opportunity.*

Vyranoth's words rose in an answering cry: *Swear to me that you will never force a primal dragon to bow to the will of the keepers.*

Alexstrasza had sworn. How she regretted those words now! If Vyranoth refused to understand something as simple as Order magic, she would never empathize with the nuances of Alexstrasza's position. Not because Vyranoth did not have the capacity to understand, but because her solution would be to forsake Order magic and return dragonkind to its more primal state. If only the answer could be so simple as Vyranoth thought it to be.

As the sun sank toward the horizon, Alexstrasza took her leave from Valdrakken. She dived from the heights of the Seat of the Aspects, reveling in the thrill of a free fall. As the ground rushed toward her, she opened her wings and beat them once, rocketing forward.

Alexstrasza loved the city. From its gleaming white towers to its glistening aqueducts, Valdrakken was fast becoming the Broodlands' bustling core. Watching its spires rise brought her so much joy. The place was a marvel, a wonder, and unlike anything else on the face of Azeroth. It brought the five flights together in ways Alexstrasza had never imagined possible. Bronzes and blues hunted together with bronze sands and arcane magic; reds and greens encouraged abundant, flowering gardens to grow in the city's quiet, shaded places; and in the black dragonflight's enclave, a new Oathstone was being prepared with the help of members of all five flights.

Everywhere she looked, Alexstrasza saw unity. Prosperity. Compassion. If the five dragonflights could find a way to work together in harmony, they could find a path to peace with Fyrakk and his followers, too.

Surely there is a way to avoid hostilities, Alexstrasza thought, sailing past the outskirts of Valdrakken. *Surely, we can find that path to peace.*

Alexstrasza flew to one of her favorite spots in the Broodlands—a small ledge on the border of the Emerald Plains and the Waking Shores, where she could watch the sunset. She lounged on the warm rock, soaking up its heat. Two large reds circled overhead, keeping an ever-watchful eye on their queen. Below her, the sunset flooded the Waking Shores with gold light, setting the valleys' pillars and arches of red stone aflame. The air smelled of sweet, dry grass and the world teemed with life. Usually, she could close her eyes and slip into the songs around her: the ancient trees shifting their boughs in the wind or a hawk's hunting cries . . . but no. Not tonight. Her mind turned and her heart ached, realizing that the living world would wake to a different dawn. One in which Alexstrasza's decision had either secured or destroyed its peace.

She was unsurprised to sense Ysera approaching on swift wings.

"I knew I would find you here," the green Aspect said as she alighted on the ledge beside Alexstrasza, setting off little whorls of dust in her wake. "How do you fare, dear one?"

Alexstrasza smiled sadly. "I sense concern in your heart, Ysera. Do not worry for me. I am quite all right."

"Are you?" Ysera said, bumping her snout against Alexstrasza's shoulder.

"I am well *enough,* thank you."

"*Well enough,*" Ysera said, "but still brooding."

"Is it that obvious?"

"You would be hard-pressed to hide your heart from me," Ysera said, stretching out beside Alexstrasza. "Do not worry, sister, we made the right choice. Taking decisive action now may preserve more life than war would take. The way we lived before the keepers was a cruel existence with moments of wild, untamed beauty. Maybe this will encourage those who stand against us to envision a gentler future with us; perhaps the whelps we save will even help us build bridges between us and our primal kin."

"That is what I tell myself," Alexstrasza replied, "yet my doubts persist. I must admit, I knew taking on the mantle of Dragon Queen would be difficult . . . but I never expected to make a choice like this."

"Let your doubts go, sister," Ysera said, leaning into Alexstrasza's side. "Your compassion is boundless—that is why the keepers made you queen. You are our beacon, our waypoint, the *best* of us. I know it is easier said than done, but you do not bear the burden of leadership alone. The Aspects stand with you. *I* stand with you."

"I know, and I thank you for it." Alexstrasza leaned back against her sister. How grateful she was for Ysera's support! The path they forged together was new, and Alexstrasza was unaccustomed to the heaviness of leadership. With time, she would adjust to the pressures of her role, but for now, all she felt was the weight of others' expectations. Tyr's, in particular.

Ysera let out a yawn, her fangs glistening in the dying light. The sisters watched the sun dip below the horizon in silence. As dusk settled over the sky, the rocks purpled. Shadows pooled at the base of the canyon. Stars emerged, then hid their faces behind clouds that crept toward the Broodlands.

The winds stirred, and Alexstrasza smelled wet earth and the sharp tang of lightning on her tongue.

"We should go," Alexstrasza said. "The hour grows late, and you already have one foot in the Dream."

"Yes," Ysera replied, her voice slow and hazy. "Yes, I suppose we should."

AS THE MOONS ROSE, Neltharion returned to the Obsidian Citadel. Or at least, he returned to the site that would eventually *become* the Obsidian Citadel. For now, his flight excavated the mountainside, tapped volcanic vents, and shaped stones for the lower levels. One day, it would be a bastion on the Broodlands' western flank, providing protection from their foes in the west.

Alexstrasza was not unwise, but she underestimated Iridikron's deep-seated distrust of the keepers and everything they touched. While Neltharion had the utmost faith in the Dragon Queen's diplomacy, even *she* would struggle to soften the Stonescaled's heart. If peace failed and Iridikron brought war to the Broodlands, Neltharion intended to be ready.

The Earth-Warder would, however, need to make his preparations with care, avoiding both Iridikron's suspicion and the Dragon Queen's ire. He summoned two of his most trusted scale-crafters to his side—Umbrenion, principal architect of the Obsidian Citadel, and Calcia, leader of the scalesmiths. Together, they descended into the large natural cavern that lay beneath the citadel and stretched for hundreds of wing-lengths under the Broodlands. The temperature rose, and the air smelled sulfurous. Lava poured from cracks in the stone, illuminating the cavern with dim red light. It ran like a red river through the cavern's center, then split in two around a wedge-shaped stone cliff. Misty light emanated from pockets of the cave, emitted by huge aquamarine crystals and phosphorescent fungi.

Neltharion paused on a ledge overlooking the space. "Now that the citadel is underway, Umbrenion, I want your engineers to turn their attention to the lower caverns."

"Of course, my Aspect," Umbrenion replied. "What would you have us do here?"

"I want armories, workshops, and additional forges," Neltharion said, pointing to the west, north, and south. "We will need training grounds for the drakonid as well. However, I want you to save Zaralek Cavern for me."

"Might I ask why we need to expand into the lower caverns already?" Calcia inquired, stepping forward to survey the space. "Is the citadel not enough to protect the Broodlands' western flank, my Aspect?"

"The citadel is sufficient for now, yes," Neltharion replied. "But we must prepare for an uncertain future with unknowable threats. Survey and map the cavern in advance of our next meeting with the flightleaders—we will decide how to allocate our resources to the construction efforts then."

Umbrenion bobbed his head. "It shall be done."

"One final consideration," Neltharion said as he turned. "This place will be for our flight alone. Tell no one of it, not even the other Aspects. Am I understood?"

"Yes," Umbrenion and Calcia said in unison.

"Good," Neltharion replied. "See to it."

As Neltharion went to leave the cavern, a wordless hiss rose in the back of his mind. He paused, looking over his shoulder, but no one followed him. Umbrenion and Calcia stood several wing-lengths back, discussing directives and making plans. So, then who . . .

"Is everything all right, my Aspect?" Calcia asked, shifting her attention back to him.

Neltharion gave her a firm nod. "Quite," he said, though it was not the first time he had heard the strange, disembodied whispers while underground. "Carry on," he said, then hurried from the cavern without another word.

CHAPTER THREE

FYRAKK SOARED HIGH OVER THE NORTHERN PLAINS, the cold air rushing across his molten scales. The frigid temperatures failed to dull the anger coursing through his veins—only the thrill of combat could do that. He craved the clash of fang and claw, the bright bite of pain, the hot rush of violence.

Today, Fyrakk would draw blood from Iridikron's stone hide.

The word on the winds said that Iridikron had guided Raszageth through the rituals necessary to become imbued with the primal elements. The fact that she had survived the process spoke to the strength of her connection to storm magic, for hundreds of others had perished in the attempt before Fyrakk's own success.

It wasn't that Fyrakk minded adding a third Incarnate to their ranks, oh no. They would need more Incarnates if they meant to face the Aspects on the battlefield. Fyrakk was furious because Iridikron hadn't even *consulted* him on the matter.

How bold of him! Fyrakk thought. *As if I were a mere pawn, and he the unquestioned leader!* He swooped lower as he drew closer to Iridikron's den of Harrowsdeep. In the south, Galakrond's monstrous rib bones arched into the sky. Though the beast had been dead for more than ten years, scraps of flesh still clung to his bones, flailing in the breeze. The stench from his flesh only stoked the fires of Fyrakk's anger. Galakrond reminded Fyrakk of Alexstrasza's victory and "rise" as Dragon Aspect. Too many dragons had chosen to follow his cousin into folly. Even Tyranastrasz, the ancient and righteous wyrm, had chosen Alexstrasza over his own primal nature.

Directly to the south, a new titan abomination took shape, rising in the shadow of Galakrond's fall. Fyrakk's scouts said that the Aspects were to name this tower Wyrmrest Temple. To Fyrakk's eye, the tower was even more monstrous than the stinking pile of Galakrond's bones. No doubt the Aspects would use the place to spy on the primal dragons—Fyrakk wanted to scorch it to the ground, but Iridikron had forbidden him from attacking the ordered outright.

Do not alarm the Aspects, Iridikron had said. *The less they suspect, the better.*

Fyrakk had scoffed at the idea. Rather than wait and watch, the Incarnates needed to strike at Valdrakken *now,* before the Aspects' dragonflights grew any larger or more powerful. The fifth and final Oathstone had been empowered in Nozdormu's bastion of Thaldraszus last spring; and Fyrakk had heard of the changes the Oathstones wrought in the flights. By all reports, the ordered were stronger now and more unified. Rumors of their strength drew more dragons to the Broodlands.

No matter. Hundreds of primal dragons had already joined Fyrakk's cause, as had thousands of tarasek—the small, bipedal dragonkind native to the Dragonwilds. If he and Iridikron flew on Valdrakken, Fyrakk was certain they could crush Alexstrasza and her allies with their combined might.

And yet Iridikron had insisted they *wait*.

Fyrakk hated that so many of his allies had turned to Iridikron for leadership. If anyone had the right to lead their new movement, it was *he*. Fyrakk had been the first to speak out against Alexstrasza and the Aspects, the first to survive being suffused by elemental energies, and the one who had rallied a rapidly growing force of primal dragons to the cause! *He* deserved to lead the growing rebellion, not Iridikron.

Which was exactly why Fyrakk had flown north from his lair in the Caldera. If Iridikron wanted to lead, he would have to take that right by wing and by talon. Fyrakk would not simply bow to Iridikron's whims—even if Iridikron had been the one to discover how to imbue oneself with elemental energies in the first place.

One massive, craggy peak speared the sky, standing taller than any other mountain in the whole range: Harrowsdeep.

At its base, Fyrakk spotted the mouth of a familiar cavern, one encrusted with glittering ice and snow. Iridikron had dug tunnels far into the world's crust, allowing him to absorb the element of stone unhindered. It was said the earth itself now responded to the Stonescaled's mastery. A formidable foe, to be sure, but Fyrakk feared no dragon.

Fyrakk landed in the snow, which melted and hissed beneath his feet. Two primal dragons, each with mottled gray scales, stood guard at the cavern's entrance.

"I am here to see Iridikron," he said to the guards. His breath plumed around his snout. "Take me to him."

The two dragons shared a look. "No, Blazing One," the first replied in his underdeveloped speech, cocking his head. "Stonescaled busy."

"Iridikron will make time for me," Fyrakk said.

The dragon narrowed his eyes. "No, he busy—"

Fyrakk stepped forward, scales blazing. A column of fire swirled around him, melting the snow in a two-wingspan diameter and desiccating the earth below his feet. The two primal dragons stumbled back, dropping their heads to protect their throats. They ruffled the protective scales around their shoulders and backed away, smelling of sharp, coppery fear. Fyrakk scoffed. He could snuff out the sparks of their lives with a single swipe of his talons.

"Do you think I cower before your master?" Fyrakk said, stepping toward the cavern. "It is because of *me* that he discovered how to attain his power. Without me, he would not *be* the Stonescaled. Step aside, or I will return you to the ground to which you so desperately cleave."

The interior of Harrowsdeep had changed since Fyrakk had seen it last: The main cavern yawned wider and higher than before, and the air smelled of sulfur and smoke. Hundreds of stalactites hung from the ceiling, toothy and sharp. A circular sinkhole dominated the floor, twisting down into tunnels and warrens. Fyrakk thought the sinkhole might be ten wingspans wide, maybe more. A new waterfall tumbled through it, plunging hundreds of talon-lengths into a dark pool at the bottom.

Stepping inside Harrowsdeep felt like walking into the maw of a giant predator—it left Fyrakk feeling ill at ease. He shook off the feeling with a growl.

The guards were right, Fyrakk thought, stalking toward the edge of the sinkhole. *Stonescaled busy.*

Everywhere he looked, Harrowsdeep bustled with activity. Primal dragons excavated new tunnels. Tarasek scurried about, carting supplies to and fro. Shouts echoed. Metal rang on metal.

Fyrakk narrowed his eyes. What was Iridikron planning without him this time?

"You there," Fyrakk said, gesturing to a small pack of tarasek with a talon. One of them squeaked and dropped the hide-wrapped package it was carrying. "Tell me where Iridikron is, *now!*"

The tarasek pointed shaking talons to a large-mouthed tunnel at the base of the sinkhole. With a growl, Fyrakk dived off the ledge and plummeted toward the blue water at the bottom. The waterfall's spray evaporated against the heat of his scales.

Fyrakk alighted on a ledge below the waterfall. The sulfurous smell grew stronger here, acrid enough to make his eyes water. He followed a tunnel into the earth. Phosphorescent green mushrooms grew along the ceiling, providing little light. The deeper Fyrakk went, the more the tunnels tightened. He bristled every time his wings scraped the walls. The ground trembled underfoot, shaken by unseen forces. Bits of rock and dust hit his scales, giving him the uncomfortable reminder of just how deep he was beneath the surface. Fyrakk wasn't meant to be underground like this, trapped like some lesser beast, the bright fires in his belly smothered. Perhaps he had been brash to think he could challenge Iridikron in his seat of power, but he wasn't about to turn back. Not now.

When Fyrakk emerged into a wide cavern, some of the tension in his chest unspooled. Unlike the upper cavern, this place had no natural light. Instead, great fires burned in clawed braziers, casting shadows across the walls. The air felt humid and damp. Droplets of water dripped off the ends of stalactites. Massive pillars bore the weight of the mountain, their forms twisted and bulbous.

If the upper cavern was the maw of the beast, Fyrakk was now in the creature's belly.

Iridikron's voice rumbled through the room, his words indecipherable. Fyrakk turned his head, following the Stonescaled's voice.

". . . to monitor the Aspects' progress," Iridikron said as Fyrakk drew closer. "Neltharion builds a fortress along the western border of the Broodlands. We must infiltrate the new construction and design an ingress point, preferably underground."

Iridikron stood in a small chamber, surrounded by seven or eight of his wingleaders. Since being imbued with primal earth energies, Iridikron's scales had hardened to stone. The Incarnate had doubled in size and towered over the other dragons in the room, a mountain among the foothills. Amber earth energies seeped out the fissure on his back, reminding Fyrakk of the volcanoes that could crack the earth wide open. Iridikron's every movement made the ground shudder.

As Fyrakk stepped into the cavern, the Stonescaled turned his bright, piercing gaze on him. The other primal dragons swiveled their heads, looking askance at Fyrakk.

Iridikron stood before a strange stone slab, one with features Fyrakk thought he recognized, just in miniature. Fyrakk frowned. Were those not the mountains of Thaldraszus? And that depression there, did that not symbolize the Emerald Plains? Though Fyrakk hadn't spent much time in the Broodlands, he still recalled its prominent features.

It was clear Iridikron was plotting something . . . *without Fyrakk. Again.*

"I do not recall inviting you to this meeting," Iridikron said, annoyed. He tapped the map of the Broodlands with a talon. It sank into the stone floor with a rumble.

"I need no invitation," Fyrakk spat, stepping into the room. "I will have an audience, Iridikron."

"You have no right to barge into *my* keep and demand an audience," Iridikron replied. "I have business to conduct. We can speak later—"

"No, we will speak *now,*" Fyrakk said. "I was the first Incarnate across the breach, the first to succeed. I will *not* bow to you, Iridikron."

One of Iridikron's wingleaders turned on Fyrakk with a growl. A second joined the first, fangs flashing. Without a word, the Stonescaled drew himself up to his full height. He thumped his tail on the ground, sending shivers through the stone floor. The two wingleaders looked to Iridikron and bowed their heads. Cowed.

Well, Fyrakk would not be cowed—he was a dragon born of fire and fury, not some spineless *lackey.*

"You hide here in your lair, using the power *I* helped you attain to build a fortress, rally an army, and craft your little schemes—which you keep from everyone, even those to whom you owe allegiance!" Fyrakk said with a snarl. A sharp pebble pricked the bottom of his foot, then another. Fyrakk shook out one foot and continued. "That was not your knowledge alone to share, especially with one as unpredictable as Raszageth!"

The Stonescaled said nothing. He watched Fyrakk with an unsettling intensity, unmoving. Unblinking. His refusal to speak only buffeted the flames of Fyrakk's fury.

"This is just like you," Fyrakk continued, fire now spouting from his tongue. "All you do is watch. *Wait.* We should have engaged the Aspects before they started turning our kind into more of those titan *abominations*! You counsel patience while you hide in your den, allowing the Aspects to grow stronger by the day. You are a *fool,* Iridikron!"

At the word *fool,* the Stonescaled's glowing eyes narrowed. His wingleaders went still. One of them looked upon Fyrakk with pity, but he ignored it—just like he ignored the trembling ground beneath his feet.

"One thing you must learn about me, Fyrakk," Iridikron said softly, tilting his head a few degrees to the left, "is that I prefer my enemies unseeing, unaware of my full strength, until it is much too late."

A great weight settled between Fyrakk's shoulder blades. He shifted, shuffling his wings, joints creaking. He tried to lift his feet, but to his horror, he could not feel or move them.

Fyrakk looked down. The floor softened beneath him, as if turned to mud. His feet sank into the rock, which grew solid once more. As the gray stone began to swallow up his shins, his heart skipped a beat. Panicked, he tried to tug himself free. When he attempted to flap his wings to generate lift, the floor held him fast.

The fury coursing through Fyrakk's veins cooled to fear.

"What—" he gasped, struggling in his stony shackles. "Iridikron, you would lift talon against me? *Me,* your brother and the very spark of your success?"

Saying nothing, Iridikron stalked forward, eyes slitted. His wingleaders scattered before him. The great energies along the Stonescaled's spine blazed ever brighter.

"Do you truly think I *hide* here in Harrowsdeep, ignorant of the threat growing in the east?" he asked quietly.

"Let. Me. Go," Fyrakk managed, nearly choking on the words. A gorge grew in his throat, making him feel as though he had swallowed a stone. Was that also the Stonescaled's power, or merely his own debilitating fear? He tossed his head, trying to break free of Iridikron's trap. Still, the fire dragon sank lower, till stone constricted his ribs and his breath.

Fyrakk was going to die here, far from the sky, starving for air. He gasped, eyes bulging, heart shuddering, yet could not draw enough air to satisfy his need. His flames withered and the heat in his body dwindled.

"Fire has the power to cleanse the world, but only molten stone has the power to shape it," Iridikron said. "We cannot face the Aspects as we are, and your wanton belligerence will prove no match for one such as Neltharion. Our new movement needs someone to temper it, mold it, *hone* it. Do you understand?"

Darkness edged Fyrakk's sight. He was drowning. Dying. "Yes," he rasped.

"Good," Iridikron said, tapping a single talon on the floor. The stone released Fyrakk, who collapsed to the ground and sucked in a deep, greedy breath. When the air hit his lungs, it sent him into a coughing fit, belching smoke and ash. Hot tears leaked from his eyes, and he clawed at the earth as his muscles spasmed.

"Do not mistake me, Fyrakk," Iridikron said. "Your fiery rhetoric will convince many of the nobility of our cause, as it did me—but you do not have the temperament to lead."

Fyrakk lifted his head to meet Iridikron's gaze. From wingtip to wingtip, every part of him ached. He swallowed hard, wincing at the rough rasp of air in his throat and lungs.

"Follow me," Iridikron said. "Together, you and I shall put an end to the Aspects and their titan defilement. I swear to you this day, I will not allow them to drive our kind to the brink of extinction."

Fyrakk wasn't sure why he said yes—perhaps he was surprised Iridikron let him live. Perhaps the last twenty or thirty heartbeats had given him a newfound respect for the Stonescaled. Or perhaps, all Fyrakk had wanted was an assurance that the Incarnates would not disregard the Aspects' tyranny, that Iridikron meant to *do* something with the power Fyrakk had helped him attain.

Now he knew.

"Come," Iridikron said, moving toward the cavern door. "Let us see how our sister has fared."

AS FYRAKK AND IRIDIKRON flew, the skies over the northern Stormscale Mountains roiled with thick, purple-black clouds, turning the day to darkest night. An enormous cyclone churned across the landscape. Bright-blue bolts of lightning danced through the storm, illuminating the clouds from within. Fyrakk could taste the energy from the bolts on his tongue. Its current crackled along his scales. The winds howled, trying to pull him into their restless maelstrom.

In all his years, Fyrakk had never seen such a terrible squall. It left a wide trail of destruction in its wake, tearing a deep gash in the valley floor, uprooting trees, and sending animals fleeing. And yet there was something thrilling about witnessing such a wanton display of power. Raszageth's strength and ability was undeniable—perhaps Iridikron was right to choose her to be the third Incarnate.

Raszageth's laugh boomed through the heavens, intoxicated with elemental power.

"These winds will snap the wings from our backs," Iridikron called to Fyrakk. "Come, let us take shelter in stone." Iridikron tucked his wings close to his body and dived toward a nearby mountain peak.

Despite what had happened just hours before, Fyrakk would be glad to have the mountain's unshakable stone beneath his feet. He folded his wings and followed, landing atop a nearby mountain beside Iridikron.

"Look at her," Iridikron said, his voice brimming with pride. "Is Raszageth not magnificent? Is she not the very pinnacle of what our kind can achieve? How could our brethren turn to the keepers when everything we need is already within our grasp?"

"I do not know," Fyrakk replied, turning his face skyward. "But this schism that divides our kind must be ended. All dragons should be free. Not just from the titans' edicts, but from Alexstrasza's false reign."

Iridikron was silent for a moment, watching the storm rage before them. He turned to Fyrakk. "And fight we shall. All I ask is for your trust. No, your *patience* . . . which I know is in short supply."

"Hmph." Fyrakk blew a hot breath from his nostrils.

Iridikron snorted, lifting his gaze back to the storm. "We will put an end to the Aspects and their masters, but we must approach the coming battle with strategy and care, and I am reluctant to strike as long as Tyr still lives. We cannot know the full extent of the magic the keepers have granted the Aspects, but they are no longer the dragons we once knew."

"Luckily, neither are we," Fyrakk said.

Before Iridikron could reply, a massive bolt of lightning shot from the heavens, shaking the earth and gashing open the clouds. A column of sunlight dropped into the storm. The light fell upon a dragon Fyrakk no longer recognized: White-blue lightning now danced down Raszageth's back, leapt across her wings, and sparked from her eyes. Her once mottled, dull scales now gleamed purple-black, the same color as the clouds that swirled around her. Raszageth was the embodiment of storm, imbued with all the wrath and brutality of the skies' fiercest tempests.

"If we mean to face the Aspects," Iridikron told Fyrakk, "we will need at least one more."

"Who?" Fyrakk asked, cocking his head. "Few dragons have the strength, will, instinct, and determination to survive the process of being imbued with the elements."

"I can think of one other—one whose presence among us would pierce Alexstrasza's heart like a talon," Iridikron replied. "But that concern is for another day. Come, Fyrakk! Let us congratulate our sister on her *ascension*."

PART TWO

A GROWING STORM

FROM THE ORAL HISTORIES OF
NOZDORMU THE TIMELESS ONE

Wan one has lived through the ages, the seasons turn faster,
ever faster. Months pass like moments, moving so swiftly that only the
bronzes take note. Our kind has long marked time only by the rise and
fall of the sun; by the seasonal migration of the herds; by the crack of
eggshells and the first breaths of new life. The concept of "keeping time"
is new to our kind; "annals" and "histories" are even more foreign and
strange, but I find myself compelled to recount these stories, nonetheless.

In the year we began construction on Wyrmrest Temple, Raszageth
the Storm-Eater joined Iridikron and Fyrakk as an Incarnate. The
news sent the first ripple of fear through the Broodlands. The Incarnate
influence was spreading; and true to her nature, Raszageth was far
more tempestuous than other members of her cohort. Perhaps Fyrakk
found joy in battle, but Raszageth derived it from killing. We believed
her bolts struck our kind from the skies . . . though we could not prove
it with absolute certainty, and could not demand justice for those killed.

Our flights continued to thrive despite growing opposition. We
finished construction on Valdrakken, then on the red dragonflight's Ruby

Life Pools. Twenty-odd years later, the black dragonflight completed the Obsidian Citadel, followed closely by the first of two great towers in the Azure Span—Vakthros, the heart of the blue dragonflight's power.

For nearly two centuries, we did everything possible to build bridges with our primal kin. Due to its proximity to Harrowsdeep, Wyrmrest Temple became a center for our diplomatic endeavors. We encouraged primal dragons to join us there, which resulted in a few scattered successes. Those efforts halted, however, when the Winterskorn vrykul captured hundreds of primal dragons and forced them to fight in the titan-forged's bloody civil war. The fighting grew so intense that Tyr called upon we five Aspects to help him end it—and we gladly flew to his aid. We not only helped him defeat the Winterskorn, but Ysera and I also wove a spell that put the vrykul into a deep, dreamless sleep.

Though we helped free our kin, the war gave primal dragons another reason not to trust the keepers, the titan-forged, and the Aspects ourselves. The primal dragons were furious that we did not destroy the Winterskorn outright for their crimes against our kind, pointing to our mercy as further evidence of our obeisance to the keepers.

Now, the path to lasting peace seems muddled and fraught. As Aspects, we will continue to work toward a bright future for all dragonkind, although we would be remiss not to acknowledge the deadly storms brewing on the horizon.

CHAPTER FOUR

As the years passed, the ordered dragons expanded their dominion—yet Vyranoth remained unconvinced of the Aspects' cause. Still, she made a point to visit Alexstrasza in the Broodlands when she could, if only to stay apprised of the Aspects' activities.

Today, Vyranoth's heart soared as she swooped over the Waking Shores, on her way to meet Alexstrasza's newest clutch of whelps. There were few pleasures so gentle as meeting newborn whelplings, natural-born *or* ordered.

The sun shone bright, warming her scales and filling her with a youthful, long-forgotten exuberance. She tucked her wings and dived through a red stone arch, enjoying the feeling of temporary weightlessness, then stretched them wide to catch the breeze. Dipping lower, she trailed her back talons in a river, startling a flock of ducks into flight. The whole world smelled *alive:* Flowers burst with the spring season, and fresh grass danced in the breeze. The Broodlands flourished under

Alexstrasza's reign, and yet Vyranoth found herself no more willing to join the flights than before.

Out of respect for Alexstrasza, Vyranoth *had* given Order magic due consideration. The dragonflights' fledgling civilization seemed inherently good, even honorable. She had watched their development with great interest, wondering if they would stay true to the lofty ideals upon which they had been founded; indeed, they fulfilled the commands of their masters with single-minded zeal . . . and that was *precisely* the problem.

Vyranoth valued her agency, her free will, her ability to go where and when she desired. The ordered enjoyed no such freedoms, having pledged themselves to the building up of the dragonflights and the defense of the world at large. And as much as she loved her friend, she needed no *queen* to do her thinking for her.

Iridikron was little better than the Aspects themselves, altering himself for the sake of power. More than a century ago, he'd taken to calling himself an Incarnate, positioning himself to be dragonkind's best hope to remain free from the Aspectral threat. He courted Vyranoth's favor incessantly— almost *obsessively* at times—sending his emissaries and promising her a place by his side.

Only one time had he come to her himself, in the year after the Aspects completed their work on Wyrmrest Temple. *I will ask you to join me but once,* he had said to her. *Deny me and I shall not trouble you again.*

Vyranoth said nothing to him then, still unsure of her own heart.

The struggle between Aspect and Incarnate left her in an unenviable position—she neither wanted to be ordered nor wished to be imbued with the planet's elemental energies, especially given the process's low rate of survival. She had grown lonely, then she had grown *tired* of being lonely . . . but that did not drive her into the wings of either faction.

Under the influence of Order magic, dragonkind aspired to things Vyranoth simply did not understand. Over the last two hundred years, Valdrakken's towers and spires had risen over the mountains of Thaldraszus. In the northwest, Neltharion had built a massive citadel and forge, where he and the black dragonflight manufactured all manner of strange wonders. On the western shores, Ysera and her greens claimed to have opened a portal into Azeroth's own dreams. And in the south, Malygos and his blues had built towers and vast . . . what was the word for them? *Libraries*. They filled these places with knowledge, recorded in stone and parchment from which future generations would learn. Vyranoth had even toured Malygos's grand tower of Vakthros, as well as the beginnings of the bronze dragonflight's Temporal Conflux.

Chief among them all was Alexstrasza's Ruby Life Pools, the seat of the red dragonflight's power. The Life Pools rested at the heart of the Broodlands, protected on all sides. They provided a place for whelplings to hatch, grow, and play— with no fear of predation. Every whelpling in the Broodlands had the chance to reach their full potential. There was joy and hope in the thought, but also *power*. In a few generations' time, the dragonflights' populations might outstrip the primal dragons' numbers.

The thought both astonished and terrified Vyranoth.

Rising from the canyons, she spotted the pools' familiar butte in the distance. Red dragons shimmered in the air around it, and gleaming pillars of marble now rose from the butte's summit. Titan-forged workers scurried across scaffoldings and moved enormous stone blocks into place. *How odd,* Vyranoth thought. *I thought the Ruby Life Pools were complete. What are they building now?*

As she drew closer, a flash of crimson caught her eye. The Dragon Queen had taken wing. Light blazed off Alexstrasza's ruby scales and gilded horns. Though Vyranoth had grown accustomed to seeing Alexstrasza in her ordered form, it still unsettled her from time to time. The chasm between them mostly went unspoken, but it seemed to have grown wider with each passing decade.

"Vyranoth!" Alexstrasza cried, doing a joyful, elegant roll in the air. "How good it is to see you, my dear! Tell me, how have you fared of late?"

"Very well," Vyranoth replied, halting to hover in the air. "You are positively glowing—I take it all in the Broodlands is well?"

"Indeed!" Alexstrasza replied. "We have been busy in the decades you've been away."

"I can see that," Vyranoth replied, peering at the polished creations below. "What are you up to now, my old friend?"

"We are adding an upper tier to the Ruby Life Pools," Alexstrasza replied. "Our flights have been so prolific, we needed more space for eggs. Come, let us fly, and I shall show you!"

"Hmph, very well," Vyranoth replied, but she smiled a little.

Together, Vyranoth and Alexstrasza cruised around the butte, enjoying the beauty of the day and the warm, gentle winds. Below them, the titan-forged were constructing open-air pools atop the butte, which were fed from the aqueduct that carried water from Tyrhold. Green dragons coaxed trees to grow, giving shade to the new pools, while the reds oversaw construction of a new landing platform.

Near the ground, young red drakes minded the whelplings, chasing them through the leafy, crimson treetops. The whelplings' giggles echoed through the canyons. The sound brought another smile to Vyranoth's lips.

"I have wanted to expand these pools for decades," Alexstrasza said with a hint of excitement in her voice. "I had to prioritize the construction of Valdrakken, then send resources to fortify our borders. But now I can finally bring my vision to life."

"Why should you need to fortify the borders of the Broodlands?" Vyranoth asked with a little chuckle. They banked under the bones of a new archway, one inlaid with gold and opalescent stained glass. "Who would dare challenge the might of the Aspects?"

Alexstrasza shot her friend a wry smile. "Neltharion takes his charge to defend the Broodlands seriously . . . perhaps a little *too* seriously at times. You have seen the Obsidian Citadel—"

"Ah, you mean the monument he built to his own *towering intellect*," Vyranoth said playfully, drawing a guilty-sounding chuckle from the Dragon Queen.

"Not everyone is as open-minded as you, my friend," Alexstrasza said. "I will always advocate for peace, but I do not trust my detractors will do the same. We do not know what dangers we may face in the future."

Ah, so you do understand the threat Iridikron poses to you, Vyranoth thought. *Even if you will not name the threat aloud, you know the Incarnates grow in strength, just as you do.* Raszageth had been a particular thorn in Alexstrasza's side, as the Storm-Eater had delighted in striking down ordered dragons along the Broodlands' borders. Raszageth sometimes flew past Vyranoth's aerie in the Frozen Fangs, reveling in the power of tempests there.

If conflict broke out between the Aspects and the Incarnates, Vyranoth would grapple to maintain her neutrality. Her affection for Alexstrasza was undeniable; however, the intervening centuries had not made Vyranoth trust the keepers or their magic. Nor did she trust the Incarnates, though she certainly empathized with some of their rhetoric.

Vyranoth's best hope was peace.

"Enough talk of philosophy," Alexstrasza said with a smile. "Come! I would now introduce you to my new whelplings."

Alexstrasza folded her wings and dived into the hollow center of the Ruby Life Pools. Vyranoth followed her down, plummeting past bursts of leafy green foliage and silvery waterfalls. At the bottom, Alexstrasza alighted on a lily-shaped landing pad, one that floated in a shallow pool. Vyranoth settled beside her friend, shaking the condensation of the waterfalls from her wings. The droplets felt almost . . . *warm*. They tingled along her wing membranes until she shucked them away.

The temperature rose as they ventured into the Ruby Life Pools proper. Alexstrasza led Vyranoth into a cavern that housed several large clutches of dragon eggs—red, black, blue, bronze, and green—all of which rested in clear turquoise pools. Lush flora thrived in the heat and humidity, filling the whole space with greenery. Warm golden light radiated from sconces in the walls. Drakonid tended the eggs in the pools, singing to them in low, soft tones, telling them stories, and cradling them in a strange magic Vyranoth did not comprehend.

As Alexstrasza moved deeper into the space, every drakonid turned and bowed. She acknowledged them with a nod, saying, "As you were," then strode onward. A few of the egg-tenders looked at Vyranoth warily, but said nothing.

"I believe they will be sleeping." Alexstrasza approached a thick curtain of ivy and vines. She nudged it aside, revealing a private pool, one filled with gigantic lily pads and delicate, glowing blooms.

Ten newly hatched whelps slept on a thick, velvety pad, their scales as soft as dragonfly wings. The whelps' golden irises moved back and forth under their translucent lids as they dreamed. An ornate fountain burbled a lullaby.

Vyranoth breathed deep, inhaling the whelps' sweet, yolky scent. The whelps curled together for security, but one boy had rolled away, sleeping on his back and kicking one tiny leg in the air. With a gentle trill, Alexstrasza nudged him back to his siblings. She nuzzled them, then blew a hot breath over their sleeping forms. One whelp, still snoring, reached up and placed a tiny forepaw on Alexstrasza's snout.

"Oh, they are beautiful," Vyranoth said in a hushed voice, realizing that she missed having whelps of her own. Her throat tightened as she said, "Congratulations." The sudden rush of emotion took Vyranoth by surprise—particularly longing and want, tinged with something that was almost . . . *jealousy*?

Vyranoth hadn't had a clutch of her own in centuries, nor had she taken a new mate since Galakrond slew her last one.

"Thank you," Alexstrasza said, smiling at the new whelplings.

Vyranoth stepped back from her emotions, examining them, confused by them. *Jealousy* was not something a dragon like Vyranoth experienced—she possessed a keen intellect, powerful ice magic, and excellent acuity in the air. Larger than most primal dragons, Vyranoth commanded respect and admiration from her peers. She wanted for nothing. Though she was inclined to solitude, she had never lacked for friends or allies.

At least, until now. Who was left for Vyranoth? So many of dragonkind's best had gone to Alexstrasza and the Aspects. Most who remained now followed Iridikron and spouted his fractious rhetoric, leaving Vyranoth caught in the midst of a growing storm. Precious few remained neutral, and those who had were too young and inexperienced, or had paired off and flown far, seeking escape from the tension between the two groups.

Yes, Vyranoth was jealous of Alexstrasza, and self-aware enough to realize that the jealousy had started to gnaw away at her heart. If left to fester, it would turn to anger. Hatred. She *wanted* what Alexstrasza had—not just a mate, not just a clutch, but a place in this world.

Eventually, she would have to choose: Aspect or Incarnate. Order or nature. She knew the choice wasn't upon her yet, but it stalked closer by the day.

"Vyranoth?" Alexstrasza asked, pulling the frost dragon from her thoughts. "Are you all right?"

The concern on the Dragon Queen's face was true—the drawn brows, the neutral lips, the slightly narrowed eyes— but Vyranoth couldn't bring herself to be honest or vulnerable with Alexstrasza. Try as she might, the Dragon Queen would not understand the conflict raging in Vyranoth's heart. And she was loath to put her struggles on Alexstrasza today, thus dampening her friend's joy.

Vyranoth touched her snout to Alexstrasza's shoulder. "It is wistfulness for a past I cannot forget and nothing more, my friend."

Alexstrasza held Vyranoth's gaze for several moments, searching her eyes. Vyranoth felt as though her chest had been laid open, and that Alexstrasza could see every beat of her heart. It was unsettling, unnerving.

At long last, Alexstrasza smiled and leaned into Vyranoth's side. "We have been friends through all the long centuries, Vyranoth. You know you can tell me anything, don't you?"

"I do," Vyranoth said, leaning into Alexstrasza.

Anything . . . but this.

AS ALEXSTRASZA ATTENDED TO her official duties that afternoon, Vyranoth lingered in the Broodlands, playing with the older whelps.

"You can't find me!" A little green, Atyrannus, giggled from the branches of a nearby tree. Vyranoth stood on an egg-tender's path nearby, pretending not to know where the whelpling hid. Two red whelplings perched on her head, Talinstrasz and Lailastrasza, siblings. A blue whelpling, Rygos, toddled in the air near Vyranoth's left shoulder, his tiny wings barely able to keep him aloft.

"He's up there!" Lailastrasza said, bouncing atop Vyranoth's head. "Look! In that tree!"

"Which tree?" Vyranoth said, pretending to be confused. She turned her great head from side to side, then pointed at a tree across the river with a large wing talon. "Is it *that* one?"

"No!" the whelplings cried in unison.

"Hmm," Vyranoth said, cocking her head. She turned around and pointed at another. "What about that one?"

The whelplings howled with laughter. Talinstrasz jumped into the air, fumbled for a moment, then managed to maneuver himself in front of Vyranoth's snout. "Here, I'll show you!" he said, motioning to her with one of his forefeet.

With a chuckle, Vyranoth followed the whelpling to the tree, while Talinstrasz, Lailastrasza, and Rygos flew up into the branches, giggling and calling Atyrannus's name. The little green squawked, and the four of them burst from the tree in an explosion of leaves. Atyrannus took a tumble, but Vyranoth extended her wing and caught him on the thick, soft membrane. He bounced once, looked up at her in round-eyed surprise, and laughed.

Vyranoth had often played these kinds of games with her own clutches. It taught whelplings how to use sound to search for their prey, how to hide themselves to avoid being seen, and how to hunt alone and in groups. Vyranoth had to admit, it was a delight to spend time with the whelplings, even if they were not her own.

Inexplicably, there were fewer whelplings in the Dragonwilds these days.

"Who wants to hide next?" Vyranoth asked, bouncing Atyrannus back into the air. "Talinstrasz? Lailastrasza?"

"No," Lailastrasza said, landing on Vyranoth's head and hiding in the frost dragon's thick mane. "I'm too scared to be alone!"

"What?" Vyranoth asked with a chuckle. "Why should you be afraid, little one?"

"I want to stay with you," Lailastrasza replied, burrowing against Vyranoth's neck.

Bemused, Vyranoth replied, "Well, I suppose you can help me look. Talinstrasz?"

"I don't want to hide, either." The little red dashed under Vyranoth's wing. "They might take me!"

"What are you talking about?" Vyranoth said with a forced chuckle. In all her years, she had never seen whelplings act like this, and their fears gave her pause. "Who are *they*?"

"The eyes in the rocks!" Lailastrasza said in a muffled voice, gripping the primal dragon's mane in her tiny talons.

Vyranoth looked askance at a nearby red drakonid. The creature lifted its shoulders in a shrug. Her frown deepened. Young whelplings sometimes had strange ideas, it was true—but in the Broodlands, they did not need to fear predation like they did in the wilds. The ordered dragons raised their young communally, and the red dragonflight ensured that all whelplings were cared for, loved, and protected. From what Vyranoth understood, parents were allowed to be as involved or as *un*-involved in their offsprings' lives as they wanted.

Red dragons lounged on ledges overhead, while drakonid patrolled the ravines and kept a watchful eye on the whelplings. No predators could get close to these little ones. At least, nothing large enough to *hurt* them. So, why were they afraid?

"You are safe in the Broodlands," Vyranoth told the whelplings, nudging Talinstrasz with her snout. He clung to her leg. "Nothing will hurt you here."

Talinstrasz turned up his big golden eyes to look at her. The trust in his expression melted her heart, just a little. "There are creatures that hide in the rocks. I've seen them! They took me when I was little."

"Took you?" Vyranoth asked. "Took you from *where*?"

"From home," Talinstrasz replied.

"Come now," Vyranoth said gently, though the conversation put her nerves on a talon's edge. *Eyes in the rocks? Whelplings who believe they've been kidnapped?* "You have nothing to fear."

Talinstrasz shook his head.

"Fine, *I'll* hide," Rygos said, shooting a little puff of arcane fire at Lailastrasza. The little red made an annoyed chirp as Rygos disappeared through a stone archway.

Despite her concerns, Vyranoth spent the rest of a very happy afternoon with the whelplings, playing their invented games, watching them hunt bugs, and asking them about their lives in the Broodlands. She tried to cajole Lailastrasza or Talinstrasz to tell her more of their fears, but both whelplings just squeezed their eyes shut and shook their heads.

Truth be told, any number of things could have happened to the siblings, from getting lost in a dark cave to an encounter with something scary. None of the other whelplings Vyranoth encountered suffered the same distress. Whether green or black, bronze, blue, or red, most of the whelplings Vyranoth met were boisterous and content. Far more so than they might have been in the Dragonwilds, even.

As the sun fell toward the horizon, Vyranoth said her goodbyes to the whelplings and Alexstrasza returned to the Waking Shores.

"Vyranoth!" Alexstrasza said, landing on the riverbank. The whelplings squealed in delight when they saw the queen, and she smiled at them as they swarmed around her and perched on her horns. "I must apologize, today's business took me away for far longer than I thought it would. Our half-giant neighbors aren't particularly friendly, and continue to vex us."

"There is no need for an apology," Vyranoth replied, lifting her head. Three whelplings still clung to her mane, begging for one last game. "I spent a lovely afternoon with the whelplings, but now I must be going."

"I am forever pulled away by my duties," Alexstrasza said with a sigh, lowering her head to allow the drakonid to collect the protesting whelps. "At the very least, I can fly with you to the borders of the Broodlands."

"I would like that," Vyranoth said.

As they flew west, dusk drew her great, comforting wing over the sky. The stars blinked awake, one by one. In the distance, the great forges of Neltharion's Obsidian Citadel burned bright. And though Vyranoth had enjoyed the day, she wanted nothing more than to leave the Broodlands and return to the familiar, icy halls of her home in the north.

The two dragons paused at the border to say their goodbyes.

"I wish you would stay," Alexstrasza said. "I can feel the loneliness in your heart, Vyranoth. Ordered or not, you are always welcome among us. My idea for the Ruby Life Pools came from the days we spent defending our clutches from Galakrond—it came from *you*. Nothing would make me happier than to see you stay."

A pang of longing resonated through Vyranoth's chest. How she wished they could go back to that less complicated time, when dragons were dragons, and their lives were full of simple joys and known dangers. For even when Vyranoth came to visit the Broodlands, Alexstrasza barely had time for her; the responsibilities of leadership weighed heavily upon the Dragon Queen.

Everything had changed—everything, except Vyranoth. Like the great glaciers in the north, she moved with deliberate slowness, taking years and sometimes decades to make up her mind on a matter.

"I cannot," Vyranoth said. "You have built something truly extraordinary in the Broodlands, Alexstrasza—but there is no place for me here, much as I wish there were."

"That is not true," Alexstrasza said, clutching her forefeet into fists. It was something she had always done when despairing. "Vyranoth, there is room enough for you in the Broodlands. There is room enough for *everyone*."

Vyranoth beat her wings, hovering in the air. "But you would not take me as I am, not truly. I would be forced to submit to the keepers' Order magic to be a part of your flights."

"I have shown you our advancements, our cities and towers, our forges and gardens," Alexstrasza said, her voice choked. "You have sat with the Aspects, played with our whelplings, flown with our finest, and shared meals with my own family. What more must I do, Vyranoth, to help you understand? You are one of my oldest and dearest friends—I want you by my side. The horizon grows ever darker, and I do not wish to face it without you."

For the space of a heartbeat, Vyranoth felt herself being taken away by the emotion of the moment. She saw that path splayed before her: a community, a mate. *Whelplings*. But at what cost? It would be so easy to compromise her beliefs, to trade them for happiness . . . But she would have to live that happiness in a different skin . . . whatever brood she had would be yoked to that choice. Vyranoth would not make that choice for them.

And the flights, they *owed* something to the keepers: the defense of the world, or so they said. In practice, Vyranoth feared it would mean relinquishing herself for the "greater good." It would mean giving them the ice in her veins and the wind under her wings . . . and that was not a sacrifice she was willing to make.

She was Vyranoth, now and always. No one would take that away from her, not even her oldest and dearest friend.

"I am sorry, Alexstrasza," Vyranoth said. "But I cannot follow you toward that horizon." And with that, she closed her wings and dived for the border, leaving Alexstrasza alone in the skies.

She thought she heard the Dragon Queen call her name.

But Vyranoth did not turn back.

FOR SEVERAL TURNS OF the moons, Vyranoth tried not to think of that day at the Ruby Life Pools, nor how Alexstrasza had asked her to join the five flights. She could not imagine allowing titan magic to change her, even if it would allow her to stay by Alexstrasza's side.

The keepers found Vyranoth and her primal kin *wanting*. They found the whole of the world wanting, which was why they forced their order upon it. But the planet was already perfect in its innate beauty—why should it be forced to submit to the titans' whims? Why should Alexstrasza and her flights hold the titans' views so much higher than those of their own kind?

After all, hadn't the *illustrious* Tyr failed to defeat Galakrond? Hadn't *five primal dragons*, working together, found a way to fell that beast? And if Vyranoth knew the story true, why then did Alexstrasza feel she needed the titans' power at all? How had her own strength not proven sufficient?

These were the thoughts that rolled in Vyranoth's mind, day in and day out, as seasons passed. While she could certainly understand the Aspects' desire for greater power, it seemed naïve to trust the keepers. Hadn't their titan-forged trapped and captured primal dragons in the north? Even if Alexstrasza and the other Aspects had fought to free those poor creatures, the damage had been done—it was obvious the titans and their creations saw dragonkind as little more than servants . . . or worse, as thralls.

Perhaps that was why the flights' oaths gave Vyranoth such pause; she would not serve a force she neither knew nor understood. Could Alexstrasza say, truthfully, that her keepers would never ask her to do something she disagreed with? And if it came to that, what then?

One afternoon, Vyranoth could not sit with these thoughts any longer. She left her aerie and took wing. The cold, icy gales that whipped around the peaks were a panacea to her, easing her troubled heart and chasing away her doubts. Overhead, the clouds rumbled and roiled. Webs of lightning raced along their bellies—an unusual sight this far to the north, where the air was usually too cold to produce such phenomena. The snows had yet to fall, but she could sense the blizzard swirling in the skies above.

Vyranoth reveled in the storm that swirled around the mountaintops, enjoying the fierce, frozen day. The sheer power of the storm was a delight . . . and perhaps in one dark, small corner of her heart, Vyranoth could understand why Alexstrasza might seek a stronger wind under her wings. Regardless, the Dragon Queen should have sought such power from the world *itself*, not from an external force.

As Vyranoth soared around one of the peaks, enjoying the wind in her mane, a familiar voice thundered from the clouds: "Vyranoth! I did not realize you enjoyed chasing the gales."

"Is that you, Raszageth?" Vyranoth halted, turning her attention skyward. It wasn't unusual for the Incarnate to follow the winds across the Dragonwilds.

With a laugh like the crackle of lightning, a large primal dragon dipped from the clouds. For a dragon so young, Raszageth nearly matched Vyranoth in size—part of that was due to having been imbued with the very element of storm, no doubt. Rumors said the Storm-Eater was capricious, volatile; but Vyranoth had never sensed any malice from the Incarnate. On the contrary, Raszageth seemed to exude a wild glee, a feeling that Vyranoth had experienced little of late.

"Who else but me?" Raszageth said, tossing her head. Sparks snapped between her four great horns. "I hope you do not mind the . . . *unannounced* intrusion. I am here to follow the storm and naught else. But since you are here, would you like to fly with me?"

"Fly with you?" Vyranoth said, giving her wings a great beat to rise higher in the skies. "And where shall we go?"

"Anywhere we want," Raszageth said with a grin. "Let us see how great a gale we can whip up with our wings! Let us make the greatest of blizzards to shake the sky!"

It sounded like the right sort of distraction to take Vyranoth's mind off the concerns that had tormented her for so long. So, with a nod of her head, she followed Raszageth into the maelstrom.

They spent a thrilling afternoon racing through those peaks, stirring the storm into a frenzy. The winds howled in Vyranoth's ears and tore at her wings. They ducked and dived, spiraling through the storm. The snows raged, each flake sharp enough to shred a lesser dragon's wings. Lightning arced through the sky, answering the Incarnate's call.

Raszageth challenged Vyranoth to wild, death-defying games—they would plunge toward the ground, and the last to halt their descent would be declared the victor. Vyranoth lost this game every time—she was far more cautious than the Storm-Eater. However, Vyranoth often bested the Incarnate in breakneck races through the Peaks, sometimes dodging past great bolts of lightning to win. Raszageth was not trying to harm her, but the Incarnate wasn't afraid of alarming the older dragon, either.

Despite the chill of the storm—and her companion's rather unnerving penchant for danger—Vyranoth's blood burned in her veins. Her heart pounded in her chest. She could not recall a time in which she had felt so alive, not in many, many long years. No, not just alive . . . *liberated*. Free. She stopped thinking about her loneliness, about the Aspects and the Incarnates, and about their keepers and their loathsome Order magic. She stopped thinking, stopped worrying, and just *lived*.

As the day began to die, Vyranoth and Raszageth let the storm ebb. They landed on a ledge just north of Vyranoth's aerie, watching the winds settle and the snows drift away.

"You realize that you could become as I am," Raszageth said, giving her head a shake. "Incarnate, ever powerful."

"Did Iridikron tell you to say that to me?" Vyranoth said without malice.

"No," Raszageth said, chuckling. "I merely sense that you are a kindred spirit. I have friends in all the far-flung corners of the world, but few of them revel in the storm as you do. Fewer still can bear the wrath of my maelstroms."

Vyranoth turned her head to the sky, watching the storm continue to ease into a gentle snowfall. "It has been many long years since I have felt so free."

"Perhaps that is because you are listening to your instincts, rather than fighting them," Raszageth said. "Can you imagine how much more free you'd feel after being imbued with the elements?" Her features twisted into a smile. "It is dangerous. *Very* dangerous. But I believe you have what it takes to embrace the elements and master their powers . . . should you so choose."

The suggestion gave Vyranoth pause, then Raszageth continued, "However, it matters not what you are to me, so long as you love the storm. Friends?"

Vyranoth's breath caught in her throat, but otherwise, she made no outward sign of her surprise. *Friends*, just like that? Vyranoth barely knew Raszageth . . . but perhaps there was a kinship there, forged in storm. In understanding. In *acceptance*.

"Friends," Vyranoth said with a nod.

The Incarnate grinned. "Come, then," she said, launching herself back into the air. "I will show you stronger winds, and we shall truly fly free."

CHAPTER FIVE

A SEASON PASSED, THEN TWO; BEFORE LONG, Alexstrasza realized she had not seen nor heard from Vyranoth in a year's time. They used to make a habit of meeting for a hunt once a season; but Alexstrasza's duties had become even more demanding of late, and Vyranoth had been less inclined to leave the comforts of her territories in the north.

The realization came as a shock as Alexstrasza listened to a report from Egnion, the flightleader of Neltharion's Shadowscales—a fledgling military wing dedicated to gathering information on the enemy. As he reported that Vyranoth had been spotted in the company of Raszageth the Storm-Eater, every eye in the Seat turned to Alexstrasza, gauging her reaction. The news cut her heart to the quick, though she didn't let the emotion show in her face.

Did Vyranoth truly prefer the company of a creature as cruel and as unpredictable as Raszageth? An *Incarnate*? Alexstrasza knew Vyranoth was lonely, and she knew her duties had oft made it impossible to visit her friend as much as she would have liked . . . but *Raszageth*?

How could Vyranoth even *entertain* the idea of befriending an Incarnate? Fyrakk had made threats against Alexstrasza's very life. Raszageth was no better, hunting and killing ordered dragons for sport.

Have our hearts truly grown so far apart? Alexstrasza wondered, turning her gaze northwest as the other Aspects prepared to take their leave. She walked to the edge of the Seat, stepping out into the afternoon light, barely able to sense the strength of the sun on her scales.

Was there anything Alexstrasza could do to keep her friend from following the Incarnates down such a cruel, crooked path? What could she say that had not already been said? She sat, staring down at the bustling streets below. Everything she did was in service of the dragonflights, and by extension for the well-being of Azeroth. Over the last two centuries, Vyranoth had seen what the dragonflights had wrought—was it not proof of the goodness of Order magic? Why did Vyranoth continue to believe that the keepers meant their world harm?

But more important . . . how could Vyranoth choose the Incarnates' cruelty over the dragonflights' hope? Over their compassion? It made no sense.

Talons clicked on the floor behind her. "Alexstrasza?" Neltharion asked. "May I have a word?"

"Of course," Alexstrasza said, turning as Neltharion joined her on the platform. "Is something troubling you?"

"I could ask you the same question." He took a seat beside her and stared out at the horizon. "I wanted to apologize for the Shadowscales' reports—I should have had them deliver the intelligence concerning Vyranoth to you privately, rather than before an audience."

"It's quite all right," Alexstrasza replied, though the situation was anything but. "Vyranoth is one of the oldest and wisest primal dragons left in existence—Iridikron knows this as well as I do. No doubt he seeks to weaponize her against me, but I . . . will not . . ."

Her words grew stiff and stuck in her throat. She swallowed down her emotion, then said, "I will not allow that to happen."

"To have Vyranoth turn against us would be a grave loss," Neltharion said. "No doubt Iridikron wishes to see her become an Incarnate."

Alexstrasza shuddered. "I cannot imagine she would choose such a path . . . but perhaps I no longer know her as I once did. I never would have imagined her befriending Raszageth, of all creatures!"

"We should discourage her from joining Iridikron, if we can," the black Aspect said. "Do you think it possible to salvage your friendship with her?"

"I do hope so," Alexstrasza said, then let out a great sigh. "I will send an emissary to the Frozen Fangs today and invite her to hunt with me."

"I will also have the Shadowscales monitor her movements more closely," Neltharion said, lifting his head. "While an Incarnate cannot hope to match the power of an

Aspect, we certainly do not need any *more* of them to contend with."

"I wish I could find a way to reach her heart," Alexstrasza said, casting her gaze back to the horizon. It felt like a betrayal, but perhaps this was the way Vyranoth had felt when Alexstrasza had become an Aspect—like she could no longer understand one of her oldest and dearest friends.

"You must," Neltharion said. "Vyranoth is seen as a paragon of wisdom in the Dragonwilds. If she joins Iridikron's cause—*especially* as an Incarnate—many will follow her example. We cannot risk that, especially now that Tyr's forces are scattered in the wake of the war with the Winterskorn."

"I know, my old friend," Alexstrasza said. "I will think of something. I promise."

"In the meantime," Neltharion said, "we should discuss the new tribe that has taken up residence in the Apex Canopy."

Alexstrasza cocked her head. "It isn't another tribe of djaradin, is it?"

"No, not this time, thankfully," the black Aspect replied.

While the Qalashi and Zaqali tribes had been in the Waking Shores for as long as Alexstrasza could remember, they had grown more aggressive in recent years.

"This new species poses our kind very few risks—for now," Neltharion said. "They are smaller, softer, and short lived. Nozdormu and I would like to try to contact them."

"Nozdormu?" Alexstrasza asked. "What interest does he have in the business of the Waking Shores?"

Neltharion hesitated, then said, "Nozdormu believes their kind will flourish and spread throughout Azeroth by the millions. He says they will have a significant hand in shaping the fate of our world."

"They are *mortal*," Alexstrasza replied, bemused. "Sentient as they may be, how can such fragile creatures hope for so grand a legacy?"

"Though their life spans are brief, they appear to be hardy and adaptable," Neltharion replied. "I have watched their hunting parties work together to kill creatures ten times their size. In large numbers, they could be a threat . . . especially if Iridikron finds a way to turn them against us."

"Be careful, old friend," she said with a chuckle. "You're starting to jump at shadows."

He huffed, giving her a sideways glance. "And yet here we are, concerned your dearest friend will join the Incarnates in their campaign against *you*."

Neltharion's words struck Alexstrasza like a bolt from above. She stepped back with a gasp, heart cracking, surprised by the violence of her reaction to the Earth-Warder's words; Alexstrasza wasn't angry at him, no, but angry at her powerlessness to convince even her oldest friend of the goodness and nobility of her cause.

She shook out her wings to rid herself of the first sparks of anger. "You have always had a knack for cutting to the heart of the matter, haven't you?"

"I consider it a talent," he said with a chuckle. She gave him a wry smile. "No—you are right, as you so often are. Summon

Nozdormu, then, and let us make plans on how best to approach our newest neighbors."

...

THE MORTALS HAD BUILT a small settlement in the Apex Canopy, far in the south of the Waking Shores. A scattered assortment of primitive huts huddled along the waterways, hidden in the shadows of towering red bluffs and lush, verdant canopies.

Alexstrasza touched down on the eastern cliff of Genesis Falls, cloaked in one of Malygos's illusory spells. Never one to be left out, Malygos had insisted upon joining his fellow Aspects, granting each one a limited measure of invisibility; Alexstrasza prevailed upon Ysera to join them as well, though the green Aspect was keen to return to the Dream.

The Life-Binder peered down at the mortal settlement, charmed. These creatures walked on two legs, similar in size to tarasek but with lankier, more hunched frames. Instead of scales, they had inky-blue flesh and bright, vibrant tufts of hair on their heads. They crouched around a fire, communicating in a guttural language and making gestures with three-fingered hands. Whelps used rudimentary traps to fish along the waterways, while four or five adults worked together to descale a basilisk.

Ysera cruised high overhead, no more than an emerald shimmer in the sky.

"Do you know from where they migrated?" Alexstrasza asked as Neltharion landed on her right side. He, too, looked like nothing more than a shadow in the air. Malygos joined him a moment later, his expression bemused.

"There are reports of similar creatures in the south," the Earth-Warder replied. "Those civilizations are reportedly larger and better established than the village you see."

"Fascinating," she said, watching a whelp catch a fish in a basket. With a joyful shriek, it leapt up from the riverbank to carry its prize back to its elders.

Ysera did a loop around the settlement then landed at Alexstrasza's other side. "This is a very young race, but a peaceful one," she said, lifting her head and speaking directly to Neltharion. "If anything, I should like to issue an edict to forbid the flights from interfering with their development."

"Tell that to Nozdormu," Neltharion said with a snort.

"The mortals may not be peaceful for long." The bronze Aspect joined them, whipping up the dust as he lowered himself beside Ysera. "In time, their civilizations will flourish. We should handle these first interactions with care, as they may have long-lasting implications for our flights."

Neltharion sat, considering the little village. "We approached the djaradin as we are, only to be met with deadly force. We should employ a different strategy with the mortals."

"Go on," she prompted.

"I've considered making contact through the titan-forged," Neltharion replied. "Even a drakonid would be less threatening than a fully grown dragon."

Nozdormu made a humming sound, thinking. "That's assuming we can decipher their language and teach it to the titan-forged in a reasonable amount of time."

"The titan-forged weren't built for diplomacy," Malygos said with a chuckle. "Look what happened with the Winterskorn! I suppose we could work with Tyr to design something more suitable for the cause . . . though I believe he's been rather busy with his own wars of late."

"That is precisely the problem," Neltharion said.

"Could we send one of your arcane constructs to them, Malygos?" Alexstrasza asked, looking to the blue Aspect. "Perhaps you could fashion one that resembles their kind?"

"I suppose," the blue Aspect replied. "But if Nozdormu speaks true, we may wish to find a more convenient way to fraternize with mortals. Something a bit more permanent."

The group fell silent for a moment, considering their options. Ysera cocked her head, watching two whelps playing on the riverbank.

"What better way to understand them than to become like them?" Ysera said after a long moment. "Even if only in their visage."

"In their visage . . ." Alexstrasza repeated under her breath. What a curious thought, and perhaps one that could only have originated from a mind that spent most of its time in the ever-shifting realms of the Emerald Dream. "Malygos, would it be possible?"

"You would wish to abase yourself and become like a mortal, my queen?" Malygos asked, lifting a brow.

"Come now, it isn't an *abasement*," Alexstrasza replied. "Ysera is right—a temporary adoption of a mortal form will allow us to empathize with and better understand their condition."

"Mortal forms might have their uses," Neltharion mused. "Particularly if the mortal races are as prolific as Nozdormu claims. We'll want our intelligence agents monitoring their movements, and that will be easier if we can mimic their forms."

Malygos sighed. "I suppose I can do some research—for now, let us test the limits of what illusory magic can do."

The Aspects spent the remainder of the afternoon on the bluffs, debating how to attempt a mortal form, or *visage*. Working together, they wove illusory magics with varying results; they first turned Neltharion into a towering mortal creature, one who stood taller than the keepers. Next, they managed to turn Alexstrasza into a smaller one, but her limbs were covered in crimson scales.

Though Malygos projected annoyance, Alexstrasza thought his eyes glowed a little brighter with each failed attempt. As the sun began to set, splashing bright fire along the horizon, the blue Aspect sat back on his haunches and rubbed his chin with his talons.

"Illusions are insufficient," he said, eyeing Ysera's now massive, illusory mortal form. The green Aspect's proportions weren't quite right—her arms were far too long, dragging on the ground. The green Aspect waved her ridiculous limbs around, sending Alexstrasza into a whelpish fit of giggles. Even Neltharion let out an amused snort.

With a touch of sadness, the Life-Binder realized it had been years since she had laughed with so much abandon. Tyr had told her that her position required dignity, majesty, and a hundred worries always weighed on her mind. Rare was the moment when she was able to be *just* Alexstrasza.

Malygos rubbed his chin with his knuckles, thinking aloud: "This will need to be something different, I think. For this to work with the desired effect, the magic will need to be deeply personal, individual—"

Before the blue Aspect could finish, a chorus of shrieks echoed through the skies.

Alexstrasza turned her gaze up. Panic spread through the Aspects' attendants, fast as wildfire. Her smile faded as she watched her majordomo, Saristrasz, dive for the butte. He landed elegantly before the Life-Binder, dipping his head to her. Fear roiled off his body like summer heat.

"My queen, we received word from Valdrakken."

"What?" Neltharion said, charging toward them as Ysera reverted back to her draconic form. "What has happened?"

"It's Tyr," Saristrasz said. "He's . . . *fallen*."

"*Fallen?*" Alexstrasza's eyes widened. She recoiled, her heart clattering through her chest. She looked to Ysera, who stood stunned and blinking tears away. "No, it cannot be, I . . . He can't be dead! *How?*"

"It matters not at the moment," Neltharion replied, as the other Aspects joined them, the heartbreak clear on their faces. "We cannot let this information become common knowledge—"

"Tyr was our greatest benefactor," Ysera said, and the grief in her voice was as deep as the Dream itself. "He helped to make us who and what we are. If this news is true, I do not wish to erase his memory. We should celebrate his many contributions and honor his life."

"I agree," Neltharion said, turning back to Alexstrasza, "but Iridikron must not learn of this development. Our alliance with Tyr and the other keepers was a great source of strength for the Broodlands. The recent wars have decimated the titan-forged, and if Tyr is gone . . ."

Alexstrasza closed her eyes and bowed her head. "Then Iridikron will have reason to strike," she said, drawing in a deep breath. "Very well, let us return to Valdrakken at once."

CHAPTER SIX

FAR TO THE NORTH, THE SKIES WERE BRUISED AND THE clouds deepened the afternoon to dusk. Iridikron slitted his eyes against the storm's fury. The Stonescaled was cautious, even in his anger. He had watched Raszageth's fury knock full-grown dragons from the sky, pluck ancient trees from the ground by their roots, and, with his help, stir up massive waves to strike the northern shores. The high winds tore at his wings, but his scales were hard and heavy as stone, giving him stability in Raszageth's storm. Even so, he was never truly *safe* in her tempests.

Raszageth, he thought, narrowing his eyes against the high winds. *What are you doing, whelp?* The Storm-Eater knew not to unleash her storms this close to Harrowsdeep, where she could disrupt the delicate, dangerous work Iridikron and his wingleaders performed underground. Like the Incarnate herself, Raszageth's storms were unpredictable. Wild. Today, her thunder had echoed into the very heart of Harrowsdeep, thwarting an attempt to shift the bones of the earth in the east.

Disgruntled, Iridikron had gone to confront the Storm-Eater himself. Raszageth would not listen to a wingleader when she rarely listened to Iridikron. At best, a lackey would be ignored; at worst, they would be killed. Iridikron would not sacrifice the lives of his commanders to Raszageth's unpredictability.

"Raszageth," he called over the high winds. "Cease this storm!"

If Raszageth could hear him, she did not respond. Instead, she boomed, "Did you think to return to us and throw yourself upon our mercy? I will tear every last scale from your hide. I will *kill* you for what you have done!"

A pained scream cut through the night. The cry was not Raszageth's—it sounded familiar, but Iridikron could not quite place its timbre in the storm. He scented blood on the air, but the snow reduced visibility.

Curious, Iridikron skirted outer gales, circling Raszageth and her prey.

With a roar, Raszageth shot great bolts of lightning from her horns, electrifying a small dragon. The dragon seized, its wings stretching wide in agony, neck arching. The brilliance of the light seared a peculiar silhouette into Iridikron's sight— that was an *ordered* black dragon. A small one, but one from Neltharion's flight nonetheless. The dragon plummeted through the air for several seconds before regaining consciousness, opened their wings, and weakly halted their descent.

What business did one of the ordered have so far north, and alone? Ordered dragons usually traveled in packs of five or six, particularly when flying through the Dragonwilds. Had the Aspects sent a spy, hoping the little dragon would be overlooked?

No, something else is at play here, Iridikron mused. He had no doubt that Neltharion had pawns in Harrowsdeep—he would expect nothing less of the Earth-Warder. No matter how often his so-called Dragon Queen declared peace, Iridikron and Neltharion had already begun a deadly dance for supremacy and survival.

Raszageth dived. Another scream tore through the storm, but this time, a familiar scent crept into Iridikron's snout, one he had known since his days as a whelp. *Ikronia?* he wondered, cruising closer. *Sister? No, it cannot be.*

Iridikron's anger bubbled from the deep, dark cockles of his stone heart, then cooled into something unbreakable and black. The little soft-scale! Iridikron hadn't seen his clutch-sister in so long, he'd thought her dead. Perhaps it would be better if she were; had he not warned her about the dangers of Order magic? Did she not understand how such magic shackled her to the whims of an unknowable force? They could not know what the titans would ask of them, nor how deep the stain of Order magic ran.

Iridikron had half a mind to let Raszageth kill Ikronia for her betrayal.

The Stonescaled circled closer, watching Raszageth continue to torment the smaller dragon. Despite his cold fury,

Iridikron could see an opportunity in this situation, too—he could study Ikronia, thus learning more about the Aspects and their abilities. Or perhaps he could send her right into Neltharion's ranks. Either way, she was worth more to the Incarnates alive.

If he saved her life, she would be a perfect pawn.

"Raszageth," Iridikron thundered. "Release my sister at once!"

The Storm-Eater halted her assault, turning her gaze on Iridikron. Ikronia called out to him, her voice hazy with pain. The little dragon could barely keep herself aloft, but Iridikron felt no pity for her; she had made her choices. Now, she would live with the consequences, or die by them.

"Ikronia has betrayed you," the Storm-Eater replied, tossing her head. "Now she thinks she can throw herself on your mercy. I will not allow it!"

"That is not your decision to make," Iridikron said.

The storm around them roared. Raszageth pivoted in the air, lightning snapping between her massive horns. "Will you try to stop me?" she asked with a wild laugh. "Will you save an *ordered dragon* from her fate? Your sister deserves death. We should kill her now and send her corpse back to her keepers!"

Iridikron growled in response.

"Has your heart grown soft, Stonescaled?" Raszageth snapped, lightning dancing across her mane. "Or perhaps your sympathies now lie with the keepers? Let us see!"

Raszageth flapped her wings forward, shooting great bolts of lightning at Ikronia. The lightning consumed the little black dragon, and she shrieked in pain. With a roar, Iridikron pumped his great wings, spiraled in the air, then turned and dived.

In the glare of her own lightning, the Storm-Eater did not see him coming.

Iridikron slammed into Raszageth, hooking his talons into her hide. Her lightning coursed through his frame, ineffective against stone. She shrieked and lashed at him, her talons glancing off his chest.

"Release me!" she bellowed.

"No." Iridikron closed his wings. Raszageth could not support their combined weight. Together, they dropped like a stone, hurtling toward the forests below. If Iridikron wanted to subdue the Storm-Eater, he needed to force her to the ground. The same stone scales that protected him from Raszageth's fury were a disadvantage in aerial combat.

Raszageth thrashed and shrieked in Iridikron's grip. The earth rushed toward them. Iridikron released her with a kick to the underbelly, sending her sprawling into the snowcapped trees. Iridikron opened his wings and caught the winds, racing over her head.

Raszageth tumbled into a clearing, covered in mud, snow, and brush. The scent of fresh sap filled the air.

He banked and landed nearby. The earth trembled beneath him.

On the far side of the clearing, Ikronia collapsed into a snowdrift and did not move. Iridikron would deal with her next.

With a wild, half-choked roar, Raszageth pushed herself to her feet. She shook her head and slammed her wing talons into the ground, sending snow spraying in all directions.

"You will pay for that!" she screamed.

"Yield," Iridikron said. "Your storms cannot break stone."

"Never," Raszageth shrieked. She opened her wings and tried to leap into the air, but Iridikron tapped a wing talon on the ground. The gravitational forces shifted underfoot. Raszageth faltered, then crashed back into the snow with a grunt. She tried to leap aloft again, only to stumble forward.

Raszageth glared at him. "What are you doing to me?" She shook snow off her snout and growled.

"Yield, Raszageth," Iridikron replied. "I have no desire to fight you."

The Storm-Eater snarled, her lip curling. "Let me kill the runt, and I will."

"No, I have use for Ikronia yet," Iridikron said. "Can you not see how she could be a great boon to our cause? Calm your storms, sister. She will meet her just fate in time, but only after she has exceeded her use."

The Storm-Eater grumbled, though her howling winds settled. The snow continued to fall, gently now, forming a thin layer on Iridikron's wings and scales. "I expect you to repay me a hundredfold, Iridikron. I want to hear our enemies' screams echoing through the Broodlands."

"And you shall, my friend," Iridikron replied, turning toward Ikronia's motionless form. "Where did you find my wayward sister?"

"Nearby," Raszageth replied. "She wanted to throw herself at your feet and beg for your mercy, can you imagine?"

"Do you know how she came to be ordered?" Iridikron asked as he strode toward the little dragon. Ikronia continued to breathe, but barely.

"No," Raszageth replied, following him. They paused beside Ikronia's bleeding form. "Does it matter? The betrayal is the same."

"It may," Iridikron said. "I would be very interested to know if Ikronia was forced or coerced to accept Order magic, or if she made that choice of her own free will."

"She seems very . . . *naïve*," Raszageth replied with a hiss. "I will never understand how the two of you came from the same clutch."

"Hmph," was all Iridikron said in response. Ikronia had always allowed others to do her thinking for her, which was less of an issue when she listened to someone with wisdom and discretion. She would make a poor spy, but still, Iridikron did not want her in Harrowsdeep. It would not do to have an ordered dragon seen among his ranks.

So, Iridikron moved his sister into a small cavern near his lair. He covered her wounded body in a blanket of soft earth, filled the deep scores in her hide with silt, and set her broken legs and tail with stone braces. He coaxed magma into the room, warming the space. While he worked, he thought about how best to weaponize his sister against the Aspects.

Over the last two centuries, Iridikron had worked quietly to undermine the Aspects' work in the Broodlands. Most recently, he and his wingleaders shifted the earth and caused quakes, disrupting the dragonflights' work.

More important, Iridikron subverted the Aspects in the Dragonwilds. He and his followers spoke to their kind about the effects of Order magic, claimed the flights pushed primal dragons out of their hunting grounds, and blamed everything from strange weather patterns to vanishing dragons on the ordered dragons. It was made all the easier to recruit followers when the Aspects mostly hid within their borders.

As for Vyranoth . . . well, he had made plans for her, too. The ice dragon had a beneficent streak he meant to exploit— and the more she felt the Aspects were harming the primal dragons, the better. He would give Vyranoth good reason to turn against the Dragon Queen . . . in time. He needed the right pawn, the right *ambassador,* to take the primal dragons' complaints to the ice dragon. Raszageth, too, could help him on this front: The Storm-Eater was known for her excursions around the Dragonwilds and beyond, and she had a wide web of friends in far-flung places. The friendship between Raszageth and Vyranoth had grown apace, and it was one upon which Iridikron meant to capitalize.

Raszageth watched from the cavern's threshold, unamused. "Ikronia is too weak to be of any use to our cause, Iridikron. The whelp can't fight."

"Wars are not won on the battlefield, Raszageth, but in hearts and minds," Iridikron said quietly. "Ikronia may serve well on that front . . . provided she is given the proper direction."

The Storm-Eater stalked into the cavern, making a disgusted noise at the back of her throat. "What are you talking about?"

Iridikron turned, his scales rasping on the stone below him. "When she wakes, take her to the borders of the Broodlands and command her to burn the villages of tarasek or mortals, I care not. Leave enough alive to spread the word. Cry chaos. Rain fire from the skies. Make the ground quake. Draw storms down from above if you must, but only Ikronia is to be seen. Do you understand?"

"Yes," Raszageth said with a cackle.

"Good," Iridikron replied, stalking from the cavern. "Go forth and destroy, Storm-Eater! It is what you do best."

CHAPTER SEVEN

FOR MONTHS, RASZAGETH APPEARED AT THE ENTRANCE to Ikronia's lair once every clutch of moons. At first, Ikronia hated their nighttime forays; they would destroy a village or two at random—tarasek or mortal, Raszageth did not care. All that mattered to the Storm-Eater was fire, terror, and *blood*.

But as the season turned and the air chilled, the tarasek's ranks began to swell at Harrowsdeep. Mortals joined them, too, fleeing the destruction wrought—seemingly—at the talons of the Aspects. Even the primal dragons took note, wondering about this change in the dragonflights' behavior.

Once Ikronia caught her brother's vision, she executed her task with *relish*.

Mortal screams echoed through the night, sharp enough to pierce Raszageth's storms. Ikronia dived through the air, breathing fire from her maw, setting a cluster of straw huts aflame. The dry grasses combusted. Small creatures burst from their entrances, shrieking in terror and pain. One mortal stumbled to the ground, eaten alive by the blaze. Ikronia sped past, her wings fanning the fires into an inferno.

Raszageth cackled overhead, hidden in the dark, swirling skies. The Storm-Eater shot lightning bolts from her perch in the clouds, bright, brilliant flashes of blue-white light.

How Ikronia hated the half-mad Incarnate! She understood her position, how these acts were needed to prove her worth and fealty to the cause. What she did not understand was the torment she suffered at Raszageth's talons. Even if Ikronia followed her brother's directives, the Storm-Eater might beat her anyway. Iridikron may have saved her life, but he had also condemned her to the Storm-Eater's capriciousness. It was a mercy and a punishment both.

Ikronia should have known better. She should have let Raszageth kill her the moment she saw her brother on the approach. From the shell, Iridikron's help had always come with caveats: He had been the bigger, faster, and more cunning of the two clutch-mates. He had protected Ikronia from the dragons who would prey upon her. But every time Iridikron saved her life, he extracted a price. A promise. A pound of scales, so to speak, but it was Raszageth who carved literal scales from Ikronia's hide.

She endured the pain because she, too, wanted to see the Aspects and their flights fall. Ikronia hadn't tarried among the flights—just for a season, maybe two—long enough for her to realize she'd made a mistake. They had promised her a place in the Broodlands, but this "place" came coupled with duty and labor. The black Aspect worked his flight to exhaustion—the black dragons commanded his forges, marched in his army, and constructed his bastion. Worse, she seemed to be the only one who did not support Neltharion's fanatical commitment to his oaths. Even among the swelling numbers of the black dragonflight, Ikronia had never felt more alone.

The little black dragon wheeled in the sky. Below her, fire rampaged across the landscape, devouring everything in its path. It chewed into the forests and coughed black smoke into the air. Birds and small creatures fled the flames. Mortals shrieked and their whelps cried. To Ikronia's mind, mortal lives were meaningless. Anything that was not a dragon was *prey*.

She closed her wings and dived toward the village. Flames erupted from her maw, consuming everything in their path. With each village she burned and every life she took, Ikronia defied the Aspects and their keepers. She wished they could see her now, burning village after village in their hallowed names, sowing fear and destruction along their borders; however, Iridikron had forbidden her from speaking of her mission to anyone, including Fyrakk.

Perhaps, someday, this charge would end, and her brother would forgive her for her mistakes. For now, she would do as her brother had bidden her.

Ikronia tilted her wings to better ride Raszageth's ferocious currents. The Storm-Eater demanded the total annihilation of the mortal villages, with perhaps one or two survivors spared— someone had to spread the news that Alexstrasza's dragonflights were cruel, murderous creatures bent on the destruction of non-draconic races. Several mortals had already managed to escape the glittering inferno.

Ikronia landed in a large central clearing. The smell of charred wood and burning flesh filled her nostrils, heady and intoxicating. The screams of the dying had quieted, leaving her alone with the roar of the fire and the howl of Raszageth's winds.

Movement drew her gaze to the left, to a gap between huts. A mortal whelp stumbled into view, tripping over its own feet and tumbling to the ground. When Ikronia turned toward it, the whelp screamed, a high, thin wail that carried over the storm. Ikronia growled, flames curling around her lips.

A sharp pain slammed into the side of the black dragon's head, barely missing her eye. A hefty stone thudded on the ground near her feet. With a snarl, Ikronia turned, surprised to see a second mortal standing in the clearing, holding another rock in one hand.

This mortal stood taller than the whelp. Its long, wild hair grew past its shoulders.

"Do you think you can lure me away from your whelp, little beast?" Ikronia said, stalking toward the mortal. The tiny creature stood its ground, knees trembling. "It would be better for you to *run*."

The creature "spoke" to the dragon in a feral, nonsensical tongue, then hurled another rock. The stone bounced harmlessly off Ikronia's chest.

Before the dragon could say anything more, a blue-white bolt of lightning shot from the skies, slamming into the mortal.

The creature spasmed; its eyes rolled back into its head as it crumpled to the ground. A long, thin wail unspooled into the night.

Now . . . where was the whelp?

Ikronia spun, seeking it. Her tail slammed into the remains of a burning hut and sent a spray of cinders into the air. The whelp burst from its hiding place, took one look at its mother's corpse, then skidded to a stop. It fell to the ground with another agonized wail, one that speared Ikronia's heart and shattered her bloodlust. This was not a cry of fear, but of a pain so deep it could crack the world. It was a cry of loss, and something more. *Loneliness.*

Ikronia knew that feeling all too well. The dragon halted, stunned by the emotion that welled up in her chest.

"Kill it." Raszageth's voice rumbled from the skies, her voice deep as thunder. "It has seen me. Do not hesitate this time!"

The very sound of the Storm-Eater's voice made Ikronia's scars ache.

"Ikronia!" Raszageth roared.

With a furious shriek, Ikronia struck the whelp down with her talons. She gave the little creature a clean, painless death. When she looked up, she thought she saw movement in the trees ahead. Whatever hid among the branches, she let it be.

As Ikronia and Raszageth withdrew from the village, the little whelp's final scream haunted her. Ikronia tucked it away in a shredded niche of her mind, remembering her hatred for the Aspects and their false promises, then followed Raszageth into the blackened horizon.

...

IN THE NORTH, VYRANOTH left her den for a night hunt, soaring under radiant ribbons of turquoise, green, and purple lights in the starry sky.

Vyranoth's mind whirled with conflicting thoughts and loyalties. Over the last few turns of the moons, Alexstrasza had been inviting Vyranoth to the Broodlands with greater regularity. Just yesterday, Alexstrasza had sent another one of her messengers to the Frozen Fangs, summoning Vyranoth to a feast at Wyrmrest Temple. Vyranoth had already declined three such requests that season. As much as she might miss Alexstrasza, she had no desire to subject herself to more heartbreak.

Alexstrasza had made her choices, and she hadn't chosen Vyranoth.

Then, just that morning, Raszageth had appeared at Vyranoth's aerie, asking the older dragon to race her through the Fangs. Now, *that* had been an invitation Vyranoth would accept with gladness. Perhaps it meant something that, of late, she felt a greater kinship with Raszageth than Alexstrasza . . . but Vyranoth was not ready to face that reality. True, the Storm-Eater was unpredictable and prone to violence. Vyranoth tried to temper Raszageth's baser instincts, teaching the Incarnate to show mercy where it was due. Whether the Storm-Eater listened to her counsel, Vyranoth could not say.

Despite her ferocity, Raszageth possessed a youthful exuberance and zest for life. She loved to summon strong winds and ride them across the landscape; she tempted Vyranoth to dive in the oceans from the great northern cliffs; but more than anything, Raszageth loved to chase storms. She often flew north to revel in the Fangs' terrible fury, often bringing Vyranoth a kill for the intrusion or news from the south. Perhaps Vyranoth taught Raszageth temperance, but the Incarnate showed her how to make the most of every moment.

Still, Vyranoth could not turn her back on Alexstrasza—at least, not completely.

To clear her head, Vyranoth flew to the northern shores, hoping to hunt the great white bears on the ice floes, or perhaps a horned whale. She craved the sweet, marbled flesh of the creatures that lived in the Fangs' perpetual winter. As she cruised past the cliffs of the northernmost reaches, the seas stretched out before her, black and fathomless. Walls of sapphire-blue ice rose straight from the waves, glowing in the bright moonlight. Icebergs speckled the waters, some as large as small islands, hosting restless seabirds and other wildlife.

To her surprise, Vyranoth spotted a small pack of dragons hunting fish several wing-lengths off the coast. Most dragons weren't naïve enough to encroach upon her territory. *Hmph,* she thought, landing on a ledge to watch.

A mottled green closed their wings and dived into the waters. Seconds later, a great whale surfaced, thrashing. Water exploded from its blowhole. A second dragon struck, raking their talons across the whale's back. Ribbons of blood spilled into the sea. The first dragon burst from the waves, a torn fin in their jaws.

The whale's low, mournful cries echoed across the water.

As the dragons hauled their kill to shore, Vyranoth circled overhead. She had no intention of stealing the whale, though her stomach rumbled when the scent of blood hit her nostrils. They were young, barely out of drakehood.

One of the dragons, a little slate-gray female, looked up at Vyranoth, her eyes widening, snout already red with gore. She bugled a warning to her pack-mates—two males, one the color of ocher, the other the mottled green of moss. Both craned their necks, looking at Vyranoth in alarm. The green one eyed Vyranoth as she landed. He lowered his gaze but stepped in front of the other two in a protective manner.

All three dragons looked as if they hadn't had a proper meal in many moons, their eyes sunken and cheeks hollow. Vyranoth could count the ocher's every rib bone. The slate-gray shivered in the cold, wrapping her tail around her feet. Of the three, the mottled green looked the most hale, but even he was too wiry for a dragon of his size. Vyranoth could smell their desperation and hear the rumbling in their bellies. She pitied them, but not too much.

"You cannot hunt here, young ones," Vyranoth said, stalking toward them, ice in her voice. "This is my territory."

The slate-gray female backed up a step, dropping her head to protect her throat. She turned her gaze down, too. "Ancient One! These waters are yours?"

"Yes, mine," Vyranoth replied.

The mottled green shifted his weight, looking down at the slate-gray female. He extended a wing over her shivering form. "Could we go far over the water to hunt?"

Vyranoth narrowed her eyes. "Too far, you die. Why did you come to the Fangs?"

The slate-gray shivered harder. "The ordered ones chased us from our grounds. It's cold here, but we're hungry. So hungry."

Vyranoth sighed. "You had no choice?"

The slate-gray bobbed her head.

Despite her loneliness, Vyranoth had no desire to share her territory with three strangers; yet she could not leave these young ones to starve, either. Many dragons had gone east to the Broodlands; those who hadn't had expanded their territories and defended them jealously, pushing younger, less experienced dragons to the fringes.

Loath to help but unable to stand by, Vyranoth sighed. "Very well. But you must obey my rules."

The slate-gray blinked and cocked her head.

"Anything," the ocher said, stepping forward.

"A kill for me every three moons," Vyranoth said. "You will not kill for sport. You will respect my solitude and find your own lairs. Agreed?"

"Yes," the mottled green said.

"Good."

Vyranoth spent the rest of her afternoon with the young ones. The stone-gray primal dragon was Nalikrona; the ocher, Szarnin; and the mottled green, Razviik. Vyranoth flew with them around the coast, pointing out fertile hunting grounds and potential locations for aeries and dens.

As Razviik and Nalikrona inspected one such cave, Vyranoth and Szarnin hovered outside. In the east, the sun peeked over the horizon, gilding the mountain peaks and coloring them in soft pinks. Overhead, the skies burned orange. The cave's mouth was draped in shadows, well hidden among the cliffs and crags.

"Many thanks, Ancient One," Szarnin said. "Their eggs were taken twice now."

"Taken?" Vyranoth narrowed her eyes. "The entire clutch? How?"

Primal parents might lose an occasional egg in the wilds, but to lose so many in a row was unusual.

"Eggs gone," Szarnin said, lifting his shoulders in a shrug. "Some say the stone-skins. Egg-stealers."

"Stone-skins?" Vyranoth repeated, picturing a titan-forged in her mind's eye. In the Broodlands, little Talinstrasz and Lailastrasza had been inexplicably afraid of "the eyes in the rocks" and being taken, and Vyranoth began to wonder if those fears weren't as irrational as she had thought. Whelplings were often cognizant of their surroundings while still in the shell. If something had taken the whelplings' eggs—no, if *someone* had taken them from their nests—that would explain their fears.

"And you have seen these egg-stealers?" Vyranoth asked.

Szarnin shook his head. "No. Just talk. Dragon talk, tarasek talk."

"Tarasek?" Vyranoth asked, confused. "Why tarasek?"

"Tarasek disappear," he replied. "Villages burn."

She frowned. Could this be true? Neltharion had always struck Vyranoth as a shrewd strategist. Like Iridikron, the black Aspect could be single-minded in pursuit of his goals. If these rumors had any truth to them, perhaps someone in the Broodlands quietly sought to bolster the dragonflights while depleting the primal dragons' numbers in the wilds. It was a cruel, heartless strategy, but Vyranoth could see how the Aspects might leverage it against Iridikron.

But she sensed Iridikron's presence in all this, too— Nalikrona even *smelled* a little like the Incarnate, which could mean they were related. The dragon's appearances in the Fangs could be as much chance as it could be one of Iridikron's well-constructed ploys. The Stonescaled did love his schemes, which was one reason why Vyranoth continued to eschew his cause.

It's a rumor, she told herself. *Nothing more.*

But perhaps all she wanted was to believe her own lie.

CHAPTER EIGHT

NELTHARION TAPPED HIS TALONS ON THE STONE floor, annoyed. He stood in the throne room of the Obsidian Citadel with three of his flightleaders, discussing the latest intelligence from the west. A sculpted map of northern Kalimdor stretched out before them, which the scalesmiths had carved from a massive piece of igneous rock. Dragon-shaped pawns stood in Valdrakken and Harrowsdeep, representing the Aspects' and Incarnates' forces.

The throne room overlooked the entirety of the Obsidian Citadel and the valleys beyond. Overhead, the clouds burned bright orange, reflecting the fires that roared in the citadel's forges. Columns of thick, dark smoke twisted into the sky. The ring of hammers echoed off the sharp cliffs. Black dragons dived in and out of sight, busy with their own tasks.

Neltharion took great pride in the bastion his flight had built—the Obsidian Citadel was the pinnacle of the dragons' fortifications, fusing imposing form with gainful function.

Over two hundred years, his flight had reinforced the mountains around the citadel, turning it into a powerful bulwark against Harrowsdeep. They built grand forges, tunneled into the mountains to create vaults, and pioneered new weapons, armor, and defenses. Of the five dragonflights, it was the black dragonflight who pushed the martial prowess of the Broodlands forward.

Today, however, those feelings were overshadowed by the news from the west. Egnion had just returned from several nights in Incarnate territory. As leader of the Shadowscales, Egnion spent much of his time afield. Upon his return that morning, he added two more dragon pawns to Harrowsdeep, signaling another hundred dragons apiece. The growth of Iridikron's forces outpaced that of the Aspects' by a wide margin. Before long, they would outnumber the dragonflights three-to-one.

Iridikron was preparing for war.

"The quakes are increasing in intensity and frequency, my Aspect," Egnion said to Neltharion. "And we still cannot prove with absolute certainty that Iridikron and the Primals are to blame for them."

"Nor can we stop them from affecting our territories." Calcia gestured to the map with her talons. "As you know, my scalesmiths have worked with the blue dragonflight to place enchanted obelisks around the borders of the Broodlands, helping to absorb the worst of the quakes," she said, tapping their western border. It lit with bright fire under her touch.

"However," she continued, "the increased frequency of the tremors has destabilized the magma chambers beneath the

Waking Shores. If left unchecked, we fear it will have dire consequences for the entire region."

"I don't need to tell any of you what will happen if the caldera beneath us explodes," Egnion said.

Neltharion drummed his talons on the floor again, harder this time, sending hairline cracks into the stone beneath his feet. On the surface, the Stonescaled appeared to be using the quakes to disrupt the Aspects' progress in the Broodlands. Iridikron's goals were rarely so superficial. Despite Neltharion's wisdom and long acquaintance with the Stonescaled—they had once been close, sharing the same interests in the bones of the earth—he could not guess the Incarnate's true aims. He had conjectures. Assumptions. *Inferences.*

The Earth-Warder shifted in place, muscles aching from the weight of the world pressing in on him from all sides. He sensed the cracks that Iridikron broke into the continent, but the *why* continued to elude him.

A whisper curled at the back of Neltharion's mind, sinuous as smoke: *You will fail,* it crooned. *You have not the strength nor shrewdness to stop the Stonescaled.*

Neltharion gave his head a little shake, but the whispers persisted: *He laughs at you from the depths—they all do!*

Even your fellow Aspects mock you, said a third. *They see you for the fool you are!*

Turn to our power, instructed a fourth voice. *We will help crush your enemies underfoot.*

Iridikron is nothing *compared to me,* Neltharion said to the whispers, frustrated with their prattle. Even before he had become Aspect of the black dragonflight, these whispers began to rise from the deep, dark caverns in his mind. Over the years, they had increased in intensity, making Neltharion question his own thoughts, his own actions. They were inescapable. Omnipresent. Neltharion had not told another soul about them—not even Malygos, who had long been his closest confidant and friend.

Embrace us . . .

No. Half a growl escaped Neltharion's throat. Before his flightleaders could so much as lift a brow, he said, "Iridikron grows more brazen by the day, and yet Alexstrasza's peace edicts bind our talons."

"We must find a way to push back, my liege." Vembrion, the embattled, one-eyed seneschal of the Obsidian Citadel's Guard, sighed as he looked over the map. "The Incarnates draw more mature dragons by the day; and while our whelplings will soon outnumber theirs, it will be centuries before our armies can match their maturity, skill, and might. At this rate, we will be unable to hold the western border in the event of a direct attack."

"I know, my old friend," Neltharion said, blowing a hot breath from his nostrils. With every passing day, the Incarnates' position grew stronger. Unlike Alexstrasza, Neltharion did not believe the Aspects would be able to make peace with the Incarnates. Tyr was gone. The rest of the keepers were scattered or dead. Whatever threats arose, the Aspects would face them on their own.

Far to the northwest, the Stonescaled shaped the ground beneath their feet. Iridikron had warned the Aspects and their dragonflights of the consequences for entering his domain, and that included its skies. So, the black dragonflight monitored Iridikron's work from afar, observing and recording the earth-rattling tremors that originated from Harrowsdeep. Fyrakk rallied primal dragons to the Incarnates' side, while Raszageth was . . . *Raszageth*. The Storm-Eater loved nothing more than to sow discord and chaos wherever she went, and often harried the flights' patrols. Raszageth had already menaced her fair share of black and green dragons along the Broodlands' western borders, and yet Alexstrasza cautioned them to stay any attempt at a counterattack. Raszageth *wanted* to incite a war; that much was clear.

Neltharion respected Alexstrasza's convictions. Publicly, he made pretenses for peace, backing Alexstrasza and instructing his flight not to engage with the Primals. Over the years, he had sent emissaries to Harrowsdeep at the Dragon Queen's behest. Each had been turned away. Several had been beaten, one to the verge of death. Iridikron had killed Neltharion's spies, refused peace talks, and spread vicious rumors about the effects of Order magic on dragonkind. He claimed the flights had kidnapped legions of tarasek and forced Order magic upon them, turning them into subservient drakonid. It was a lie, of course, but many were quick to choose fear over truth.

Iridikron would not be reasoned with—he would set all of Kalimdor aflame before he bowed to anyone, much less to those who served the keepers.

So, quietly, Neltharion prepared for war, just as Iridikron was doing.

He tapped his talons on the ground a third time. "Calcia, I think we can indeed *push back*. Develop an obelisk that senses the vibrations in the earth and emits an interfering wave of equal strength. The quakes must stop if we are to continue our work."

"We could do that," Calcia said, pressing one of her forefoot knuckles into her chin, thinking. "I will set to work on the prototypes myself."

"Good," Neltharion said. "The question of our numbers is much more difficult to solve, however. It takes dragons far too long to reach adulthood. We have decades, not centuries."

"So, we conscript the eldest drakes to fight," Vembrion said.

"Not against fully grown dragons," Neltharion replied. "Elder drakes may serve on patrols and in support roles, perhaps, but they will not be able to hold their own in the skies."

"Can we not breed more drakonid?" Egnion said.

"Drakonid cannot fight in the skies, and they possess only limited control of magic," Neltharion replied. "If we want to disrupt the Primals on the battlefield, we may need to create a new type of soldier entirely. Let me think on the solution."

A blaze of crimson caught Neltharion's eye. He looked up, surprised to see Alexstrasza landing on the terrace of the throne room. A second dragon alighted beside her, a blue-tinged primal dragon of ice. *Vyranoth,* Neltharion thought with a frown. Vyranoth had not been seen in the Broodlands for several years—what brought her to their territories now?

Neltharion knew Vyranoth by reputation alone. The primal dragon had long been friends with Alexstrasza; however, the Shadowscales had spotted her with Raszageth on more than one occasion. With conflict brewing on the horizon, a dragon of Vyranoth's stature could not stay neutral for long.

Neltharion did not trust her to choose order.

"Speak to no one of this," Neltharion said to his flightleaders of their plan. The three black dragons nodded to their Aspect, murmuring their assent. Egnion stretched his wing over the map, turning all the pawns on its surface into shadows.

"Alexstrasza," Neltharion said, forcing a smile as he strode toward the terrace. "What brings you to the Obsidian Citadel this day? A look at our forges for our friend Vyranoth, perhaps?"

"No, Neltharion," Alexstrasza said, her tone grim. The Dragon Queen flicked her tail back and forth, almost as if she were . . . *nervous*? Nervousness was not a state in which Neltharion was accustomed to seeing Alexstrasza. "I fear we bring distressing news."

Vyranoth turned to him. A thin layer of frost grew under her feet and spread out across the floor. "Perhaps you can explain, Earth-Warder."

"Explain what?" Neltharion asked, looking to Alexstrasza in confusion. His flightleaders fanned out behind him. "What has happened?"

Alexstrasza swished her tail again, agitated. "Two nights ago, Vyranoth believes she saw an ordered dragon ravaging a local tarasek village. The entire settlement was burned to the ground."

Neltharion narrowed his eyes. "From which flight?" he asked through his teeth.

The Dragon Queen sighed, giving him a fraught look.

"Ah," Neltharion replied. "I see."

"I wanted to bring these allegations to you in private, rather than to the Seat of the Aspects," Alexstrasza said. "Do you know anything of this?"

"No," he replied, and the word rumbled through his chest like cracking stone. "I have issued no such orders."

The Dragon Queen held his gaze for a full heartbeat, her golden eyes sharp. Intelligent. Questioning.

She thinks you a liar, one of the whispers said. *A warmonger. Undermining her command.*

Silence, Neltharion told them, then he said, "You know I would not lie to you, Alexstrasza."

You already lie, the whispers curled at the back of his mind. *She knows of the weapons you forge in the dark.*

"And what of your flightleaders?" Alexstrasza asked, turning her attention to Egnion, Calcia, and Vembrion. "Have you seen any such behaviors from your flight?"

"No, my queen," Vembrion said, bowing his head. "The black dragonflight is ever loyal to your decrees."

"Very well," Alexstrasza replied. "Vyranoth, will you tell them what your friends witnessed at our borders?"

"In the autumn, I took several drakes under my wing," Vyranoth said. "During the last dark moons, one of them spotted an ordered black dragon burning a tarasek village to the ground. They say the mortals have been attacked as well."

"That cannot be," Egnion said, stepping forward. "We would not attack innocents, especially unprovoked! If such a thing were happening, surely *we* would know about it—"

"Egnion," Neltharion said, his tone carrying a warning. Few knew of the Shadowscales or their mission, and the black Aspect intended to keep it that way.

"I flew the length of your western border," Vyranoth said, "and found evidence of other sites that have been destroyed. Many tarasek have fled west, telling stories of dragonfire and ruined villages. I also found black scales at several sites."

Vyranoth extended a collection of scales to the Earth-Warder. Each one gleamed obsidian.

Neltharion plucked a scale from her grasp, turning it this way and that, examining it from all angles. The scale belonged to an ordered dragon, of that there could be no doubt. Several of the scales were cracked or hatched with old claw marks. At least two looked dull, almost cloudy.

"These scales did not come from a healthy dragon," Neltharion said, passing the scale to Egnion. "The scales' size and shape are consistent, however, which leads me to believe they were taken or shed from the same creature. Due to their poor condition, I would guess this dragon is not living in the Broodlands or among the flights."

Alexstrasza frowned. "Are there any black dragons missing from the Obsidian Citadel?"

"Perhaps," he said. "Egnion, can I entrust you with this matter? Take the scales to the flightleaders. See if you can identify them."

"Of course, my Aspect." Egnion bobbed his head once, collected the scales, and hurried off.

"In the meantime," Vyranoth said, "I will take you to the burned villages, if you wish."

Neltharion tilted his head, thinking. This situation smelled like a plot—if Vyranoth had chosen to side with the Incarnates, Iridikron could have sent her forth with this story, hoping to lure Alexstrasza from the safety of the Broodlands. In her infinite mercy, the Dragon Queen would rush across the borders, hoping to alleviate suffering and bring those responsible to justice. Thus exposed, it would be an ideal time to capture or kill the Dragon Queen. Iridikron had to know the dragonflights would not last without Alexstrasza—no creature could survive without its beating heart.

However, Neltharion could not turn away from this situation. Trap or no, he needed to investigate Vyranoth's allegations.

"I will go with you," Neltharion said.

Vyranoth dipped her head. "Very well. I shall be glad of your company."

"I will go, too," Alexstrasza said.

"There is no need, my queen," Neltharion said to Alexstrasza. "Allow me to go in your stead. I will be your eyes." Better for Neltharion to go alone—especially if Vyranoth spoke true and the black dragonflight was responsible for significant loss of life. If that was the case, he would want to control the perception and reputation of his flight.

Alexstrasza shook her head. "If our flights are responsible for the suffering of others, I want to see the pain we have wrought with my own eyes."

"Come, then," Vyranoth said. "We should take wing before the hour grows late."

THE MORTAL VILLAGE HAD been reduced to nothing more than ash. Neltharion and Vyranoth were the first to arrive— the Dragon Queen had to let at least the black dragonflight take the vanguard. Neltharion circled the demolished village in the air. When Vembrion and his Obsidian Guard signaled that the area was secure, the Earth-Warder banked and glided toward the ground.

So, Vyranoth had not been lying about the villages, which meant Neltharion had a different problem now.

The Earth-Warder landed amid the remains of a wrecked hut. Charred wood disintegrated under his feet, and a skull rolled into the space between his toes. Disgusted, he batted the remains away, kicking up a cloud of ash.

The little village might have been charming once, at least by tarasek standards. Tucked away beneath the protective wing of a mountain range, fifteen huts had once stood on a pretty riverbank. Now the village was naught but blackened bones and burned corpses. The air smelled of charcoal, and the breeze rattled in what was left of the trees. Under Neltharion's feet, the earth still cried out in pain. Embers seethed inside the soil, burning deeper into the world's crust.

The Dragon Queen will blame you and your flight for this destruction, said a whisper.

They will say you are unfit to lead.

Neltharion frowned, pushing the words from his mind. To his chagrin, the magic that called to him from the ground was *ordered,* and unmistakably from *his* flight, too. As his flightleaders landed around him, Neltharion exchanged a wary glance with Vembrion. Clearly, the old guard captain sensed it as well.

"Say nothing," Neltharion said under his breath. "Especially to the Dragon Queen. We will deal with this issue ourselves. Search the area and bring every scrap of evidence to my attention."

"At once, my Aspect," Vembrion said, bowing. "I will inform the others."

Neltharion turned. Alexstrasza landed among the ruins, her features twisted in despair. She stirred her talons in the ash, exposing a set of skeletons clinging to one another. The Dragon Queen set her foot down and stared at the bones.

Neltharion cared little for the burgeoning mortal races and even less for the tarasek. Yet the absolute wretchedness in Alexstrasza's bearing struck him to the core. The Dragon Queen closed her eyes and lowered her head. Her wings drooped. Several heartbeats passed in silence.

A whisper curled in the back of his mind, beckoning to him: *She is too weak to lead,* the sibilant voice said, its vowels warped. *Why weren't you chosen? Are you even weaker than she?*

She will not have the strength to do what must be done.

There are many different kinds of strength, Neltharion told the whispers in his head.

But only one triumphs in war, the whispers said.

Alexstrasza's voice tore Neltharion from his thoughts: "Terror permeates this place," she said. "These creatures died, screaming, and their cries still echo off the mountains that surround this place. It is unfathomable to think one of our kind could have done such a thing. And you say there are more places like this?" Alexstrasza lifted her head and looked to Vyranoth, who stood a few wingspans away from the queen.

"By my count, at least ten," Vyranoth replied, her gaze full of accusations.

"So many," Alexstrasza lamented. "Order magic is meant to call us ever higher, away from our baser instincts. This makes no *sense*."

"Perhaps Order magic is not what you were promised," Vyranoth replied.

Alexstrasza gritted her teeth and said nothing.

While the Dragon Queen mourned, Neltharion began investigating the village and its surrounding environs. Working with Vembrion, the Earth-Warder dug in the ash, examined the burn patterns on the ground, and noted the depths of embers burrowing deeper into the soil.

"Six moons past," he mused to himself, rubbing some of the ash between his talons. The village had burned barely a clutch of moons ago. Neltharion frowned. He saw the *what* all around him, but he was once more missing the *why*.

The Earth-Warder walked to the sandy riverbank, gazing at the turbulent white water as it rushed over the rocks. Underfoot, he sensed a strange yet familiar energy. Curious, Neltharion pressed his forefoot into the wet sand, asking it to part for him. The sand cracked and split, yawning open to reveal a thick, twisted branch. Thin fingers of lightning rose from the ground and sizzled around the damp bank. The scent of storms filled Neltharion's nostrils, fresh and sharp.

With a frown, Neltharion reached into the earth and extracted the branch. No, not a branch—a *fulgurite,* a tube of vitrified sand. A fulgurite took the fury of lightning and trapped it in glass. At two talon-lengths, this was one of the larger specimens Neltharion had seen in his life. Only a massive thunderbolt could have created such a thing.

Neltharion hefted the fulgurite in his forefoot, thinking. Such an object may have been created by natural means— after all, it was not uncommon for powerful storms to strike along shorelines and roil among mountain ranges—but this particular artifact bristled with elemental magic.

Not long ago, he had seen one of the Storm-Eater's creations on the horizon: a great, churning maelstrom that blotted out the sun. The residual magic in the fulgurite reminded Neltharion too keenly of Raszageth's wild, unpredictable power.

The Storm-Eater was not clever enough to devise a plot like this—no, this was Iridikron's doing. The Stonescaled must have found a way to coerce a black dragon into helping Raszageth with her grim work.

The Earth-Warder turned his head, eyeing Vyranoth. The primal dragon stood with Alexstrasza on the other side of the clearing, examining a copse of burned trees. Overhead, black dragons wheeled in the sky, ever vigilant.

Did Vyranoth know of Raszageth's involvement? The primal

dragon was wise. If she had known about Raszageth's part here, she likely would have come to the same conclusions as Neltharion had and confronted Iridikron, not Alexstrasza. Iridikron must have fed her a partial truth through a third party, knowing Vyranoth would go straight to the Dragon Queen.

What was Iridikron playing at? What sort of trap had he set for the Aspects, via mortals and tarasek, no less?

The fledgling mortal races were insignificant creatures—they should have been far below the notice of a dragon like Iridikron. Their lives burned bright for a moment, but that was all.

"My Aspect," Vembrion said, alighting beside Neltharion. "The others are ready to move on."

"Very well," Neltharion replied, blinking his thoughts away. He offered the fulgurite to Vembrion. "Send one of your guards back to the Obsidian Citadel with this at once."

"A fulgurite?" Vembrion said, taking the glassy tube from Neltharion. He sat back on his haunches, eyes widening as he turned the tube between his talons. Vembrion held it up to his snout and inhaled. "Is this . . . was this made by Raszageth's bolts?"

"Perhaps," Neltharion replied. "Take it to Umbrenion and tell them to look into the matter."

"Titans be good," Vembrion breathed. "Berian is our swiftest flier. I will send him forth at once."

"Do not be seen," Neltharion said. "For now, it is best the Dragon Queen does not know. She is too trusting, and we dare not risk Vyranoth learning what we know."

"Understood," Vembrion said.

With worry pressing heavily on his mind, Neltharion took wing, rejoining Alexstrasza and Vyranoth in the skies.

EVERY VILLAGE THEY VISITED was nothing more than a dark smudge upon the landscape.

Alexstrasza stood amid the ruins of another settlement, her seventh that day. Charcoal dust coated her limbs to the knee and blackened her belly and tail. Her heart, too, felt as ashen as the grime on her scales.

Ordered dragons had burned these villages. *Her* dragons. Neltharion had confirmed it, as had Malygos, who had been summoned to survey the arcane energies in the area. Alexstrasza called Nozdormu to their side, too, hoping that the bronze Aspect might peer into the past and help them understand what had happened in this place.

I am sorry, Nozdormu said to her, *but the threads of time are delicate, and I am still mastering this art. I dare not risk meddling with the timeways until you have exhausted all other options.*

Very well, my friend, Alexstrasza had replied with a sigh. *We will find another way.*

This village was different from the others—this was a *mortal* settlement, not a tarasek one, and the destruction was fresh. Embers burned low among the charcoal huts. Ash fluttered in the air like snowflakes. Half the trees surrounding the village had been reduced to blackened bones. Overhead, the day faltered. The sun sank toward the horizon, stretching long, tarry shadows across the ground.

Alexstrasza's nostrils were full of the stench of death, and her eyes watered from the debris in the air, but she could not look away. She counted every corpse, tallying up the dead. All told, their numbers were over a hundred. Adults. Whelps. Every death left another rent on her heart.

As Dragon Queen, it was her responsibility to ensure the flights flew straight and true. As Life-Binder, she had a charge to safeguard all life on Azeroth. She found herself failing both duties. How could any dragon, ordered or not, kill so senselessly and without need?

Alexstrasza's guards found tracks outside the settlement, indicating several mortals had survived. The thought brought her little comfort. Even if some *had* survived, they had lost their homes. Their families, too. Alexstrasza knew some things of the mortal condition—they had been continuing to explore visages, after all—and she knew they could not survive long without shelter, food, and clean water.

She tried to find solace in watching her flights work together: Neltharion stood on the perimeter of the settlement with Malygos, examining traces of magic in the burned structures. Later, the black dragonflight would gather the remains and draw the earth up over the corpses. The bronzes and blues worked together, searching for evidence among the ruins. Meanwhile, the reds used their cleansing fire to heal the landscape and coax new growth from the ashes. Together, they would find the dragon or dragons responsible.

"Tell me," Alexstrasza asked as Vyranoth landed beside her, "where do the victims go when they flee this destruction?"

"The mortals disappear," Vyranoth replied. "Whether they die in the wilds or travel to neighboring settlements, I do not know. The tarasek, on the other hand . . ."

There was a beat of silence.

"They go to Harrowsdeep," Alexstrasza said.

"Indeed," Vyranoth said. "Can you blame them? Their families burned to death before their very eyes. Would you not also take up arms in your own defense?"

Alexstrasza eyed Vyranoth. "No. I would first seek understanding."

"You cannot ask that of them, Alexstrasza," Vyranoth said, her stare cold. "You cannot ask that of *any* of us."

"Us?" Alexstrasza asked, tossing her head as she turned to face Vyranoth. "Do you sympathize with the Incarnates, then? With *Iridikron,* who would burn the Broodlands, slaughter all my kind, raze this world to see his will done?"

"I know your heart, my friend," Vyranoth said. "But there are other matters I have not broached with you about *your kind.*"

The words *your kind* were laced with so much bitterness, they churned in Alexstrasza's stomach. Vyranoth had said too much, accidentally revealing a bias that she, in all her wisdom, had not realized she possessed. Even if she apologized, the wound to their friendship would remain.

"Meaning *what,* exactly?" Alexstrasza asked through her teeth.

Ice slipped into Vyranoth's tone. "The primal dragons who brought this issue to my attention were driven from their territory by your flights. I thought their concerns might be a chance occurrence, but now to see your flights attacking defenseless mortals and tarasek—"

"My flights are not attacking the settlements," Alexstrasza said to her friend. "Neltharion believes these attacks are the workings of a single rogue dragon."

"Is that the truth?" Vyranoth said. "Or is that simply what you want to believe? Do you know what your flights do when your back is turned?"

"Not this," Alexstrasza replied with a firm shake of her head. "The dragonflights swore sacred oaths to protect life, not to take it without cause. You must understand, Vyranoth, this is not who we are—this is *not* what we do."

"Do not ask me to try to understand," Vyranoth said. "You are changed, Alexstrasza. Everything about you, from your scent to your very essence, is unrecognizable. You have rejected who—no, *what* you are."

"I am what I have always been. I am Alexstrasza," she said, stepping forward. "Ever have I fought to defend the helpless. And if you cannot see that now, perhaps it is because your heart has frozen. *You* are the one who keeps company with the cruel, the *merciless*." Alexstrasza spread her wings wide to gesture to the ruined lands around them. "It would not surprise me to learn that the Incarnates had something to do with this destruction."

"You would point a talon at your enemy and blame them for the faults of your flights?" Vyranoth said, eyeing Alexstrasza with distaste.

"And you would accuse me on hearsay," Alexstrasza said. "You did not see these attacks for yourself—how do you know Iridikron isn't manipulating you as he has done to so many others?"

"Because I can trust my kind!" Vyranoth said in a half-roar, her words echoing off the cliffs around them. The sentiment seemed to surprise her as much as it did Alexstrasza—the ice dragon took a step back, stricken. Silence rushed in, hushing every voice in the valley.

The Life-Binder loosed a deep sigh. After the horrors she had seen that day, she did not want to end it with harsh words and hurt feelings. She had been trying to salvage her friendship with Vyranoth of late; but every time she tried to cross the chasm between them, the gap only grew wider.

"Vyranoth," she began softly, but the ice dragon turned away, shaking her head.

"There is nothing more to be said between us." With that, Vyranoth took wing and disappeared into the growing dusk.

Alexstrasza neither followed the ice dragon nor tried to call her back as she might have once done. Instead, she turned and beckoned to the other Aspects. "We have immediate need of ambassadors to the mortal races—finish the work on the visages, or else I fear Nozdormu's predictions will come to pass."

VYRANOTH RETURNED NORTH, RELIEVED to take comfort in the chilly peaks of her mountain aerie. As she neared it, the chill soothed the pain of her broken heart, patching the cracks with ice. The day had shown her that she and Alexstrasza had grown too far apart for their friendship to survive. Vyranoth had expected it to happen, but perhaps not so soon.

She had no doubt that Alexstrasza wanted to protect this world, but to alter the natural order of things was imprudent at best and deadly at worst. Could Alexstrasza not see how this situation could spiral out of control? What if a significant force of ordered dragons turned against their Aspects? What if an *Aspect* turned their monstrous strength against their own kind, as Galakrond had? Vyranoth shuddered at the thought. Galakrond, left unchecked, would have consumed them all.

Vyranoth could not return to the Broodlands—not in good conscience. Not now. Perhaps not ever.

Gloomy, unnatural clouds collected over the Frozen Fangs. As Vyranoth approached her aerie, she spotted Raszageth lounging at the cave's mouth, a pair of slain stags at her side. The clouds rumbled, heralding their mistress, but the storm did not break.

"Your visit is not unwelcome, Storm-Eater," Vyranoth said as she alighted on the icy ledge outside her home. "Though I am in no mood for games."

"No, I would imagine not," Raszageth replied, getting to her feet. "I came north today to see if you would like to join me for a hunt but found you missing. Little Nalikrona told me you had gone to the Broodlands. I figured you would be hungry after the long flight." The Storm-Eater gestured to the two stags.

Vyranoth cocked her head. As much as she liked Raszageth, the Storm-Eater did not often think of others' needs—not out of maliciousness or self-centeredness, but merely from a lack of awareness. Raszageth, like a storm itself, cared naught for anything but her own fury. Perhaps it made this display of friendship all the more remarkable; perhaps the Storm-Eater would be able to learn kindness, or at the very least, something akin to it.

The frustration melted from the wing-muscles in Vyranoth's back. "Your thoughtfulness is appreciated, my friend. Today has been . . . *trying.*"

"The Aspects have forgotten what it means to be a dragon," Raszageth said. Taking one of the stags in her jaws, she tossed it at Vyranoth's feet. A little warmth still radiated from the creature. "Alexstrasza and her kith have been tamed by their keepers—you should have forsaken them long ago."

"Perhaps," Vyranoth said.

"Why should you still waste your time with them?" Raszageth asked, then tore into her prey. Flesh ripped. Bones crunched. Viscera spilled out onto the ice, still steaming. The scent hit Vyranoth's nostrils, heady enough to make her stomach growl.

"I thought I could hold Alexstrasza to account for her actions," Vyranoth said, turning her head to look south. "Instead, she turns the blame on the primal dragons for the wrongs of her flights."

Raszageth lifted her head, her snout smeared with gore. Bits of lightning snapped between her horns. "Whatever do you mean?"

"Her flights burn tarasek and mortal settlements along the Broodlands' borders," Vyranoth said. "Yet, Alexstrasza seeks to lay the blame at Iridikron's feet."

Raszageth's glowing silver eyes narrowed. Overhead, thunder rumbled. "What would make her think we were to blame for such atrocities? Does she have any evidence, any reason to believe Iridikron would strike at the tarasek? They are his allies."

"No," Vyranoth said, though she thought she heard a sliver of uncertainty in Raszageth's voice, and that gave her pause.

"Hmph," Raszageth said. "If the Aspects are already turning on their neighbors and chasing primal dragons from their territories, it won't be long before they come for *us*."

"Alexstrasza does not want war with the Incarnates," Vyranoth replied.

"Perhaps not," Raszageth said. "But can you say the same of Neltharion? Of Malygos? Do you believe they will leave our kind in peace? Because I do not."

"You sound too much like Iridikron, my friend," Vyranoth said.

"After everything you have seen in the Broodlands, how can you disagree?" Raszageth said, a growl creeping into her voice. "Can you say with certainty that we have nothing to fear from the Aspects and their hateful flights? Perhaps the fact that you haven't joined them yet is proof enough of your doubts."

Vyranoth blew out a breath. "Perhaps." *Or perhaps it is because I can trust Iridikron no more than I can trust Alexstrasza.*

"No more *perhaps*. Eat," Raszageth said, gesturing to the stag at Vyranoth's feet. "Then tell me what the Aspects know of these attacks on the villages."

CHAPTER NINE

FOR FIVE YEARS, NELTHARION WATCHED THE MORTALS who had settled in the Waking Shores—first in suspicion, then with keen interest. In that time, the little settlement in the Apex Canopy had grown. New groups migrated to the area. The number of huts along the riverbanks doubled, then tripled. New whelps appeared, riding on their parents' hips and backs in fur slings.

These mortals had realized that the dragonflights were mostly benevolent; Alexstrasza and Ysera had sent emissaries forth in experimental versions of Malygos's new *visages*, ones that allowed the dragons to appear mortal in every way. Their temporary forms matched those of the mortal races that had been victimized in the attacks, but Malygos thought he was close to developing a more permanent form of the visage, one that each individual could fashion and adopt as their own.

Still, the idea had already borne fruit—the mortal hunters below had spotted Neltharion lounging on the butte near the

Obsidian Citadel, but they paid the Aspect no mind. Outside the Broodlands, mortals fled in terror when a dragon approached their village, ordered *or* primal. There was little Neltharion could do to assuage that fear, at least not within the century. Mortal generations would pass away before the wounds from Raszageth's storms would heal.

Raszageth, Neltharion thought, curling his upper lip. He could prove the Storm-Eater was responsible for the attacks on the villages, but the Aspects' petitions to Harrowsdeep went unanswered. To stop her, the flights would need to catch Raszageth in the act . . . and she had proven herself to be remarkably wily for one so mercurial.

Overhead, gray-bellied clouds darkened the day, grumbling in the distance. The mortals pursued a small herd of grazers, creeping through the misty foliage below. Curiously, they now had a wolf hunting alongside them, one that sniffed the ground and led them toward the herd. Perhaps they had trained it to compensate for their poor aural and olfactory abilities? It made Neltharion wonder how such creatures would adapt to hunt dragons.

He cocked his head, curiosity piqued.

Could mortals be trained to hunt dragons? They certainly proliferated and reached maturity faster than dragons did—perhaps they could be used to augment the Aspects' forces in the coming war.

Neltharion hummed in thought. The world around him faded as the great forge in his mind set to work: Could he build a soldier on a mortal's frame, but with the scales, wings, and magical acumen of dragons? Fuse mortal adaptability with the powers of the five flights, perhaps? Thus appointed, such soldiers could serve as both ground and aerial infantry; in a group, they might strike full-grown dragons from the sky. Perhaps they could reach maturity in twenty or twenty-five years, rather than the hundreds it would take a dragon to grow into their full strength.

Iridikron would never expect such a tactic, nor would he have time to adjust his strategies against such a foe.

Neltharion narrowed his eyes. It would take years to create, propagate, and train such an army, even for one as talented as he. He might have sixty, perhaps seventy years at most—he expected the Incarnates to declare war before the century was out.

It was an impossible task; there was not enough time. But did he have any other choice? Tyr was gone. The Primals' numbers were swelling, and all the whelplings at the Ruby Life Pools would not an army make. Nor would their drakes, for that matter, and the Aspects had precious few other allies to call upon.

Neltharion took wing, barely hearing the hunting whistles and the screams of the grazers on the ground below. Before he stepped into Aberrus, the laboratory he'd hidden deep within Zaralek Cavern, ideas had already sparked in his mind and caught fire.

He commanded his flight to bring him mortals from beyond the Broodlands, *alive*. Working in secret, he conducted endless experiments, unspooling mortal musculature to understand their anatomy, testing the limits of their endurance, and augmenting their bodies with various draconic essences.

Seasons passed, then years. Trial after trial resulted in a heap of useless flesh or mindless abominations. Adult specimens never woke from augmentation, their physiology twisted. Altered clutches failed to quicken. Mammalian pregnancies ended in stillbirths. The soldier Neltharion envisioned eluded him at every turn.

These failures did not deter Neltharion, however—the survival of dragonkind depended on his success, and by extension, the fate of the entire world. The Earth-Warder worked with a single-minded zeal, accompanied only by his brightest and most trusted flightleaders; he could not entrust this task to anyone else, nor call upon the likes of Ysera or Malygos for assistance. Alexstrasza could not learn of what he plotted from the depths of the earth.

Not until the time was right.

When that day came, the Dragon Queen would thank him for his foresight and his brilliance. The other Aspects would stand in awe of his achievements, and the Broodlands would celebrate him as their finest protector. Despite what the whispers told him, he *was* dragonkind's most distinguished mind.

On a quiet, unremarkable afternoon, Neltharion descended into the depths of Aberrus, into the Shadow Crucible, smiling as furious roars echoed through the caverns. His flight had recently captured one of the Zaqali djaradin's elders, a powerful creature known as Rashok. At first, the Earth-Warder only meant to remove the djaradin threat from the field . . . but now he had *other* plans for such a robust source of living flame.

As Neltharion passed the elementium forges, black drakonid snapped to attention and saluted him. Aquamarine light from the incubation tanks bled along the walls, mixing with the crimson light from the magma falls. Sparks swirled through the air, carried on ever-moving currents. The whole place smelled of molten metal and sulfur.

As he stepped into his laboratory, hydra pups scampered out of his way. Red flames danced freely in large braziers, tossing inky shadows across the room. Five black dragons crowded around a shattered incubation tank, whispering to one another in hushed tones. A foul-smelling liquid from the tank flooded the room. He curled his lip.

"What has transpired here?" Neltharion asked, shaking fluids from his right forefoot with a grimace. Several dragons jolted, swinging their heads around in alarm.

The most senior flightleader in the room, Livia, turned her sleek head as the others dipped into hasty bows. "Ah, my Aspect!" she said. "As always, you have impeccable timing. It seems we may have had our first success—something finally managed to survive."

As Neltharion approached, Livia stepped aside. There, at the base of the shattered tank, sat a small, shivering form. The creature hugged its knees to its chest. Gleaming black scales covered its long, lanky limbs. Wet wings clung to its back. The creature had a mortal's physique, but it was not mortal. Nor was it a dragon, nor a drakonid, nor like any race this world had yet seen.

It lifted its wedge-shaped head. Two intelligent golden

eyes locked with Neltharion's. The creature did not flinch or look away, even as the Earth-Warder's shadow fell over it.

The black Aspect's grimace turned into something sinuous, devious—it wasn't quite a smile, but he was certainly pleased.

Another failure, a whisper said. *Look at how it shudders!*

A second voice slipped into his ear, saying, *It is futile—you will never achieve the heights you seek.*

Your life will end in failure, said a third.

Neltharion narrowed his eyes. What did the whispers know of his future, a thing not even the bronze dragons could divine? The proof of the Earth-Warder's brilliance sat at his feet; he would turn these creatures into soldiers who could strike an Incarnate from the skies.

"How many more survived?" Neltharion asked Livia.

"Four others," the flightleader replied crisply, nodding to tanks containing dark silhouettes suspended in liquid. "Though they are not yet awake."

"Wake them now, and bring them to Zskarn for testing," Neltharion said. "We shall see if this is the soldier I seek."

PART THREE

THE WINDS OF WAR

Over the last fifty years, tensions have risen between the Aspects and our Incarnate kin. Now, they draw all manner of creatures to Harrowsdeep, rallying primal dragons, tarasek, and even mortals to their cause. Iridikron makes no secret of his warmongering, though he has yet to make an overt attack.

As Aspects, we continue to campaign for peace, for one fact is indisputable—a war between our flights and the Incarnates would result in a catastrophic loss of life. I have seen it in the timeways, as have my bronzes. We are not willing to risk the lives of so many, not when peace may yet be achieved.

Thus, the Dragon Queen continues to nurture the seeds of hope. Recently, she reached an accord with Iridikron over hunting grounds in northern Kalimdor: His followers have permission to hunt in the territories around Wyrmrest Temple, provided they do not harass the ordered dragons who make the temple their home. It feels like a victory, no matter how small. We have made inroads with some of the unaffiliated primal dragons in the area and are building relations with the mortal tribes who call those lands home, too. Malygos's visages have been used to great effect with this latter group.

The Storm-Eater and her underlings continue to attack tarasek and mortal villages, though we have yet to catch her in the act. Unlike Fyrakk, or a primal dragon leader like one called Vitelenoth, Raszageth is nigh unto impossible to track. She hides within the fury of her storms, often changing directions and frustrating any attempts made to follow her. Additionally, the Shadowscales have seen Raszageth conversing with a small black dragon, one who matches the description of a dragon named Ikronia. The black dragonflight thought her dead. Neltharion worries about the secrets she may have told Iridikron, for it is possible she worked the forges in the Obsidian Citadel before her defection.

The Stonescaled has ignored our calls to restrain Raszageth, insisting she has committed no transgressions.

On that matter, Neltharion's instinct to keep Tyr's death from the dragonflights has served us well, as the Incarnates do not seem to realize Tyr is gone. Alexstrasza has called most of our allied titan-forged home to Valdrakken to bolster their numbers, but a few continue their work in the Dragonwilds. The longer we can keep this knowledge from Iridikron, the better—Tyr and his titan-forged were an excellent deterrent to an Incarnate invasion, as Iridikron was loath to take on an allied force of keepers and Aspects.

Despite these dangers, the Broodlands continue to thrive. Have we not just finished construction on the Temporal Conflux, the seat of the bronze dragonflight's power? The Temporal Conflux will be an anchor to our flight in the timeways, allowing us to explore as never before. Ysera and her greens have opened portals straight into the Emerald Dream, allowing us to step through and see the wonders the Dreamer sees when she closes her eyes. The greens have also taken to our new visages the most naturally, building strong relations with our mortal neighbors. Many such beings have moved to the Emerald Plains, where they now thrive under the greens' gentle care.

In the south, Malygos and his blues have been busy expanding their knowledge of the arcane, while the Dragon Queen has invested herself in creating, raising, and training legions of new drakonid for each flight. Scalesworn now patrol the streets of Valdrakken at all hours of the day and provide support at the border. She claims these creatures are meant to support us in our oaths, but secretly, I wonder if she isn't preparing to defend the Broodlands in her own way.

Only Neltharion's aims remain hidden from us—while he hosts his sparring matches, war games, and other displays of strength, he spends most of his time in the northern reaches of the Broodlands, far to the north of the Scalecracker Peaks. He has forbidden other flights from venturing close, calling it a testing ground for aerial weaponry.

The futures I see in the timeways grow darker, ever darker. There are a thousand ways war might come to our lands and few ways to escape its rampant destruction.

We shall see how the winds will stir the sands of time.

CHAPTER TEN

IRIDIKRON SHIFTED HIS WEIGHT, CONSIDERING THE NEWS his Rockfury agents relayed: Tyr, the Aspects' beloved keeper, was dead.

Good, he thought. The Stonescaled stood in his war-cavern in Harrowsdeep with Fyrakk and Raszageth, considering his campaign map. The massive chamber looked like the hollowed-out insides of a great beast. A large spine of stalactites ran across the ceiling. Lava pumped from the mountain's heart, filling a lake with molten rock. Several large islands floated atop the magma's bright surface, though Iridikron conducted business from the central platform.

It had been many long years since Iridikron's agents had seen the keeper in the Broodlands; the Aspects had hidden the keeper's death from their flights. To this day, only high-ranking flightleaders and commanders knew Tyr was gone, which was precisely why it had taken the Rockfuries decades to confirm the fact.

"Who gave you this information?" Iridikron asked the agent, a stone Primal named Zakarnos.

"I overheard one of Neltharion's scalesmiths talking about it with a stone-skin," Zakarnos replied. "Calcia is her name. They were building a statue of a titan on the outskirts of Valdrakken."

"I mislike that you got this information from one of Neltharion's own," Iridikron said with a growl in his throat. "Are you sure you were not seen? Calcia is one of the Earth-Warder's most trusted lackeys. It would not surprise me to learn she fed you false information in the guise of a private conversation."

"For days, I appeared as nothing more than a rocky outcropping in the shadows of the foliage," the Primal replied. "If they had known I was there, they would have driven me out."

"The keeper is *gone*, Iridikron," Fyrakk said loudly, rolling his eyes. The Incarnate of flame lounged on the far side of the island, stirring the lava with his talons. "You're out of excuses— it's time to strike."

"Hmph," Iridikron said. While he trusted his agents, he would not be surprised if Neltharion and the black dragonflight tried to goad the Incarnates into attacking prematurely. The Stonescaled had been leery of declaring war on Valdrakken while Tyr still lived—the keepers commanded powers the Incarnate did not understand.

However, if the keeper was dead, it meant the Aspects were alone in the world.

"I agree," Raszageth said with a toss of her head. "We must do more than growl and snap at their borders! We should release the full fury of the storm on their skies."

Iridikron narrowed his eyes, turning his attention back to his campaign map. The pawns on the board trembled as an earthquake rolled through the cavern. True, the Incarnates' forces now outnumbered the Aspects' by a substantial margin. True, many great champions had flown north to join the cause . . . but the strongest still eluded him. Vyranoth had been particularly resistant, as had Oxoria and her brood.

However, Iridikron's main concern had nothing to do with the size of their respective armies: "There is still much we do not understand about the Aspects and Order magic," he mused. "Even now, their flights adopt mortal forms to build alliances with the tribes on their land. We cannot explain how they assume such forms, though it is likely due to them using more of their accursed arcane magic."

"Aaargh!" Fyrakk said, getting to his feet. "Why should it matter if they want to adopt mortal forms? They will just be easier to kill!"

"We cannot defeat an enemy we do not understand," Iridikron said. "Numbers alone will not carry us to victory. Alexstrasza commands fanatical devotion from her followers, and Neltharion's cunning cannot and *should* not be underestimated. We must strike with care. Perhaps the ability to take a mortal form has its tactical uses."

"I would never lower myself to take on the appearance of these mewling mortals!" Raszageth said with a scoff.

"I agree," Iridikron said, "though a smaller form that is rooted in the elements would give us the same advantage the Aspects have—moving about the Broodlands without alerting Neltharion's intrusive scouts."

"Let's use visages then, too!" Fyrakk said, eyes alight.

"It is certainly worth exploring," Iridikron mused.

Raszageth hissed. "Fine," she said begrudgingly. "But how?"

"We shall discuss the particulars of assuming such forms later," Iridikron said. "If Tyr is truly gone, we have more pressing concerns to discuss—namely, how to destabilize the Broodlands and force the Aspects into war." Iridikron turned his sights onto Raszageth. "That, I believe, will start with you."

The Storm-Eater's face split into a hungry smile.

IN ALL THE WORLD, there was nothing Raszageth loved more than chaos. Tonight, she had driven a brutal storm all the way to the northernmost reaches of the Broodlands—an empty, sparse expanse, one long ignored by the Aspects and their flights. The clouds grew dark as night. Raszageth took a deep breath and grinned. She gathered the storm's natural power under her wings, reveling in its might.

Tonight, she would strike at the Broodlands for the first time.

Raszageth couldn't remember the last time she'd been so excited.

While the Storm-Eater would have loved to unleash such power upon the Aspects' garish city of Valdrakken, Iridikron had demanded caution. He insisted that Raszageth begin by testing remote targets in the Reach, ones populated only by wild tarasek. Thus, Raszageth and Ikronia settled on a small tarasek village far to the north.

For more than fifty summers, Raszageth and Ikronia had destroyed settlements in the Aspects' names. Not once had they been caught, nor could the Aspects prove or stop it without provoking the Incarnates to war. So, Raszageth continued to destroy villages, just a few each year, to continue her reign of terror. It not only infuriated the Aspects, but also bolstered the Incarnates' ranks and turned more minds against hateful Order magic.

To date, Raszageth and Ikronia had managed to drive a wave of tarasek to Harrowsdeep, where a new movement had sprung to life. Iridikron named the faction the Primalists to honor the primal dragons who imbued themselves with the elements of fire, stone, and storm. Upon hearing of these new powers, legions of dragons came to Harrowsdeep, pledging to support the Incarnates over the Aspects. Mortals had gone west, too, lured to the movement by the promise of strength and security.

Before long, the Incarnates would turn their fury on the Broodlands and bring them down. The very thought brought a wild, untamed joy to Raszageth's heart. The Dragon Queen had brought dragonkind such misery; Raszageth only wanted to return the favor. The Storm-Eater would burn villages, kill ordered dragons, and laugh over their smoking remains. She wanted to watch Alexstrasza weep over the corpses of her kin. She wanted *vengeance* for all the hurts the keepers and their Order magic had inflicted upon dragonkind.

But most of all, the Storm-Eater wanted to turn one of Alexstrasza's best and dearest friends to the Incarnates' cause. Vyranoth was close to joining their side; Raszageth could feel it in her bones. She had already explained the process to the primal dragon . . . now all Vyranoth needed was one last little betrayal. One last little hurt.

Raszageth landed on an icy ledge, high above a village of tarasek. A few tribes had expanded in the north, where the dragonflights were less active due to the frozen climes. Night filled the valley below with shadows, which made the village's tiny watchfires flicker and glow like embers in a dying fire. Such a small, isolated village would not recognize her storms for what they were, nor would they see her hidden among the fury of the clouds.

The winds started to stir around her, restless. The Storm-Eater sensed Ikronia in the west, ready for the signal.

Spreading her wings wide, Raszageth leapt aloft. As she climbed into the clouds, she radiated the storm's elemental power from her body. Lightning snapped and danced across her scales. The wind howled. Snow swirled off the mountaintops and flurried in the air, obscuring everything for anyone trapped within.

Then, with a growl, Raszageth sent the first thundering bolt into the ground below. Moments later, a dark shadow passed over the village, setting three grass huts alight. The winds carried screams up to Raszageth's ears.

"Yes, yes," she said with a snicker, whipping the fires into an inferno with the winds. The flames ripped a gash through the darkness, consuming the village and the forests around it with speed. But then, something she did not expect: The winds carried the sound of a distant dragon's bugle to her ears and tugged on her mane in warning.

Raszageth turned her head, listening. The sound had come from the southeast. A second call trumpeted over the mountains, closer this time. Cutting. With a growl, Raszageth sent her winds forth, searching for the hunters who now stalked them in the night.

There! On the valley's ridge, a patrol of black dragons rode the gale. Two of them dived toward the valley floor, heading for the village. Ikronia had been spotted. The other two remained in the air, gliding under the clouds. Cautious.

Raszageth had no love for Ikronia. However, if the black dragons managed to capture her, she might turn on the Incarnates and reveal their secrets. Raszageth had been careful not to tell her too much, but who knew what Fyrakk had spewed in the little dragon's presence?

So, Raszageth chose violence. Chaos. Death. Manifesting lightning from within, she sent a massive, branching bolt down toward the ground, striking one of the dragons headed for the village. The lightning outlined the creature in blue light. The dragon seized, releasing an agonized scream as their head arched back, their limbs and tail straining. The lightning faded, leaving the silhouette of the dragon's final moments impressed upon her eyes.

As Raszageth sparked the energy for a second bolt, the winds shifted to her left and right. Black shadows rushed at her from either side. With a growl, the Storm-Eater closed her wings and dropped through the air. The black dragons followed her, close in pursuit.

Snapping open her wings, she propelled herself over the black dragons' heads, catching them both by surprise. The dragon on the left darted away. The one on the right was slower. Raszageth slammed into his back, piercing his hide with her talons. Bones snapped, scales cracked. Exuding electricity, Raszageth pushed the energy into the dragon's unprotected body. Spidery legs of lighting burst over his frame. The dragon writhed in her vicelike grip. Hot blood gushed over Raszageth's talons and slicked her toes. The dragon screamed, then went limp. The thunder of his heart fell silent.

Hmph, Raszageth thought, sensing movement in the winds behind her. On instinct, she beat her wings and spun, unsurprised to see the third black dragon rushing toward her. Summoning a fast updraft under her wings, Raszageth rose and kicked the corpse at its companion. The black dragon dodged, but the body clipped her left wing. The dragon faltered in the air.

Taking advantage of her opponent's instability, Raszageth struck. She sent whorls of wind off her wings, capturing her enemy in a vortex. The black dragon spun in the air, thrashing and flailing, wholly at Raszageth's mercy.

"Is this the vaunted strength of Order magic?" Raszageth tossed her head and laughed. "Pathetic!"

Raszageth sliced both wing talons down, commanding the winds to hurl the black dragon to the earth. The elements dashed the dragon against the mountaintops, shattering every bone in the creature's body.

"You are no match for me!" Raszageth roared in the night. She hovered in the air, sensing the movement of the winds, searching for the fourth and final black dragon. The winds tugged her attention back to the village, where the surviving creature had Ikronia pinned beneath one of his massive forefeet.

With a wicked grin, Raszageth dipped lower. She stirred the winds on the ground, rattling the debris from the burning huts. The fires circled the two black dragons, flames burning high and hot. The black dragon had his claws around Ikronia's throat and kept her pressed against the earth.

"We will bring you to Neltharion for judgment," he snapped at Ikronia, his teeth flashing in the firelight. "You will face justice for what you have done, monster!"

"We?" Raszageth cackled, pausing to hover in the air in front of the black dragon. "You poor fool, there is no more *we*. Your friends are *dead*."

"Then my Aspect was right," the black dragon said. "*You are* responsible for all this destruction. For thousands of lives lost!"

Raszageth dipped her head and said, "Including yours." With a snap of her wings, she sent a torrent of wind into the village, stoking the flames. A bright-red column of fire shot into the sky, lighting the terrain for hundreds of wing-lengths in every direction. Ravenous, the flames consumed the very air they breathed. Smoke whirled, hot and acrid. The black dragon stumbled off Ikronia, coughing.

Raszageth cackled, drawing the lightning from her body. As she unleashed the killing bolt, the black dragon sank his claws into the earth. He pulled a rough shield of stone up in front of his body. The lightning slammed into the rock and fizzled out, leaving writhing worms of electricity in its wake.

"My, my," Raszageth said, laughing with glee. "You are more clever than your companions. Let us see how long you last against an Incarnate!"

The black dragon rose, shaking the earth off his wings. He glared at Raszageth. "The black dragonflight will make you pay for your cruelty, Storm-Eater. This I swear."

"Your oaths mean nothing to me," Raszageth spat, still hovering over the village. "My winds will drag your flights from the skies and you will die screaming, just like your kin!"

"But not today." The black dragon sprinted past her and leapt aloft, flying fast for the mountain ridges to the east.

"After him!" Raszageth shouted to Ikronia, who struggled to her feet. Wheeling, the Storm-Eater crested the treetops. Despite the pleasure Raszageth was taking, this game was now in deadly earnest—she would not allow her prey to escape.

Big, blue-white bolts arced through the air around them, thundering off the sharp mountain peaks. Flying at this speed, Raszageth could not aim them as accurately. She whipped up a headwind against him, but that only forced her to fly faster and harder, too.

The black dragon darted into a rocky chasm to escape. Raszageth gave chase, but the channel tapered, leaving her little space to navigate. Thin, wan gray light highlighted the dangers ahead: She dived under a sharp jut of rock and dodged the ancient roots of a tree, keeping the black dragon in her sights. A waterfall roared down the right wall. The black dragon hit it first and disappeared into the chasm's shadows.

Raszageth flew through the waterfall, electrifying it as she passed. The light shocked the rock walls around her, illuminating the black dragon's tail as he leapt skyward.

"Coward!" With a growl, Raszageth summoned the winds and vaulted herself from the chasm. She spiraled high into the air, lighting up the skies with her fury.

But the black dragon had disappeared.

Raszageth patrolled the area, her frustration growing. The sky resonated with her fury, raining lightning bolts down upon the world. She called a gale to clear the skies as they searched for the black dragon, but her winds returned to her with empty whispers.

As the Storm-Eater turned back, the natural winds shifted directions, blowing in from the northeast. They brought Raszageth the smoky, rich smell of burning wood and the earthen scent of black dragon scales. What were the Aspects doing so far to the north? Beyond the jagged peaks of the mountains, an orange light tinged the bellies of the clouds.

Curious, Raszageth flew toward the mountain range, keeping out of sight. Tall, toothy peaks ringed the valley below. Fires burned in massive braziers, illuminating the forms of at least a hundred black dragons and thousands of drakonid from the black, red, blue, green, and bronze flights. Several flightleaders cruised in the skies above. To Raszageth's eye, the sparring on the ground and in the air looked like military exercises.

The black dragonflight appeared to be training for war.

Wait, Raszageth thought, watching the lithe creatures leap into the air. They spread their wings, gliding easily toward the valley floor. *Those are not drakonid!* Drakonid were not winged, nor were they capable of flight.

What new abominations are these? Raszageth thought, backpedaling before she could be spotted by so massive a force. With a cackle, she turned southward, speeding toward her own aerie in the Whorl.

Raszageth did not wait for Ikronia, for what did it matter? The little fool could find her way back to her own lair, and besides . . . the Storm-Eater needed to prepare for a new hunt.

IKRONIA MOVED TO FOLLOW Raszageth, but the little dragon had broken at least two of her ribs. Though she could fly—albeit slowly—the fury of Raszageth's storms made it impossible to stay aloft for long. Ikronia made it a few hundred wing-lengths from the village before she collapsed on a stone ledge, breathing hard. The raging winds swirled over her, piling snow against the edges of her scales.

It did not take long for the black dragonflight to find her.

Four black dragons escorted Ikronia to the Obsidian Citadel. The citadel's towers looked like behemoth claws reaching up into the soot-stained sky. Forges glowed red, while dragon-headed fountains spewed great gouts of lava. She had spent too many wasted days here, toiling in the forges, surrounded by dragons and yet still so alone.

The black dragons forced Ikronia to fly higher, ever higher, until the pain grew so strong, she nearly tumbled from the sky. Sighing, one of the larger black dragons extended a wing. Ikronia accepted his help out of exhaustion, not gratitude.

When they landed on a high ledge, Ikronia sank to the ground and shuddered. The black dragons moved her inside, where drakonid swarmed around her and shackled her front legs to the ground. Ikronia hissed and snapped, but the drakonid dodged her slow, weakened attacks.

"No dragon should have to suffer this," Ikronia said to them, tugging at the iron shackles that bound her forelegs to the ground. The Order magic in the metal buzzed through her bones and rattled in her teeth. "Why not just kill me outright?"

"It is not for us to decide your fate," one black dragon said. "You are a member of our flight—only our Aspect may pass judgment on you."

"Can you not think for yourselves?" Ikronia spat. "Or must you do everything according to your master's will?"

The black dragon snorted. "You defected from our ranks, did you not?" he asked, turning away from her. "You know the answer to that question better than I."

The black dragons left her alone, save for the drakonid who tended her wounds. Ikronia was confused by the drakonid's gentleness, wishing they would kill her and have done with the matter. Raszageth was an ally and she beat Ikronia even in victory; what horrors would Ikronia suffer at an Aspect's talons after crossing them?

The longer she waited, the larger her fears grew. Great braziers threw strange, twisting shadows over the walls, but Ikronia could not help but stare at the stone map that dominated the space. Iridikron had a similar map at Harrowsdeep. She had spent many nights in her brother's empty council chambers, staring at his maps and guessing at his strategies. She had learned much over the years, despite his attempts to keep his plans from her.

They were so very much alike, Iridikron and Neltharion. Before the titans began their meddling, the two had been as close as clutch-mates, closer than Ikronia and Iridikron had ever been. They shared similar goals and interests, though Neltharion ever said he was a builder, while Iridikron enjoyed watching the earth break. Tension eventually tore them apart—though what had happened, Ikronia could not say.

It was late before a deep voice interrupted her musing: "I am unsurprised to learn that Iridikron and his kin are responsible for so much mortal misery."

Ikronia turned her head. Neltharion, the Earth-Warder and her brother's greatest rival, alighted on the landing behind her. Two of his lieutenants flanked him as he stepped inside the throne room, the firelight dancing across his jet-colored scales. His eyes burned with orange fire, as brilliant and brutal as the engines of war below.

Fear struck Ikronia's heart. She had always been small for her kind, but Neltharion dwarfed her and every other dragon in the room. The floor trembled under his steps. Not even Iridikron stood as massive and mighty as the black Aspect, and the thought sent fear through Ikronia's entire being. She cowered back a step, her chains straining against her scales.

Neltharion stopped a few paces in front of Ikronia. "Tell me," he said, lowering his head to look her in the eye, "did your brother force you into the black dragonflight's ranks to perpetrate this ruse?"

"N-no, I chose to come to Valdrakken on my own," Ikronia said, turning her head away. "But I regretted my choice and fled. Raszageth caught me, and . . ."

"Are there others like you?" Neltharion asked, his voice rising, his tone sharp as a rake of talons. "Are there other black dragons who have fallen under Iridikron's sway and now burn the villages of the innocent? Or are you responsible for the whole of it?"

"It was me," Ikronia said, pressing her belly to the ground and her wings to her back, trying to make herself look as small as possible. "My brother forced me to burn the villages. If I refused, Raszageth would kill me."

Neltharion shook his head. "Your brother is a perpetual disappointment, but the scars in your hide are proof enough of Raszageth's brutality. Still, Ikronia, you have taken many lives in the name of the black dragonflight. That is not something I can forgive."

Neltharion stepped forward. She cringed, her shoulder blades tensing, waiting for death to come. But the black Aspect did not strike her down.

After a long moment of silence, Neltharion said, "Cruelty may be Iridikron's way, but it is not mine. While you have committed horrific acts, you are still a member of my flight, and therefore, one of my own. You are to be imprisoned on the Reach, where you will never be able to speak of what you have seen to anyone."

"Imprisoned?" Ikronia asked, her voice hardly above a whisper. "I would prefer death."

"Death would be a mercy, and you now owe a debt to this flight. No, you may yet be of service to me," Neltharion said, turning away. "Come, we will descend into Neltharus, where you will tell me everything of your brother's plans."

"I will tell you nothing," Ikronia spat.

"I did not say you had to be willing," Neltharion said. Without another word, the black Aspect strode toward the landing. The shackles around Ikronia's legs fell open with a groan, and she went reluctantly to her fate.

CHAPTER ELEVEN

MESSENGERS FROM THE BLACK DRAGONFLIGHT ARRIVED at the Ruby Life Pools at dawn, carrying terrible news: Tarasek villages had burned in the Reach. Three black dragons lost their lives in the skirmish that followed, but the main perpetrator—*Raszageth*—had escaped. Settlements had burned outside the Broodlands for decades, but this was the first time that villages *within* the Broodlands had been targeted. To inflict such pain so close to ordered holdings was bold, and clearly it was a risk that hadn't benefited the perpetrators.

The sun had barely opened a glittering eye on the horizon, but despite the early hour, Alexstrasza called an emergency meeting. Nozdormu, Malygos, and Neltharion came at speed, gathering at the Seat of the Aspects. Ysera remained behind in the Emerald Gardens, overseeing the creation of the Eye of Ysera—a space within the Dream that allowed the green dragonflight to watch over both realms. The green Aspect did not dare leave the delicate first blooms of her work unattended. Instead, she sent an apparition of herself to attend the meeting. Ysera's Vision looked like a ghostly version of the green Aspect, one that glowed like a portal to the Dream itself. It could speak and interact with the Aspects as Ysera herself might, but Alexstrasza found herself missing her sister's quiet warmth and strength all the same.

Far below the Seat, Valdrakken still slumbered, its skies quiet. A light breeze drifted through the tower, cool and gentle. It was a perfect morning for flying, though Alexstrasza's mood was anything but free.

"Can we take no action to stop Raszageth?" Alexstrasza said, frustration seeping into her tone. "She has wrought only havoc for fifty years, and now she strikes so close to our home with reckless abandon. Harrowsdeep has sent our emissaries away, and I fear more strident actions will provoke them to violence."

"The Incarnates know our talons are tied," Neltharion replied. "We have no authority over Raszageth, and we would be ill advised to strike at Harrowsdeep."

"So what do we do?" Malygos said. The Spell-Weaver usually looked so nonchalant; but today, even his scales seemed ruffled. "Their next strike could be on the Obsidian Citadel, the Azure Archives, or even the Emerald Gardens."

The Vision of Ysera flared her nostrils in annoyance. "I don't believe they would dare strike so boldly at us—it is one thing to burn a tarasek village, but *quite another* to engage the full strength of a dragonflight at the seat of its power."

"We cannot pretend that war is not an eventuality, not anymore," Neltharion replied, nodding to Ysera. "Even Nozdormu has said as much."

"I did not say war was an *eventuality*," Nozdormu replied, looking sideways at Neltharion. "I said the pathways to peace grow fewer by the season, and that the *probability* of war was now higher than before. The more our council seeks conflict, the more like we are to find it."

Neltharion curled his lip. "I do not seek war with the Incarnates, Nozdormu."

"Perhaps not in this exact moment," the bronze Aspect said, clearly unconvinced.

"That's enough," Alexstrasza said. But in the deep, dark recesses of her heart, she wondered if Neltharion would welcome a war.

No, no, she told herself, chasing away her unfounded thoughts. Alexstrasza couldn't cast such aspersions on one of her oldest and fiercest allies. Neltharion had never done anything to deserve her mistrust, nor had he been untruthful with her or the other Aspects.

Still, her concerns shadowed her heart.

Alexstrasza had no doubt that Iridikron had every intention of putting them between a rock and a hard place, so to speak. Diplomacy was failing her—but that was what war meant, was it not? The absolute and utter failure of diplomacy? She could no more compel the Incarnates to peace talks than she could forbid the sun to rise.

How could she reason with zealotry? With hatred? How could she soften a heart as hard as stone itself, or melt the ice that now encased Vyranoth's? But most of all: "How do we defend ourselves from the Primalists without starting a war?" Alexstrasza mused aloud. "We cannot close our borders—not every primal dragon is affiliated with Harrowsdeep, and pushing them out of our lands will only send them into our enemies' ranks."

"That is true," Neltharion began. "However, so long as our lands remain accessible to everyone, we lose the strategic advantage. If we cannot close our borders, then we should move to banish all primal dragons from our seats of power.

"It's been centuries since Iridikron began this movement against us," Neltharion continued. "By now, he has likely mapped our holdings, numbered our ranks, and discovered our weak points. That is why primal dragons cannot approach the Obsidian Citadel from the west, nor are they allowed to fly over the Apex Canopy or Life-Binder's Conservatory."

"And how have you enforced such an edict?" Malygos asked.

"How else? With force," Neltharion said with a snort. "Though I am certain the blue dragonflight could achieve similar results by magical means."

The Vision of Ysera tilted her head. "While I support this plan, it would be wise to make a statement reiterating that all *peaceful* primal dragons are welcome in the Broodlands. I do not wish to further antagonize our primal kin."

"Titans know they are already harassed enough," Nozdormu said with a sigh. "I assume you've all heard the news concerning some of our drakes?"

"What news?" Alexstrasza asked.

"I've had recent reports that our youngest drakes are harassing the primal dragons who hunt in the Broodlands," Nozdormu said. "I intended to bring up the point at our next formal council meeting, but it seems relevant now."

Alexstrasza sighed as a dull ache began to pound under her temple. "And how long has *that* been happening?"

"A flightleader caught a small pack of them fighting a primal dragon three moons ago," Nozdormu replied as Malygos rolled his eyes. "But we believe the drakes have been at it for some time."

"Why do our young ones feel the need to attack primal dragons?" the Vision of Ysera asked Nozdormu.

"The primal dragons have been taunting them," Nozdormu replied. " 'Tis no excuse."

Alexstrasza turned to her majordomo, Saristrasz, who sat at her right wing. "Gather the drakes in question to the Ruby Enclave at sunset—I wish to address them myself."

"It shall be done," the majordomo replied. As he quit the Seat with the other majordomos, Alexstrasza turned back to the Aspects.

Malygos spoke first: "Neltharion makes a good point—we should consider keeping primal dragons away from our flights' bastions. While I cannot stop the Incarnates from attacking our territories by magical means, I may be able to deter them."

Alexstrasza lifted her head, curious. "Go on."

"It would be best to show you," Malygos said, twisting a bit of arcane fire around his talons. Sparks fell to the ground, expanded, and swirled up into a miniature funnel. The air snapped with electricity as the energy began to coalesce, then settle. An elemental emerged from the vortex, crackling and glowing like a hunk of mana crystal. Two eyes burned like stars in its head.

"An arcane elemental?" Neltharion asked, lifting a brow.

"Correct," Malygos said. "My flight has recently developed techniques to summon and command these beings."

"Forgive me, Malygos," the Vision of Ysera said, cocking her head to one side. "I fail to see how we might employ these to our benefit."

"Ah, that's where the magic comes in, my dearest Ysera," Malygos replied with a wave of his claws. The arcane elemental shimmered and transformed, growing blue scales, a tail, wings, and a crested neck and head. In seconds, a full-grown blue dragon stood before them, swishing its tail from side to side.

"Titans be good, is it real?" Alexstrasza said, eyes widening. She strode forward, reaching out to touch the blue dragon. Her talons swept straight through empty air. The dragon-elemental swung its head around to look at the Life-Binder, but its eyes stared straight through her, lifeless.

"No," Malygos said as Neltharion joined Alexstrasza. "However, my flight could summon an army of arcane elementals and glamour them to look and act like dragons. Were we to place such simulacrums in strategic locations around the Broodlands . . ."

"We could make our forces appear to be three or four times larger than they are," Neltharion said, his eyes flashing with bright fire. He paced around the dragon-elemental. "We could have an illusory army, which would allow us to redirect the Primalists' attention away from weak points in our defenses."

"Precisely," Malygos said with a nod. "The elementals can be augmented to provide shielding and defenses of strategic locations. Or, if you prefer, *defenseless mortal and tarasek villages*."

Alexstrasza shifted her gaze to the Spell-Weaver. "How much of a strain would that place on your flight?"

"A considerable one, but well worth the price," Malygos replied. "We would need to have a blue or two at each location to shepherd the elementals, but drakes or even drakonid may suffice."

"Very well," the Life-Binder said. "Are there any objections to this plan, or are we of one mind? Nozdormu, what say you?"

"It is a sound strategy," the bronze Aspect said. "Though I would caution you to implement it slowly, so that hundreds of dragons don't appear along our borders overnight."

"I agree," Neltharion said. "With your leave, Alexstrasza, I will work with Malygos to select the initial locations for our new 'troops.' "

"Good," the Life-Binder said, turning to Ysera's Vision last. "And what of you, sister? Is there anything we have overlooked?"

The Vision of Ysera closed her eyes and hummed in thought. "Only this—I want to extend a wing of protection to the mortal villages with whom we have worked hard to build relations. I do not want the Storm-Eater to undo decades of hard work."

"But of course," Malygos said. "Will you send your ambassadors in their visages to introduce the mortals to the elementals? Both the red and green flights have demonstrated a remarkable ability to understand and assist them."

"With pleasure." Ysera's Vision bobbed her head.

"It is decided, then," Alexstrasza said. "Let us be about our work."

THAT EVENING, THE BROODLANDS' young drakes gathered at the Ruby Enclave.

Alexstrasza was fond of the stone pavilion in the enclave, the one that stood on the cliff's edge. Its arches faced northwest, allowing her to watch over the Ruby Life Pools. Flowering vines twisted up the structure's columns, filling the air with their sweet scent. Enchanted flames danced in opalescent sconces. A small waterfall tumbled from the mountain's heights nearby, cooling the air around her.

While the pavilion lacked the grandeur of the Seat of the Aspects, it was an ideal setting for addressing a group of wayward youths—more intimate, less imposing. These drakes were among the first generations of dragons to be born to ordered parents, and she was keen to ensure they flew straight and true.

Alexstrasza stood at the top of the pavilion's steps as the drakes arrived, flanked by her consort Tyranastrasz and her majordomo, Saristrasz. The sunset light flashed off the drakes' red, black, bronze, green, and blue scales. Most were still in their adolescence—most of them had seen fewer than a hundred summers, a fraction of Alexstrasza's own years. They were so young, knew so little about their world.

The Life-Binder could sense the drakes' nervousness. They shifted their weight and shook out their wings, casting anxious glances toward the pavilion. As Saristrasz announced Alexstrasza, the young ones bowed to her, the gesture awkward and unpracticed. Whispers rippled through the assembly.

"Greetings, my young ones," Alexstrasza said, sitting atop the pavilion's stairs. "How my heart soars at the sight of you! When I look upon your young faces, I have nothing but faith in the future of our flights."

Alexstrasza swept her gaze over the enclave. "However, I have heard disquieting news of late: I am told that you have instigated fights with primal dragons both within and outside our borders. I cannot fathom what would drive you to such a thing. For centuries, we have endeavored to make peace with our primal kin—yet your behavior only serves to divide us."

More than half of the assembled drakes dropped their gazes to the ground. The Life-Binder paused for a moment, giving them time to consider her words. "Our charge is not to take life, but to protect it—these were the oaths we made to the world as the dragonflights first came to be. It is my duty to ensure our flights uphold the oaths we made, which is why I cannot condone your actions—"

"We did not choose this life," a voice said from the back, interrupting her. "We took no oaths. We made no promises."

Gasps echoed through the enclave. Saristrasz stepped forward, but Alexstrasza held up two talons, preferring to handle the situation herself.

"I would say that I am surprised by your audacity," Alexstrasza said with a chuckle, "but I suppose it is your *audacity* that brought us here this evening. Step forward, young one, so that we may speak face-to-face."

The drakes turned their heads, then parted, allowing a young red to step to the front of the crowd. He stood of average height and wingspan for his age, but his movements were lithe and graceful. Two long, elegant horns curved off the top of his head. But Alexstrasza thought the most remarkable thing about him was his utter lack of fear—he stood before an Aspect, yet he held his head high while his fellows cowered.

"Talinstrasz," Alexstrasza said, recognizing the brazenness in him, the fearlessness. The young red's eyes widened when he realized the Life-Binder knew his name. He should not have been surprised, for she knew the name of every dragon hatched and tended at the Ruby Life Pools. Judging by his relative age, he had been a whelp there some years ago, not quite among one of the first generations of successfully ordered eggs, but not long after, either.

She tilted her head, scrutinizing the drake. "When you say you *did not choose this life,* what do you mean?"

Talinstrasz lifted his head, holding the red Aspect's gaze. "We are taught that in the days before Valdrakken, every dragon was allowed to choose whether they wished to be ordered. But I was given no such choice. I *remember* being infused with

Order magic while I was still in my egg. I have dreams about it, as does Sirigosa." Talinstrasz nodded to a blue drake who stood to Alexstrasza's left, just on the cusp of the crowd.

It wasn't unusual for a dragon to be aware of their surroundings before they hatched, particularly as their time grew close. The egg-tenders told Alexstrasza that many of their whelps claimed to remember being infused with light and warmth and comfort, but Alexstrasza failed to see why such a memory would cause these drakes to question their ordering.

Curious, Alexstrasza turned to the blue drake. "And what do you remember, Sirigosa?"

Sirigosa sat on the ground and wrapped her tail around her feet. Unlike Talinstrasz, she did not meet and hold the Life-Binder's gaze. "Perhaps *remember* isn't quite the word—Malygos tells us to always be precise with our language, and to say that I *remember* being ordered isn't truthful. When I sleep, sometimes I think I can still feel magic sliding across my scales, changing them from one thing to another. Perhaps it is more dream than memory? I cannot know."

Scales flashed as several of the drakes nodded in agreement.

"You all dream of this?" Alexstrasza asked the assembly.

More nods. A chorus of, "Yes, my queen," rose from their lips, some voices loud, others no more than a whisper.

"It is not surprising that you remember being ordered," Alexstrasza said. "We, as Aspects, have always allowed parents to bring their eggs to the Broodlands to be infused with Order magic. I suppose it may also be possible that your mothers were with clutch on the day of their ordering, as we placed no restrictions on such things.

"However," she continued, "I fail to see how this issue intersects with the unsanctioned attacks on primal drakes."

Talinstrasz stepped forward. "The primal dragons taunt us, my queen. They call us abominations, soft-scales who live only to serve the titans' whims. We try to ignore them, and sometimes we fight with them . . . but lately, I cannot help but wonder if they have the right of it."

Previous generations of ordered drakes had never voiced such before.

"And if they do, then we did not choose this life," Talinstrasz said, his tone shifting, breath fluttering faster. "None of us did!"Alexstrasza exchanged a glance with Tyranastrasz. Primal dragons taunting ordered drakes, planting incendiary ideas in their minds? It sounded very much like something Iridikron would do—how many of the Stonescaled's agents roosted in the Broodlands, waiting for a chance to spread their vile poison among the dragonflights' ranks? The notion only strengthened her desire to expel the primal dragons from the dragonflights' individual seats of power.

What would happen if the unaffiliated dragons in the wilds heard these rumblings? If *Vyranoth* heard them? Why, it could cause untold chaos.

To counter his rising temper, Alexstrasza exuded an aura of patience and serenity, hoping to reach the little red's heart. "Talinstrasz, you were born to the red dragonflight, which means the magic in your veins grants you great wisdom, courage, and compassion," she said gently. "You must see that answering the primal dragons' resentment with violence is folly. They are too shortsighted to see the gifts that Order magic bestows upon our kind."

"Why should I allow them to berate me for a choice that was not my own?" Talinstrasz said. "Our red historians have said that every dragon was allowed to choose for themselves—why were we denied this opportunity?"

"Eggs born from ordered parents are ordered themselves," Alexstrasza said gently. "It is for your parents to explain why they made this choice for themselves and for their bloodline."

"I don't know who my parents *are*," Talinstrasz said, raising his voice. "I understand the red flight allows parents to choose their involvement with their brood. I understand how this helps to empower our flights, but I have not been claimed by any among our number, nor have many of the drakes here. Those who know their ordered parents may find these answers, but *I* cannot. From most every drake who stands here today—"

"*Talinstrasz,*" Saristrasz said sharply. "Mind your tone when you are speaking to the queen!"

"He is not wrong," one of the black drakes cried.

"We should have been given the right to choose," said a green.

Sirigosa tilted her head, however, and said, "That isn't entirely correct, Talin. Several drakes here have memories of being ordered, and yet they know the faces of their parents. My Aspect always says that memory is malleable, which is why we *write things down*. Your so-called *memories* may not be what you believe them to be."

"What about what the bronze saw?" a blue drake said.

"Oh, please," Sirigosa said, rolling her eyes and tossing her head. "Nolizdormu cannot see what he hunted last week in the timeways, much less what happened to him before his Hatching Day!"

"Hey, that's not true!" a bronze said with a sniff.

Voices began to burble and snap, tensions rising. Alexstrasza lifted her right wing, commanding the attention of the room. The drakes fell silent, but Alexstrasza could sense how Talinstrasz's words had ruffled their scales.

"Do you see how the primal drakes' words divide us?" she said softly, but her tone was deadly. "As we speak, Iridikron and his Primalists do everything in their power to destroy our flights. They will tell any lie, exploit any weakness, and murder innocents in pursuit of their goals. I have no doubt that Iridikron now seeks to turn your hearts against your home, your families, and your flights. You may not yet know your parents, Talinstrasz—and so long as it is their right to keep such knowledge, you may never know them—but the red flight protects you, guides you, uplifts you in their stead. The Primalists would have you isolated from your flight, weak without our support, easy prey.

"We must all guard against the Stonescaled's lies," Alexstrasza continued. "Though I empathize with your concerns, I ask that you come to me directly for an audience and not entertain idle gossip and wild speculation. I would also counsel you to be cautious in your dealings with primal drakes, for many will not have your best interests at heart. Do you understand?"

Most of the drakes bowed their heads in assent. Talinstrasz held the Life-Binder's gaze, and for a heartbeat, Alexstrasza thought the drake would be foolish enough to challenge her a second time. But he, too, closed his eyes and lowered his head.

"As your queen, I forbid you from fighting with the primal dragons unless lives are at stake," Alexstrasza said, and as she spoke, one of her red scribes seared the words on a parchment, binding them into law. "For your indiscretions, each of you shall serve for a season at Wyrmrest Temple, where you will assist our ambassadors with outreach efforts. Perhaps then you will understand the gifts you have been given."

The drakes groaned, but their voices rose in a chorus of "Yes, my queen."

"Now go," she said with a patient smile. "Venture forth and be paragons of your flights. A bright future lies ahead for each one of you."

With the pronouncement made, Saristrasz stepped away to usher the drakes out of the enclave. The Life-Binder watched them go, mulling over their words. As the young drakes took wing, filling the skies with brilliant bursts of color, Tyranastrasz nudged her shoulder, then gestured for her to join him at the edge of the pavilion.

Alexstrasza sank down beside her consort with a sigh. In the distance, the sunset gilded the spires of the Ruby Life Pools. The vista, though striking, brought her no peace.

"I knew it would be difficult to be queen," Alexstrasza said as the drakes' silhouettes shrank into the sky. "But I feel as though I am failing everyone—the flights, the other Aspects. *Tyr.*" In moments like this, she wished Keeper Tyr were still here to guide her. While she may not always have agreed with his methods, his results spoke for themselves.

"You are not failing anyone, Alexstrasza," Tyranastrasz said, lifting his head to look to the horizon. "We knew the skies before us were full of strong headwinds. While the charge to collect eggs from the wilds might be controversial to some, none of us choose the circumstances of our birth. The vast majority of drakes hatched from adopted eggs have been a credit to their flights."

"Still, I can't help but worry," Alexstrasza replied. "The Primalist threat grows by the day. Neltharion, who has ever been one of my closest allies, works in the shadows and tells me little of his activities. Members of our rising generation seek to reject the very essence of their being. And perhaps they are right to be angry." Though she didn't speak Vyranoth's name aloud, Alexstrasza's thoughts turned to her oldest friend, too. The Life-Binder had been careful to keep this secret through all the long years, hoping it would never reach Vyranoth's ears. Some trusted members of her flight knew, of course, because how could they not? They were responsible for accepting, ordering, and caring for the eggs, after all.

The old wyrm chuckled, nuzzling Alexstrasza's snout. "Such is the folly of youth, my love. In time, they will see the great gift you have bestowed upon them. This is a grand experiment you have undertaken, and none could have embodied the position with as much vigor and wisdom as you."

"You are kind to me," Alexstrasza said, casting her gaze over the Broodlands. In the distance, the drakes wheeled and dived through the skies, thinking themselves free of Alexstrasza's watchful gaze. "I do not regret the decision we made as Aspects, all those years ago . . . just look at them! So full of potential and possibility, granted abilities that do not even exist in the philosophies of our primal cousins. And yet . . ."

In the quiet moments, Alexstrasza wondered if she had made a mistake. She had only expressed this fear once, long ago, and only to her sister. Since then, she had grown into her role as queen and realized there were some burdens she would need to shoulder alone.

"Do not fear," Tyranastrasz said. "Ever have I watched you rise to meet your challenges with courage and compassion— this time will be no different."

She smiled, very much wanting to believe him.

CHAPTER TWELVE

THE BLACK DRAGONFLIGHT IMPRISONED IKRONIA IN A small, windowless cavern, one deep within the mountains of the Reach. The floor was rough-hewn underfoot. Wan light crept in from the braziers in the hallway outside. Unbreakable elementium bars sealed the entrance. Two black dragons guarded her, day and night, keeping the stone wards around her prison strong.

After her interrogation, Ikronia's guards never spoke more than a word or two to her at a time. However, her drakonid minders took pity on her and brought her books and malleable stones. Ikronia did not know what to do with the books—to her, knowledge was ever the domain of the blue flight—but she found she could stack and manipulate the stones, which gave her something to do when the boredom set in. To keep time, she counted the changes in her guard, surmising she had been imprisoned for at least a full clutch of moons, maybe two.

To Ikronia's surprise, guilt was one of her constant companions. Without Raszageth's thunder ringing in her ears, Ikronia couldn't escape the memories of the villages she had attacked: Mortal screams clawed at the edges of her sanity. The smell of burned flesh and fur curled in her nostrils. In her mind's eye, she could still see the dancing silhouettes of the dying.

Perhaps there was some titan magic in these cells that forced the occupants to relive their crimes, over and over again; but whatever it was, it did not soften Ikronia's heart toward the Aspects or their flights. In particular, her hatred for Neltharion and the black dragonflight remained. Some days, she wished Neltharion had seen fit to kill her. Ikronia had no reason to hope for salvation. Iridikron had been clear that if she were to be captured by the Aspects or their dragonflights, he would not come to her aid. Nor would Raszageth, who thought of Ikronia as nothing more than a plaything. Hers was a meaningless, dull existence, devoid of any hope save that of a quick end.

Until one night, when a roll of thunder shook Ikronia awake.

Shouts echoed down the corridors outside her cell. Ikronia lifted her head, blinking and bleary-eyed. More thunder shivered through the mountain, a sound she did not hear with her ears but rather felt in her bones.

Raszageth? she wondered, turning her head toward the source of the sound. *No, it cannot be . . . Iridikron would never allow it.* But who else could bring such storms to bear, ones with the power to make the very earth tremble? Had Iridikron's stony heart softened toward his sister? No, it seemed like too much to hope—her brother would not risk premature war with the Aspects on her behalf. She'd eavesdropped and learned that the Aspects' keepers were gone, but the Stonescaled was still gathering his armies and making plans.

Of all the Incarnates, nobody respected the Aspects' power more than Iridikron . . . which was precisely why he'd spent so many years preparing to destroy them.

Outside the cell, Ikronia's guards shared a look. Hurried footsteps echoed off the stone. Dragons rushed past, shouting orders at one another. Their shadows rippled across the walls of Ikronia's cell. Curious, she rose to her feet and eased forward. She craned her neck, watching the activity outside. Armored drakonid marched by, armed with lances and axes.

One of Ikronia's guards, a large black dragon named Endemion, stepped forward. "Flightmaster Levarian!" he shouted at someone Ikronia could not see. "What's happening?"

"It's Raszageth," a third black dragon replied, pausing just on the cusp of Ikronia's field of view. Levarian stood taller than both of Ikronia's guards—the black was a muscular, powerful creature outfitted in the same gleaming plates the drakonid wore. "The Primalists march on the Reach."

Ikronia's heart leapt.

"Impossible," Endemion replied. "Has Raszageth gone mad? She must know the Reach bristles with the strength of the black dragonflight. And for her to strike *tonight* of all nights—"

The black dragon glanced behind him, cognizant of Ikronia's presence. He frowned and did not finish his statement.

"How did she mobilize her armies so quickly?" the other guard said, a smaller female with hooked horns. Ikronia thought her name was Sandesia. "How did we not *know* about this in advance?"

"The Storm-Eater hid her forces inside the eye of a powerful tempest," the flightmaster said, lifting his head and flaring his nostrils. "The Shadowscales could not penetrate the fury of her maelstrom, but that is neither here nor there. Our Aspect has summoned all available wings to the battlefield, where we will fight alongside the dracthyr in earnest. It's to be the first test of the weyrns' strength."

Ikronia narrowed her eyes. Her guards had whispered of Neltharion's newest abomination, the dracthyr, made from the blood of mortals and the essence of dragons. She'd even seen one or two passing by—they were lighter than drakonid, winged, and capable of knocking full-grown dragons from the sky with their aerial attacks. Neltharion created the dracthyr for one purpose, and one purpose alone: to kill primal dragons, and perhaps more specifically the Incarnates.

"Will you need additional reinforcements?" Endemion asked.

"As of yet, no," the flightmaster said, looking past the guards at Ikronia. "We have yet to ascertain the Storm-Eater's purpose. It is best you remain."

"Very well," Sandesia said with a nod. "Winds be with you, friend."

The flightmaster returned the gesture. "And with you."

When he was gone, Endemion turned his head to Ikronia. "Do not hope for rescue—the dracthyr will make quick work of Raszageth and her forces. They were created to protect the Broodlands from the Incarnates' brutality."

"I have seen Raszageth's 'brutality' a hundred times over," Ikronia replied with a hiss. "Every scar scratched into my hide was left by her talons. The fury of her winds will strip the very scales from your back and peel the soft flesh from your wings. Do you think you can stand against the power and might of the Incarnates?"

The second guard remained cold. "We will see who still stands by morning."

"That we will," Ikronia replied with equal malice.

With that, Ikronia's guards turned their attention away, but Ikronia smelled the tension in the air. Every time a bolt struck the mountainside, the two black dragons shook shivers from their wings. When the ground trembled from the power of the storm's fury, they exchanged a glance. As the screams of the wounded echoed through the mountain corridors, they shuddered.

Hours passed. The battle raged on. Dragons and drakonid came and went. As the hour grew late, a battered, bleeding black dragon limped into the dungeon and said, "Endemion, Sandesia, our flight needs every fresh wing it can get. Go to the front. I will guard your prisoner with what strength I have left."

"We cannot abandon our posts, Ignion," Endemion said. "We have instructions that this prisoner is to be guarded by two members of our flight at all times."

"And you are badly injured, my friend," Sandesia added. "You need the healers, not guard duty."

"You do not understand," Ignion replied. "If the Reach falls, the Primalists will free Iridikron's sister anyway. You must go. Fight. I cannot fly, but I can certainly rest here and maintain the wards."

Ikronia sidled a little closer to her cell's seals, curious. Endemion looked to Sandesia, the question clear in his gaze.

"He is right," Sandesia said softly. "The Reach cannot fall this day."

But it will, Ikronia thought. *Your miserable flight is already failing to push Raszageth back!* Neltharion was powerful, it was true, but even the ground trembled with the Storm-Eater's fury.

Endemion gave the old black dragon a nod. "Very well, we will trust our charge to you."

"Fight well," Ignion said to them.

The two black dragons hurried away, leaving Ignion as Ikronia's sole guard. The dragon towered over Ikronia, taller, broader, and far older than any of her previous wardens. Ikronia could feel the weight of the dragon's strength in the stone around her—even injured, he was far more powerful than anyone she had seen here in the dungeons.

"So," Ignion said, sinking down beside Ikronia's cell. "I finally meet the dragon who betrayed our flight."

"Your *flights* betrayed all of dragonkind," Ikronia said with a hiss. "I will revel in watching Raszageth strike your Aspect from the skies—"

As if Raszageth could hear those words, thunder struck the mountain.

The old dragon looked up, as though he could see the storm outside through the stone. "Tell me something, Ikronia, sister of Iridikron. If you hate us so, why did you choose to be ordered?"

Neltharion had asked Ikronia a similar question, though she doubted the Earth-Warder believed her answer. So it sounded like a lie when she said, "I wanted to believe in the dream of your flights."

"And why did you find us wanting?" Ignion replied. Blood pooled under his body, gleaming dark in the low light. Whether the old dragon realized it or not, he was dying—and with him, the strength of the wards around Ikronia's prison.

"I thought I might find a place among you, somewhere I truly belonged," Ikronia continued, watching the puddle widen under the old dragon. "But Order magic turned me into something hideous . . . *unnatural*. I could not stand the thought of what I had become, so I fled the Broodlands and returned to my brother."

"Because Iridikron is known for his *mercy*," Ignion said with a snort. "Knowing him, it would not surprise me if he somehow manipulated you into coming to the Broodlands in the first place—the Stonescaled excels at that sort of thing."

"I made that choice on my own," Ikronia replied with a growl.

"Did you, now?" he replied. "I am sure your brother made you think as much."

"My brother would *never* manipulate anyone into accepting Order magic," Ikronia said with a snarl, ignoring the seed of doubt Ignion sought to plant in her heart.

"Iridikron would do anything to see the Aspects fall," Ignion said. "He would compromise the very values he holds inviolate and burn the Broodlands themselves. Why, then, would he not find a way to weaponize his own sister in this pursuit?"

"Lies," Ikronia said, backing away from the door. "You wish to turn me against him."

His next breath rasped, and he said, "No, little one. I merely wish for you to see Iridikron for what he is—a master of schemes, who treats others no better than the errant pebbles beneath his feet." Ignion coughed. Flecks of blood spattered over the stone floor. "I do not know, truly, what caused you to come to and then turn from us, but I do not think it is as simple as what you said. I do believe that there is still a place for you here . . . but there is no future for you at your brother's side."

"Lies, lies, *lies*." Ikronia curled up in one corner of her cell, glaring at Ignion. "I hope Raszageth leaves your flight in *tatters*."

The old dragon did not respond.

Outside, the sticky red pool around him stained the stone. It crept over the floor seeping past the bars of her cell. Ignion put his head down, his breath labored, his mastery over the mountain stone growing ever weaker.

Before long, Ignion's consciousness faded. His wards in the mountain crumbled like wet earth, and the stone came alive under Ikronia's feet. She did not wait—despite the chaos, *someone* would notice her wards had fallen. If she wanted to escape, now was her only chance.

Thrusting her talons into stone, she tore down the wall beside her cell bars. She slipped from her cell, keeping to the shadows and heading for the exit. With the chaos in the dungeons, none paid her any mind. After all, she *looked* enough like one of them, and no one had any reason to think Iridikron's sister had escaped.

Ikronia burst from the mountain and into the storm. Rain pelted her scales as she bounded out onto a landing platform. The clouds churned in the sky, gathering so thick and dark, Ikronia could not tell if it was day or night. Lightning flared. Thunder clapped, intertwining with the howls and screams of battle. The winds shrieked in her ears. She closed her wings against her back, cowering in the safety of stone.

Though she had flown with Raszageth for more than fifty summers, Ikronia had never seen the Storm-Eater's full fury. But this might be close . . . and it was *terrifying*.

A massive vortex swirled along the northwestern mountain ridge, beating itself against the cliffs' mighty face. The cyclone tore trees from the ground, hurled boulders through the air, and sucked a river into the sky. No doubt Raszageth herself flew at the center of that maelstrom, commanding her forces from the safety of its fury.

However, Neltharion's dracthyr had broken the Primalists' aerial front line, leaving the Primalists fighting in scattered packs on the winds.

The dracthyr were merciless. Brutal. They would leap into the skies with targeted precision, slashing at the Primals' delicate wing membranes. Ikronia watched as two dived upon a primal dragon's back in perfect synchrony, then drove their talon-shaped weapons into the poor creature's muscles. With a scream, the dragon plummeted to the earth. The dracthyr leapt away and glided to their next target.

The Primalists' tarasek forces on the ground fared little better—they, too, fell before the combined might of Neltharion's dracthyr and drakonid. As in the skies, the dracthyr on the ground moved in perfect concert. It was an unnerving thing to watch, even from this vantage point. Their coordination left thousands of tarasek bodies broken in their wake.

Ikronia wasn't sure she could help Raszageth and her armies, but she had to try. Summoning up her courage, Ikronia leapt from the landing. It took every ounce of her strength to stay aloft. The Storm-Eater's winds were furious, frantic; and though Ikronia had long experience flying in Raszageth's storms, she had never seen them rage quite like this before. The air currents changed paths faster than Ikronia could predict. One moment, the air filled her wings. The next, it darted away, forcing Ikronia to dive to maintain her momentum. She spiraled and danced, hiding among the ranks of the black dragonflight, avoiding the Primalists who would not recognize her, looking for Raszageth all the while.

In the distance, enormous braziers blazed at the base of a mountain. Neltharion stood in his visage on an open platform, alone. To think that he would stoop to take the form of a mortal! Perhaps his visage was a disguise. Few Primalists would think to look for a mortal. Ikronia curled her lip.

The little black dragon had heard of Iridikron speaking of the Aspects' visages with disgust, and she would recognize the black Aspect no matter which form he assumed. Though the Earth-Warder could not exert power over her conscious will, she was drawn to him, almost as if he exerted a gravitational force. Inquisitive, she banked in his direction. She sailed over the drakonid and dracthyr, unnoticed. Unremarkable. To their eyes, Ikronia was just another black dragon returning from the front.

Several flightleaders patrolled the skies above the black Aspect, drawing Raszageth's fury away from him. In his mortal form, Neltharion wore a titan-made artifact on his right forelimb. Ikronia did not have a name for such a thing—it was wrought in gold and shaped like a mortal hand. The artifact glowed so bright it held the very shadows around him at bay.

Neltharion held the artifact aloft; watching the battlefield with fanatical intensity. As he did so, the dracthyr shifted their positions, moving as one. When he cast his arm in front of him, speaking words that were stolen by the winds, the dracthyr in the skies turned their attention to one of Raszageth's commanders. They sent the poor creature hurtling to the ground.

A shiver racked Ikronia's scales. It seemed the Earth-Warder controlled the dracthyr just like the keepers controlled him, perpetuating the cycle of domination and oppression. Ikronia hated herself—she hated that moment of weakness that drew her to Tyrhold so long ago.

She had half a mind to strike now and take the Earth-Warder by surprise, but she could not stand against an Aspect. Raszageth, on the other hand, would be a worthy match. If the Storm-Eater hoped to turn the winds of war, she might start by destroying that artifact. Raszageth had to know what Ikronia had seen.

Wheeling, Ikronia made for the front lines.

She dipped low, hoping the mountains' strong backs would shelter her from the worst of the winds. As she skirted a ridge, she felt a predatory gaze crawl up her spine.

Ikronia glanced over her shoulder, just in time to see a large, fiery Magmatalon dive toward her. A rush of adrenaline shot through her heart. On instinct, she rolled sideways. The primal dragon missed her by inches, the heat of his scales searing the flesh of her wings. She winced, feeling her delicate wing membranes stretch taut with the heat.

"Hold your fury, my friend!" Ikronia tried to shout, but the winds stole her words away. The fire Primalist wheeled in the air and dived at Ikronia a second time. With a powerful flap of her wings, she darted right, landing on a vertical cliff face and digging her claws into the stone for support. As the Primalist rushed at her, Ikronia thumped her tail on the rock, sending a shower of razor-sharp stone shrapnel into the air. The stone fragments pierced the Primalist's wings—it wasn't enough to kill him, but the attack forced him to the ground. He slammed into the mud below, rising to his feet with an angry howl.

Before she could draw the attention of his comrades, Ikronia launched herself off her perch.

This time, she kept to the mountains, careful to stay out of sight. In all the chaos, she managed to slip past the Primalists' lines and fly straight toward Raszageth's vortex. The violent winds, however, forced her to land on a mountain ledge nearby, where she sank her claws into the rock and turned her head to the heavens.

"Raszageth," Ikronia called out, hoping her voice carried over the winds. "You must strike at Neltharion! He has taken a mortal form and uses a titan artifact to control his forces!"

A deep laugh echoed from within the whirling clouds. Veins of lightning swirled around the vortex. Suddenly, the whole of the storm exploded out with a crack of thunder, sending debris flying in all directions. A tree slammed into the ledge below Ikronia, shattering on impact. A boulder cratered the mountain's face behind her, and the whole of the world shook.

Ikronia cowered, then looked up. Raszageth hovered just below the cloud line, lightning dancing over her wings. The Incarnate faced the battlefield and let out a roar that made the entirety of the valley tremble.

"Is that so, whelp?" Raszageth said with a cackle, turning her attention to Ikronia.

"Let me help you," Ikronia said. "I can show you the way!"

"Do you think I need your *help*?" the Storm-Eater said, lightning snapping across her horns. "This war has begun in earnest now—I have no more need of you or your brother's games. I shall drown the Broodlands in an unending storm, starting with Neltharion and his little insects!"

The Storm-Eater turned away. In desperation, Ikronia leapt into the storm, shouting, "Raszageth, wait!"

A bright flash of lightning enveloped the little black dragon, setting every nerve in her body alight. As she fell from the skies, the world went dark.

CHAPTER THIRTEEN

THE WIND BEGAN TO KEEN, WHIPPING NELTHARION'S hair around his face. It carried the bright, brassy clash of talon on armor to his ears, along with the screams of the dying. He stood atop a stone staircase outside Froststone Vault, observing the battle conducted in the air and on the ground.

By the titans, Raszageth's storm felt so much worse in his visage. A mortal body had its uses, but it was far too soft for his liking. He was a creature of earth and stone. To feel so vulnerable and small, even when clad in armor, was ... *unpleasant.*

Neltharion had assumed his mortal form so that he might command his dracthyr via the Oathbinder, a gauntlet he had found deep within a titan vault. When he realized how *good* the dracthyr were at killing dragons, the Earth-Warder had asked the titan-forged to modify the device to fit the purposes of controlling the dracthyr.

Raszageth would be an ideal first test.

The Storm-Eater and her Primalists sailed closer, riding her winds with monstrous speed. Neltharion couldn't believe her audacity—did she truly think she could match the power of an Aspect? Had she not watched his dracthyr decimate the primal dragons in the skies?

The dracthyr had outperformed his expectations in every way: On the western front, Azurathel and his Obsidian Warders held the front line at the Weyrn Training Grounds, forming the bulwark against the Primalists' legion of tarasek. The Dark Talons, led by Cindrethresh, leapt into the skies with deadly accuracy. They landed on the backs of the primal dragons, slashing at their wing muscles and tails. Injured dragons hurtled from the skies and slammed into the ground, dead on impact. Smaller parties of Sarkareth's Ebon Scales were scattered throughout, as were Viridia's Healing Wings. The weyrns provided powerful offensive and defensive support for their comrades on the front lines.

It was a most impressive display, one the Earth-Warder hoped would shock the Primalists into thinking twice before attacking the Broodlands again.

You will fall, a whisper snuck into his mind, impossibly loud despite the din of war. *Your flight will abandon you.*

You cannot weather this storm, said another. *Not without our power.*

Our strength is eternal, said the first. *Even the elements bow to us.*

No, they will bow to me, Neltharion told the whispers, watching as Cindrethresh tore one of the Primalists' champions from the sky. The fire dragon screamed his rage as he plummeted like a comet toward the ground. *The Primalists cannot hope to contend with an Aspect!*

Black dragons trumpeted on the front lines, warning their comrades of incoming danger. One of Neltharion's flightmasters, Levarian, landed beside him on the platform. Though Levarian was an accomplished combatant, the battle had left him marred and bruised. His armor bore deep scores, but it had not broken.

"My Aspect," Levarian said, "the Storm-Eater flies on our position."

"So she does," Neltharion said through his teeth, watching Raszageth approach. "Shall we see how my dracthyr contend with an Incarnate?"

Neltharion stretched his hand forth, calling, "Cindrethresh! Take your Dark Talons and strike Raszageth from the sky! Sarkareth, bring the Ebon Scales' flames to bear upon the Storm-Eater!" He sensed more than saw the dracthyr's attention shift to the Incarnate, their collective rage as bright and hot as magma.

"Kill her," he said, watching as a host of Dark Talons leapt skyward, their silhouettes outlined in a bright flash of lightning.

NEVER IN HER LIFE had Raszageth felt so *alive*. The storm around her ran wicked and wild, unyielding in its power. Soon, she would strike at the black Aspect himself, but first, she would make him watch his precious flight die screaming.

As Neltharion's twisted little whelps leapt toward her, the Incarnate cackled. She gathered the winds in her wings and whipped them downward, creating a microburst. The gust tore through the skies, scattering the Primalists and the ordered alike.

But Neltharion's insects sliced straight through it, their wings tucked against their backs.

With a snarl, Raszageth dived toward them. She concentrated the storm's brutal power in her chest as she dropped. The beasts fell upon her in an instant—she released the elements stored up in her chest, turning herself into a brilliant, blazing ball of lightning. Its fingers arced across the sky, reaching for every living thing within fifty wing-lengths, racing through their blood and bones, frying them from the inside out. The winds warped their screams. Corpses rained from the skies.

The Storm-Eater preened in victory. As she began to gather the power for a second strike, a flash of crimson scales darted past. The little beast swirled once in the air, snapped its wings open, then plunged toward Raszageth.

Growling, Raszageth began to propel herself higher, but the vermin got a hook in her scales. They soared skyward. A bright pain stabbed into Raszageth's neck, a sharp talon that dug deeper, ever deeper, until the pain ripped down her left shoulder and into her wing-finger. Screeching, Raszageth rolled in the air, but the beast held on.

"It was a mistake to come to the Reach, Storm-Eater," the little beast shouted over the winds.

"Ha! Coming from nothing more than a *whelp*!" Raszageth roared, but as the words left her lips, the beast shoved its blade in deeper and wrenched it sideways, nearly incapacitating her with pain. They tumbled into a free fall. As the thunder sang through the skies, more of Neltharion's hateful little fiends careened toward them.

"I am Cindrethresh," said the beast on her back, "and my weyrn will break you in our Aspect's name!"

"Your *Aspect* is *weak*," Raszageth said. Furious and half mad from the pain, she dived into the rising pack of Neltharion's insects and twirled, drawing all the winds around her body. A cyclone erupted around her, tearing Cindrethresh from her back and scattering the dracthyr on the winds.

With a roar, Raszageth snapped her wings open and sent the winds fleeing. Neltharion's twisted creations were far more dangerous than she had first surmised—she could not let them live.

Reorienting herself in the air, she spotted Neltharion on the far side of the valley. She growled, and lightning snapped and danced along her jaws.

As she started toward him, a flaming rock whistled past her head. A second slammed into her wing membrane, sending more sparks of pain through her shoulder. The Storm-Eater looked up. To her horror, a rain of meteorites shot from the clouds, casting the sky in a hellish light.

Raszageth dived, bottoming out and swooping over the heads of the tarasek. The rain of fire crashed into her forces. Furious, she gulped down air, feeling the storm crackle in her lungs. She rushed toward the front line, spitting a torrent of lightning at Neltharion's forces. It hit their phalanx and sent them flying in all directions. She cut a swath through their ranks with more lightning, charging straight toward their Aspect.

Tonight, the titans' terrible power would bow to the elements. Raszageth sucked the storm into her chest again, delighting in its chaotic energy and strength.

Despite the Storm-Eater's charge, Neltharion still hadn't transformed back into his draconic form—he was either arrogant or insane. He stood on a platform at the base of a mountain, his full attention on her, one hand extended in her direction. The titan artifact glowed on his forelimb.

An easy target.

Too easy.

So gleeful was she, Raszageth almost didn't see the shadows that dropped from the clouds. *Black dragons!* Dragons to her left and to her right, over her head and on her tail. Below her, Neltharion's little beasts regrouped to attack.

"Do you think you can face the full might of an Incarnate?" Raszageth bellowed to her attackers, her voice echoing off the mountaintops. She whipped the winds into a cyclone with her wings and pulled the clouds down from the sky. The wind funnel slammed into the ground, cracking stone and shoving her attackers back.

Lightning corkscrewed around her. Thunder roared in her ears. Her heart pounded in her chest, flooding her veins with white-hot sparks. Then, from the heart of the chaos, Raszageth gathered lightning into a ball between her fore-talons. When released, the surge would electrify the whole of the storm at once, killing every living thing for hundreds of wing-lengths in every direction. Perhaps it would be strong enough to kill an Aspect.

Raszageth could not let Neltharion's dracthyr proliferate—they could destroy everything the Incarnates had worked so hard to achieve. No, *no*. She would destroy them all in one glorious, brutal storm, and take their damn Aspect with them.

But a shout tore past the drum of her heart and the crack of thunder: "For the Vigil!" a voice called. "For Neltharion!"

A small weight slammed into the base of Raszageth's neck, only to be joined by a second, then a third. Still caught in the throes of her spellcasting, the Storm-Eater bucked and roared, trying to shake Neltharion's abominations from her back.

"Hobble her wings," the voice shouted.

Sharp pains pierced the Storm-Eater's shoulders, forcing her to angle her wings downward.

"Little beasts!" Raszageth shrieked. She lost control of the winds as her wings seized. The ball of lightning in her talons destabilized, sending shocks dancing in all directions.

A third blade bit into the base of her skull and wrenched forward. Bright shocks of pain exploded through Raszageth's head. With an agonized roar, she plummeted through the skies. As she collided with the ground, the ball of lightning in her talons exploded. Brilliant. Unbelievably bright. A shock wave shook the very foundations of the earth, breaking it beneath her.

For a few breaths, the world went dark. Quiet. A warning shout of thunder shook Raszageth back to consciousness.

Stunned, the Storm-Eater staggered to her feet, rolling her shoulders, her wounds aching. She stood inside a massive crater. Worms of electricity sizzled along the ground. Hundreds of corpses surrounded her—Primalists, ordered, and little abominations alike. Curling her lip, she turned her attention northeast. Even from this distance, Raszageth could feel Neltharion's gaze upon her.

"Emberthal!" The black Aspect's voice carried through the valley and into the crater. "Finish her!"

Lightning flashed. A black-scaled little fiend landed before the Storm-Eater, her eyes flashing gold. She carried a long, bloodstained polearm in her grip.

"You have murdered many good dracthyr this day," she said, her voice soft. Dangerous. *Familiar.* "Even if my Aspect had not commanded your death, I would *gladly* deliver it to you."

"You are *powerless* against me, whelp!" Raszageth snapped.

"I knocked you from the skies," the little beast replied, brandishing her polearm at the Incarnate. She spread her wings, preparing to strike. "I have power enough to destroy one such as you."

"What, with your little *stick*?" Raszageth said through bared teeth. "Ha! I think not. I tire of your master's games—it is time for Neltharion to face me himself!"

Before the insect could strike, Raszageth gathered the storms in the skies and sent a bolt barreling straight for the black Aspect.

BLUE-WHITE LIGHTNING SHOT FROM the heavens and struck the Oathbinder, shattering the gauntlet utterly.

A shock of pain flared through Neltharion's arm. Metal shrapnel exploded in every direction, embedding itself into his armor and flesh. With a roar, Neltharion turned his face away and grasped his injured arm to his chest. His ears rang in the aftermath of a clap of thunder. The scent of ozone and burning flesh filled his snout.

The Oathbinder lay on the ground before him, blackened and broken.

The dracthyr paused their collective assault, looking to one another, confused, their bond snuffed out like a choked flame.

Raszageth took wing, her wild laughter echoing through the Reach. Neltharion narrowed his eyes. How had the Storm-Eater known about the Oathbinder? It was one of his most closely guarded secrets, one he'd shared only with his allies here on the Reach.

You see? one of the voices whispered.

You are weak, said another.

You cannot win, said a third.

The Earth-Warder gritted his teeth and turned his attention back to the fight. Without the Oathbinder's magic, the dracthyr's ranks scattered. Raszageth swept over the battlefield, spitting lightning and driving them into further disarray. Primal dragons pushed the black dragonflight back toward the vault, closing in. On the ground, the tarasek broke through Azurathel's front line.

Without the Oathbinder, Neltharion was powerless against the Primalist assault—he had not been prepared to fight a battle on such a scale. Except for the dracthyr, he had kept only a token force in the Reach.

Tendrils of desperation and fury rose in him, black as a moonless night. He could not lose—he had managed to keep the dracthyr hidden from Alexstrasza's watchful eye for decades. They were the pinnacle of his creations, the very embodiment of the black dragonflight's excellence. He would not watch them come to naught now, nor could he leave them to the slaughter. He would *not* fail to defend the Reach from Raszageth, for how would that look to the other Aspects? To Alexstrasza? How could he be the Broodlands' greatest protector if he failed to save a miserable scrap of land in the north?

Neltharion beckoned to his flightmasters on the ground beside him. "Command the dracthyr to fall back and regroup." Garion, the closest, nodded and leapt into the air.

Raszageth now flew over the War Creche, engaging the remnants of Emberthal's embattled Adamant Vigil. "I will cleanse this place of your abominations, Neltharion!" she cried, drawing the storm's electricity into her wings.

Even from here, Neltharion could see the shattered remnants of the Adamant Vigil spring into the air, ready for one final, desperate assault on the Storm-Eater.

The clouds erupted, creating a web of lightning with her at its center. It lit the whole valley as though it were daylight, catching the dracthyr of the Adamant Vigil in its threads. Bodies twisted. Contorted. A torrent of shrieks and screams swirled on the Storm-Eater's winds. The light went out, plunging the caldera into darkness.

Neltharion's chest heaved as his fury welled, everything around him fading but *her*. He would destroy Raszageth for this, pluck every scale from her hide and feed her corpse to the maggots.

"You have lost, Neltharion!" Raszageth cackled, landing on the platform behind him. She bared her teeth and said, "You are *pathetic*."

Call upon our power, the whispers said, a chorus now, louder than they had ever been before. *Call upon us and claim your vengeance! We can end this storm!*

With a roar, Neltharion released his suppressed fury, desperation, and fear. The emotions flared around him in a torrent of purple light, widening the cracks in his mind. In that whorl of darkness, Neltharion thought he could feel something looking *back* at him, something vast and unknowable, something cosmic and horrifying. He ignored it, pressing onward, turning the whole of his fury on the Storm-Eater.

Do it! the voices said, ever louder. *Take your vengeance!*

Neltharion reached out with his injured hand, directing that dark power to take root within the mountain behind Raszageth. A swirling vortex of shadow and eerie purple light opened behind her. It cast violet light over the caldera's twisted stones. Neltharion could feel the vortex's staggering hunger, one that could swallow entire worlds and still not be satiated.

"What?" Raszageth shrieked, turning to look behind her. The vortex grew in size, drawing her toward its maw. The Storm-Eater screamed and dug her claws into the stone below her, but her strength was no match for the power of this void.

It sucked Raszageth into its portal, trapping her within the hollow vaults of the mountain. Then it winked out, leaving no trace save for the laughter rolling on the wind. Neltharion told himself it was naught but the last dregs of thunder.

The rain eased to a gentle patter. One last, lonely gale blew in the Storm-Eater's wake, scattering the Primalists to the far corners of the Reach.

The hungry power drained from Neltharion, leaving him gasping. Trembling, too, for he knew he could not turn from that darkness now. In his moment of weakness, its tentacles had slipped through the hairline cracks in his resolve. Whispers filled his mind, a constant, never-ending susurrus that writhed on the edge of his consciousness.

He knelt, scooping the fractured shards of the Oathbinder into his hands. A single spark of Order magic remained, filling the tips of his fingers with warmth. Enough magic to issue one final command, perhaps.

As Neltharion rose, cradling the remains of the Oathbinder, he felt the eyes of his flight turn toward him. Black dragons circled in the skies, protective. Flightmasters Garion and Levarian returned to his side, wide-eyed but silent.

The dracthyr on the battlefield turned their gazes up to him, their weyrns shattered, surrounded by the corpses of both friends and foes. To think that such a brilliant experiment would end here in the shadows, in obscurity! For he could not possibly let the dracthyr walk free, not after what he had done. He could barely allow his own *flightleaders* to live after what they had seen. Flightmasters Garion and Levarian would be loyal, of that there was no doubt—they knew of Neltharion's work in Aberrus. However, the five surviving flightleaders would need to be sworn to secrecy, perhaps on pain of death.

As for the dracthyr . . . no, there were far too many of them to manage without the Oathbinder. The Earth-Warder would need to contain them on the Reach, just until he could devise a new way to control them. Alexstrasza could *never* learn the truth of what had transpired here—not of the dracthyr, and *certainly* not of how Raszageth had been imprisoned.

Raszageth's absence would not go unnoticed.

He would need a credible story to tell in place of the truth.

"Garion," Neltharion said quietly, "gather the flightleaders and any other black dragons who still live. None are to leave the Reach without my express permission."

"At once, my Aspect," Garion said, taking wing.

"Levarian, my old friend, I have a different task for you," Neltharion said.

"Anything, my liege," Levarian said, stepping forward.

"When I order the weyrns to return to their creches," Neltharion said, "I want you and your flight units to ensure they remain there until I can give them further instructions."

As Levarian dipped his head to acknowledge the command, Neltharion extended the fragments of the Oathbinder toward the surviving dracthyr. Perhaps not all was lost—perhaps he would find a way to bring his dracthyr back to the battlefield. Perhaps they would yet be useful to this world and its defense.

The fragments glowed. The dracthyr's eyes flashed.

One by one they turned away from him, heeding that final order.

And with that, the Oathbinder's light dimmed, then died.

CHAPTER FOURTEEN

AT NELTHARION'S BEHEST, MALYGOS FLEW FOR THE Reach at dawn, accompanied only by the black Aspect's own majordomo, Nalaxa. Neltharion had asked Malygos to come alone, and quickly.

If he was being summoned to another sparring match or demonstration, Malygos was going to *strangle* Neltharion. But something about the majordomo's demeanor told the Spell-Weaver this was no ordinary request—Nalaxa was usually so self-possessed, almost aloof, but even her voice had trembled when she had relayed Neltharion's entreaty.

What have you done now, my old friend? Malygos wondered as they soared over the Scalecracker Peaks, heading north. The black Aspect had always been rather secretive, keeping to the citadel and his training grounds in the Reach; but lately, Neltharion had become ever more withdrawn. There used to be a time when the black Aspect would confide everything in the blue. Now, Malygos would be hard-pressed to say aught of his friend's business.

They crested the mountain ridge and dropped into the Reach. Malygos's eyes widened. The entire valley looked like a gaping wound in the world. The air crackled with hostile energy. Every tree and shrub had been stripped away. Rivers no longer ran through their original beds but found new paths over juts of rock and fallen logs. The once proud spires of the great vaults were cracked, and broken bridges protruded into empty space.

Worst of all, thousands lay dead—dragon, drakonid, and tarasek alike. The survivors worked to remove the corpses of the flight's fallen and prepare funerary pyres. Per the customs of the black dragonflight, the dead would be burned, with their bones interred in mausoleums in Valdrakken. Their ashes would be scattered across the magma falls in the Waking Shores, so they might return to the same stone that once gave them power.

As Malygos alighted on the platform outside Froststone Vault, he found the scalesmiths of the black dragonflight working to reinforce a towering door. Neltharion turned, and Malygos wanted to believe he saw relief flickering in his friend's eyes.

"By the titans, Neltharion," he said, tucking his wings against his back, "what happened here?"

"Thank you for coming on such short notice," the Earth-Warder said, joining Malygos on the edge of the platform. "Raszageth attacked the Reach last night."

"*Raszageth* did this?" Malygos asked, turning to appraise the battlefield again, his tail rasping on stone. "We must send word to Alexstrasza at once—Iridikron may be planning another assault on the Broodlands."

"We can do nothing of the sort," Neltharion said sharply.

Malygos looked at his friend askance.

The Earth-Warder gestured to the battlefield. "Raszageth acted alone—her offensive strategy was wild, erratic. No maneuver of Iridikron's making would have been so mercurial and ill conceived, and if Harrowsdeep had been preparing for war, we would have known about it in advance. My Shadowscales would have seen to that."

"Where is the Storm-Eater now?" Malygos asked.

"I managed to defeat and imprison her," Neltharion said.

The words hit Malygos like one of Raszageth's own thunderbolts. "*What?*"

"We fought wing-to-wing and talon-to-talon," Neltharion replied, gesturing to the vault behind them. "At one point, I knocked her from the sky and into the earth's embrace, rendering her unconscious. Once her forces saw she had fallen, they fled."

"Unbelievable," Malygos said, surveying the vault door. "So, the Storm-Eater lives, trapped in an old titan vault, no doubt to grow more and more furious with each passing day?"

"Correct," Neltharion said. "I am certain Iridikron has already been informed of her capture, so we seek to fortify her prison before he can mount a counterattack."

"What a comforting thought," Malygos said drily, turning back to the battlefield. "As for the warriors on the field . . . some of them do not appear to be drakonid, nor are they tarasek. Are those Primalist forces? I've not seen them before."

"No, they are not," Neltharion replied, shifting his weight. Was that a note of regret in his tone, or grief? The Spell-Weaver could not decide.

"They were mine," Neltharion said after a long moment. "My *dracthyr*."

"Dracthyr." Malygos furrowed his brow and cast his gaze back over the battlefield. By the titans, there were *hundreds* of them, if not more. "What are they, and why didn't you tell us about this? *Me*, at the very least?"

"I sought to create the perfect soldier, but no one could know," Neltharion replied. "Especially not Alexstrasza—she would see them for what they were, no, for what they *are*: tools to destroy the Incarnates and their Primalist rebellion."

Malygos sighed, a heavy, resonant sound. "Well, I suppose your *perfect soldiers* will be indispensable once Iridikron learns of Raszageth's defeat and subsequent imprisonment. His wrath will be unstoppable."

Neltharion shook his head. "Many still live, but we cannot allow them to fly free."

Malygos lifted a brow. "Did you not say they were the ideal soldiers?"

"When I could control them with Order magic, yes," the Earth-Warder said. "But Raszageth shattered the vessel I used to control their will—"

"*Control their will?* Neltharion, I . . ." Malygos trailed off, shaking his head. What use was it to lecture the black Aspect now? The mistakes had already been made, and Neltharion had never taken even the most constructive criticism in stride.

Instead, Malygos said, "I suppose you did not summon me from the Azure Span simply to tell me this—you need my help, don't you?"

"I do."

"And I take it I will not be able to tell the Dragon Queen?"

Neltharion lifted his head. "Alexstrasza can never know about the dracthyr."

"Never?" The blue Aspect lifted a brow. "*Never* is a long time. What happens when the Incarnates assail our borders and we have need of your 'perfect soldiers'? Surely, Alexstrasza would thank you for your foresight?"

"I will find another way."

"Hmph." Malygos understood Neltharion's furtiveness to a point—the Spell-Weaver kept his own secrets from the Dragon Queen. However, hiding *Neltharion's* secrets from Alexstrasza was another matter. If Alexstrasza discovered this deception and Malygos's role in it, he would pay dearly for the mistake.

Worse, Malygos sensed his friend wasn't being entirely honest with him. Neltharion usually liked to wax poetic about his exploits and achievements. Today, he seemed circumspect, almost unnerved. His wingleaders were startled at shadows. Behind them, the scalesmiths worked silently, saying nothing, retrofitting the old titan vault into a prison. There were no songs of victory, no tales of valor; no relief among the living.

Whatever had happened in the Reach last night, it had traumatized an entire flight. For now, it would not do to bring the Dragon Queen's ire down upon their heads, too.

Malygos looked at Neltharion out the corner of one eye. "I have conditions."

"Such as?" Neltharion replied with a stony grumble.

"One, if I help you conceal what happened here from the Dragon Queen, I will expect you to repay me in kind," the blue Aspect said. "Should my flight be in dire need, swear to me that you will come to our aid without question or compunction."

"I swear it," Neltharion said. On this point, Neltharion seemed to speak true.

"Two, when we have finished our work here, we will fly straight for Valdrakken and tell Alexstrasza that the Incarnates attacked the Reach—"

Neltharion winced. "Malygos, I—"

"Don't," Malygos interceded, holding up a single talon. "*More secrecy* will not lend any credibility to your story. Tell her as much as you can and be as truthful as you can. Fail to do this, and I will tell her the *full* story myself. Dracthyr included." The blue Aspect waved his talons at the fallen soldiers on the field.

"And here I thought you my friend," Neltharion said, cocking his head to look at the blue.

"I am," Malygos said. "I'm the best friend you have, Neltharion, and that is precisely why I will not let you make any more mistakes than you already have."

The Earth-Warder snorted but said, "Fine. Come, I will show you what we must do."

They took wing, and were soon alighting on the platform outside the vault of the Weyrn Grounds. Neltharion shifted into his visage in a swirl of cinders, motioning for Malygos to do likewise. Bemused, the blue Aspect stepped into his own mortal guise.

Two black drakonid bowed to Neltharion as they stepped into the vault. "I do not wish to destroy them, but would prefer to place them in a deep, dreamless sleep." He winced as he adjusted the gauntlet on his right hand. Beneath the armor, the skin of his forearm appeared red and blistered. "I may yet find a new way to control them."

"Why must you control them at all?" Malygos asked as they descended the staircase, heading into the shadows. A warm—almost hot—updraft of air rushed up to greet them. "If they are such excellent soldiers, do they not deserve their own agency?"

"The dracthyr were bred to be dragon-killers," Neltharion said simply. "I cannot risk Iridikron turning them against us."

The Spell-Weaver frowned but did not respond.

"Do you not agree?" Neltharion asked as they paused at the threshold of a massive underground chamber.

"You place outsized emphasis on Iridikron's powers of persuasion, my friend," Malygos said, adjusting the collar of his robes. By the titans, it was *hot* in this place—the cylindrical chamber was lit from below by a bubbling magma pool. A thin waterfall of lava fell through the center of the room. Malygos lifted his gaze, awed by the sheer number of doors set into the chamber's stony walls. They spiraled higher, ever higher, until they disappeared into the shadows.

"I know the dracthyr as I know my own mind," Neltharion said. "You must trust me."

"I do . . . but never more than strictly necessary," the blue Aspect replied, shooting the Earth-Warder a smirk. Neltharion rolled his eyes, but some of the tension drained from his face.

"I can place them in an icy stasis," Malygos said, stepping into the chamber and gesturing to the doors with a spread of his hands. "It will allow them to sleep for a year, or sleep for a millennium, it matters not. They should suffer no adverse effects from the magic—they will be as you left them, fit in body and mind."

"Excellent," Neltharion replied. "When can we begin?"

"Now," the blue Aspect replied, waving one hand in the air. Violet-blue sparks flew from the tips of his fingers. "Unless you would like the opportunity to say goodbye?"

The Earth-Warder shook his head. "Best to take them unawares."

Together, they entered the dracthyr's creches one by one. Malygos's arcane aura crept across the floor like a rime of ice, freezing each dracthyr it touched. The joy on their faces at seeing Neltharion, their creator, turned to confusion, then fear, as Malygos's magic flowed into their limbs. Many called out for their friends or loved ones, or even for Neltharion himself . . . and in each creche, Neltharion turned his back on them. Again, and again, and again.

The blue Aspect pitied them, these creatures he imprisoned for the crime of fulfilling their creator's ambitions a little too wonderfully and well. Though Malygos would never admit it aloud, the fact that Neltharion would use Order magic to deprive another sentient being of their free will made him apprehensive. Order magic was not meant to be used to dominate, but to *liberate*.

When it was done, Malygos and Neltharion stepped from the final creche near a freshly made crater in the ground. The sun's light filtered through the lingering gray clouds, laying all Raszageth's destruction bare.

The blue Aspect doubted the Reach would ever be the same—everywhere he looked, the shocking power of Raszageth's storms had ripped every tree from the valley, displaced entire rivers, and even beaten the mountain peaks into submission. Great spikes of lava had been pulled into the air and spun into sharp black claws, where they had cooled to stone. It would be beautiful if it weren't a monument to death.

"I will return tomorrow with a cabal of my trusted Spellscales and Spellsworn drakonid," Malygos said as they paused on the landing. "They will stand guard over the creches and help defend the Reach from Primalist invasion—you know Iridikron will fly for our borders when he hears of this."

"We will be prepared for them," Neltharion replied.

"For the Primalists, perhaps," Malygos said, "but are you ready to tell *Alexstrasza* what has happened?"

"I had hoped you'd forget about that part of the bargain," the Earth-Warder said with a grin.

"Ha!" Malygos said, shifting back into his Aspectral form. "To Valdrakken, then?"

"To Valdrakken," Neltharion replied.

THE NEWS FROM THE north shattered Alexstrasza's dreams of peace. While the clear skies around the Seat of the Aspects held a swath of winking stars, storms now roiled on their horizons. And powerful as she was, even Alexstrasza could not command a storm to cease.

The Life-Binder stood with the other Aspects in the Seat, holding back a swell of fury as she listened to Neltharion's story: Raszageth had attacked the Reach. Neltharion and a handful of wingleaders had managed to hold off the Storm-Eater's assault, imprisoning her inside one of the Reach's many stone vaults. From all accounts, Neltharion and his wingleaders had barely survived the encounter.

"How dare they?" Alexstrasza said, lifting her head and maintaining an outward semblance of calm, even if she shook with rage on the inside. Her muscles quivered in her legs, shoulders, and abdomen. Heat flushed her face. "What have we done to merit such an attack, and in the Reach, of all places? Do you think this attack was directed by Harrowsdeep, or was Raszageth operating independently?"

"I am still waiting on word from the Shadowscales," Neltharion said, "but I believe Raszageth acted on her own. Iridikron would not have fumbled in such a manner, nor has he seen fit to declare war."

"That possibility becomes more distinct by the day," Nozdormu said, staring off into the distance past Alexstrasza's shoulder, a flash of gold in his eyes. "Few paths to peace remain open to us now."

"If any," Malygos said. "Iridikron will be furious when he learns of Raszageth's imprisonment."

As will Vyranoth. Alexstrasza gritted her teeth. In one night, Raszageth had managed to undo centuries of peacekeeping and diplomacy. Yes, relations with the Incarnates had been tense for more than two hundred years, but Alexstrasza had still managed to keep war at bay. Once the Incarnates learned of the Storm-Eater's imprisonment, tensions would rise higher and grow more violent. The Life-Binder tapped her talons on the ground, thinking.

Ysera turned to her. "Perhaps we can take comfort in the fact that Raszageth has been removed from the field, sister. She will threaten us no longer."

"You are ever the optimist, dearest," Alexstrasza said with a smile, though it died the moment it hit her lips. "In light of recent events, we must continue to strive for peace even as we prepare for war. Malygos, how goes the development of our so-called ghost army?"

"Rather well, actually," the Spell-Weaver said. "Sindragosa and Beregos have already managed to adapt our arcane constructs to the task—in a few days, we will be able to introduce hundreds of new 'dragons' to our borders."

"Good," she said. "Neltharion, can your scalesmiths fashion a tactical map of both the Broodlands and Greater Kalimdor for the Seat of the Aspects? We will need to decide where best to deploy the blue dragonflight's constructs."

"Of course," he said.

"If Raszageth is in the Reach, we should devote a sizable force to defend her prison," Alexstrasza said.

"I will pledge a cabal of blues to the cause," Malygos said

with a nod to Neltharion.

"And you shall have support from the reds at the conservatory," the Life-Binder said, then turned to her sister. "Ysera, would you send messengers to every mortal village in the Broodlands and those that lie near our borders? Let them know that Raszageth has been captured but that the Incarnate threat remains."

"My greens shall fly at first light," the Dreamer said.

Alexstrasza nodded, looking lastly to Nozdormu. She sighed. "Long have you warned us that war would be nigh unavoidable, my friend, so I know I ask for the impossible: If any avenue to peace remains to us, I wish for you and your flight to attempt to find it."

Nozdormu bowed his head.

"In the meantime, I shall try to make the impossible happen myself," Alexstrasza said. "I shall meet with Iridikron and parley for peace."

"He will *never* agree to that," Neltharion said, tossing his head. "The Stonescaled wants one thing, and one thing alone—*war*."

"And what of you, Neltharion?" Alexstrasza turned her head to look the Earth-Warder in the eye. The Seat fell silent. "Do *you* want war?"

Neltharion appeared impassive as mountain stone, but the conflict within his heart echoed within her own. She could feel the strength of his desire to protect the Broodlands, as well as the lingering fury over the losses his flight had suffered at the Reach. Alexstrasza empathized with these emotions, for she felt them, too. She would be a poor queen, indeed, if she did not want justice for the fallen, and to protect her flights from those who meant them harm.

Still, she refused to give up on peace.

Beneath Neltharion's bubbling anger and his unshakable determination, Alexstrasza sensed something . . . *else*. Something that flitted away from her when she turned her attention toward it, like a shadow skittering on the edge of her sight. It left her with a sense of unease, though it might have been her imagination.

"No," the Earth-Warder said after a long moment. He swallowed hard. "I have seen the Incarnates' wrath for myself and would not wish such destruction upon the wider Broodlands."

"Then we should do everything in our power to avoid it, even if our enemies rebuff us," she said. "Our treaty with Harrowsdeep is now null—until I can stabilize relations with the Incarnates, all primal dragons are hereby banned from the Broodlands and Wyrmrest Temple. Close your borders. Fortify your defenses. We will not be caught unawares again."

RASZAGETH HADN'T RETURNED TO Harrowsdeep for several moons, Iridikron noted. Current reports said her aerie in the Whorl was abandoned. The Storm-Eater tended to be capricious—she would disappear for days, chasing storms all over the continent—but for the whole of the Whorl to be empty, now *that* was a concern. Of the three Incarnates, Raszageth's aerie was the closest to the Broodlands; however, there was no sign of an attack.

Ikronia was missing, too, and Iridikron thought his sister's absence indicated disaster. The two had managed to avoid capture far longer than Iridikron imagined they would, but perhaps fate had finally caught up with them.

So, when the Rockfuries heard whispers of a great storm in the Reach, Iridikron commanded his wingleaders to search for the missing Incarnate. He said nothing of Ikronia, however. Very few of the Primalists knew of his sister's existence, and the ones who did never spoke her name. Far better for the tarasek and the mortals to never know and instead curse the Aspects for their misery.

Primalists flew to every corner of the Dragonwilds, scouring the skies for Raszageth. The search parties hoped to find some sign of the Storm-Eater. One pack ventured to the Frozen Fangs, asking Vyranoth if she had seen Raszageth or knew where she might have flown. Vyranoth, worried and confused, joined Iridikron's wingleaders in their search.

Another day passed with no word, then two.

On the third day, Iridikron stood in his war cavern, brooding over a stone map of the Dragonwilds. The room lay mostly dark, lit only by the murky light of the lava flows.

While Iridikron would never outwardly express something so trite as a worry, Raszageth's disappearance caused him grave concern. His Rockfuries reported the Storm-Eater hadn't been sighted within the Broodlands' borders; nor was she imprisoned in the dungeons of the Obsidian Citadel. Raszageth's pawn on the map still stood at Harrowsdeep, but she was not there; it was almost as if she had been swallowed up by the world.

Wings stirred the cavern's still air. "Stonescaled, I bring news," a voice called to him.

Iridikron turned away from the map. One of his wingleaders, Rava, landed on the great stone platform before him. Rava was ever one of Iridikron's favorites—clever, bold, and assertive. Her talons had already claimed many lives of the ordered. The skillful primal dragon had scales that gleamed like shards of obsidian in the low light, and her eyes burned with a fierce, brutal intelligence.

Rava touched one of her wing talons to her chest in salute. "I have brought you something from the east."

"What is it?" Iridikron said, trying to hide his agitation. "Have you found her? Have you found Raszageth?"

"I wish I could bring you such happy news, my lord," Rava said. "But I fear I have brought you something . . . *else*. Perhaps it will please you."

"Bring it forth, then."

Rava motioned to her lieutenants, Ryanog and Kagoznos, who stood at the war cavern's entrance. With a nod, Iridikron raised a stone platform from the lava, bridging the two islands. Her lieutenants started forward. Behind them, ten tarasek dragged a pile of white rubble on a sledge. The wooden poles rasped against the stone. The tarasek pulled the sledge across the lava lake and onto the center island, bowing their reptilian heads to Iridikron.

The sledge contained the remains of a fallen titan-forged, rent into pieces. Several large talon marks crisscrossed the creature's torso. Its stone skull had been hewn in half, and it was missing one arm.

Curious, Iridikron stepped forward. Rava came to stand at his right wing, while her lieutenants flanked the sledge. The tarasek backed toward the rim of the island, keeping their eyes on the floor. They knew to keep silent, having seen too many victims of the Stonescaled's displeasure.

"What is this?" Iridikron asked, turning to Rava.

"A titan-made egg-thief," she replied.

Iridikron felt as though she had sucked all the air from the room. "Where did you find such a thing?" he asked, gaze flicking back to his wingleader.

"Near Wyrmrest Temple, my lord," Ryanog replied.

Iridikron's thoughts churned into a maelstrom: For centuries, he had blamed the Aspects for the dragon eggs that went missing in the wilds . . . but he hadn't thought it to be actually *true*. For all her moralizing, perhaps the Dragon Queen was more devious than he'd thought.

Long had he awaited a day like this! Many of the most powerful primal dragons refused to turn against the Aspects—dragons like Vyranoth, Cysanz, and Igyniar, all of whom had old friendships with dragons in the Broodlands. But *this* revelation would force them to admit that the struggle between Incarnate and Aspect wasn't a matter of opinion, but one of *survival*.

Despite the thoughts whirling in his head, Iridikron simply said, "Explain."

Rava nodded. "Ryanog? Show the Stonescaled the device."

The ice drake took a spherical object from the sledge in his jaws. He dropped his head and approached Iridikron, setting the object on the ground before the Stonescaled.

Iridikron lifted it from the floor to study.

The device was of titan make, round like a bubble, and slightly larger than a dragon's egg. Its curved sides were clear as quartz, but cracked, and swirling designs had been carved into its surface. An opaque, yolky substance coated the interior walls. Iridikron could see fragments of an eggshell inside, along with the fragile imprint of a whelpling's wing.

Iridikron narrowed his eyes, saying nothing.

"This titan abomination took a dragon's egg from an untended nest and placed it inside this device," Ryanog said with a snarl. "I attacked it before it could steal another."

"Hmm," Iridikron said, his voice rumbling like a rockslide. So, his suspicions were correct. Vyranoth had told Raszageth that the whelpling number of ordered dragons outpaced that of primal ones. She said it was the red flight's stewardship, the safety of their holdings compared with the Dragonwilds, but even Vyranoth had found that strange. The Dragon Queen had promised the primal dragons that Order magic would be a choice, but she had not clarified that she only meant a *choice for those already born*. Or had Neltharion seized the eggs without the Dragon Queen's knowledge? Such a scheme smacked of the Earth-Warder's cunning.

How many eggs had the Aspects kidnapped? How many young drakes in the Broodlands deserved to be free of the titans' stain? How badly had the primal dragons' numbers been culled, right under Iridikron's snout?

Fury bubbled in the Stonescaled's veins, slow and hot as magma. Unlike the other Incarnates, Iridikron's anger was not explosive or capricious—it had built over the centuries, its heat increasing with every indignity the primal dragons suffered at the Aspects' talons.

The theft of the eggs was too much to bear.

"This is how the Aspects mean to eliminate our kind," Iridikron said quietly, lifting his head. "Rava, I want you to take this news to Cysanz at once. Send messengers to Igyniar and his pack in the west. Tell them I have proof of the Aspects' treachery. As for me, I must fly to the Frozen Fangs at once— I would speak with Vyranoth myself."

AS THE FIRST GRAY talons of dawn reached across the sky, Iridikron swept toward Vyranoth's lofty aerie. The Fangs' peaks emerged from the cloudy skies, and he trumpeted his approach; he did not want to take the frost dragon or her pack unawares. He knew from experience that Vyranoth did not like surprises.

He alighted on the ledge outside her aerie, his stone talons slipping on the ice. If the air was chill, Iridikron could not tell—he had ceased to feel the cold when his flesh had turned to stone.

"Iridikron." Vyranoth's voice echoed from the depths of her cave. Her talons rasped on the ice as she stalked into view, her intelligent eyes glowing in the frosty shadows. "What brings you to the Fangs at this hour? Have you managed to find Raszageth?"

"No, not yet," the Stonescaled replied.

"Hmph," Vyranoth said. "I suppose she would have come here herself if you had . . . Well, then? Out with it."

"Long ago, I said that if you refused to join my cause, I would not ask you a second time," he said, setting the titan-made device down on the ledge. Vyranoth tilted her head, her gaze flicking to the device then back to him.

"Today," he said, "I must break that promise."

"What is that?" she asked, stepping from her aerie and wrinkling her snout.

"It is the device that Alexstrasza's titan-forged used to steal eggs from our kind," Iridikron said softly.

Vyranoth paused mid-step, going so still that it were as if she had turned into the very glaciers around them. She stared at the device with wide eyes, her lips parting, a tremor racing through her lower jaw. At last, she drew in a deep, shaky breath.

"How do you know it was Alexstrasza, and not Neltharion?" she asked.

"The Dragon Queen raises our whelps in the Waking Shores," Iridikron said, adding a growl at the edge of his words. "It does not matter whether she gave the command—she sees the eggs are primal. She *knows*."

Vyranoth drew in a second shaking breath, then a third, until a shiver ran through her body. "No, you must be mistaken . . . my friendship with Alexstrasza may have withered, but I refuse to believe she would lie to me about something like this. She would not do this. *She swore it to me*."

"You may believe what you want," he replied, "but my scouts saw it for themselves—"

"Iridikron! My lord!" A panicked voice cracked the skies. With a frown, the Stonescaled turned, surprised to see a storm dragon riding into the Fangs on swift winds. "I followed you as quickly as I could, but could not catch you—the Rockfuries have found Raszageth! She was taken captive by the Aspects in the Reach! Neltharion has sealed her in a prison of stone!"

What? A stony growl rumbled in his chest. The Stonescaled narrowed his eyes, his rage burning ever brighter. But even his wrath was dwarfed by Vyranoth's roar of fury, a sound that set avalanches into motion. Snow cascaded down the faces of the Fangs, shrieking with the dragon as her rage manifested itself in the elements. The air filled with ice crystals that burned in Iridikron's lungs and shut out the sky. The ground shook underfoot, and Iridikron worried the mountains might crack all the way to their roots.

After what felt like an eternity, there was silence. The ice crystals in the air settled, forming a thin rime on Iridikron's scales. Vyranoth stood unmoving, her head bowed, eyes squeezed shut.

"I ask you a third time," Iridikron said quietly. "Join me."

Vyranoth blew out a breath, though it sounded more like a sob. For a heartbeat, he thought she might deny him again, but she lifted her head and met his eyes.

"For the eggs that were stolen," she said with a nod. "And for Raszageth."

CHAPTER FIFTEEN

A S IRIDIKRON THREATENED WAR, ALEXSTRASZA INVITED the Incarnates to a parley. Iridikron wanted Raszageth's release, while the Life-Binder wanted a promise of peace. However, Alexstrasza was not naïve enough to think those goals were congruous—if freed, the Storm-Eater would only continue to wreak havoc along the Broodlands' borders.

Still, Alexstrasza wished to speak to the Stonescaled face-to-face; for the last two centuries, all their communications had been handled through the embassy at Wyrmrest Temple. If she was going to war against Iridikron and his Primalists, she at least wanted the opportunity to take his measure. Titans knew he wouldn't listen to reason, but perhaps Alexstrasza could find a way to delay all-out war. Exceptional as they were, her flights would be outnumbered. They needed more time to prepare to meet the Primalists in the field.

Alexstrasza landed on the tundra of northern Kalimdor in the gray light of dawn, in a lonely, nameless stretch of land between Harrowsdeep and the Broodlands. Her talons broke through a light crust of ice and snow as the vastness of the northern tundra stretched before her. She sensed no sign of the Incarnates or Primalists. For now, the Aspects and their forces were alone.

Mark my words, Iridikron only agreed to the parley as a distraction, Neltharion had said. *He will take this opportunity to attack . . . but where and how, I cannot guess.*

To prepare for a surprise attack, the Aspects worked together to plan their defenses. Malygos's army of illusory dragons took up positions in the Reach, on the Emerald Plains, and at the Azure Archives, making the Aspects' forces appear a great deal larger than they actually were. Neltharion selected strategic choke points along the Broodlands' borders to lay with traps, then armed mortal villages with projectile weapons. The tribes in the Apex Canopy adopted the technology with surprising speed, but they had been associating with the black dragonflight for many years.

If Alexstrasza craned her neck, she could just barely see the great spires of the Obsidian Citadel on the southern horizon. Neltharion had positioned a sizable battalion of blacks and reds there, along with scores of drakonid foot soldiers.

If the Incarnates proved treacherous, the Aspects would fall back to the citadel while Neltharion took command of their forces. Alexstrasza did not expect Iridikron to attack the citadel outright—the Reach was a more likely target. For that reason, Alexstrasza had sent wing units from every flight to defend Raszageth's prison, as well as a legion of drakonid.

Because the Incarnates could strike anywhere, the Aspects had to prepare for war everywhere.

"I mislike this," Saristrasz said, sniffing the air. His lip curled. "Something is amiss. The air is too cold for this time of year, and the small creatures of the earth tremble in their burrows. We should keep to the skies."

"I agree, though Neltharion has asked us to remain grounded," Alexstrasza replied, turning her gaze to the Earth-Warder, who communed with the ground not ten wing-lengths from where they stood. Ysera joined Alexstrasza, her emerald scales glimmering in the morning light. Alexstrasza took comfort in her sister's stabilizing presence.

"The black dragonflight has established a perimeter of the area," Alexstrasza continued. "I trust they will warn us of any impending danger. Besides, Iridikron would be unwise to test the might of five Aspects at once."

Ysera swept her tail along the ground, sending up a great fan of snow. Stalwart and brave as the green Aspect might be, she hated conflict.

"Even so," Saristrasz said, giving his wings a restless shake, "I can't help but be nervous."

"I share your concerns, my friend," Alexstrasza said gently. "But I will not send another dragon to speak to Iridikron in my place. We must parley for peace. War would mean that we have failed—no, that *I* have failed—in my charge to protect the flights and Azeroth at large."

"You could not fail us." Saristrasz made a rumbling noise in his throat. "Besides, our kind was made for the defense of this world. To its defense we must come, even if it is against those we once called kin."

"I thank you for your faith, my old friend," Alexstrasza said, though she couldn't help thinking of the look upon Nozdormu's face during their last Aspectral Council. She had asked him for news from the timeways, and all he'd done was shake his head solemnly. The bronze flight was hard-pressed to find a future that avoided this conflict. Alexstrasza could not bear to hear that the final pathway to peace had been lost, so the bronze Aspect had said nothing at all.

Nozdormu landed on Alexstrasza's left, pulling the Life-Binder from her reverie. He gave her a nod. Malygos joined them on the ground, just to the right of Neltharion. Half their escort remained in the skies, ever watchful for danger.

In the east, the sunrise lacerated the horizon, leaving a bright gash of red light over the Broodlands. Alexstrasza's anxiety grew, and she began to wonder if the Incarnates would appear at all. Tension stretched each second taut. Dragons paced and watched the skies. Others went about their duties, weaving enchantments and wards, communicating in low tones. Even Neltharion fidgeted, tapping his talons on stone.

"There they are," Saristrasz said quietly, narrowing his eyes.

A small band of primal dragons appeared on the western horizon, led by Fyrakk. As they drew closer, Alexstrasza frowned. "If I'm not mistaken, no dragon of Iridikron's description flies with Fyrakk."

"No," Saristrasz said, his eye widening. "I've seen the Stonescaled before—he isn't among them."

"Titans be good," Alexstrasza breathed. A spike of adrenaline hit her heart. Iridikron and Fyrakk had agreed to meet her at dawn. If the Stonescaled was not here, did that mean he had gathered his forces to strike elsewhere?

"Neltharion," Alexstrasza called, turning to the Earth-Warder. "Do you sense the Stonescaled in the vicinity? He is not among the Incarnates' delegates."

"No," Neltharion replied, but gave his escort hasty orders to search the area. Four black dragons flew for the cardinal points, no doubt to warn the blacks at the Earth-Warder's obelisks.

"I will send messengers to the Broodlands," Malygos said, opening several portals for his blues. Alexstrasza recognized the Obsidian Citadel, Vakthros, and Valdrakken in the portals' gleaming faces.

Dread crept across the snow as Fyrakk approached. Alexstrasza had not seen her cousin since he had become an Incarnate. Like the Aspects, Fyrakk was wholly changed: The elements had charred his scales black and set his horns aflame. Great gouts of fire erupted along his spine, and his eyes blazed red.

When he landed on the ground before Alexstrasza, the snow hissed under his feet. Fyrakk stood as tall as Alexstrasza did, a behemoth among the smaller primal dragons in his retinue. Even though she stood ten wing-lengths away from her cousin, she could feel the blistering heat rolling off his scales. Somehow, his hatred for her burned hotter.

The Life-Binder stepped forward. "Let us dispense with the pleasantries, cousin—where is Iridikron?"

"The Stonescaled sends his regrets, *cousin*," Fyrakk said with a deep, mountain-cracking chuckle. "He is unable to attend today's parley."

Neltharion growled, tossing his head. "That was not the agreement—enlighten me, what business of Iridikron's is more important than deciding the future of dragonkind?"

"I am not interested in a discussion of dragonkind's *future*," Fyrakk said, turning on Neltharion. "I am here to negotiate for the release of Raszageth the Storm-Eater. Until she is freed, there shall be no peace between the Incarnates and the Aspects."

"Never," Neltharion snapped, his fangs flashing. "Raszageth attacked the Reach without cause, killing hundreds of members of my flight. Such wounds cannot be forgiven or forgotten."

The flames blazed brighter along Fyrakk's spine. "You would speak of wounds when your very flights are a corruption of our kind? Fools! I should take your wings for that insult—"

"Enough!" Alexstrasza shouted, slamming one forefoot into the ground. Ruby light burst from the impact, sending out a calming emanation to everyone around her. Fyrakk snarled, stepping back from the light. "We did not come here to fight over past injuries, but to discuss the terms of Raszageth's release *and* a path to peace. If we must move forward without Iridikron, so be it."

"There can be no peace, Alexstrasza," Fyrakk said. "Not while my sister remains imprisoned."

"It is a fitting punishment for her crimes against the black dragonflight," Alexstrasza said. "Had she not attacked the Reach, we would never have had cause to imprison her."

"If that is the case," Fyrakk said, "then you should renounce your titles, Alexstrasza, and submit yourself to the judgment of the Incarnates for your own crimes against *our* kind."

"What *crimes* have I committed against you?" Alexstrasza cried, stepping forward and spreading her wings to emphasize her words. "For centuries, I have worked to build peaceful relations between our kinds. I would never do anything to harm the Incarnates or the primal dragons who—"

Before Alexstrasza could finish, Fyrakk snatched something from one of his retainers and hurled it to the ground. It slid for several wing-lengths in the snow, coming to a stop in front of Alexstrasza.

It was the talon-sundered corpse of a titan-forged.

Alexstrasza's heart stuttered in her chest. She lifted her gaze to Fyrakk's, wary. All around her, the other Aspects went still. She could feel Neltharion's fury welling like magma, which contrasted with Malygos's icy hatred. Ysera lifted her head, appraising Fyrakk coolly. Ysera had never liked Fyrakk—his fiery temper had always been at odds with her gentle nature.

Only Nozdormu remained unmoved. The bronze Aspect's words came back to Alexstrasza in that moment, haunting her from so many years past: *This course of action may provoke the very conflict you wish to avoid.*

"For centuries, you and your keepers have stolen our eggs," Fyrakk said, his voice full of deadly malice. "You took them, forced Order magic upon them, and raised them as your own—"

"What proof do you have of these allegations?" Alexstrasza said, stepping forward and curling her lip.

"Griminoth!" Fyrakk said. A frost dragon stepped forward, carrying a round object between his small forearms. With great care, the Primalist set the artifact down on the ground between Fyrakk and the Aspects. Weak sunlight glanced off the artifact's metal rings and toothy, shattered glass. Inside, Alexstrasza could just see the remnants of a crushed whelp.

Alexstrasza recognized the artifact immediately—it was one of the titan-forged's egg-carriers, a device they used to protect wild primal dragon eggs while enroute to the Broodlands. She stared at the artifact, sinking her claws into the ground to steady herself, her mind racing as fast as her heart.

"What say you to this?" Fyrakk bellowed at Alexstrasza, his words ringing across the empty plain. "You, who swore that every dragon would be given a choice. You, who swore our kind would not be forced to serve your titan masters!"

"Lies," Neltharion replied, making the whole of the earth quake under their feet. "You say this to slander us again, just like you did by burning villages in our names!"

"That was *you*," Fyrakk said with a snarl.

"No, cousin," Alexstrasza replied, "it was *Raszageth* who burned the villages to the ground, aided by defectors from the black dragonflight."

Neltharion stepped forward and continued. "For decades, Iridikron sent her forth to burn villages in the Aspects' names, sowing terror and discord along our borders. I can see through your deception, Fyrakk! You seek to turn more against us with your lies."

"You would compare the lives of our *whelplings* to those of *insects*?" Fyrakk snapped. "Mortal lives are *meaningless*."

"No," Neltharion growled. "But unlike you, I can see Iridikron's pathetic warmongering for what it is—"

With a roar, Fyrakk charged at Neltharion. The Earth-Warder bristled. Alexstrasza, acting wholly on instinct, launched herself forward and slammed into Fyrakk's unprotected flank, sending the Incarnate sprawling backward. Fyrakk slid in the snow, sending up a plume of steam in his wake. Alexstrasza landed with grace, then rose to her full height.

"This was meant to be a *parley*," she boomed, her scales blazing with ruby light. The primal dragons cowered before her, hiding their faces from her glowing form. "Instead, it has devolved into petty accusations and lies. If we are to find a path forward, we must put our differences aside and try to form some sort of understanding."

"I have already said there will be no peace, Alexstrasza," Fyrakk said, getting to his feet. He shook out his wings, glaring at her. "The Incarnates would never consider peace with monsters like you."

Alexstrasza narrowed her eyes and lowered her chin, expecting Fyrakk to strike. Neltharion and Nozdormu flanked her.

"If you want to discuss peace," Fyrakk continued, "either free Raszageth or submit your own queen to us for penance. The Incarnates will accept nothing less—"

"No," Neltharion said. "Raszageth attacked the Reach without provocation and did significant and lasting harm to the black dragonflight. My flight *will* have justice."

"Do you think we Incarnates care about your petty *justice*?" Fyrakk asked, flames curling around his fangs. "No more talk! Produce Raszageth, or the Primalists march on Wyrmrest Temple *now*."

"Is that where Iridikron is?" Alexstrasza asked with a snarl. "Is he breaking our pact and marching on neutral territory?"

Fyrakk merely grinned.

The Life-Binder drove her talons into the earth, shredding the ground underfoot. Wyrmrest Temple had but a small defense force—even Iridikron had agreed that it would be a neutral location, so long as the primal dragons were still allowed to use the surrounding territories to hunt. If the ordered dragons there were beset by the Incarnates and Primalists, they would be slaughtered outright. Alexstrasza could not abandon them, nor allow Wyrmrest Temple to fall. Beside her mounting casualties, it would signal to their enemies that she was too weak to lead the dragonflights.

"What will you have us do, my queen?" Neltharion asked.

"We will not abandon our own in this hopeless hour," Alexstrasza said, staring straight into Fyrakk's eyes as she said the words aloud. Her cousin's grin only widened. "Tell Iridikron, *cousin,* that if he goes through with this plan, I will claim all the territory from Wyrmrest Temple to Valdrakken. Our greens will drive the herds from your hunting grounds. Your grand armies will *starve*."

Fyrakk snarled. "We will set fire to the Broodlands, and you shall burn with us!"

"Then you will fall like Raszageth!" Alexstrasza snapped. "Neltharion, deal with my cousin. I must go to Wyrmrest posthaste."

"I have already knocked one Incarnate from the skies," Neltharion said through clenched teeth, stepping toward the Blazing One. Overhead, the black dragons circled lower. Fyrakk cackled, thumping his tail on the ground.

"Malygos! A portal for me and my escort to Wyrmrest Temple," Alexstrasza said, gesturing to Saristrasz. "The rest of you, return to the Broodlands and gather an advance force."

"You cannot go to Wyrmrest alone!" Ysera cried. "It could be a trap."

A blue portal appeared before Alexstrasza, shimmering like a watery mirror. Alexstrasza could see the top of Wyrmrest Temple in its depths. She looked at Neltharion out the corner of one eye. "Of course it's a trap, but I will not abandon our flights. See to it that I am not alone for long. Reds, to me!"

She would brook no further argument. Alexstrasza leapt through the portal, feeling a moment of physical disassociation—a breathless, weightless leap through space—before solid ground materialized under her feet, slippery and cold. A frozen wind bit between Alexstrasza's scales, and a rime of ice coated the membranes of her wings, making them feel heavy. Sluggish. The scent of blood saturated the air. Alexstrasza slitted her eyes against the snow. The platform around her was empty, but in the skies above, the silhouettes of dragons ducked and dived through a storm.

Saristrasz emerged from the portal. Squinting, he asked, "A storm? Did Malygos send us to the wrong location?"

"*No,*" Alexstrasza said. She wasn't speaking to Saristrasz, but to the terror rising in her heart. She knew the elemental powers that swirled around Wyrmrest Temple like she knew her very soul. Trembling, she walked to the edge of the platform and looked to the skies.

There, churning the clouds above Wyrmrest Temple, was *Vyranoth.*

The mere sight of her drove shards of ice into Alexstrasza's heart. Vyranoth no longer looked like the dragon Alexstrasza remembered: Her scales had deepened to cerulean blue, the same color as the heart of a glacier. Sharp, gleaming chunks of ice studded her horns. With each wingbeat, she summoned the blizzard into being.

Vyranoth was ice incarnate.

Alexstrasza's next breath was a sob.

The massive Incarnate turned her attention to the temple's peak, as if she sensed the Life-Binder's presence.

"Oh, Vyranoth," Alexstrasza whispered. "What have you done?"

Vyranoth roared over the fray, her voice cracking with anguish. Beneath it all, the Life-Binder sensed a maelstrom of hurt, anger, desperation, and something else . . . *betrayal.* In that moment, all the weight of Alexstrasza's choices as queen came to bear. Beyond the expectations and the pressures, the responsibilities she had to her kind, she had failed on perhaps the most intimate level: She'd made an oath to a friend . . . and broken it with her next breath. She could never take that back, even as she knew it was in service of the greater good.

The Dragon Queen lifted her voice into the winds. "Vyranoth! My friend, please—you were ever an advocate for peace! Talk to me! We may solve our differences another way—"

"*No!*" Vyranoth howled. "You shattered that peace when you allowed your titan masters to steal the first primal dragon's egg. We once defended our own nests together. *Monster! Oath breaker!* Your words are poison. I will hear no more of them!"

Vyranoth closed her wings and plunged toward the tower.

Adrenaline shocked Alexstrasza's muscles. In a single great bound, she leapt forward and dived off the side of Wyrmrest Temple. As she hurtled toward the ground, she opened her broad wings and filled them with wind. Just before she hit, she engaged her back muscles, beat her wings, and shot forward, leaving an explosion of snow in her wake.

To Alexstrasza's horror, the skies and grounds of Wyrmrest Temple had been consumed by war. Dragons—ordered and primal alike—were locked in a battle of tooth and talon. A legion of tarasek outnumbered the temple's small force of drakonid on the ground. To fight Vyranoth here would be to put more lives in the path of danger. Alexstrasza had heard the tales of Raszageth's attack on the Reach—she could not, in good conscience, put her flights in the path of Vyranoth's fury.

Alexstrasza banked around the temple, dodging a blast of Vyranoth's frosty breath. Ice and snow slammed into the temple's western flank. A flash of ruby scales caught Alexstrasza's attention. Two red dragons swooped down to flank Alexstrasza.

One called out, "My queen, Vyranoth is in pursuit! What would you have us do?"

"I will deal with Vyranoth myself," Alexstrasza shouted over the winds. "Tell the others to defend Wyrmrest Temple until Neltharion arrives with reinforcements."

The red bobbed his head. He ducked and swooped under Alexstrasza, banking northeast. His companion followed him.

"You cannot outfly me, Alexstrasza," Vyranoth roared behind her.

Alexstrasza tacked her wings with the wind, turning sharply, and barrel-rolled through an open platform of the temple, heading north. Behind her, Vyranoth roared in frustration.

On the ground, an embattled squadron of drakonid defended the tower's north entrance. Alexstrasza dived lower, breathing a hot, healing breath on their ranks, restoring them. The injured rose from the ground and took up their weapons, cheering the Dragon Queen.

She flew onward, hoping to draw Vyranoth far from the fray. Up ahead, Galakrond's enormous rib bones arched into the sky. Galakrond had been dead for centuries, but the cold temperatures of northern Kalimdor had frozen his decaying flesh. Long, desiccated scraps of hide still clung to his bones, swaying in the breeze like battle standards. His eyes had disintegrated into putrefied, tarry pits, and his blood had stained the ground black.

The skies roiled with rumbling clouds as Alexstrasza wheeled around the crater. The wind picked up, whistling past the bones, hollow and lonely. She'd thought her choice of location a veiled threat—if the Aspects could fell a beast like Galakrond, why should the Incarnates think they had a chance?—but now she feared it had been received as a provocation, a challenge. Fortunately, the crater around Galakrond's remains was devoid of life. Even the tiny creeping things had abandoned this place . . . no innocent life would be lost amid the crossfire.

Over Alexstrasza's head, the clouds darkened. Vyranoth burst into view, her body bristling with ice. On instinct, Alexstrasza folded her wings against her body and dived beneath the Incarnate, hurtling toward the crater.

"Alexstrasza!" Vyranoth roared. "You will answer for your betrayal!"

But not with my life, Alexstrasza thought. *Nor will I take yours.*

Alexstrasza swooped through Galakrond's rib cage; then, with a powerful beat of her wings, arced high in the air with her snout to the sky. As she turned, Vyranoth slammed into her. The ice Incarnate hooked her back talons into the scales that protected Alexstrasza's midsection. The force of the blow took the breath from Alexstrasza's lungs, nearly knocking her senseless. Alexstrasza scrabbled for purchase against Vyranoth's icy hide as the two dragons tumbled, end-over-end, toward the earth. Wings thrashed. The ground rolled in and out of sight, falling closer.

With her longer forelegs, Alexstrasza slashed at Vyranoth's throat. Her claws glanced off pure ice. With a furious roar, Alexstrasza blasted a fiery breath at Vyranoth, melting the ice that protected the Incarnate. Vyranoth grunted, perhaps in pain. Before the Dragon Queen could strike, Vyranoth shoved her away.

Alexstrasza somersaulted backward, opened her wings, and descended toward the crater at high speed. She had given Vyranoth an opening—foolishly—and she couldn't afford to make a mistake like that again. The next one could cost Alexstrasza her life.

Out of the corner of her eye, Alexstrasza spotted Vyranoth ascending toward the gray, low-hanging clouds. Alexstrasza banked to the right, cruising along the crater's rim. Vyranoth had all but disappeared.

Hiding, are we? Alexstrasza thought, beating her wings and climbing through the air. She wasn't foolish enough to try to engage Vyranoth inside those icy clouds, oh no. Vyranoth was known for her cunning. If she wasn't attacking Alexstrasza outright, she had good reason.

The wind swirled around Alexstrasza with intention, as if it sought to knock her off course. Did Vyranoth bid the wind to howl so hard? No matter, Alexstrasza had new abilities of her own.

Alexstrasza hovered above the crater, careful not to touch the unnatural clouds that swirled overhead. "Vyranoth!" she called. "This day need not end in further bloodshed. You and I both want peace! Let us speak as we once did, as friends, as sisters—"

"*Sisters?*" Vyranoth cried, her voice carried to Alexstrasza on the wind. "You have *taken* my *true* sister from me! There can be no peace until you free Raszageth!"

The temperature plunged, riming Alexstrasza's scales with more ice. A chill spread down the membranes of the Life-

Binder's wings and stiffened her joints, making it difficult to stay aloft. Her muscles grew sluggish.

Alexstrasza faltered in the air, sensing Vyranoth's spell a moment too late. A thunderous *boom* echoed overhead. An axe of frigid air split the clouds and crashed into Alexstrasza, throwing her to the ground. She slammed into the bottom of the crater, sliding through the black muck until she collided with Galakrond's stinking skull.

"Do you know what I hope for, friend?" Vyranoth called, dipping below the cloud line. "I hope that what I once feared most has come to pass—that your masters' Order magic has altered your mind. You cannot be the dragon I once knew!"

Alexstrasza stumbled to her feet with a groan, then shook the muddy snow from her hide. The left half of her body ached. Her scales were scuffed and stuffed with dirty ice. Wincing, she flexed one foot, then stretched out her wing, testing each limb. Bruised, but not broken.

She lifted her gaze skyward. Even from this distance, Alexstrasza could see Vyranoth's injuries, including the heat that licked at the Incarnate's throat. Those burns would sink deep into the Incarnate's flesh.

But the pain of betrayal in Vyranoth's eyes, oh, it was *worse*. The Incarnate's grief ran deep, and Alexstrasza suffered it with her; it was as if the Life-Binder's own heart was being torn from her chest and clawed to pieces. Even as Vyranoth turned against her now, Alexstrasza would not hate her for it—no, she could empathize with her friend's position. Alexstrasza had made a promise to Vyranoth, and in her pursuit of protecting others, she had turned her back on her oldest and dearest friend.

"I empathize with you, Vyranoth, I do," Alexstrasza called into the skies. "But that does not mean I *agree* with you. Raszageth, your *sister,* marched on the Reach with no provocation, killing hundreds of innocents. Before her imprisonment, she spent decades slaughtering defenseless mortals and tarasek in villages across Kalimdor! And now you point a talon at *me?*

"No, my old friend," Alexstrasza continued, dropping her chin to her chest and ruffling the scales around her shoulders. Spreading her wings, she leapt aloft in a blaze of crimson flame. "You have thrown your lot in with warmongers and *murderers*—and if you insist on following this path, then it is *I* who no longer recognize *you.*"

Vyranoth roared, lunging toward the Life-Binder. Alexstrasza beat her wings harder, whipping the flames around her into an inferno, faster and faster until she glowed like the sun. Vyranoth checked her descent with a snarl, wincing at the light.

"Hear me now," Alexstrasza said. "I will not stand aside while the Incarnates continue their reign of cruelty across this world, not while I am Life-Binder and Dragon Queen. If that places us on opposite sides of the conflict, so be it!"

With those words, Alexstrasza swept her wings up with intention. Her crimson flames exploded outward with a roar, blasting Vyranoth's blizzard back for ten, twenty, then fifty wing-lengths. Sunlight tumbled through a freshly made crater in the clouds. The sky above was blue as dragon scales.

Vyranoth beat her wings, backing away from the Life-Binder. "I pity you, Alexstrasza," she said. "Your precious oaths have blocked you to the noble aims that once guided you. Now, you see the horrors of the means by which you have achieved your ends! Would you have stolen my clutch, given the chance? What would you have done if I had kidnapped yours?

"When you are convinced of your own righteousness, no act becomes unconscionable," the Incarnate hissed. "Think on that when your flight calls you queen."

Those words cut to the quick—Alexstrasza drew a sharp breath, but before she could reply, a dragon's bugle sounded over the tundra. She turned her head, spotting the black Aspect sailing forth with an entire wing unit of black dragons. *Neltharion!*

"Retreat, Vyranoth!" Neltharion roared. "You cannot hope to stand against five Aspects and their armies!"

"I shall give you three moons to release Raszageth, Alexstrasza," Vyranoth said, tossing her head. "Else I shall fly on the Broodlands and take my vengeance. I cannot save the young you stole from us, but I *can* save one of our kind. I will take my sister back, even if I must carve a path through your dragonflights to do so!"

As Vyranoth retreated with the remainder of her forces, Alexstrasza felt the adrenaline in her system ebb, leaving her feeling empty. Exhausted.

Neltharion approached. "Are you hurt?"

"A few bruises, nothing more." Alexstrasza rolled her shoulders and tested her wing muscles. "She struck my heart true, though—I have failed her, Neltharion. I have turned her against us, and now our flights will pay the price for the secrets I kept."

Neltharion turned his head, watching Vyranoth retreat. "It was no fault of yours, Alexstrasza. The Aspects' goals have ever been opposed to the Incarnates', and it was only a matter of time before our efforts to defend the Broodlands came into conflict with their activities. True peace was never an option with Iridikron. Our path was soaked in blood from the beginning."

"I wish it were not so," Alexstrasza replied. "I wish he would see reason!"

"One cannot argue with the stubbornness of stone," Neltharion said, casting Alexstrasza a knowing look.

"That may be the truest thing you have yet said," she replied. With a heavy heart, she turned away from Vyranoth's fading form. "Very well, Neltharion. Let us prepare the Broodlands for war."

VYRANOTH RETURNED TO HER home in the Frozen Fangs, commanding her wingleaders to leave her in peace. The frigid winds of the north would numb her to the fractures in her heart. Rage had driven her to turn wing and talon against a dragon she had loved so long and so well; but now, in the quiet moments, Vyranoth still had to reckon with the pain of Alexstrasza's betrayal. She wanted to do so alone.

As she drew closer to her aerie, she noticed a little shadow following in her wake. When she turned her head, she sometimes spotted a flash of red among the Fangs' snowcapped peaks.

With a growl, Vyranoth launched herself into the icy, low-hanging clouds overhead. Thus concealed, she pivoted and hovered in the air, watching.

A small red—no more than a drake, and a young one at that—crawled from a crack in the mountain rock, turning his head left, then right. He scrambled forward onto a ledge, his talons slipping on the ice, scanning the horizon. If he was an agent of the red dragonflight, he was a poor one.

Still, Vyranoth was in no mood for games. She summoned up a long, sharp spear of ice, then sent it whistling toward the red. It slammed into the ledge beside him, frightening him so much that he nearly slid off the ledge and tumbled into the chasm below.

"What do you want, spawn of Alexstrasza?" Vyranoth roared from the clouds. "I have no patience for your kind today."

"I do not mean you harm, great Incarnate," the little red shouted, bowing his head and trembling. "Nor am I here at the behest of the Dragon Queen! I only wish to ask you a question."

"Be gone!" Vyranoth replied with a curl of her lip, preparing to send another spear of ice straight for him. This time she wouldn't miss.

"Is it true the Aspects kidnapped eggs from primal dragons?" the red called out.

Vyranoth paused, snarling. "Yes," she said.

"I . . . I believe I was one of those eggs." The drake took wing, rising toward her in the sky. "My name is Talinstrasz, and I am one of several drakes who remembers being taken."

Talinstrasz. Vyranoth recalled that name from days long past. Back then, he had been a shivering little whelp who sought shelter beneath her wing. He and his sister, Lailastrasza, had been afraid of being taken. Now, Vyranoth finally knew why.

"I know your face," Vyranoth said, cocking her head to one side, her heart softening. "What do you want, little one?"

"The truth," Talinstrasz replied as Vyranoth descended from the clouds to meet him. "The Dragon Queen lied to me about where I came from . . . who I am."

"Alexstrasza has lied to us all. Come with me, young one. We should talk."

CHAPTER SIXTEEN

AFTER CENTURIES OF OPERATING IN SECRET, NELTHARION could finally put his flight's true genius on display before the other Aspects. He had kept his work a secret to avoid raising the ire of the Dragon Queen, but who could object to his foresight? Now, the other Aspects would hail the black Aspect and his flight as heroes.

"Over the last two centuries," the Earth-Warder said, stepping into one of Neltharus's darkened storerooms, "my flight has endeavored to build a comprehensive armory to serve in times of great need."

The other Aspects filed in, one by one. Even Ysera attended in the scales, having left the Dream to lead her flight through the oncoming conflict.

Neltharion paused in the middle of the room, waving a forefoot to bring up the lights. The clawed braziers around him blazed, illuminating the massive cavern. Behind him, the other Aspects gasped.

Neltharion's scalesmiths had filled the vault with armor for dragons, elder drakes, drakonid, and mortals alike. The light glinted off rows of gleaming breastplates designed to add a layer of protection to a dragon's throat and chest. Vambraces were stacked in shoulder-high pyramids. Thousands of helms hung on the room's enormous, square-sided pillars. The smiths of the black dragonflight had designed tail armor that ended in a wicked, razor-sharp fin; talon sheaths that provided additional power to puncture scales; and studded pauldrons that would prevent wing muscles from being lacerated while in flight.

"Neltharion, what . . ." Alexstrasza said as her gaze roved across the room. She blinked, then turned back to him. "How long have you been working on this . . . this *war room*?"

The Earth-Warder dipped his head in a half bow. "My flight set to the forges the day after we empowered our Oathstone."

"What?" Alexstrasza and Ysera cried in unison.

"That was almost three hundred years ago," Nozdormu said with a frown.

"And even then, I knew Iridikron's hunger would only ever be satiated by war," the black Aspect replied.

"Yes, yes, you are very smart and wise, oh great Earth-Warder," Malygos said drily, crossing the room to stand beside Neltharion. The blue Aspect gave him a cheeky grin. "Are these all your designs?"

Neltharion snorted, taking a cuff from a nearby shelf. "Not all. My scalesmiths developed new forms of blacksteel and elementium, both of which provide lightweight protection in the air," he said. "These cuffs, for example, will clip around a dragon's outer wing-finger to give a layer of protection. Our aim was to increase a dragon's defense without limiting mobility."

"May I?" Malygos asked, extending his talons.

"But of course." Neltharion handed the cuff to the blue Aspect.

"We could easily imbue each piece of armor with wards for additional protection," Malygos said, turning to face the group. He levitated the cuff over his talons; then, with his other forefoot, he cast a spell over the armor. The metal shimmered with an azure hue. "Not only would our armor provide protection from physical attacks, but we could also give it the ability to absorb or reflect elemental ones, too."

"That would be a boon in the skies," Alexstrasza said, stepping forward to examine the cuff. "How long would it take to enchant everything in this chamber?"

"That is precisely the issue," Malygos replied. "Even if I were able to spare a hundred mages—which I am not able to do at present—it might take us years to properly enchant each piece of armor."

"And this is not the only armory in Neltharus," Neltharion said.

Alexstrasza turned her golden gaze upon him. "How many of these chambers do you have?"

"Five for armor," Neltharion replied, "and another two for weapons for the drakonid and mortal races. With our current numbers, we should be able to outfit every active battalion in the Broodlands."

"By the titans," Ysera breathed, coming to sit beside the Dragon Queen. "That's thousands of dragons."

"My goal will ever be to save as many lives as possible," Alexstrasza said, turning the cuff in her talons. "But you should not have kept this from us, Neltharion. I have given each Aspect the authority to direct the affairs of their flight, with the understanding that I be kept apprised of your activities. And yet . . . you said nothing of this to me."

She looked up at him, a challenge laid bare in her gaze. For all her talk of peace, Alexstrasza could declare war with a single look.

The Dragon Queen can see into your heart, a whisper said. *She knows you lie.*

"Nay, Alexstrasza," Neltharion said. "I told you that I worked to bolster the Broodlands' defenses, though I admit I did not detail all that this encompassed. Tyr himself had warned us of the enemies that seek to claim our world . . . but I could not know that the first threat was like to come from our own kind."

The Dragon Queen narrowed her eyes. Yes, he had hidden the extent of what he had been working on from her; but if she had known why the citadel's forges burned day and night, she would have forbidden the work, leaving the flights bereft of advantage against the Incarnates.

The Dragon Queen knows what you hide from her, a whisper crawled into Neltharion's head. *Aberrus. The dracthyr. Iridikron's sister—*

Ikronia is dead, Neltharion replied.

But what did she say to your enemies before she died? asked the second.

Iridikron knows you called upon us at the Reach, said another. *He thinks you weak for being unable to control even the least of the Incarnates without our help!*

Neltharion refused to listen to them, as hard as it might have been. Admittedly, they had grown louder since that fateful battle with Raszageth, more insistent and, at times, all-consuming. In his greatest moments of weakness, Neltharion retreated deep into Aberrus, his workshop buried in Zaralek Cavern, the birthplace of the dracthyr, to suffer in silence.

Some days, the whispers grew so loud they filled his ears with a ceaseless buzzing. Sometimes, the chaos in his head reduced him to nothing more than a shivering whelp on the floor of his sanctum.

Though he was loath to admit it, Neltharioan feared that he wouldn't be clever enough, strong enough, or decisive enough to stop a dragon who would see the Broodlands burn. That in the end, he would be found *wanting*.

Neltharion refused to lose to one such as Iridirkon.

Thus, Neltharion had forbidden his flight from speaking about the events that led to Raszageth's imprisonment. The other Aspects could *never* know what had happened in the Reach. Neltharion had called upon the very dark powers Tyr had warned him about . . . An unforgivable action, no matter how desperate the hour. Alexstrasza would never understand.

As the Aspects exited the vault, Alexstrasza said, "Neltharion, a moment, please."

Neltharion stepped aside, allowing the other three Aspects to exit the chamber. Malygos shot Neltharion a pitying look before he left the room.

The Earth-Warder had expected Alexstrasza to confront him over his flight's activities in Neltharus. He had even gone so far as to prepare a defense: After all, he *was* fulfilling the measure of his order, was he not? Hadn't Tyr charged him with the defense of the Broodlands and, by extension, the whole of Azeroth? It was only natural for Neltharion to do everything in his power in pursuit of that goal.

As the other Aspects' voices faded down the hallway, Alexstrasza turned to Neltharion. "As Earth-Warder, it is only natural that you be named general flightcommander in the coming war."

She hasn't the strength to lead them without you, came a whisper in the back of his mind.

And you are nothing without us!

"But you have hidden so much from me, my old friend," Alexstrasza continued, her golden eyes full of empathy, rather than the condemnation Neltharion assumed he would face. "You told me nothing of your work at the Reach, nor did you call for aid when Raszageth attacked. Now, I learn that your flight has spent centuries building weapons of war. It only makes me wonder what else you have hidden from me."

Alexstrasza gestured to the armory with a graceful sweep of her wing. "I admit, this is an impressive display and a credit to your flight. But if you are to fulfill your role to its utmost, there can be no more secrets between us. I need to be able to trust you, Neltharion."

Alexstrasza turned her weighty, knowing gaze back upon him. There it was again, the feeling that Alexstrasza could see into the darkest places of his heart and soul. The whispers slipped away, cursing her. Neltharion wavered in their absence. How he wanted to trust in those golden eyes and tell Alexstrasza everything; how he wanted to relieve the burden that rested upon him, heavy as all the world!

But just as he curled his tongue to speak, a whisper slipped through: *And just what will you tell her, Neltharion?*

A second voice seeped in, joining the first: *Will you tell her about Raszageth?*

Will you tell her that you were too weak to defeat an Incarnate on your own?

Be silent! he snapped at them, though he held his tongue. He did not want to fall in the Dragon Queen's estimation, nor to be seen as anything but the strong, stalwart protector of the Broodlands, ever prepared to stand in its defense.

"Now and ever onward, Alexstrasza," Neltharion said, "I swear there shall be no secrets between us."

Alexstrasza searched his gaze for a moment, then nodded, the corners of her lips turning up. "Very well, Flightcommander. Let us rejoin the others."

As the Dragon Queen turned away, the whispers in Neltharion's mind snickered from the shadows. How he hated them! He knew he should not bow to their tyranny, for he sensed a dark, unholy power about them. While the titans had offered to uplift him, the whispers only sought to drag him down, down, *down* into the shadows. He sensed their eyes on him at all hours of the day, ever watchful, waiting for a chance to slip through the cracks forming in his resolve. He could not afford a repeat performance of what had happened at the Reach—Raszageth's screams still haunted him in his sleep.

Before he could think about what he was doing, Neltharion said, "Alexstrasza, wait."

The Dragon Queen paused at the armory's threshold, turning her head. "Yes?"

No, the whispers said. *Do not tell her the truth of the Reach.*

Do not tell her the truth of us, said another.

She will strip your titles from you, said a third. *She will strip your flight from you!*

She will lock you in a prison of your own making until you forget the very color of the sky.

He gritted his teeth, wincing at the thought.

"Is something wrong?" Alexstrasza asked. Worry flitted across her expression. "You look almost . . . pained."

He blew out a breath, at odds with himself and the voices inside him.

Do not tell her, said a whisper. *You know we speak true.*

"It is hard for me to apologize," Neltharion said with a dry chuckle, which he used to hide the struggle in his heart and in his head. The lies slipped through his teeth easily, for an apology was easier to speak aloud than the truth: "You are right, I should not have hidden Neltharus's armories from you. Each Aspect brings a unique perspective to our councils, and I want you to know that I value your insights, Alexstrasza. I am sorry."

The Dragon Queen dipped her head. "It is all right, and I want you to know that I am grateful for your foresight. Going forward, our enemies will do everything in their power to shatter our unity. Let us not forget the lessons of Galakrond and endeavor to remember that we are stronger when we work together."

This time, Neltharion's smile was true. "Of course, my queen."

AFTER TOURING THE REST of Neltharus—including the armories and training grounds—the Aspects convened at the Seat to discuss strategy. Despite the vastness of the vaults at the citadel and the dragonflights' considerable advantages against primal dragons, an Aspectral victory was far from assured. The Incarnates' forces were considerably larger. Worse, Iridikron cared little for honor, which would allow him to employ cruel and more ruthless tactics on the battlefield. Where the Aspects would have rules of engagement, the Incarnates would do anything within their power to win.

It was a terrifying thought.

Neltharion mulled over these concerns as he alighted at the Seat of the Aspects. The sun had already begun to sink toward the horizon, the temperatures plummeting. Normally, a chill did not bother him, but today it sent a shiver through his scales.

Alexstrasza walked to the center of the room, then breathed crimson fire across the floor. The bright flames traced a map of the Broodlands, the Dragonwilds, and northern Kalimdor on the flagstones. The twin fortresses of the Obsidian Citadel and Harrowsdeep appeared first, followed by Wyrmrest Temple and the heights of Valdrakken. Stone figures of the Incarnates appeared at Harrowsdeep, the Caldera, and the Frozen Fangs, along with hundreds of pawns to represent their forces. The Aspects' tokens materialized next, each one fashioned from glittering gemstone, with pawns that represented their flights, drakonid, and mortal and tarasek allies.

In the air and on the ground, the Incarnates' forces outnumbered the Aspects' almost three-to-one.

Concern flickered across Alexstrasza's features. "Are these numbers correct?"

"No older than ten moons," Neltharion replied. "Though yesterday's battle at Wyrmrest Temple may have swayed more primal dragons to the Incarnates' cause."

Alexstrasza's frown deepened. "The Primalists will assail our borders in three days' time. Though I should like to think every one of our dragons counts for three of theirs, especially armored"—she nodded to Neltharion—"we are still outnumbered. We must devise and implement a strategy to repel them, ideally one that will minimize loss of life."

"War creates an infinite number of branching paths in the timeways, and at present, we cannot know which direction our timeline will take," Nozdormu said, assuming his usual place on Neltharion's right side. The bronze Aspect gave his wings a shake, then sat on the ground, considering the map before them. "However, one thing is certain—the longer the conflict draws on, the less likely we are to be victorious."

"I, too, would like to see this conflict ended quickly," Alexstrasza replied, "and with casualties on both sides kept to a minimum."

Dragon should not fight dragon. Her own words echoed in her mind.

"So, let us kill Iridikron and be done with it," Malygos said.

"That would require a full-scale, prolonged offensive on Harrowsdeep," Neltharion stated. "We would need all our strength to fly from Wyrmrest Temple, which would leave the Broodlands woefully under-defended. I will not leave the Obsidian Citadel and the Reach without proper defense—I'm sure you feel much the same about your own strongholds."

"Then we target him specifically," Malygos replied. "In a more subtle manner."

Neltharion cocked his head, chuckling. "Do you think I have not tried? My Shadowscales are talented, but the tunnels of Harrowsdeep are maze-like, ever quaking, and shift at the Stonescaled's whim. We have never breached the darkest depths of his keep."

"On this point, I agree," Nozdormu replied, though his voice sounded faraway, detached. "Assassination attempts will only provoke retaliation in kind. And you, Neltharion, have a few particularly ignominious ends that I am quite certain you would prefer to avoid."

The Timeless One's gaze slid sideways, looking straight through Neltharion. The Earth-Warder shuddered inwardly. What, if anything, had Nozdormu seen of the Reach? Neltharion knew very little of how the bronze Aspect's abilities worked . . . probably because his dragonflight was still discovering that for themselves.

Ysera gestured to the map with her talons. "More to the point, Iridikron's death would do little to stop the Primalist movement now—Vyranoth would make an equally formidable leader, and she is now supported by ancient dragons like Cysanz and Vitelenoth."

"There are also rumors that Oxoria and her brood have left the southern jungles." Alexstrasza drummed her talons on the floor. "The news of Raszageth's capture has turned many hearts against us—the Storm-Eater flew far and had many friends."

"Oxoria has not yet been seen at Harrowsdeep, but such news would not surprise me," Neltharion said with a sigh. Oxoria's brood was impressive—unlike other primal dragons, who often abandoned their young when they grew into drakes, Oxoria encouraged her young to stay close to her lair, where they had higher survival rates and forged strong familial bonds. If Oxoria flew north, she would bring a sizable colony of primal dragons with her, all of whom were strategically minded and could work together like a flight.

Alexstrasza continued. "Our main objective is to defend the Broodlands and preserve our way of life. I would like to find a way to shield the Broodlands from the Incarnates' advance and take the fight to the wilds between the Obsidian Citadel and Wyrmrest Temple."

"I, too, would like to keep the Incarnates as far from our borders as possible," Neltharion said, thinking of Raszageth and the secrets she could tell if freed. "The strategy would depend entirely on whether creating a shield or barrier around the Broodlands is feasible—Malygos?"

"A barrier? Over the whole of the Broodlands?" Malygos asked with a snort. "I would say that's quite *im*possible, Neltharion. Even a barrier over a fraction of our holdings would drain my flight of its magic within days."

Neltharion gave Malygos a sly smile. "I thought your flight excelled at making the *impossible,* possible. Am I mistaken?"

"No," Malygos said with a little huff, "but it is not a task my flight could attempt alone. However, there may be a way to harness the abilities of each flight to augment our existing defenses."

The Spell-Weaver tapped the stone map. Little points of blue lit up along the Broodlands' borders.

"Centuries ago," Malygos continued, "the blue dragonflight helped the black construct obelisks to stabilize the earth's crust beneath the Broodlands, making our territories impervious to Iridikron's earthquakes. Each one of these obelisks is connected to Vakthros through a fabricated ley line."

Blue lines shot from each point of light, reaching back to Vakthros in the Azure Span.

"We may be able to augment those obelisks to provide the Broodlands an additional layer of protection," Malygos said, "such as an enormous domed shield."

Neltharion shifted his weight. Without the obelisks' defense, Iridikron would strike the earth's crust beneath the Broodlands. Or worse, try to crack the tectonic plate beneath them.

"We cannot afford to lose the protections in the earth," Neltharion said. "It would leave us defenseless against Iridikron and his Rockfuries."

"I'm not suggesting we rededicate the obelisks so much as *enhance* them," Malygos said, gesturing to the map. The ley lines in the Waking Shores, the Emerald Plains, and Thaldraszus lit with red, green, and gold light, respectively. "If each flight can augment the ley lines in their territories, we may be able to offer the entirety of the Broodlands a shield of sorts."

"What sort of magic would this require?" Alexstrasza asked, mulling over the suggestion.

"Perhaps we could employ poisons or withering magics in the Emerald Plains," Ysera said, running her talon along the border of her territory. "Such a spell could be crafted to target primal dragons and tarasek alone, allowing all other forms of life to pass through the barrier unharmed."

"I like it." Alexstrasza sat on her haunches and pressed a knuckle into her chin, thinking. "I could ask the reds to channel an enervation spell, something that would sap our enemies of their strength, willpower, or courage."

"You've caught the vision, my queen," Malygos said.

"The bronzes can accelerate or decelerate time for the invaders quite easily," Nozdormu said. "How long would it take to augment the obelisks?"

"With your assistance, days," Malygos said. "Though you must realize that these measures will only be temporary—the obelisks are quite old, and the strain will precipitate their end."

"How long?" Alexstrasza asked.

"Neltharion and I will have to conduct an examination to be sure," Malygos replied. "But I would be surprised if the obelisks lasted a year under such strain."

"That's enough time," Neltharion said, nodding at Malygos. "In a year, we could significantly weaken the Primalists' forces and prepare to launch a coordinated attack on Harrowsdeep."

"How do you propose we weaken them?" Malygos asked.

Alexstrasza narrowed her eyes. "We will starve them into peace if we must. Iridikron has violated our treaty, thereby losing access to the hunting grounds we control. We will chase them from the lands between the Broodlands and Wyrmrest Temple. Additionally, Ysera and I can work together to encourage the herds in Primalist territory to migrate east."

"They do have an extraordinary number of dragons to feed," Malygos said drily.

Nozdormu shifted his weight. "Hunger will weaken them, but it will also make them more desperate. However, it could also cause discord within their ranks, or force them to abandon the Primalist cause entirely . . . It could work."

"Moving the herds would drive more of the nomadic mortal tribes into our lands," Ysera said, "many of whom may not be friendly to our flights."

"Our flights have proven themselves to be remarkable mentors to the mortal races, sister," Alexstrasza said to the green Aspect. "I have full faith that we will overcome any obstacle in that regard, together."

Ysera smiled and bobbed her head. "Very well."

"They may even become useful allies," Neltharion said, thinking of the dracthyr. "The mortal races are clever and adaptable—they certainly do not approach problems the way dragons do."

If only the Oathbinder hadn't been destroyed! Even a small force of dracthyr would have been a *considerable* advantage against a Primalist invasion. Why, Cindrethresh had leapt into Raszageth's storm and driven the Incarnate to the ground. Had it not been for Raszageth's lightning, the Incarnate would have died in Stormsunder Crater.

Neltharion closed his eyes. What would the dracthyr have achieved, had he not been forced to seal them away? What would have *been,* had the Earth-Warder and the black dragonflight been truly victorious at the Reach? Would the Aspects be having this conversation now, or would they simply deploy the dracthyr to drive the Incarnates from the sky?

The Earth-Warder had told Malygos he would find an alternative answer to the Incarnate threat, and that was precisely what he intended to do.

Even without the dracthyr, the Aspects' strategy showed promise. Alexstrasza's instinct to keep the war out of the Broodlands was sound; if they could hold Iridikron's forces at, say, Wyrmrest Temple, their opportunities for a full assault on Harrowsdeep would increase.

This plan will fail, the whispers said. *You will watch your precious Broodlands burn.*

You are no match for the Stonescaled and his armies. You will fail, for you are neither as clever nor as strong as you imagine yourself to be.

The whispers continued to taunt him.

The Reach was only the beginning.

You will watch every last one of your black dragons fall from the skies.

You will burn the shattered corpses of your friends!

There is nothing you can do to save them.

Neltharion sneered, opening his eyes to slits. *Calling upon you in the Reach was a mistake,* he thought with a growl. *Do not think I will make such an error in judgment again—*

"Neltharion!" Alexstrasza said, snapping the Earth-Warder from his thoughts.

He lifted his head, surprised to see all four Aspects looking at him askance, wide-eyed.

Alexstrasza spoke first: "Is everything all right?"

"Yes, yes, I apologize," he said, waving off her concerns with a swirl of his talons. "In terms of our western flank, I will organize the forces at Wyrmrest Temple. They will be on the front lines, so we will need to send our best—"

Malygos chuckled. "We are talking about how to imprison the Incarnates, my friend. Just how long have you *not* been paying attention?"

"And you *may* have growled aloud at Nozdormu's most excellent suggestion," Ysera said gently, though she exchanged a mirthful glance with the bronze Aspect.

Neltharion cleared his throat, ignoring the way Alexstrasza was now dissecting him with her gaze. "My apologies, Nozdormu, I was thinking about strategy, and remembering the Primalists' attack on the Reach. Will you please repeat what you said?"

"As I was saying," Nozdormu said, giving Neltharion an indulgent smile, "if the Dragon Queen does not want to kill the Incarnates, we can imprison them here."

The bronze Aspect reached out and tapped a mountain range just east of Tyrhold.

"I can work with the titan-forged to build a great vault where we can hold the Incarnates in perpetual stasis," Nozdormu said. "It will take considerable time and effort to build, however."

"Why don't we just kill them?" Neltharion asked, looking to the Dragon Queen.

"No," Alexstrasza said. "I cannot and will not allow Vyranoth to be executed—or any of them, for that matter. If they fall in battle, that is one thing. *Execution* is another."

"Fine," Neltharion said. "Let us build a vault of Incarnates, then. My flight will assist you in this endeavor, Nozdormu."

"I would welcome your expertise," the bronze Aspect said.

Alexstrasza smiled. "Very well! Are we all in accord?"

"Aye," Ysera said. The gem on the verdant-green banner behind her head flared with bright fire.

"Aye," Malygos and Nozdormu said in unison, their banners lighting with azure and bronze flames, respectively.

Alexstrasza turned her gaze on Neltharion again, expectant.

"Aye," Neltharion said, though the whispers snickered at him.

"Good!" Alexstrasza said. "Now let us set to work—our enemies will be at our borders swiftly, and there is much we must do to prepare."

As the others turned away, the whispers taunted Neltharion again:

You will fail, fail, fail—

"Neltharion?" Alexstrasza's voice broke through the whispers. Her golden gaze was on him again, eyes narrowed with concern. "Are you certain you're all right? You've seemed uncharacteristically . . . *distracted* today."

"Quite," Neltharion replied, donning a smile with the hope of putting her at ease. It *would* be all right, because he would make it so.

The whispers were wrong.

He would not fail.

THE MORE TALINSTRASZ LEARNED of the world before there were Aspects, the angrier he became.

The young drake spent two moons with Vyranoth, listening to her stories and meeting her adopted family. They spoke of Galakrond and the dawn of the Aspects while Nalikrona's whelplings scampered around their feet.

Talinstrasz knew the old story—it was taught to every whelp in the Broodlands, after all—but he didn't know the Aspects sent the titan-forged into the wilds to kidnap eggs from primal dragons' nests. Nalikrona and Razviik told him about the clutches they lost, though they had never left their nests longer than a day or two and ever only to hunt. They guarded their whelps jealously, though they suspected their clutch was safe so far to the north.

Vyranoth also told Talinstrasz of how she became an Incarnate, and how Razviik bestowed the moniker "the Frozenheart" upon her, for the Incarnate's once-gentle heart had hardened to ice.

Despite her frozen heart, the Incarnate treated Nalikrona's whelps with tenderness, allowing them to scamper on her back and wings. With a pang, the red recalled how Vyranoth had played games with him in the Broodlands—he envied the whelps who would know the dragons who gave them life.

What would it be like to see the faces of his parents? What would *he* have been like before order? Would he have had rust-colored scales, red as the bluffs in the Waking Shores? Or would his scales have assumed a different hue entirely?

In turn, Talinstrasz recounted his memories of the dark shadow that had fallen over his egg, the glaring flash of light, and the memory of being submerged in warm, gentle waters. The infusion changed him—body, mind, and soul. Of that, he was sure.

As the red drake prepared to return to the Waking Shores, Vyranoth approached him. "You are welcome to stay, young one. The Fangs are far to the north—you need not fear retaliation from your ordered cousins."

"Thank you," Talinstrasz said. "But I must take what I've learned to the other drakes in the Broodlands. They deserve to know the truth, too."

"Of course," Vyranoth replied, though she sounded weary. Talinstrasz knew the Incarnate didn't quite trust him, and why should she? The very color of his scales reminded her of the betrayal she had faced at the talons of her oldest and dearest friend.

"Should you wish to know more," Vyranoth said, "my aerie is always open to you."

CHAPTER SEVENTEEN

As the sun rose, Ysera hovered in the skies above the Emerald Gardens, looking to the west. Three hundred wing-lengths from where she flew, a delicate green shimmer lifted from the borders of her territory, so slight only the members of the green dragonflight would be able to perceive it.

Any Incarnate or Primal who flew through that barrier would wither like an autumn leaf.

Today, not even the gentle breezes from the Dream could calm Ysera's nerves. Small birds fluttered around her horns, singing their sun-warmed songs to her, but their sweetness could not touch the green Aspect's heart. All attempts at diplomacy and peace had failed.

Now, the Aspects would test the strength of their barriers. If magic failed, the flights stood ready to defend the Broodlands by wing and by talon.

Behind her, the full might of the green dragonflight filled the skies, ready to repel a Primalist attack. Her flightmasters flanked her—three on the left, two on the right—while her majordomo, Vathira, flew at her right wing. Their numbers looked twice as large, thanks to the blue dragonflight's illusory army. Ysera had those "dragons" positioned to the south, hoping to encourage the Incarnates to attack to the north of the gardens.

A regiment of Neltharion's Ironscales joined them, led by Garion, a veteran of the Battle of Stormsunder Crater. The Ironscales took point, forming a bulwark between the green dragonflight and the border.

On the ground, green drakonid bristled around the portal to the Emerald Dream. Elder drakes had also taken positions inside the portal, prepared to dispatch any enemy who tried to force their way through.

If the barriers failed, the Verdant Preservers stood ready to defend their flight, but Ysera desperately hoped it would not come to that. Fifty of her best warriors had already gone to Wyrmrest Temple, where they'd helped to raise defenses, move herds of northern caribou west, and chase the Primalists from the surrounding environs.

"War is a waste," Vathira said softly, so only the green Aspect could hear. "I am not afraid to stand in defense of the Emerald Plains, my Aspect . . . but I wish it had not come to this."

"As do I, but our flight's magic is strong," Ysera replied. "The barriers around our lands will hold."

"They will," Vathira said with a resolute nod. "They *must*."

The first bugle sounded. On the western horizon, a horde of Primalists crested a nearby mountain range. So numerous were they, the dragons looked like ants spilling out a mounded nest. Though the green dragonflight flew in full force, they were still far outnumbered.

"Steady!" Garion shouted from the front line. "Tahlien, Zorastia! Take your wing units and prepare to flank them in the south. We do not want to fight in the skies over the gardens!"

As the Ironscales adjusted their ranks, the Primalists flew closer, ever closer. Ysera could now see Fyrakk flying in their midst—her sister had told her to expect the Blazing One, as Vyranoth would likely assail the Reach while Iridikron tried to break the Obsidian Citadel. The three Incarnates would slam into the Broodlands' western flank, forcing the Aspects to fight on three fronts, rather than one.

Neltharion was at the Obsidian Citadel, and Alexstrasza had gone north to defend the Reach from the Life-Binder Conservatory.

Fyrakk and his armies drew closer.

"Courage, now!" Ysera called, still hoping her flight would not have need of it this day.

As the first wave of Primalists crossed into the Emerald Plains, a bright flash of viridescent light exploded across the sky. The primal dragons seized and contorted in the air, shrieking, their living tissue withering on the bone. As they plummeted to the earth, their wingleaders trumpeted a halt. A thousand primal dragons crashed to a stop, nearly knocking more of their front lines through the barrier.

A great cheer exploded from the green dragonflight.

Fyrakk flew up to the barrier, which sparked and snapped in his presence. "Ysera," he roared. "What is the meaning of this? Come and face me on the field of battle, you coward!"

"You will not slake your thirst with the blood from our throats, Fyrakk," Ysera said, launching herself over the heads of the Ironscales. "Return to Harrowsdeep! Return to your foul dens! The battle you seek is not here."

With a furious roar, Fyrakk spat a fireball at the green Aspect. She dived backward, dodging it with ease.

"Mark my words," Fyrakk said, "when I return, the first thing I intend to do is burn your precious gardens to the ground."

As Fyrakk and the Primalists turned tail, Garion joined Ysera in the skies.

"Would you like us to give chase, Lady Ysera?" the flightmaster asked.

"No," Ysera said. "Let our enemies seek out bloodshed. We will remain here unless we are needed. Let us hope the other Aspects have fared just as well."

AS THE ASPECTS' NEW barriers glimmered on the Broodlands' borders, Talinstrasz gathered his friends in the maze-like waterways of the Waking Shores. More than twenty drakes from all five flights met in the backwaters beneath the Life-Binder's Conservatory, hidden from their elders' watchful gazes. The red's closest friends, Sirigosa and Nolizdormu, came immediately, as did many of the drakes he had befriended at

Wyrmrest Temple. Obezion and Ravia, the twin black dragons who saved his life on the battlefield, joined them, too.

Sirigosa bounded up to him, her azure scales shimmering. "Talinstrasz, we feared you dead!" She butted her head against his, gently. "You dense dragon, I'm glad you're safe."

"I'm all right, I promise you," Talinstrasz said with a laugh.

"It's been three moons since the battle at Wyrmrest Temple," Nolizdormu said, sand dancing through his golden gaze. "What happened to you, my friend? I admit, I can't see aught in your past."

"Come, I will tell you everything," Talinstrasz said, beckoning them to follow him into a large-mouthed, ivy-draped cave. When the last drake sidled inside, twenty pairs of curious eyes turned his way.

"After the battle at Wyrmrest Temple," he began, "I followed Vyranoth the Frozenheart to her aerie in the Fangs."

Several drakes gasped, rearing back in alarm. *"An Incarnate?"* someone hissed. Heads cocked to catch whispers. Several dragons shifted their weight or narrowed their eyes. Sirigosa and Nolizdormu exchanged a glance but said nothing.

Talinstrasz continued. "Not more than a clutch of moons ago, the Incarnates caught a titan-forged stealing eggs from a primal dragon's nest in the wilds. Over the last two centuries, Vyranoth estimates that hundreds—if not thousands—of eggs have been kidnapped from the wilds . . . and I believe that every drake here was among the stolen clutches.

"We were raised together in the Ruby Life Pools," Talinstrasz went on. "It would have been so easy to hide us among the true-born ordered—but can you name your parents, Zenodormu? What about you, Tallegosa? Other drakes have parents, but *where are ours?*"

The drakes' murmurs deepened to growls. Obezion and Ravia shared a look. Iremos, Zenodormu, and Mirigosa spoke together in low tones, their fangs flashing. They, too, had memories much like Talinstrasz's.

"We were not given the choice our brethren had," Talinstrasz said, stepping forward and spreading his wings. "Why did the Aspects take us from our parents and force order upon us, when others were granted a choice in the matter?"

"Are you sure, Talinstrasz?" Sirigosa said, the confusion clear on her face. "But the Dragon Queen . . . she promised—"

"Did she lie to us?" Tallegosa asked with a gasp.

"No," another voice said. "The Dragon Queen would never lie!"

"What evidence do they have of this?" said another.

"And how do you know the Frozenheart is not lying to *you*, Talinstrasz?" Ravia said, lifting her voice above the crowd's. She turned her gaze on him. "I heard Vyranoth speak at Wyrmrest Temple, too, but I am unable to trust her words. She also called Raszageth sister. *Raszageth!* The very dragon who turned tooth and talon against my flight. Many good dragons died that day, including my own wingleader and mentor."

Her brother, Obezion, curled his lip. "You would have us fly with the monsters who would set our home aflame?"

"They are not *monsters*," Talinstrasz snapped.

"I had to put a fistful of Zoltica's ashes into the lava cauldrons of the Obsidian Citadel because of Raszageth," Ravia said, stepping forward, her voice rising. "Tell me what *you* have lost besides your so-called *choice*."

Ravia's words rattled in Talinstrasz's teeth. For a moment, he wavered in his determination, but no. *No.* Raszageth may have been violent, even cruel, but Vyranoth was not the Storm-Eater. Vyranoth was as ancient as the glaciers: wise, kind, steady. If *she* had turned against Alexstrasza after all the long centuries, she must have had good reason to do so.

"A choice is power over one's own destiny," Talinstrasz said, echoing something Vyranoth had said to him. "All the drakes in the Broodlands deserve to know about the Aspects' treachery."

"Treachery?" Obezion said, shooting Talinstrasz a cool, measured look. "Who in the Broodlands will believe you? Do you think the dragonflights will trust the word of an Incarnate, a *betrayer,* over the word of our queen?"

"Vyranoth is not a *betrayer,*" Talinstrasz said, lifting his voice. "It is Alexstrasza who has betrayed us all."

Obezion growled, a deep and throaty rumble that silenced every other conversation around them. Though not the oldest, Obezion was easily the largest among the assembled drakes. He stood a full talon-length taller than Talinstrasz did at the shoulder, and the black drake was broader, too, thanks to his work in the forges of the Obsidian Citadel.

The other drakes backed away from Obezion, sensing violence. Ravia, however, remained at her brother's side, watching the scene with dispassion. Talinstrasz tensed, ready for a fight.

"You would speak ill of the Dragon Queen?" Obezion said.

Talinstrasz snarled, flashing fang. "I speak the *truth,* Obezion. It is not my fault if you refuse to hear it."

"Then I wish I had not saved your sorry scales at Wyrmrest," Obezion said, pushing his forefoot into the earth. "Perhaps I will rectify that . . . *mistake.*"

The earth rumbled with a small quake, knocking Talinstrasz off balance. Obezion leapt at him, the light glinting off his massive talons. Talinstrasz rolled out of range, found a foothold, and whirled. Obezion moved faster, pivoting and slamming his barbed tail into Talinstrasz's cheek. Bright lights exploded across Talinstrasz's vision. He staggered, shaking his head.

Just as chaos erupted in the cavern, someone roared, "That is *enough!*" with all the fury and authority of a flightleader.

Talinstrasz's heart stuttered in his chest. He pivoted, fully expecting to face the wrath of Alexstrasza, or at least one of the flightmasters.

To his surprise, it was only Lailastrasza, his sister. His *sanctimonious,* moralizing sister, the golden whelp of the Waking Shores! She had barely seen fifty summers and the wingleaders of the red dragonflight already compared her to the Dragon Queen herself.

Lailastrasza shouldered the curtain of ivy aside, striding into the cavern. Three drakes accompanied her—a second red, Aymestrasz, who followed Lailastrasza like a shadow, sworn to protect her; a green, Atyrannus, her dearest and closest friend;

and a blue, Rygos, who had often been at odds with Talinstrasz thanks to his sharp tongue and quick wit. Lailastrasza still enjoyed the friendships of their whelphood, though Talinstrasz had turned to Sirigosa and Nolizdormu decades ago.

"Lailastrasza," Talinstrasz said with a little growl, "this is *none* of your business."

"I came at your behest," Lailastrasza said. "Were you not sent to Wyrmrest Temple for fighting, brother? Now that you have been forbidden to fight the primal dragons, you choose to turn your talons on your kind?"

"Whether they are *my kind* is debatable."

"Your brother spoke ill of the Dragon Queen and the Aspects," Obezion said to her. "I struck to defend Alexstrasza's name."

"What?" Lailastrasza blinked, giving her head a small shake. "What would compel you to speak ill of the queen? Of our flight's own Aspect, Talin?"

"The Aspects stole our eggs from the wilds, sister," Talinstrasz said, though he felt sure his words would fall on closed ears. "After the battle at Wyrmrest Temple, I met with Vyranoth the Frozenheart—"

Lailastrasza drew back from him with a hiss. "You spoke to that betrayer?"

"Listen to me," Talinstrasz said. "Alexstrasza lied to us about how and when our eggs were taken, Lailastrasza! The Aspects *kidnapped* us from our true parents—"

"No doubt because she foresaw how the Incarnates would tear dragonkind apart," Lailastrasza snapped.

"It is the *Aspects* who tear us apart," Talinstrasz said, glaring at his sister. "They have driven a wedge into the hearts of our kind, and now we go to war in further service of their treachery!"

The group seemed stunned by this outburst, but Talinstrasz couldn't stop himself. "The Dragon Queen chose what shape I would take in life; I will not let her choose my death. I would sooner join the Primalists."

The other drakes looked at him in shocked silence, eyes wide. Obezion was the first to move, blowing out a breath and muttering a curse. He strode from the cavern, followed closely by his twin, Ravia.

"You are my clutch-brother, Talinstrasz," Lailastrasza said. "Never doubt my love for you, but I will not follow you down this path. If you wish to rebel against the Aspects, you will do so on your own."

With that, Lailastrasza turned and followed Obezion out of the cavern.

"You cannot mean that," Talinstrasz said. "They took your choice away from you—"

"My choice to be *what*?" Lailastrasza said, whirling. "A primal drake in the wilds of Kalimdor, bereft of the magic, struggling for survival? To be unexceptional, unremarkable, *unenlightened* as to what dragonkind can achieve? To struggle against my own kind for resources, instead of banding together to overcome our shared challenge? No, brother. I would not choose to walk when I can fly."

Talinstrasz frowned. "You don't understand—"

"No, it is *you* who do not understand," she said, lifting

her voice. "You choose not to understand the power of the gifts you have been given, of the *life* you have led. You let past injuries undermine your future. But I swear to you this day, if you raise wing and talon against our queen, you will not live to see the morrow."

With that, Lailastrasza left the cavern and took wing. Her comrades followed her, shooting wary gazes over their shoulders.

"Anyone else?" Talinstrasz asked, his voice rasping, throat tight. Scarce ten drakes stayed, including Sirigosa and Nolizdormu. Let his soft-scale sister go! Her words could not restore the choice that had been stolen from him.

When no one else left, he said, "Good. Then let us discuss our first move."

PART FOUR

THE RISING INFERNO

For twenty-four years, the barriers have protected the Broodlands from invasion. Neltharion's Shadowscales turned Iridikron's own tactics against him, spreading rumors and lies that the barriers would order any primal dragon who touched them. Neltharion also threatened to collapse Raszageth's prison should the Stonescaled continue his earthquakes. The ground beneath us fell silent.

For a time, the primal dragons stayed away from even our farthest-flung borders . . . but the Primalists' territory could not support their burgeoning numbers. Hunger set in, and the Primalists began to question Iridikron's leadership. Concerned, the Stonescaled ordered a strike on Wyrmrest Temple, which later became known as the Battle of Dragonblight. Our flights successfully held the temple against Fyrakk and his legions, but we lost every wing-length of territory between Wyrmrest and Harrowsdeep. Now our flights keep the temple ensconced in shields and protective magics. The flights use arcane elementals to ferry supplies through portals, and the Shadowscales of the black dragonflight use it as a base for their intelligence activities.

As we have fought our battles in the west, we have slowly lost ground against the Primalists' greater numbers. We snatched several victories from the jaws of defeat; and though we have lost territory, we have whittled some thousand dragons out of the Primalists' ranks. Some have defected. Others have died, starved, or been struck down on the battlefield.

Vitelenoth fell at Icewing Rift to the leader of the Heart's Guard, Bojsanz, removing one of Vyranoth's most trusted lieutenants from the field. Levarian, flightmaster of the black dragonflight, slew Oxoria's mate at Cinderfrost Vale, then went talon-to-talon with the grand matriarch herself. He lost an eye for his trouble, but Neltharion promoted him to flightcommander of the black dragonflight for his exemplary service. At the Molten Abyss, the blue dragonflight used illusory magics to trick an entire Primalist legion to fly underground . . . where the black dragonflight promptly cracked the earth's crust and buried them beneath the ground. Beregos, the archlibrarian of the Azure Archives, was responsible for engineering that feat.

By relying on unconventional tactics in the field and leveraging our flights' abilities to their full extent, we have lost no more than a hundred dragons over the years. We have several advantages over the Primalists—for one, we have been primal dragons, but they have never been ordered. The Primalists do not understand how we think, but we are intimately familiar with the inner workings of their minds.

However, we retreat from two battles for every one we win, preserving the lives of our flights over digging our talons into an empty tundra. But with each year that passes, the Primalists push a little closer to the Broodlands . . . and before long, we won't be fighting to cull their numbers. We'll be fighting for our lives.

The barriers won't hold forever. Even if Iridikron isn't aware of this fact, we Aspects are. We have not wasted the time given to us, working tirelessly to prepare our flights to defend the home front.

Alexstrasza holds war games, skirmishes, and tournaments to encourage a spirit of cooperation among the flights. She created flight academies for the drakes—elder and younger—to encourage them to build the skills they need to defend the Broodlands and, later, Azeroth at large. Elder drakes now join border patrols with fully grown dragons.

The hammers in the Obsidian Citadel never stop ringing, and Neltharion's Shadowscales have eyes throughout the Dragonwilds. From the Emerald Gardens, Ysera mobilizes the considerable number of mortal tribes that have migrated to her lands, teaching them to tend the fields and fostering a respect for nature. The greens drive herds from the wilds into the plains, preparing for a siege. Malygos and the blues have reinforced the ley lines throughout the Broodlands, giving them access to a robust font of arcane power; and we bronzes have increased our mastery of the timeways, able to see future events with more clarity, if not more certainty.

Our time grows short—we are at war.

CHAPTER EIGHTEEN

On a late summer's day, Alexstrasza stepped from the Vault of the Incarnates, alone. She paused on the edge of the terrace in the sunshine, sensing a chill upon the wind. For nigh unto twenty-five years, the Broodlands had enjoyed relative peace . . . but she knew it would not last.

Still, the flights had not wasted the time. The Vault of the Incarnates was a testament to the black and bronze dragonflights' ingenuity: With its white marble columns and golden pediments, the vault was a stunning addition to the sights of Thaldraszus. Blooming flora cascaded from the mountainsides. Blessed rivers crashed down on either side of the vault, filling a sparkling pool at its base. Birds filled the air with song.

Had she not known the true purpose of this place, the Life-Binder would have found it peaceful. Serene. But the vault was little more than a beautiful prison, a small kindness for those they had once called kin, *friend*.

Alexstrasza tried not to think too much on its purpose.

Neltharion had seated the Vault of the Incarnates on an underground bed of magma, allowing its foundation to better absorb certain types of seismic waves. Inside, Nozdormu and the titan-forged had created three spherical cells, each one designed to hold an Incarnate in perpetual stasis. Raszageth would remain in the Reach, where her prison was reinforced with Malygos's most potent wards.

As of today, Nozdormu and the bronze dragonflights were finishing the time enchantments on each cell. Everything—at least for the vault—was ready.

Heavy footsteps thudded across the platform. "Is everything all right, Alexstrasza?" Nozdormu asked, pausing beside her, his scales gleaming like gold in the afternoon sunlight. "Perhaps that was not the best way to word the question—not much is *all right* at the moment, is it?"

Alexstrasza sighed, looking out over the crater toward Tyrhold. "Tell me," she said quietly, knowing the gravity of the question she asked, "was there a wiser Alexstrasza in the timeways, one who managed to lead the flights through this conflict without war?"

"Some managed to avoid war, yes," Nozdormu said. "But I would not say they were *wiser,* as it always came at a terrible cost. In one timeline, Alexstrasza hunted down each Incarnate and challenged them herself, slaying them one by one. The actions poisoned her heart, turning her into a dark queen who eventually broke the very world she had pledged to save. In another, she forced all dragons to accept Order magic on pain of death. Thousands were slaughtered."

Those words brought Alexstrasza no comfort. She shuddered, wondering what sort of power would drive her to break the world in two.

"I know you blame yourself, Alexstrasza, but this conflict is no fault of yours," Nozdormu said, smiling as two messengers swooped toward the terrace, belying the weightiness of his words. "Know that a clean victory is not achieved easily in any timeline—the battles we fight will be brutal and bloody, and they will harrow our flights to the core. But there is only one predictor of failure that seems inescapable."

"And what is that?" Alexstrasza asked.

"Your death," Nozdormu replied, turning his incisive gaze on her, his smile falling. "In no timeline do the flights survive without you. In the coming days, if you risk your own life, you may risk the lives of us all."

She drew a sharp breath but gave him a nod.

"We need you, our queen," Nozdormu said. "You may not realize it, but you are the beating heart of our flights. The only way *any* of us will survive the coming war is if you have the strength and courage to follow yours."

The beating heart of our flights. How often had she heard those words, said by her sister, her consort, her allies, all of whom thought them a compliment, a kindness. But Alexstrasza knew them now for what they were: a weight.

"Oh, Nozdormu," she said as the messengers alighted on the terrace. "Sometimes, I wonder why Tyr named me Dragon

Queen when I have made so many mistakes. I . . ." She trailed off, picturing the fury and pain she had seen in Vyranoth's eyes. She thought of the drakes who claimed to remember being taken from their nests in the Dragonwilds, and the primal dragons like Oxoria who had flown to Harrowsdeep in defense of their broods, fearing Alexstrasza might come for their whelplings next.

When you are convinced of your own righteousness, no act becomes unconscionable.

For so many years, Alexstrasza thought she was serving the greater good, following the wisdom of the keepers, but now she realized that the *greater good* had no single definition. Even her best intentions led to unforeseen ends, complications she had scarcely imagined . . . and trying to oblige two conflicting sides only fanned the flames of war.

"Know that I have never questioned Tyr's choice," Nozdormu said, interrupting her thoughts. "His charge was the stewardship and safety of Azeroth. You will achieve that and more, Alexstrasza. Take heart."

"Thank you, my friend," she said. "I shall remember your words as the hour grows ever darker."

Nozdormu bowed his head. "I hope you shall."

"My Aspects!" The red dragon Timaeustrasz alighted on the terrace and dipped his head in a hasty bow. "We bring an emergency summons to the Seat of the Aspects from Malygos the Spell-Weaver."

"What has happened?" Alexstrasza asked, stretching her wings to prepare them for flight as she strode toward the edge of the platform.

"The blue dragonflight caught several drakes attempting to compromise the mana crystal that powers our barriers," Timaeustrasz said. "The Spell-Weaver says it may not last the day."

No. The breath left Alexstrasza's chest.

"That is not all." The black dragon Stahlien bowed. "The Primalists are moving their forces toward the Reach, under the command of Vyranoth the Frozenheart. We believe they are preparing for an attack."

"What?" Nozdormu asked, recoiling.

"Let us fly for the Seat at once," Alexstrasza said, leaping into the air before the words were off her lips. The others scrambled to follow her. As she soared past Tyrhold, flying fast as her wings could carry her, she felt they would not dodge this blow as easily as the last one. War now came to their lands in earnest—she could not, nay, *would not* fail her kind.

Alexstrasza slammed into the terrace at the Seat of the Aspects, not surprised to find a crowd of dragons milling about the council chambers—Aspects, majordomos, consorts, and flightleaders alike. Tension hung so thick in the air, Alexstrasza thought she might slice it with her talons.

Dragons scrambled out of the way as the Life-Binder strode into the main chamber, shouting. "Malygos, tell me what has happened!"

The blue Aspect lifted his head wearily. The decades of supporting the arcane fonts at Vakthros and the Azure Archives had taken their toll—his scales had faded to a dull blue, and the vibrant fire in his eyes had all but gone out. His cheeks were hollow, his shoulders hunched, and his wing membranes were dry as the pages of the books he so loved. His consort, Sindragosa, stepped forward to speak on his behalf, but Malygos waved her down.

The Spell-Weaver sighed. "I am sorry, Alexstrasza, but I fear the barriers will not hold much longer."

"It is all right, my friend," Alexstrasza said gently, taking her place among her flight. Tyranastrasz curled his tail around hers, providing unspoken support, while Saristrasz shifted a few steps to the Life-Binder's left, giving her room.

She continued, looking to the blue Aspect. "You and the blue dragonflight have given so much to defend us all, and our gratitude is boundless. We knew this day would come, but you must tell me how our drakes hastened it along."

Malygos nodded. "Less than an hour ago, Sindragosa caught six drakes attempting to shatter the mana crystal that lies far within the depths of the Azure Archives."

"This crystal feeds the ley lines to the obelisks?" she asked, heart fluttering.

"The very same," he said.

"How severe is the damage?" Alexstrasza asked.

The Spell-Weaver opened his mouth to speak, but exhaled and shook his head instead.

Sindragosa put a forepaw on Malygos's shoulder. "We cannot fix it, my queen. Not in time to save the barriers. I am sorry. The young drake, Sirigosa . . . employed Primalist techniques to disable the archives' defenses. Ice, in particular."

Alexstrasza pressed her lips together. "Our drakes have been consorting with *Primalists*?"

"With *Vyranoth*," Neltharion spat. "The red drake Talinstrasz admitted it proudly."

Cries erupted around the Seat. *Talinstrasz*, the Life-Binder thought and narrowed her eyes. She remembered the brazen little red too well—though she had never imagined that youthful insolence would turn into full-scale *rebellion*. The news only stoked Alexstrasza's anger. How *dare* they consort with the enemy, thereby putting thousands upon thousands of lives at risk? Did they think Fyrakk would spare the whelps at the Ruby Life Pools? That Vyranoth would not sink the Broodlands into an age of never-melting ice? That Iridikron would not pull the very mountains down on their heads?

"Who else?" Alexstrasza asked. "Name them."

It was Sindragosa who spoke: "Ellegos, Nolizdormu, Azarian, and Ivarus. One from every flight, and two from mine."

"Have they been apprehended?" the Life-Binder asked, looking to Neltharion.

"The Shadowscales are questioning them in the dungeons of the citadel as we speak," the black Aspect said.

"Good," Alexstrasza replied. "Majordomos, capture every drake who might be associated with Talinstrasz's 'movement' and send them to the Obsidian Citadel for interrogation. The rest of us should prepare for the attack—"

"You cannot pretend they did not have a point!" a voice rang out from the blues' wing, interrupting the Life-Binder.

Silence descended over the chamber like a shroud. Every eye in the chamber turned toward Stelegos, a wingleader with Malygos's Spellscales.

"Stelegos," the blue Aspect said with a sigh. "We've spoken of this before—now is not the time."

"We all heard what Fyrakk said at the peace summit," Stelegos said. "And later, what Vyranoth said over Wyrmrest Temple. We *all* heard her accuse the Dragon Queen of stealing eggs from the nests of primal dragons!"

"I said that was enough," Malygos snapped.

Stelegos continued. "You cannot hide it any longer—"

"*Enough!*" Malygos whirled on Stelegos, his fury sparking as fast as the arcane fire along his talons. Stelegos recoiled, dropping his head to protect his throat and ruffling his scales. Talons shrieked against stone. Even Sindragosa, calm, unflappable Sindragosa, curled her lips in a snarl. Fear spiked the chamber, and the greens and bronzes recoiled from the blues.

"It is all right, everyone," Alexstrasza said, sending a gentle pulse of ruby light through the room, hoping to soothe tensions. "Malygos, please, do not strain yourself for my sake."

The Spell-Weaver looked to her, blew out a breath, and sat back, hanging his head not in defeat or shame, but in simple fatigue.

She did not fault him for his temper. Malygos had never suffered fools gladly, and he was tired, so tired. She could sense the relentless exhaustion he shouldered every day, testing not only his spirit but the very bonds of loyalty he had with the other Aspects, his friends. She had asked much of the blue Aspect—too much—and he had given his all.

Stelegos turned his gaze on Alexstrasza, raising his voice. "Would you deny it? Is it true you sanctioned the theft of dragons' eggs from the wilds?"

The blue's voice rang through the skies, so loud that fliersby turned to look in the direction of the Seat. Alexstrasza kept her features neutral, careful not to show her consternation. She did not look to Neltharion, nor her sister; instead, she held the blue's gaze, unflinching, unrelenting, till he dropped his eyes and stared at the ground.

Once, long ago, Nozdormu had warned her it might come to this—that the very futures of her flights might hinge on the outcome of that fateful decision: *I see a thousand futures before our flights, but I could not tell you which way the sands of time will flow. Taking primal dragon eggs from the wilds may be a boon to our flights—it also may be the choice that ends them.*

The flights needed to survive. They *had* to survive, and she could no longer pretend that the Aspects hadn't made difficult choices in pursuit of that goal. She could feel Neltharion's gaze boring into her scales, imploring her to hide the truth, begging her not to say the words that were about to flow straight from her heart.

But Alexstrasza was Dragon Queen, and she had learned through sad experience what happened when she did not trust those closest to her with the truth.

No more secrets.

"Listen to me, and listen well," Alexstrasza said to everyone in the chamber, "for if you have any love for your flights, you will understand why we, as Aspects, made a difficult choice more than three centuries ago."

Neltharion closed his eyes, saying nothing.

As a wave of uncertainty washed over the chamber, Alexstrasza continued: "At Tyr's behest, and in order to fulfill the oaths we made to one another and to this world, the Aspects sanctioned the retrieval of primal dragon eggs from the Dragonwilds."

She paused for a moment, giving the assembly a moment to reckon with her words. It wasn't a revelation, but the Life-Binder's confirmation of the truth changed everything.

The reds at her side and back, however, did not so much as question her, their resolve unshaken. The bronzes, too, looked wholly unsurprised. Unruffled. The blues and greens took this confirmation with less forbearance, looking to one another askance.

The black dragons looked impressed, almost smug.

"We struggled with this directive," Alexstrasza said, looking to Ysera. "We had no desire to take eggs from their rightful parents. As compromise, I ordered the titan-forged to take only the eggs from untended nests in the wilds, which might just as easily have been snatched up by predators. Still, I struggled with this decision.

"When Fyrakk imbued himself with the power of the elements, a new movement took hold—the Primalists labeled us as abominations, aberrations, thralls to the titans. They said we were dangerous, that we should be eliminated. We knew he would not stop until the Broodlands burned, and every ordered dragon along with it."

Alexstrasza swept her gaze across the room. "Tell me true: Would you not have made a similar decision, faced with the horrors that now bristle on our borders? Would you not have moved to strengthen your own numbers while weakening those of your opponents? Would you not have done all in your power to ensure the survival of your kind?"

One green spoke up from the back, saying, "But wasn't this why the Incarnates refused peace with the Broodlands? This information turned Vyranoth against us!"

"They would have come for us anyway," Saristrasz snapped, stepping forward to flank Alexstrasza. "Iridikron *wanted* a reason to declare war on the Broodlands."

"But we could have had more *time,*" Stelegos said. "Perhaps we could have had a thousand years of tentative peace, rather than a few hundred! In time, we might have found a way to coexist with them."

"There can be no talk of peace, no *coexistence* with those who believe we should not *exist,*" Egnion of the Shadowscales said, making a rumbling noise in his chest. "I have watched them for centuries, and I tell you now—the Incarnates never wanted anything but an end to our kind!"

Stelegos squared his shoulders and lifted his head. "I refuse to believe there was no other path to peace."

"It was not the eggs that tipped the scales of war, Stelegos, but Raszageth's capture," Alexstrasza said softly, and yet her words made all the other voices in the chamber fall quiet. "Would you have me release the Storm-Eater, even to win another century of peace? She would not give it to you. Remember, she attacked us first."

The blue stepped back, chastised. Every eye turned back to the Life-Binder, expectant. Though the dragons remained outwardly stoic, their fear, anger, and confusion simmered through the chamber. She needed the leaders around her to see the situation with clarity, or else many lives would be snuffed out this day.

"As we speak, our enemies fly on our borders," Alexstrasza said. "Our flights, our families, and our very way of life will soon be under attack. I do not need to explain to this assembly what will happen if the Broodlands fall.

"I empathize with your frustration and anger," she said as she looked to Stelegos, who bent his head, "for this is the way I felt when Tyr first asked the Aspects to recover the eggs from the wilds. My heart cried out against the command. Now that you know the truth of the matter, I will not fault you if you choose to depart Valdrakken and tarry with the dragonflights no more. The choice to remain is yours, and yours alone; I will never sanction the removal of individual agency again.

"You are the leaders of our flights," she said, lifting her gaze and squaring her shoulders. "If we are to weather the coming storms, the hearts in this room must be in accord. I cannot promise that I will ever be a perfect leader, but I *can* promise that I will ever work to preserve your health and happiness. I will fight to my dying breath to protect you, celebrate your victories with you, and lift you up in times of need. But above all, I swear this day that I shall never hide my work from you again."

Alexstrasza had broken a promise once, and she and her flights would pay dearly for that mistake. She would not make such an error again.

Resolute, she lifted her voice and said, "Our skies grow dark—will you stand with me now and defend our beloved home?"

Ysera said, "Always," before the words were off the Life-Binder's lips.

Tyranastrasz thumped his tail on the ground, sending tremors through the floor. "I am ever by your side, Alexstrasza."

"As are all in our flight!" Saristrasz said. "We will not allow our kind to abandon hope."

Neltharion stepped forward. "The black dragonflight stands ready to defend the Broodlands with you, my queen." The black dragons around him lifted their heads and trumpeted their war-calls. Their flight had been preparing for this day for centuries.

"As does the blue," Malygos said, lifting his head. For the first time in many years, a spark of arcane fire lit the Spell-Weaver's eyes. Behind him, Stelegos closed his eyes but dipped his head in a nod.

"So, too, shall the bronze dragonflight bring all our talents to bear," Nozdormu said. Before he could say aught else, a sob echoed from his camp, shattering the tremulous thread of hope that had formed.

"Soridormi," the bronze Aspect said, turning to his consort with a frown. "Whatever is the matter?"

Gold light glazed Soridormi's eyes. Bright tears leaked down her cheek. Tremors raced through her legs, and she pressed her wings against her back. "The p-plains are burning," she said with another sob. "I-I can see it, close in the distance—Fyrakk is burning the Emerald Gardens with an army of Primalists. I-I don't know . . . there's not much time. But the portal to the Dream, oh!"

Ysera cried out, sending all the little birds that nested in her horns scattering. The greens panicked, looking to their Aspect for orders.

"Go, sister!" Alexstrasza said. "We may not have much time—go!"

Ysera gave her queen a nod. "Titans be with you, sister."

"And with you," the Life-Binder said, wishing they had time enough for a proper goodbye.

As the greens leapt into the skies, chaos broke out in the Seat. Aspects conferred with their flightcommanders, barking orders and sending dragons scattering in all directions. Alexstrasza returned to the chamber, summoning up her campaign map from the floor. The Seat emptied, leaving the remaining four Aspects alone.

"So, it begins," Neltharion said, joining Alexstrasza at her right wing.

"Don't sound too excited," Malygos said, shooting the Earth-Warder one of his looks. Despite the Spell-Weaver's exhaustion, he never tired of ribbing the black Aspect.

Neltharion frowned, but before he could respond, Alexstrasza interrupted. "Much as I enjoy your banter, our time is limited. We must defend the Reach and the Emerald Gardens from a Primalist assault. Neltharion and I will go north to defend the Reach, with the reds taking a position at the conservatory." She tapped the Life-Binder Conservatory with her talon, setting it alight with red flame. Her ruby pawn slid across the floor toward the keep, while Neltharion's moved to the border of the Reach.

Neltharion slid one of his battalions to the Emerald Plains. "I have sent Garion and his Ironscales to provide front-line support to the greens."

"Good," Alexstrasza said. "Malygos, I suspect you will want to return to the Azure Archives posthaste?"

"Preferably," the blue Aspect said. "I may be able to win us a few more hours of time."

"Very well, do what you must," she replied, sliding his sapphire pawn to the archives. "Nozdormu, you should return to the Temporal Conflux and prepare for an attack—we don't yet know if Iridikron is on the field."

"At once," the bronze Aspect said.

Alexstrasza scanned the campaign map, looking for weaknesses. "Am I missing anything, Neltharion?"

"No," he replied. "I sent Levarian to the Obsidian Citadel to lead a combined force of the Earthen Bulwark, drakonid, and mortals hidden in the canyons of the Waking Shores. We have ghost armies in position to force our enemies to engage us in more favorable locations that will incur less loss of life, and we have drakonid along the border operating the dragon-killer artillery."

"Let us hope it will be enough," Alexstrasza said. "By wing and by talon, I will not let the Broodlands fall this day."

...

VYRANOTH STOOD ON A ledge outside the Reach, studying the vermillion barrier that enclosed the whole of the Waking Shores. Tendrils of ruby light curled toward the sky, tinging the clouds pink. The sun sank toward the horizon, and on the other side of the barrier, she could see the destruction her sister had wrought in the Reach. She knew Raszageth could be reckless, but she also knew her sister would not have attacked the Broodlands without reason.

Neltharion was hiding something in the Reach, and her sister had paid the price.

I will set you free, Raszageth, Vyranoth thought. *No matter what it takes, I will see the wind fill your wings once more.*

This moment had been almost twenty-five years in the making. The Frozenheart had taken the young ordered drakes under her wing, speaking with them infrequently to keep from arousing the Aspects' suspicions. It had taken years to teach Sirigosa the right spells, then to position the drake inside the Azure Archives as a trusted under-librarian.

Razviik landed beside Vyranoth, touching his wing talon to his chest. Over the last fifty years, the mottled green had become indispensable to her, serving as her right wing, adviser, and confidant. He and his mate were family, and their whelps looked to Vyranoth as their grand-dame. It was Razviik who stood guard as Vyranoth had been imbued with the element of ice; Razviik who had dubbed her the Frozenheart in the wake of Alexstrasza's betrayal; Razviik who flew at her right wing as they sieged Wyrmrest Temple for the first time.

"The sun flies toward the horizon," he said, lifting his head and scenting the air. He had learned much from Vyranoth about tactics and coordination. "Your drakes are late."

"Patience," Vyranoth said. "If they had failed, the black dragonflight would not bristle at the border as they do. Is everyone in position?"

"Indeed," Razviik said.

"Good." Vyranoth had engaged the Earth-Warder on multiple occasions, taking as many losses as she had wins. Neltharion's battalions were better trained than any other force on the field—one could not simply strike his armies with a hammer of force and expect them to break. No . . . one needed a modicum of strategy to face Neltharion.

"This war brings me no joy," Razviik said. "One day, I may face my own flesh and blood on the battlefield."

Vyranoth made an empathetic rumbling noise in her throat. "We must trust that the truth has spread among the drakes of the Broodlands. Talinstrasz knew he had been ordered in the egg—other kidnapped whelps must know it now, too. They will not raise their talons against their primal kin."

"I believe you," Razviik replied. "Still, the thought haunts me."

"How could it not?" Vyranoth replied. "I find no glory in combat, but the Aspects leave us little choice. I will not bow to the will of their masters, nor will I stand by as they decimate, corrupt, or imprison our kind. And I will *not* let them bury my sister under that hateful mountain."

Vyranoth cast her gaze across the valley. Along the eastern mountain range, she could just make out a large, glimmering blue ward set into the mountain's face. According to Iridikron's Rockfuries, *that* was where Neltharion kept the Storm-Eater imprisoned.

What had Raszageth done to deserve such a well-defended prison? Or, more like, what other horrors had she witnessed here in the Reach, crimes the Aspects would not want their primal kin to know?

Razviik nodded. "I will fight by your side, Vyranoth, until we have justice for the atrocities committed against our kind."

"When the barriers fall, we attack at once," Vyranoth stated. "Have Cysanz engage the Earthen Bulwark, and send the Icetalons to destroy the drakonid's dragon-killers on the border. Our objective is to push to the Weyrn Grounds, but we will not throw lives away if both Neltharion and Alexstrasza take to the field. I will not fight two Aspects at once."

"Understood," Razviik said, bobbing his head.

Another hour passed; then two. As the sun touched the horizon and set the western mountains aflame, the air began to crackle. Red sparks exploded across the border like a curtain of fireworks. Embers rained from the sky.

As they cascaded to the ground, Alexstrasza's barrier was no more. Bugles erupted; the black dragonflight formed their ranks over the mountains. The flightleaders' voices rose over the sound of hundreds of wingbeats, confident and sure.

A half smile turned up one corner of Vyranoth's lips. She leapt skyward. With a single beat of her wings, she froze the moisture in the air, blanketing the peaks in a thick fog. She whipped it toward the Reach as her wingleaders roared, signaling the attack. Razviik followed her, along with Mithruz, a primal dragon she'd chosen as her third-in-command.

The mists tumbled into the Reach, filling its great valleys and giving her forces cover. Her Frostscale warriors cruised through the fog, which coalesced around their bodies and solidified to icy armor on their scales.

The Frostscales fell upon the black dragons, whistling through the air. The two armies collided with such force that the sound of their congress echoed off the sides of the mountain. Roars and screams swirled high. The drakonid launched burning lava into the sky with their catapults, illuminating the fog from within. The scent of blood tinged the air.

Vyranoth's mobile Icetalons dived beneath the Frostscales, heading for the drakonid positioned on the mountain ranges below. Massive wooden javelins shot through the fog, striking several Icetalons in the chest or wings. Others fell upon the drakonid, tearing them limb from limb and smashing their weapons. But the Earth-Warder's Shadowscales appeared from cracks and crevices in the mountains, as if chiseled out of the stone itself. The black dragons leapt upon Vyranoth's

Icetalon soldiers, driving them away from the drakonid and the heavy artillery.

"Mithruz, join them on the front lines," Vyranoth said. "Stoltria is leading the Earthen Bulwark in Levarian's place— she was one of the dragons responsible for Vitelenoth's death. Kill her."

Mithruz bobbed his head and dived for the front lines, heading for an armored black dragon who fought three Primalists at once. Stoltria flipped in the air, slamming her tail into a Stormtalon's head and breaking its neck.

"Once we've destroyed their artillery, have the Frostscales push the black dragonflight into the valley," Vyranoth said to Razviik. "If we fight them over the mountains, their light infantry will try to pin us against the peaks." She had seen Neltharion's Onyx Reavers fall from the sky like hunting hawks, slamming their targets into mountaintops and snapping wings, spines, and necks. The maneuver was difficult to defend against—the Reavers could reach blisteringly high speeds while falling and dropped from the sky like meteorites. Neltharion had employed the strategy at Emberstone and the Glacial Maw, as well as smaller skirmishes throughout the Dragonwilds.

Vyranoth hadn't seen the Reavers at the Reach, but that didn't mean Neltharion wasn't holding them in reserve.

Where is Neltharion? Vyranoth wondered, ill at ease. The black Aspect dwarfed even the largest of ordered dragons, making him easy to spot on the battlefield. Vyranoth let loose a frustrated growl. *Where are you hiding . . . ?*

As a wing of Icetalons rocketed past, destroying more of the black Aspect's toys, Vyranoth spun the icy fog around her talons, forming a lance of ice. Rotating once in the air, she propelled it at a group of drakonid working the ballistae on the mountain flank. The ice shard crashed into one of the catapults, freezing it and everything within twenty wing-lengths of its position. She shot a second lance at one of Neltharion's wingleaders on the front line. The dragon dropped from the sky and shattered into icy fragments on the rocks below.

Neltharion would not leave the Reach undefended. Had he gone to the Obsidian Citadel, expecting Iridikron to attack there? The Stonescaled had not joined the other Incarnates on this foray, preferring a two-pronged approach that would allow him to trap Neltharion's stronghold in a pincer. If Fyrakk could manage to smash his way into Stonefray Falls— which might be asking too much of the hot-tempered Incarnate—he and Vyranoth would assail the citadel from the north and the south.

No, something was *wrong*. Vyranoth could sense it in her gut, even as she launched lance after lance, watching Neltharion's dragons fall from the skies. As the last of the drakonid were dispatched below, Mithruz and Cysanz trumpeted an advance. The Frostscales surged forward, pushing the black dragons into the valley and surrounding them on three sides.

Still, the Earth-Warder did not appear.

Vyranoth followed her forces into the Reach, wary. Razviik fell back, joining the Incarnate above the battle.

"Have you seen the Earth-Warder?" she asked him.

Razviik shook his head. "He may be fighting on another front."

"No, I know Neltharion well," Vyranoth said. "Neither his flightcommander nor his flightmaster is here, which means he must have direct command of the forces in the Reach—"

As Vyranoth said those words, the fog shifted overhead. Her ears picked up a faint whistling sound. When she looked up, she saw fifteen black dragons plummeting straight toward her.

"Reavers!" she shouted, spreading her wings wide to shock the air with frost. She dived. The Frozenheart knew she could not outfly such monsters, but the chill would make them less maneuverable when they opened their wings again.

As she plummeted toward the foot of the mountain, her fog thinned. Sparks caught fire in the earth below. First two, then ten, then twenty.

No, not fire . . . *eyes*. Twenty-five pairs of eyes, all watching her every movement.

The soil began to roil and churn. To Vyranoth's dismay, a company of black dragons rose from their hiding places in the loam, shaking the dirt from their backs. The earth cracked open, and a massive, black-scaled forefoot shot out and sank its talons into the ground.

Neltharion! Vyranoth thought, her heart rising into her throat. The ground rushed closer, and the Reavers fell faster than she. They would be upon her in another heartbeat or two.

Vyranoth opened her wings and shot over the heads of her enemies. Up ahead, Neltharion emerged from the earth, eyes blazing. With a toothy grin, the black Aspect dug his talons into the ground and hurled a chunk of earth at her. Vyranoth closed her wings and rolled left, but the boulder slammed into her right hip. Soil and stones exploded on impact. A painful series of shocks and bright pops burst along her spine. She lost her momentum, crashing into the ground as the Reavers screamed over her head.

Before Vyranoth could regain her footing, Neltharion leapt on her side, pushing her into the earth as his fore-talons punctured her scales. She shrieked at him, punching her thorny wing talon into the gap in his shoulder armor. The Earth-Warder roared and leapt back. Blood welled from his wound, slicking his onyx scales.

Vyranoth scrambled to her feet, panting. Her pulse thrummed through her chest and in her eardrums, so loud she almost couldn't hear the din of battle. She lowered her head to protect her throat.

So the Earth-Warder had managed to take her unawares, using his Reavers to chase her to the ground. Had he also planned to have his Earthen Bulwark fall back, luring the Frozenheart and her forces into a false sense of security? Then, he had taken advantage of her survival instincts to force her into a vulnerable position. She growled at the thought.

Overhead, Razviik trumpeted four short blasts, warning the Primalists that Vyranoth had been grounded. The Frostscales panicked, their formations deteriorating. Cysanz bugled a response; but before the Primalists could dive to protect their Incarnate, the black dragonflight surged forward, pushing the Primalists back to the ridge and trapping the Incarnate behind enemy lines.

High in the skies, the Reavers began a second descent through the fog. Fifty, maybe sixty dragons plunged toward the front-line scrums.

Vyranoth narrowed her eyes, turning her attention back to the Earth-Warder. Four black dragons flanked him, while others circled in the air above. The mountain blocked her retreat. Two twin waterfalls crashed down the mountain's rocky face, filling the air with mist.

Neltharion had outplayed her, yes, but that didn't mean he had *won*. Vyranoth drew in a deep breath, letting her blood chill and her heart slow. She would need her wits to be razor-sharp if she was going to survive this encounter.

The Earth-Warder rolled his injured shoulder, then tilted his head to crack his neck in a languid manner. "Do you think you can win against me, truly?" the black Aspect said with a sneer. He lifted his head. "Our campaign in the Dragonwilds was *whelps' play* compared with what we will unleash upon you in the Broodlands."

Vyranoth curled her lip, baring a fang. "You have lost every wing-length of territory from here to Harrowsdeep, Neltharion. Do *you* think you can stand against the might of the Incarnates? I will free my sister, and together, we shall lay the Broodlands and all your hateful cities low."

"I was the one to trap your *sister* under the mountain," Neltharion said, his words edged in malice. He stalked toward her, his eyes burning with hate. "And now I think I shall do the same to you."

"Unlikely," Vyranoth said through gritted teeth. As the

Earth-Warder lunged at her, she leapt into the air, sending out a shock wave of frigid cold from her chest. The waterfalls froze in an instant; when she shouted her fury, they shattered into a million glittering, razor-edged pieces. With a forward snap of her wings, she sent the shards barreling at the black Aspect and his forces.

The ice sang as it shredded wing membranes and splintered scales, sending the black dragons around her tumbling through the mists like dark shadows. Armor cracked in the cold. Screams cut through the fog. The black Aspect howled in rage, consumed in a cloud of sparkling ice.

Before he could launch another attack, Vyranoth fled. She took the ice that whirled off her wings and condensed it, forming thick icicles that hung in the air over her shoulders. She found the weakest flank in the black dragonflight's front lines and smashed the spears through the gaps in their armor.

With a roar, the Frostscales leapt into the breach, clearing a path for their Incarnate. Vyranoth sailed past them, banked, and turned to hover behind a wall of her Primalists.

Too close, Vyranoth thought bitterly, breathing hard. Below her Neltharion slew ten of her Frostscales with single swipe of his tail. The other Frostscales scattered before the Earth-Warder.

"Vyranoth!" Razviik shouted, climbing toward her, the fear clear in his eyes. "I saw you drop, but nothing that happened after. Are you unhurt?"

"I'm fine," Vyranoth replied with a little growl, one meant for herself and her own denseness. Neltharion obviously intended to try to capture her, rather than kill her . . . but she wasn't sure why that would be. In prior encounters, it had seemed Neltharion and the other Aspects had tried to kill the Incarnates with brute force—why, she still had scores in her hide from some of their talons, and her left shoulder had never been the same after a particularly violent encounter with a bronze flightleader.

What new strategy is this, Alexstrasza? she wondered, watching with dispassion as Neltharion ravaged the Frostscales. *What are you doing?*

As if summoned by the Frozenheart's thoughts, a faint ruby glow appeared on the southeastern horizon. Vyranoth turned her head. The light spread across the valley, illuminating the Reach in a gentle warmth. It melted Vyranoth's icy fog and cleared the storms from the skies, pushing them back to reveal a glittering wing of stars.

Alexstrasza stood atop a tower at the edge of the Reach, blazing like a miniature sun. Her reds pushed back the cold with crimson fire. The very sight of her old friend filled Vyranoth with icy rage; there was a time when she could look upon the Dragon Queen with empathy, but all she saw now was an *enemy*.

One day, she would tear Alexstrasza from the skies with her own talons—this she swore on Raszageth's name, and on all the eggs crushed under the heel of Order magic.

"Sound the retreat," the Frozenheart told Razviik. "We will fight another day."

ALL TOLD, THE BLACK dragonflight had lost eighteen dragons to Vyranoth and her Primalists on the first advance. A paltry number compared with the losses the Primalists incurred, but Neltharion still mourned every fire-hearted dragon who left the sky.

The black dragonflight placed the pitch-covered pyres along the shores of the lagoon in the Caldera of the Menders. The moonslight slicked the obsidian scales of the dead. No matter how stony his exterior, Neltharion still found himself stricken with grief at the sight of them all. His flight had already given so much at the Reach; how many more would fall in the coming days? How many more would be asked to give their lives for peace?

Alexstrasza might believe Neltharion had wanted this war, but he hated it as much as she did. The Earth-Warder had ever been a builder and protector, not a breaker. He loathed seeing so many bright lights extinguished at the talons of their enemies—so much potential, wasted, just like it had been at the Battle of Stormsunder.

The Earthen Bulwark of the black dragonflight gathered silently on the beach. They perched on the mountain cliffs, not ready to say goodbye to their comrades and friends, their family, their flight. Unlike the Primalists who left their dead for the worms, every fallen member of the black dragonflight had been retrieved and placed upon pyres by the drakonid. Neltharion would send the dragons' remains into the heavens on cinders, so that they might fly free; what bones were too heavy for the winds would be interred at the Veiled Ossuary. The fallen deserved to rest in stone.

"You have flown your last, my friends," he said, voice strained, throat tight. "Your sacrifice allows us to fight another day—for that, your names shall never be forgotten."

Neltharion closed his eyes and drew in a deep breath. His lungs superheated the air until flames curled around his fangs. Neltharion lifted his head and dug his talons into the soft sand. Then, with the power building in his diaphragm, he swept his head down in an arc and let the fires inside him erupt.

The pyres burst into a massive conflagration. All around him, the black dragonflight lifted their voices and named the fallen—what started as a whisper grew into a roar, carving their comrades' names into their memories as fire consumed their physical vessels. The flight kept a vigil till the pyres burned low.

As the drakonid stepped forward to gather the embers and bones of the dead, a familiar voice interrupted Neltharion's thoughts: "Congratulations, my Aspect, on your victory against the Frozenheart."

The Earth-Warder turned his head, glad to see it was only Levarian. The flightcommander bowed his head and said, "May I have permission to join you?"

"But of course," Neltharion said, turning his gaze back to the ashes. "I am told the Stonescaled did not appear on the battlefield today, neither at the citadel nor in Thaldraszus or the Azure Span."

"He did not." Levarian sat beside Neltharion, watching the drakonid scoop ashes into lightweight metal vessels. "I admit, I am surprised . . . I expected the Incarnates to bring their full strength to bear against us once the barriers fell."

"Hmm," the black Aspect said, thinking. "His absence may indicate that he knows about the vault and is unwilling to risk capture." If Vyranoth had been the Incarnates' point of contact with the rebellious drakes, it was possible she knew of the vault, too, and simply did not care about the danger. The Aspects hadn't spread word widely of the project, but they certainly hadn't hidden it, either.

The flightcommander turned to his Aspect. "Speaking of the vault, the flightleaders tell me you nearly captured the Frozenheart on your first attempt."

"Hmph," Neltharion replied. "*Nearly* is not a success, nor is it something to be celebrated."

Levarian smirked. "As you say, my lord."

"They will be upon us again," Neltharion said, turning away from the ashes. "Come, Levarian. We have much work to do ere the sun rises."

CHAPTER NINETEEN

NELTHARION CURSED HIS FAILURE TO CAPTURE Vyranoth—had he succeeded, he would have dealt a crushing blow to the Primalists' campaign in the north. Instead, the Primalists returned the next day, seeking to win a talon-hold in the Broodlands. The black, red, and green dragonflights rebuffed them.

They attacked at dawn of the third day, undeterred, and again on the fourth day. Ten times the number of Primalists fell from the skies as did dragons from the Aspects' forces. Still they raged on. Alexstrasza's reds flew in to provide support in the Reach, bringing reinforcements to flagging defenders and healing magics to the wounded.

Vyranoth's tactics grew cleverer with each encounter, testing Neltharion's strategies, seeking to whittle down the black dragonflight's strength. The Earth-Warder could not tell if Vyranoth had improved as a commander or if Iridikron influenced her approach. The Frozenheart used her greater numbers to devastating effect; still, the Primalists struggled to capture even a wing-length of the Reach.

With each passing day, the Incarnates' grand strategy grew clearer to Neltharion—they meant to seize the territories directly north and south of the Obsidian Citadel, catching it in a pincer attack. In the Reach, Raszageth was a secondary objective; for if the citadel fell, the whole of the Waking Shores would fall, too.

On the sixth day, Vyranoth pulled the Reach's many rivers into the skies, using them to create a great glacier that punched through the mountains south of the Zskera Vaults. Neltharion commanded his forces to fall back, for the Frozenheart and her allies drew immense strength from the thick ice. It would spread, slowly, until it engulfed all the Reach.

Concerned, Neltharion asked Alexstrasza to assemble the Aspects at the Seat on the evening of the sixth day. The mood was somber—the Dragon Queen fretted over the campaign map, speaking in low tones to Nozdormu. Malygos sat opposite them, appearing more hale than he had in decades. Arcane fire sparked from his eyes when he saw Neltharion stride into the Seat.

Ysera drooped like a withering flower beside the Spell-Weaver, having spent the last six days keeping Fyrakk at bay. Black, bubbly burns charred the left side of her neck and shoulder, the wounds packed with glowing peat moss. Butterflies danced along the moss, emanating glittering magic into the wound.

Ysera's greens and the black dragonflight's Ironscales had kept Fyrakk from setting fire to the plains, but Fyrakk was much less circumspect than Vyranoth. He aimed to spread as much pain, terror, and fear among the dragonflights as possible.

Malygos chuckled as Neltharion took a seat beside the Dragon Queen. "Late to your own meeting, I see," the blue Aspect said.

"Would you like to come out of your stuffy libraries and fight Vyranoth on the front lines with me?" Neltharion replied.

The Spell-Weaver wrinkled his snout and shook his head.

"That's what I thought," Neltharion said with a snort. He turned to the green Aspect. "How fare you, Ysera? Garion tells me the fighting at Stonefray has been fierce."

The Dreamer yawned, then gave her head a little shake. "Well enough, though I would appreciate if we could keep this short—Fyrakk's thirst for battle is nigh unto unquenchable. He is the first on the battlefield and the last to retreat."

"Then with Alexstrasza's permission, I'll take the floor," Neltharion said.

"It is yours," the Dragon Queen said with a wave of one forefoot, still mulling over the pawns placed along the Broodlands' border.

"After careful consideration," Neltharion began, "I believe Iridikron's strategy is to catch the Obsidian Citadel in a pincer movement, or perhaps in a three-way siege. That is why Vyranoth and Fyrakk are fighting on separate fronts—they mean to capture the territories directly north and south of the citadel, then attack the fortress as one." The Reach and the northern section of the Emerald Plains lit up on the war map as the Earth-Warder mentioned them. The golden light hugged the Obsidian Citadel, almost swallowing the stronghold in its brilliance.

Alexstrasza narrowed her eyes. "That does appear to be a possibility. The citadel cannot fall—if it does, the Ruby Life Pools will be defenseless, and it would give the Incarnates a fine position to strike at Valdrakken. What are your suggestions, Neltharion?"

"We focus our considerable talents on removing one Incarnate from the field immediately," Neltharion replied. "Vyranoth is too canny—it will take time to find a way to capture her. Fyrakk, on the other hand . . ."

"Is as smart as a clutch of rocks," Malygos said, which prompted an uncharacteristic snort from Ysera.

"Precisely," Neltharion said.

Nozdormu drummed his talons on the ground. "In many timelines, Fyrakk is the first or second to fall—there's no reason that can't happen in the one true timeline as well."

Alexstrasza cocked her head, making the dangling gems on her horns swing. "I assume you have a plan?" she asked, her gaze flicking to the Earth-Warder.

"I do." Neltharion sighed. "Well, at least part of a plan. I fear you will not like it, Ysera."

The green Aspect flared her nostrils. "Why is that?"

"I want you to give him Stonefray Falls," Neltharion said.

Ysera recoiled. Alexstrasza's gaze snapped to him, questioning.

"Are you mad?" Ysera said with a half gasp. "We lost forty good dragons from the green and black dragonflights at Stonefray!"

"I know," Neltharion replied. "I need Fyrakk to think he's *winning*. We give him Stonefray and have the green dragonflight fall back to defend the plains." Neltharion moved the green dragonflight to the river near Stonefray Falls, then slid the Earthen Bulwark's five pawns into the Apex Canopy. "Levarian and his battalion will taunt Fyrakk and engage his forces here at the canopy, with instructions to slowly fall back to the citadel. We can use our mortal allies positioned in the canyons to thin the Primalists' numbers as they approach."

Malygos frowned. "And what makes you think Fyrakk will follow your forces into the Waking Shores? That may be counter to the Stonescaled's orders, and even Fyrakk won't be unwise enough to defy Iridikron."

Neltharion smiled and slid Alexstrasza's ruby pawn onto the citadel's ramparts. The light gleamed off the pawn's sharp, precise facets.

Malygos's eyes widened. "Fyrakk does hate the Dragon Queen."

"No," Nozdormu said as Ysera cried out. "Under no circumstances can we *ever* risk Alexstrasza's life, especially as *bait*."

Alexstrasza shifted her weight but said nothing, her gaze fixed on her ruby pawn.

"With any luck," Neltharion replied, "Alexstrasza won't *need* to engage Fyrakk."

"I'd rather not rely on *luck*." Malygos made a rumbling noise in his throat, plucking his pawn from Vakthros and considering it. He turned the sapphire piece this way and that, letting it catch the light, then levitated it in a whorl of arcane fire.

The blue Aspect smiled, flashing fangs. "Perhaps I shall *leave my stuffy libraries* after all," he said to the Earth-Warder. "It seems you will need my help."

Malygos's pawn disintegrated, reappearing on the map at the Obsidian Citadel in a flash of blue light.

Neltharion looked up at the blue Aspect and grinned.

THREE DAYS AFTER FYRAKK and his armies established a talon-hold at Stonefray Falls, he received a curious message from Vyranoth: *Be careful, Fyrakk,* the Frozenheart said via a messenger. *The Aspects may be trying to capture us.*

Fyrakk thanked Vyranoth's messenger, but he laughed as he did so. The old ice Incarnate tended to be as paranoid as Iridikron himself. Fyrakk would die before he allowed the Aspects to capture him as they did Raszageth. He was not so *weak.*

In the aftermath of Fyrakk's victory at Stonefray Falls, Neltharion sent the Earthen Bulwark to the Apex Canopy to harry the Primalists. Alexstrasza now had command of the citadel, where she led a combined host of Ruby Flamebringers, Onyx Reavers, the Obsidian Guard, and several battalions of drakonid.

Fyrakk was intrigued by the news—if he could smash through the Earthen Bulwark, he could challenge the Dragon Queen at the citadel. For centuries, Fyrakk had looked forward to facing his cousin in battle—he wanted to raze her stone monstrosities that twisted the land to the titans' whims, to wipe the righteous smirk off her titan-sculpted face, and to listen to her last, gurgling breath as he crushed her windpipe like a wet reed.

When they were young, he had taught her how to hunt and fight, the force one needed to snap bone or tear flesh. If Alexstrasza was worth anything in the air, it was because of *him*. He knew her every move, her every weakness. And he knew he was the better fighter.

Alexstrasza would give him the fight he so craved. Since becoming an Incarnate, Fyrakk had found no other dragons to satiate his bloodlust—they were all too weak or timid to threaten him. Fyrakk had grown bored, even with the promise of war. None of the ordered could match him in the skies—he had even left scores in Ysera's hide.

Now he could see a path to an *actual* challenge. All Fyrakk wanted was Alexstrasza, dead by his own talons. Killing the Dragon Queen would scatter the flights. Fyrakk could win the war in one battle, then spend the remainder of his days hunting the ordered down to the last.

It sounded *delightful*.

Fyrakk considered waiting for the word from Iridikron, but he did not need the Stonescaled to chart his course like a whelp. Besides, was Iridikron at the Battle of Dragonblight? *No.* Was he at Frostfire Chasm? *No.* What about Icewing Rift? *No!* (The victory at Icewing Rift was Vyranoth's, but she would not have won without Fyrakk's timely intervention.)

Speaking of the Frozenheart, he wasn't about to tell *her* his plans. She was already Iridikron's favorite, and the last thing Fyrakk wanted was for *her* to come in and steal *his* glory.

So he instructed his Magmatalons to prepare for a night attack.

As the sun fell, Fyrakk roosted on a tall, lonely peak on the edge of the Emerald Plains, looking toward the citadel. Excitement bristled in his belly, making him feel as though he had swallowed a hive of angry wasps. Every so often, he twitched, barely able to contain himself.

"Mighty Incarnate!" Vazerrion, one of Fyrakk's wingleaders, landed at the Blazing One's side in a rush of hot wind. "The citadel lies quiet, and the majority of the patrols are on the ground. Even the Earthen Bulwark appears to have bedded down for the night."

Fyrakk cackled. "Excellent—we strike at moonset."

When the moons dipped below the horizon, Fyrakk and two of his battalions took wing, flying by starlight. In the distance, heavy clouds hung low over the Obsidian Citadel, their bellies bright with the light reflected from Neltharion's forges. Tonight, the Primalists would shatter the Aspects' western defenses. Iridikron would have Fyrakk to thank for it, too. Perhaps the Stonescaled would finally appreciate his strength and resourcefulness. Vyranoth was too principled, too cautious; only Fyrakk could unleash chaos over the Broodlands, leaving nothing but cinders in his wake. The Frozenheart would destroy only those she could not subdue. In Fyrakk's mind, that hesitancy made her feeble.

As they sailed closer, a war horn sounded in the night, a singular and lonely warning. Fyrakk grinned. Adrenaline punched through his veins, brilliant and hot. Magma sizzled between his teeth. Today, he would make the black and red dragonflights bleed. They would watch their precious queen tumble from the skies before a new day dawned.

He hadn't thought to take the enemy completely unawares—the Aspects had spies and scouts everywhere. No doubt the Incarnate and his battalions had been seen leaving their camps and flying north. Even so, the Earthen Bulwark would have to scramble to organize their forces. Fyrakk would feast on the chaos.

A second war horn blared out, closer this time. Fyrakk narrowed his eyes. The thought struck him almost a second too late: *That's not a dragon bugle . . . that's a* mortal *hunting horn.*

A whistling shadow shot past Fyrakk's ear, colliding with the primal dragon on Fyrakk's left wing. The dragon gurgled around the splinters of wood lodged in its throat, then dropped, lifeless. A second salvo hit one of Fyrakk's wingleaders, and a third dragon shrieked as a javelin pierced its wing.

"Climb!" Fyrakk roared, stretching his wings and vaulting himself higher. His Magmatalons on the front line didn't react quickly enough—a dark volley of javelins screamed from the jungles below, shattering skulls, puncturing guts, and dousing the fiery wings of more than fifty dragons at once.

Fury bubbled in Fyrakk's veins as the rest of his forces gained altitude. He would *destroy* these insects for their audacity. How *dare* they interfere with an Incarnate's plans!

"Burn the forest!" Fyrakk shouted into the skies. "Burn them *all*!"

He dived, leading the charge, building up a powerful glut of fire in his chest. A third horn sounded, but the timbre of this one wasn't a warning. It was a *challenge*.

Nearly a hundred red dragons burst from the trees, armor gleaming, forms silhouetted against the citadel's burning skies. At their head was Cristalstrasz, flightleader of the Ruby Flamebringers, a powerful brute who had killed more Primalists than Fyrakk had numbers for. Fyrakk's scouts had not informed him that Cristalstrasz was positioned to the south, too, but no matter. All would die in primal flame.

"Come, then!" Fyrakk roared, answering the dragonflights' challenge with his own. With a powerful thrash of his wings, he sent twisting columns of fire toward his enemies. The reds maneuvered around them, undeterred, and fell upon his Magmatalons. Fyrakk thought he spotted a glimpse of crimson and gold on the front line, but it winked out in a burst of cinders.

Alexstrasza, he thought. *Good! Now watch as I dismantle your flight, limb by limb!*

Fyrakk had always taken to the business of killing with glee. He grabbed a red out of the sky and sank his teeth into the creature's unnaturally long neck. Its bones snapped under the pressure of his jaws. Dropping it, he darted forward and slammed into a pack of five, shocking them with a burst of heat. Not even the dragons' armor and scales could reflect an Incarnate's flames, and their delicate wing membranes caught fire. Their raw screams were a melody to Fyrakk's ears. The sweet scent of their charred flesh filled his nostrils. They tumbled toward the ground, snatched from the air by their comrades. Ruby light ensconced the fallen, healing their wounds.

No matter. Fyrakk had the numbers. He would delight in tormenting them a second time.

Two large reds rushed at him. Grinning, Fyrakk leapt toward the first one and feinted left, dodging its first attack. The second red was on Fyrakk in an instant, hooking its front talons into the big muscle near his shoulder. Pain sparked through the Incarnate's body, but he reveled in it. With one powerful twist of his back, Fyrakk flipped over, surprising the red. He seized the dragon in his powerful wings and yanked it against his torso. The red struggled, unable to break free.

"That was a *mistake*," he said with a wild laugh.

Together, they plummeted through the air, slamming into a scrum of dragons below. Bones broke. Skulls cracked. Armor shattered. Nine dragons fell in a storm of thrashing wings and talons. Howls of pain and terror lit up the sky and set Fyrakk's heart aflame. He dug his powerful back talons into the red's abdomen and ripped, gutting it easily. Then, Fyrakk kicked the red away, leaving his prey to break upon the rocks below.

"The Broodlands will *burn*," Fyrakk raged, opening his wings and beating them powerfully, shooting back up into the skies. He basked in the heat of the bloodshed.

This was all Fyrakk wanted.

This was what he lived for—the *fight*.

His battlefield was chaos; the Blazing One cared little for strategy. He found Iridikron tedious and Vyranoth dull; instead, Fyrakk lost himself in the pulse of the battle, relishing the sight of every red dragon he struck from the sky. He dipped and twisted around his enemies, using hot air currents to send them into death spirals, superheating the dragons' armor and punching molten metal past their scales, setting all the skies alight. Perhaps the black dragonflight's armor was effective against a primal dragon, but Fyrakk tore through it as easily as he might a whelp's scales.

It was *glorious*. He hoped Alexstrasza watched the masterpiece of violence he was painting with her precious flight, sending dragon after dragon to their death. Unlike Vyranoth, Fyrakk did not cower behind the lines of the dragons who followed him. No, he plunged into battle alongside his soldiers. His dragons took strength from Fyrakk's martial zeal. Together, they were an unstoppable brute force, raining fire and chaos down upon their enemies.

From the middle of the Ruby Flamebringers' line, Cristalsrasz trumpeted the retreat, falling back toward the citadel.

"Will you run, then?" Fyrakk said, his laughter nipping at their tails. "Fine! Admit the elements are greater than your precious Order—"

Before he could finish, a battle shout echoed from behind Fyrakk's forces. The Incarnate turned in the air, hardly surprised to see Neltharion's favorite little one-eyed wingleader, Levarian, leading a battalion of black dragons against the Primalist rear guard.

"Strike the Magmatalons from the sky," Levarian shouted to his battalion, "but leave the Incarnate to me!"

"Ha!" Fyrakk shouted. "I should like to see you try, whelp!"

Levarian tucked his wings against his body and dived toward the Incarnate. With a grin, Fyrakk sucked a greedy breath into his lungs. The flames along his spine blazed brighter as he loosed a torrent of fire at the black wingleader. He had watched his breath melt the very scales off dragons' hides. Nothing could survive such heat.

But Levarian burst through the flames untouched, his scales, wings, and armor glittering with arcane magic. Shocked, Fyrakk drew in a gasp, almost choking on his own breath. It burned in his gullet. The wingleader fell upon the Incarnate, tearing away some of Fyrakk's magma-hardened scales. Pain oozed from the wounds.

"You can't burn me, Fyrakk," the wingleader said, so softly that Fyrakk almost couldn't hear the words.

"I can still tear out your throat," Fyrakk said with a roar. He twisted and tried to grab Levarian, but the wingleader was faster, propelling himself out of range of Fyrakk's wings and talons. As Levarian dodged Fyrakk's second attack, a blaze of crimson scales swooped in. The red dragon slashed one of the Incarnate's wing membranes, then darted away in a blaze of sparks.

The two dragons teamed up on Fyrakk, diving and ducking his attacks. Both Levarian and the red—Fyrakk thought he recognized Alexstrasza's favorite champion, Bojsanz—had heat-shielded scales and wings. They used quick, ruthless strikes, never letting Fyrakk get too close or land a blow.

Furious, Fyrakk gathered his wings against his chest then spread them wide, sending a localized explosion through the air. He knocked the dragons away, sending them careening toward the world below.

With a growl, the Incarnate hovered aloft, getting his bearings. He'd been so distracted by the Aspects' little gnats, he hadn't realized that the black dragonflight had pushed his forces to the southern edge of the Obsidian Citadel.

He vented a hot breath through his nostrils, ignoring the ember of trepidation that smoldered in his chest. Why had the Earthen Bulwark pushed the Primalists *closer* to the citadel? Perhaps they thought they could win an advantage if they brought the Primalists to the artillery on the citadel's walls? Bah! He could kill an entire battalion of drakonid in one breath.

Fyrakk had only seen the citadel from a distance. The place was far larger than he'd imagined, sprawling across the westernmost edge of the Black Mountains and using the natural caldera beneath the rock to fuel its forges. Even from here, Fyrakk could sense the lava moving beneath the stone.

Hundreds of dragons flew between Fyrakk and the citadel's walls—the Obsidian Guard took wing, rising over the ramparts, while the Ruby Flamebringers rallied behind them. Two units of Malygos's Spellscales took up the rear guard.

Odd, none of the reports he'd heard had mentioned the blue dragonflight's presence at the citadel. No matter—even if Fyrakk had lost a third of his forces on the advance, the Primalists still outnumbered Alexstrasza's forces.

The Obsidian Guard charged. As black dragons slammed into Fyrakk's line, the Incarnate surged forward on a wave of boiling air. It desiccated the guards' wing membranes, drawing the moisture from their flesh. The Primals tore into the black dragons. With a roar, Fyrakk joined them. And in that blaze of battle, Fyrakk almost didn't see the stars twinkle and shift far overhead.

Almost.

A hammer of Onyx Reavers dropped through the skies. Fyrakk trumpeted twice—a warning. His primal dragons had seen this maneuver before at Wyrmrest Temple and Cinderfrost Vale, but it was a difficult formation to counter. The black dragons would hit their marks moving so fast they could break the primal dragons' armored backs, knock them senseless, and smash their bodies against the ground. The attack was almost impossible to dodge, especially at night.

Superheating the air beneath his wings, Fyrakk launched himself at the oncoming Reavers. Relying on his upward momentum, he spiraled in the air to draw the heat around his body. Just before the Reavers struck him, he whipped his wings open wide, creating a thermal explosion. The eruption rocked the black dragons, sending them tumbling through the air, head-over-tail. Those who managed to keep their wings fled before the Incarnate, but not fast enough. He fell upon two at once, tearing the wings from their backs and leaping toward a third.

He did not hit his target. Another black dragon struck Fyrakk from behind, sinking its talons into his hide. Fyrakk blasted the fires along his spine brighter, catching the black dragon in the face. It roared in pain but held on. A second black dragon attacked from his right. Fyrakk rolled and dived to shake off his attackers, then banked back toward the Primalists' lines.

The Primalists still made forward progress, but the Obsidian Guard proved to be much more resilient than the reds. They were slower but nearly impossible to kill thanks to the heavy armor and tight formations. The Earthen Bulwark kept pushing the Primalists closer to the citadel, too, placing them within range of the drakonid's ballistae.

Out the corner of his eye, Fyrakk spotted another flash of vermillion scales and shimmering rubies. He turned, but the Dragon Queen disappeared into a shower of sparks.

"Alexstrasza!" he roared at the Dragon Queen. "Craven! Meet me in battle, else I will slay every dragon in the Waking Shores!"

But Alexstrasza was gone.

With a growl, Fyrakk plunged back into the fray, killing anything and anyone who came within reach. Dragons fell from the skies. His. Theirs. Screams cracked off the Black Mountains. Death filled his nostrils and rang in his ears. He saw a third flash of the Dragon Queen, then a fourth—she appeared on the front lines for just a moment, using her cleansing flames to heal the Obsidian Guard.

Was Alexstrasza so cowardly as to refuse to meet him on the field of battle?

Hmph. If he could not stir the Dragon Queen to action by killing, perhaps he could threaten the very Obsidian Citadel itself. He wasn't far from its gates now, perhaps a few hundred wing-lengths, no more. As he hovered over the smooth volcanic hillsides of the Black Mountains, he sensed the burning blood that flowed beneath the world's crust. It would not listen to Fyrakk the way it listened to Iridikron—the Stonescaled could manipulate molten rock as if it were mud or clay. Fyrakk couldn't force the lava to form mountains, but he could coax its quiet heart into violent volatility.

Calling out to his forces for support, Fyrakk began to channel the fires in the earth below. The Primalists rallied around him, defending him as he drew upon the power of the elements. A tendril of fire twisted from the rock, reaching for the Blazing One, sinuous and small. A second tongue of fire stretched forth, only to be joined by a third, a fourth, then a *multitude*. The flames twisted and writhed around the Incarnate in the skies. They roared with the voices of a hundred dragons, lighting up the lands for fifty wing-lengths in every direction.

Fyrakk gorged himself on the flames. The heat from the earth built up in his spine and lungs, augmenting his power. His flaming horns blazed brighter. His wings burned blood red. Fyrakk roared and the earth answered. Stone cracked, then melted under the heat. Lava pools formed around the citadel, growing wider by the breath.

Fyrakk was the element of fire, unleashed. He reveled in it, in this brilliant, burning promise of destruction and death.

All his pain and exhaustion faded into the flames. Today, Alexstrasza the Life-Binder would fall, and the Broodlands would fall with her.

In the distance, the black dragons trumpeted. Frantic. Some dived toward the earth, perhaps to stop the citadel's foundations from melting in the heat that Fyrakk brought to bear. The other primal dragons fled from him, too, as the air grew so hot it hissed against his scales.

Fyrakk threw back his head and laughed. "Come, Alexstrasza!" he said with a roar. "Fight me, or all you have wrought shall *burn*!"

Through the swirling flames, Fyrakk saw a shimmer of ruby scales, but the Dragon Queen did not answer his challenge. *Fine.* He would blast a hole in the citadel's flank, then!

"The queen!" one of the Primalists shouted. Warning bugles erupted on the front lines. "It's the Dragon Queen!"

A glint of gold caught his eye, plummeting through the skies overhead.

Fyrakk glanced up. He saw a flash of talons first—he ducked, but not fast enough. Alexstrasza raked her talons across his snout, shattering his channel. The great inferno around him collapsed, fizzling into cinders on the wind. He snarled; she flipped in the air, kicking him under the jaw and sending bright sparks popping across his vision. His fangs nicked his tongue, filling his mouth with the taste of blood.

With a husky chuckle, Alexstrasza folded her wings and plummeted toward the citadel's gates.

"There you are, Alexstrasza!" Fyrakk roared, spitting blood. The Primalists parted in terror as Fyrakk charged forward, swooping after the queen. She opened her wings before she hit the ground, flying fast for the citadel's walls. He couldn't let her get back across friendly lines.

Bolts from the ballistae on the citadel's walls whistled past him. Fyrakk ducked beneath them, and with a mighty thrust of his wings, he leapt at the Dragon Queen. He feinted left but sprang right. He caught Alexstrasza in a dodge, jaws snapping at her armored neck. He could crush her throat in a single bite. He missed.

Alexstrasza growled, a low reverb that caught him in the gut. She swung her head around, bludgeoning him in the cheek and eye socket. Pain exploded through the hinge of his jaw. Her horn slashed through his hide. With a massive sweep of her wings, she kicked him back.

"A decent hit," Fyrakk said with a hiss. The two dragons spiraled around each other, though warm air currents lifted Fyrakk faster, higher. "But you'll have to do better than that to defeat me. Do you think you can win, *Dragon Queen*?"

"Against you? *Obviously,*" she said, but the timbre of her voice sounded different. Deeper, almost. Fyrakk hadn't noticed a change in her voice at the parley.

"Hmph! Let us see if you remember what I taught you. How to fight like a *real* dragon!" Fyrakk snapped his wings forward, setting the air between them aflame. He dived through the fire, taking Alexstrasza by surprise and slamming into her left flank. He tore off a panel of her chest armor with his talons, leaving light scores in her shoulder muscles. The scent of blood hit Fyrakk's snout. A faint flash of bluish light sparkled along her scales. *Another shield?* Fyrakk wondered, flaring his nostrils.

Alexstrasza flipped over in the air, sinking her talons into Fyrakk's belly. The Incarnate howled in pain, struggling to keep them both aloft and scrabbling at her chest with his forelimbs.

"There's only one problem, Fyrakk," the Dragon Queen said, her voice growing rougher, deeper. She tugged him closer. A flash of purple fire burst from her golden eyes. "I am not Alexstrasza."

Fyrakk gasped. "Malygos!"

The Aspect grinned, folding his wings and diving backward, dragging Fyrakk with him. As they plummeted through the skies, the red color wicked off Malygos's scales, revealing their true azure gleam. Fyrakk thrashed in Malygos's grip, but the blue Aspect held him firm. With a roar, he sent out a broiling burst of heat, but the blue Aspect dragged him down in a blaze of fire.

With a sweep of his wings, Malygos opened an enormous, shimmering portal below them. Fyrakk shrieked in rage, kicking, biting, slashing. *Falling.* They hit the portal's surface and tumbled through it. Cold shocked Fyrakk's senses, dousing his bright flames. For a single heartbeat, he went numb, surrounded by silence.

Just before he started to panic, the world roared back. Fyrakk collided with solid ground, tumbling head-over-tail until he scraped to a stop.

"Not my most elegant portal exit," a voice said through a haze. "But it *is* rather difficult when your cargo is trying to kill you."

Fyrakk scrambled to his feet, catching himself on one wing as his legs gave out on him. He rested on a round platform in a darkened cavern. Pale light filtered through the room. Nozdormu, Ysera, and Malygos stood on the platform before him, just out of range of attack. The Aspects regarded him with curious expressions.

Behind them, three massive titan-made machines reached down from the ceiling. Each machine clutched an enormous glowing orb in its claws. In the shadows, the Incarnate thought he could see the titan-forged staring at him, but the world swam before his eyes. He could barely make out other platforms and ledges in the room, but what they were used for, Fyrakk could not guess.

"Welcome to the Vault of the Incarnates, Fyrakk," Nozdormu said in a measured tone. "You're just in time."

"What is this?" Fyrakk said, trying to step forward. A wave of vertigo hit him, sending him sprawling to the ground. For several seconds, he couldn't tell what direction was up. He winced. "What . . . what did you *do* to me?"

"Ah, I remember my first portal," Malygos said with a chuckle. "It takes the body a few hours to adjust to the disorientation, but the effects are not permanent. Usually."

"I will . . . kill you for this," Fyrakk said. "Malygos . . ."

"No, dear cousin," Ysera said as she stepped forward. "You will sleep a deep, dreamless sleep. Forgive me when I say I hope we never meet again."

Fyrakk scrambled to sit up. "Ysera, wait—"

The Dreamer drew a deep breath, then exhaled a green cloud that smelled of sweet summer grass and wildflowers. Fyrakk tried to back away, but it descended upon him like a thick fog, sneaking into his nostrils and filling his lungs.

In three breaths, his eyelids began to droop.

"Goodbye, Fyrakk," Nozdormu said as golden sands danced across the Incarnate's sight. "This is where your time ends."

"VYRANOTH!"

The voice tore the Frozenheart from sleep. She lifted her head. A bolt of fear zinged through her body and jolted her awake. The Incarnate slept inside the great glacier, encouraging it to grow and expand as she slept.

Even if it took her a hundred years, she would cover all the Reach in ice and lay Neltharion's mountains low. She would see Raszageth freed; and once the Storm-Eater rejoined her in the skies, they would hold Alexstrasza to account for her crimes against dragonkind.

"Vyranoth," the voice said, echoing through the icy halls. This time, she recognized it as Razviik's. "There is news from the south!"

"I'm here," Vyranoth said, emerging from one of the many caverns inside the glacier. Razviik hurried down the corridor toward her, panting, so panicked that he stumbled and slid on the ice.

"It is unlike you to be so careless," Vyranoth said, helping him up from the floor with a wing talon. "What is wrong?"

"There was a battle," he said, gasping, "over the Obsidian Citadel. Fyrakk . . . the Aspects have captured Fyrakk."

Vyranoth drew a sharp breath, stepping back from Razviik as if the news had burned her. A tremor raced through her jaw. She clamped her mouth shut, unwilling to show any emotion or reaction. *No,* she thought. *No, the Dragon Queen can't take another one of us from the skies! Fyrakk, you fool, what have you done? Did I not warn you of the dangers?*

Would the Aspects lock Fyrakk away in a prison of stone, too? Deprive him of the skies, of the very air that fed the great fires of his heart? Vyranoth had never been close to the Blazing One—they were as opposite as the very elements they embodied—but his loss cut her to the quick, dredging up the feelings she had experienced after Raszageth's loss. The glacier groaned and cracked, expanding as it fed on her fury. The floor trembled, and the temperature grew so cold that even Razviik trembled.

Long ago, Alexstrasza had turned her tail on Vyranoth; now, did she think the Frozenheart would stand by while her flights stole everything the Incarnate held dear? No, *no*. Vyranoth would call an age of ice down upon the Broodlands, waging a ceaseless war until her comrades were freed.

It had taken Vyranoth centuries to find her place in this new world—she would not allow the Dragon Queen to take it from her now. Not after all the cracks Alexstrasza had already put in her heart.

"Vyranoth?" he asked, voice tremulous.

"Do you know what happened?" Vyranoth asked quietly.

"I have reports from the survivors."

"Good," Vyranoth said, stalking past him. "We fly for Harrowsdeep at once."

PART FIVE

A Frozen Heart

F yrakk's last battle became known as the Battle of Flamesfall, commemorating Malygos's heroic plunge through the skies over the Obsidian Citadel with the Incarnate. In addition to the loss of Fyrakk, five hundred Primalists were slain that night, caught between the dual flanks of Neltharion's Earthen Bulwark and the Obsidian Guard.

Up to that point, it was the single greatest loss of life during the war. Three days later, the green dragonflight expelled the remainder of Fyrakk's forces from Stonefray Falls. Vyranoth's battalions remained rooted in the Reach, along with her ever-expanding glacier.

For a time, we saw neither Vyranoth nor Iridikron on the battlefield. The Frozenheart left enough of her forces in the Reach to defend her glacier, which continues to creep closer to Raszageth's prison to this day. Alexstrasza and her reds regularly place barriers of fire to slow the glacier's progress, and Neltharion redirects the magma flow to heat the ground beneath it, but the glacier moves on, fed day and night by Vyranoth's frost dragons. It now covers half the Reach.

Roughly fifty years ago, Vyranoth emerged from seclusion. She sent the shattered fragments of a dragon figurine to Alexstrasza—the Dragon Queen told me it was a gift she gave to Vyranoth during one of the Frozenheart's last forays into the Broodlands, one carved from never-melting ice. Alexstrasza gave the shards to the scalesmiths of the black dragonflight to see if the figurine could be repaired; it could not, but they reconstructed it by filling the figurine's cracks with molten gold.

When the Frozenheart rejoined the battlefield, she did not return to the front in the western Reach. Instead, she established camps in the eastern Dragonwilds to assail Thaldraszus and the eastern Reach.

The Incarnates' priorities had shifted: They sought to free their imprisoned brethren at all costs. However, Thaldraszus and the Vault of the Incarnates are not easy targets to siege—both are protected on the eastern flank by one of the tallest mountain ranges in northern Kalimdor, one whose heights are matched only by the Storm Peaks. Vyranoth turned her attention north.

Swiftly, Vyranoth managed to capture the Veiled Ossuary, using the halls of our honored dead as a military base for her Primalist zealots. The Primalists defiled those revered halls, disrupting tombs and desecrating the resting places of champions who had fallen in the war.

Alexstrasza tried to parley with the Frozenheart, offering an exchange of territories. Vyranoth refused, saying there would be no mercy for the Dragon Queen nor her flights, not until Fyrakk and Raszageth were released from imprisonment.

Understandably, Alexstrasza refused.

From their position at the Ossuary, Vyranoth sent Oxoria and her brood north to try to claim Raszageth's prison at Froststone Vault, forcing Neltharion and Alexstrasza to fight on two fronts. They faced Oxoria in the east and the longtime veteran of the Reach campaign, Mithruz, in the west. Neltharion countered this strategy by striking at both from the Life-Binder Conservatory in the west and from the Talonlord's Perch in the east.

Meanwhile, Vyranoth took her forces to Algeth'ar Academy, where Malygos and I met her with an allied force. The academy is the northern gateway to Thaldraszus—were it to be captured, the Primalists would have an ideal position to fly on Tyrhold, Valdrakken, and the Vault of the Incarnates.

The Primalists, however, were not equipped to fight mages and Timewalkers; Vyranoth struggled to take the academy from us, especially as the blue dragonflight designed more complex arcane maneuvers, allowing them to flank an enemy and move flight units between strategic points with ease. We bronzes discovered how to reverse wounds with time magic, making our flight hardier and more durable in the air. Shielded by the blues, we faced the Primalists on the front lines, slowing their advance by both magical and martial means.

Hundreds of Primalists fell from the skies. We suffered our own losses, too; but unless the Primalists could strike a dragon dead in a single blow, they would return to the skies in moments. Our forces weren't immortal, but five Primalists fall for every one of ours.

For many years, Vyranoth was circumspect in her strategy. She never appeared on the battlefield, preferring to watch the outcomes from behind her lines. When the flights frustrated her attempts in both the Reach and Thaldraszus, she turned to attrition tactics to wear us down. Vyranoth raided the Emerald Plains, slaughtering prey animals and burning vegetation. Primalist guerrillas ambushed our patrols. Our forces in the Reach were assailed night and day. Neltharion often says that "war never sleeps" in the Reach.

Later, more than a thousand dragons fell at the Battle of Emberfall, a desperate gambit to stop Oxoria's advance into Stormsunder Crater. It was the deadliest battle in our history, claiming nearly two hundred lives from the black dragonflight's Ironscales, Earthen Bulwark, and Onyx Reavers alone. It was the first match in a scaling offensive, one that has only become more bitter and cold with the passing years.

On the western front, the red dragonflight also contends with an increasingly violent force of djaradin half-giants. For the last few years, the djaradin have pushed east into the Waking Shores, seeking to capture the Scalecracker Peaks as their own. Alexstrasza has commanded our elder drakes to deal with the djaradin incursion, and thus far, they have managed to keep the threat at bay.

Still, the war has gone on far too long; our flights are stretched thin, and with each passing year, they only grow more tired, more heartsick, more defeated.

Our kind fear for their lives each day, but I have begun to fear more for the day that lies beyond this conflict, and for how this age of war has shaped us.

CHAPTER TWENTY

LAILASTRASZA LANDED ON A CLIFF JUST OUTSIDE THE Life-Binder Conservatory, bristling under the shadow of night. Below her, thick bands of smoke billowed from a thin canyon. The trees burned and crackled, set alight by a sizable band of Qalashi djaradin dragon-hunters.

The red curled her lip. This was the third time in as many days that the djaradin had attempted to advance into the canyon. Now they burned trees along the borders, perhaps intending to lure the red dragons to their position. It was a common tactic, as the djaradin had learned the red dragonflight would not abide the senseless destruction of life. The Qalashi did not employ stealth tactics—they were *always* looking for a fight.

The djaradin had inhabited the Waking Shores as far back as any remembered, but over the last century or so, their tribes had become increasingly hostile, capitalizing on the flights' war in the Reach. The Qalashi in particular killed black and red dragons with reckless abandon, stole ballistae from the front lines, and actively tried to compromise the Obsidian Citadel's walls. The young reds worked under the direction of Saristrasz, the queen's majordomo, to defend the Broodlands' western flank from non-Primalist threats.

As the war dragged on, more drakes took on responsibilities usually entrusted to dragons. The young adults and elder drakes trained new drakonid regiments, assisted healers, worked the forges, educated whelplings, and stood guard at the borders. The flightleaders would not send drakes, or even near-adults to the front lines to fight full-grown primal dragons—Alexstrasza had forbidden that—so the younger generation contributed to the Broodlands' defenses as best they could.

Eight other dragons cruised overhead, their silhouettes shadowing the stars. Saristrasz himself had given Lailastrasza command of this patrol. The young red had been proud to accept; Lailastrasza was happy to do anything to offset her brother's crimes, desperate to be seen as loyal to Alexstrasza and the red dragonflight.

The flights hated Talinstrasz for what he had done, and one hundred years had done nothing to soften their hearts. The reds were ashamed one of their own had caused so much suffering and death; for no one could say how much longer the barriers would have lasted, had he and his comrades not shattered the mana crystal inside the Azure Archives. By now, the specter of betrayal haunted every flight—Sirigosa was so reviled among the blues that her name had been struck from their mouths, never to be said again. Neltharion's strategy for the Battle of

Emberfall had been compromised by a Shadowscale working as a double-agent for Oxoria; bronzes tried to turn back time to give the Primalists the advantage; and once, a green and red had conspired to kidnap eggs from the Ruby Life Pools.

The war had turned so many dragons against one another—brother against sister, friend against friend. It was so much pointless suffering and death! So many lives wasted on the altar of other dragons' hatreds and ambitions. How many Primalists would have to die before they saw fit to withdraw from the Broodlands and leave the dragonflights in peace?

Aymestrasz, Lailastrasza's second-in-command and longtime friend, landed beside her on the cliff. He scented the air, wrinkling his snout. "Ah, the unmistakable stench of a djaradin war band—smoke, sulfur, and half-giant sweat. I believe this is what obtuseness must smell like—have they not learned that charging up a canyon *full* of red dragons will only end in disaster for them?"

"They brought magmammoths this time," Lailastrasza said, gesturing to the large, char-colored pachyderms that rumbled up the canyon, setting everything alight with their tusks. "That tactic will obviously turn the tide."

The djaradin resembled the titan-forged with their two-legged frames and wingless backs, but that was where all resemblances ended: The djaradin were half-giants, massive, hulking beasts strong enough to grapple dragons and pull them from flight. Their inky, deep-blue skin was covered in markings that danced with living flames. But the thing that struck Lailastrasza most about them was the cruelty in their eyes—like the Primalists, they thrived on their hatred for the dragonflights.

"We only have one blue tonight," Lailastrasza said, mulling over their options. "Adugos could drop a wall of ice at the mouth of the canyon, but with that many magmammoths, I worry the djaradin would charge straight through it."

"Perhaps they *were* employing some strategy by bringing magmammoths along," Aymestrasz said with a chuckle.

"Don't give them too much credit," Lailastrasza said with a toothy grin. "Let's have Ravia and Obezion send landslides into the canyons—that will smother the fires, while the magmammoths will stampede and stomp their own masters to death. We can pick off any survivors who emerge on the northwestern side."

"Excellent," Aymestrasz said with a dark chuckle. "You'll be a fine flightleader someday, Laila, you know that?"

Lailastrasza froze, feeling a talon of fear stab her chest. Several of her older friends had already been called to the front lines, and if the war didn't end soon, the flightleaders would call Aymestrasz to the Reach, too.

Aymestrasz was a year or two older than she, taller at the shoulder and longer from snout to tail. Over the last few decades, he'd grown into his ungainly wingspan and added muscle to his frame. Elegant horns now crowned his head. Aymestrasz wasn't a dragon grown—at least, not yet—but he *had* started to look and fly like one. The flightleaders had already pointed him out during training exercises, making notes. She had little doubt that he would join the Ruby Flamebringers, the red battalion directly under the Dragon Queen's command. She was proud of him.

But she was terrified for him, too.

Every red and black dragon in the Waking Shores knew the horrors of the war in the Reach. Mithruz and Oxoria were cruel, capable leaders, willing to sacrifice any number of lives necessary to free the Storm-Eater from her prison. The black and red dragonflights had barely hung on at the Battle of Emberfall, felling so many Primalists that Oxoria had been forced to withdraw for a season.

Lailastrasza slept little these days, plagued by nightmares of standing beside a pyre with Aymestrasz's body upon it, or Rygos's, or Atyrannus's. Or Aspects be good, maybe even her own *brother,* as much as she would like to see him rot in the citadel for the rest of his days. Every time she closed her eyes, Lailastrasza lit her friends' pyres and watched them burn, whispering their names as their cinders rose into a moonless sky. She woke every morning with heavy wings and an aching heart. Yet the Primalists continued to assault the Broodlands, relentless, unending.

Lailastrasza hadn't told anyone about her dreams, but her friends could always read the emotions on her face. She had never been able to hide it—unlike her brother, she had very little guile.

"Why do you look so sad, brave heart?" Aymestrasz asked with a soft chuckle. "Wait, don't tell me—do I smell as bad as the djaradin?" He pretended to sniff himself, then grimaced.

She let out a little laugh. "No, it's not you, I just . . ." But she trailed off, unable to say the words aloud. The pause felt awkward, almost juvenile in the way it shouldered between them.

At last, he said, "You're worried Saristrasz or Cristalstrasz will send me to the front."

"No," Lailastrasza said with a tiny shake of her head, but even she could taste the lie on her lips. "No, *no*. It would be an honor to serve the flights on the front lines, and there is nothing I would rather you do than fight to protect the Broodlands."

"Laila," he said, giving her a light nudge with his wing, "we both have a little more growing up to do before we can go to the front, don't you think?"

She didn't want to admit she was afraid—not to die, perhaps, but to watch her friends and loved ones suffer the horrors of war. So many had been lost! And yet there seemed to be no end to the violence in sight.

"One day, the flightleaders may not have a choice," Lailastrasza said softly. "What will we do if Iridikron emerges from Harrowsdeep and decides to siege the citadel? He and his legions of Rockfuries lie in wait . . . I don't know if we could face him while Vyranoth assaults us in the northeast."

Unlike hotheaded Fyrakk, Vyranoth had proven impossible to capture. She stayed off the battlefield, directing her maneuvers and strategies from afar. Lailastrasza could not believe that the kindly dragon who had played hide-and-seek with her as a whelp could have such a monstrously cruel heart, going so far as to turn her own brother against her. Lailastrasza would never forgive Vyranoth for that, for shattering what little family Lailastrasza had and for putting a dark mark on her bloodline.

However, in the wake of her brother's betrayal, Lailastrasza had realized that her family was so much bigger than one brother—it had grown to encompass her friends, her flight. She would do anything to protect them.

"Take heart, Iridikron would never leave Harrowsdeep undefended, or perhaps even at all," Aymestrasz replied, giving her a cheeky grin. "Come now, this isn't the Lailastrasza I know. The heat of battle will lift your spirits. Let us make quick work of these brutes and chase them from our territories!"

"All right," Lailastrasza said, returning his smile.

They leapt skyward. Lailastrasza sent Aymestrasz to the south cliffs with Ravia and two reds, while she went north with Obezion, the blue, Adugos, and one green, Filora.

The drakes gathered on the eastern end of the canyon. "Adugos, Filora," Lailastrasza said under her breath, watching the djaradin move toward their position. "Once the magmammoths stampede, you'll be in charge of putting out any lingering flames. We don't want the fires to reach the conservatory, but take care and don't risk your lives."

The blue and the green dipped their heads.

Obezion sank his talons into the stone beside her. "On your command, then," he said. Across the canyon, his sister Ravia crept into position, careful to stay hidden in the shadows.

Below them, the djaradin advanced, wary. Lailastrasza counted ten half-giants in total and five magmammoths. Two djaradin took point, setting the canyon alight with their torches, alert for dangers. She did not see Warlord Sargha or the so-called Fleshrender among their ranks tonight, which was an unexpected boon.

As the first djaradin stepped below them, Lailastrasza lifted her head and trumpeted once, signaling the attack.

A shout went up from the djaradin. Obezion punched his talons into the cliff, fracturing the stone. A fissure tore across the cliff's face for almost ten wing-lengths, cracking like thunder. For a heartbeat, there was silence; then the rock shattered and slid down the steep slope, speeding toward the djaradin war party. The southern side of the canyon collapsed seconds after, sending a mountainside crashing into the canyon floor. Another terrifying *crack* echoed through the night. A spire of rock sheared off and fell, blocking the path forward.

Screams tore through the gorge. The rockslide roared as it smashed down, crushing the vanguard. Boulders bounced like whelps' toys. Flaming trees tumbled through the rubble. The magmammoths shrieked, scrambling backward as they were struck on all sides. One stumbled sideways, crushing its master as the rubble buried them both. Djaradin clambered out of the way, but the shattered stone swallowed them whole.

Clouds of dust, smoke, and searing embers billowed into the air. On the southern cliffs, Ravia cackled in delight. Her peals of laughter rang over the chaos.

"I see my sister is enjoying herself," Obezion said with a grin.

"It's a good day when we can cull the djaradin's ranks," Lailastrasza said, and the black drake nodded. "Come on, let's chase off any survivors."

...

ON THE FLIGHT BACK to Valdrakken, Lailastrasza quit her friends with great reluctance. She'd made a habit of visiting Talinstrasz in the dungeons of the Obsidian Citadel, but she had been too busy to visit in a full clutch of moons. On top of her regular duties, she had volunteered to mentor a few young drakes who were interested in becoming djaradin-hunters.

Even Adugos, who was usually so indifferent and withdrawn, told Lailastrasza to abandon her brother for one evening and join the drakes at the Ruby Feast.

"Talin's not going anywhere," Aymestrasz said with a hearty chuckle.

"In fact," Ravia said with a giggle, "he hasn't gone anywhere in about a hundred years!" Obezion snorted at his sister's remark, and Lailastrasza felt a little wriggle of jealousy in her heart. What she would give to fight alongside Talinstrasz in defense of the Broodlands, like Ravia and Obezion did!

"Come on," Filora said, swooping around Lailastrasza and performing a little spin in the air. "You can go tomorrow!"

"I have guard duty at the Ruby Life Pools tomorrow," Lailastrasza said with a smile. "And whelp-brained as he might be, Talin's still my brother. Besides, he'll enjoy hearing about how we brought a mountainside down on the djaradin's heads."

Ravia cackled and trilled. "I bet the djaradin won't come up that canyon again!"

"They will," Adugos said with a sigh. "And they'll bring Chargath with them next time."

"Ooh, Chargath!" Ravia said, wiggling her fore-talons at the blue. "Bane of Scales, Terror of the Waking Shores!"

"Think he can dodge a rock?" Obezion said drily.

"Not if it's bigger than him!" Ravia said.

Aymestrasz rolled his eyes. "Are you really going to leave me to deal with them alone, Laila? I need help when they're like . . . *this*." He gestured to their comrades with a smirk.

"Wait until we get to the wine," Ravia crowed. "We'll have Adugos dancing about the Roasted Ram!"

"Unlikely," the blue said flatly.

"My heart goes with you, but I should visit my brother," Lailastrasza said, performing an aerial halt with Aymestrasz. The two siblings cruised past them, waving, with Adugos close on their tails.

"Before I go," Aymestrasz said, "I want to be sure that you know that nobody blames you for what Talin did, and no one would blame you if you left him to rot for the rest of his long life, *alone*."

"Some do," Lailastrasza said, thinking of the reds who still shunned her to this day. "I have days I never want to see him again . . . but then I remember our Aspect's wise words: *If something lives, it can change and grow.* I want to believe that's true with all my heart."

"He does not deserve you," Aymestrasz said.

"Aymestrasz, let's go," Obezion shouted. "Else they'll be out of cakes by the time we arrive!"

"I will see you on the morrow, Laila," Aymestrasz said, lifting one forefoot in farewell. Lailastrasza smiled and waved, wishing she would be flying the rest of the way to Valdrakken by his side.

Instead, she turned southwest, setting a course for the Obsidian Citadel. Even if he was a headstrong fool, Talinstrasz was still her brother. Nothing could change that. Not Order magic, not a difference of beliefs, not even his own monstrous choices. Many reds avoided her for being related to Talinstrasz, and still others disliked her for speaking to him. Lailastrasza understood their anger; after all, everyone had lost loved ones on the day the barriers fell . . . but she did not want to lose her brother as well.

As she flew closer, she realized the signal fires burned along the Black Mountains—the citadel was on alert. Concerned, Lailastrasza flew faster. As she drew close to the ramparts, the Obsidian Scalesworn recognized her and waved her through. She glided past the great forges, surprised to find them abandoned. Where were the scalesmiths? Where were the drakonid? The citadel usually rang with the sounds of hammers day and night, but now its halls lay silent.

Anxiety swelled in her gut. She hurried into the citadel's depths, worried for her brother's safety. She hated the dungeons of the Obsidian Citadel and their dark, oppressive walls, but not as much as she hated the reasons her brother had spent more than a century here.

Black dragons rushed to and fro, too busy to stop and explain the situation to a red. Drakonid, too, shouted orders at one another. Lailastrasza descended to the lowest cellblock in the citadel, the one reserved for the dragons who had betrayed the Broodlands.

Lailastrasza smelled blood before she even reached the dungeons.

As she stepped into the cellblock, she gasped. Dried blood coated the stone floors. Shattered, gore-splattered black scales littered the room. Every cell in the room yawned open, their arcane wards *gone,* along with their occupants.

Lailastrasza's heart clattered against her ribs. Talinstrasz, Sirigosa, and their ilk weren't the only ones being held here—Ryzindormu, the Primalist double agent responsible for the fall of the Veiled Ossuary, had been three cells down from her brother. Zaethanus, the green who tried to destroy the Dream Portal, was around the corner; and Lyldora, the black dragon who had leaked the Shadowscales' plans to assassinate Mithruz, had been across the lane.

Two of the guards, Hemation and Sabria, spoke to a flightleader of the black dragonflight on the far end of the cellblock. Several blues examined the cells, talking in technical terms about magical theories that Lailastrasza did not understand. Tension made the air feel taut, almost as if it could snap and sizzle. Words echoed down the hallways, clipped and fast.

"Talinstrasz?" she whispered, easing forward. Her brother's cell was the third on the left, across from Sirigosa's. With a sob, she rushed to her brother's cell.

It was empty, save for his lingering scent. Lailastrasza felt light-headed, as if all the blood had drained from her head. Stumbling back, the red slumped, sitting on the ground.

Talinstrasz had left her. How many times would her brother break her heart? Had they not curled up together as whelps, promising to always protect each other? Through her hundreds—thousands!—of visits over the last one hundred years, she had hoped to have planted a seed of understanding in her brother's heart . . . but apparently, she was wrong.

Lailastrasza closed her eyes, swearing she would not cry.

Behind her, talons scraped against stone. Sabria sat beside the drake, her obsidian scales glittering in the low light. Lailastrasza had gotten to know all her brother's guards over the years, but she considered Sabria her friend. The black dragon treated her with kindness and respect, going so far as to fly to the Ruby Life Pools to update Lailastrasza on her brother's condition after he tried to gnaw his own foreleg off. They had shared meals and laughter, their losses and grief. If there was a silver lining to her brother's imprisonment, it was Sabria.

"What happened?" Lailastrasza asked, unable to look away from her brother's darkened cell.

"The Primalists mounted a small-scale rescue," Sabria said softly. "They turned several black drakonid against us, who then helped your brother and his comrades escape. Neltharion is . . . *questioning* the drakonid now. That's why the forges stand empty."

Questioning? Lailastrasza wondered, but she did not give voice to her thoughts. Everyone knew the Earth-Warder punished traitors severely.

"Was anyone hurt?" Lailastrasza asked.

"Two guards were killed," Sabria said. "Two others badly injured, and we cannot be sure if they will make it through the night."

A tremor started in Lailastrasza's legs, though she could not be sure if she shook in fear or fury. How many nights had she spent in the dungeons with Talinstrasz, talking and laughing, bringing him news of the outside world? While the black dragonflight had forbidden her from telling her brother anything about the Aspects' grand strategy, she could tell him about their victories and about her work fighting the djaradin.

Lailastrasza didn't want her brother to spend his life in a prison cell, bereft of sun and sky . . . but she *certainly* did not want him working for Vyranoth. Over the years, Talinstrasz's love for the Frozenheart had not dimmed. He spoke of her tenderly, almost like he might a mother. Had Vyranoth's operatives breached the citadel to help Talinstrasz escape? And if so, what further use did Vyranoth have for the drakes? Was bringing down the barrier and raining death upon the Broodlands not enough?

"Vyranoth must have a plan for them," Lailastrasza said, her voice trembling. "Else she would not risk a strike on the citadel."

"I don't know, my friend," Sabria replied with a sigh. "But we had nearly fifteen drakes imprisoned here, all of whom have fled. The Shadowscales are hunting for them now."

"Sabria!" the flightleader called, beckoning to the black dragon with one wing. "May I have a moment?"

"At once!" Sabria said, then turned back to the drake. "You may stay as long as you like, but I ask that you don't disturb your brother's cell for the time being."

"Of course," Lailastrasza said, looking at her brother's barren room. He hadn't many possessions of note.

Sirigosa's cell was a different matter—the blue had great stacks of books lining one wall, with spines as bright and varied as the flights themselves. Come to think of it, Sirigosa had seemed content to while away the hours in her cell, studying. Perhaps her choice of reading material would give Lailastrasza a clue as to why her brother had been freed.

Lailastrasza wandered inside, cocking her head sideways to read their titles.

"*Ley Line Mysteries: An Adept's Guide,*" she read under her breath, glancing at the cell door. There was a tome called *Time Weaving: A Treatise on Chronomancy* stacked atop a hefty volume called *The Arcane Labyrinth: Unlocking the Secrets of Mana*. She swept her gaze over the entire pile but found no unifying theme. However, a glowing slip of paper stuck between two volumes caught her attention.

Lailastrasza tugged it out with her talons. The paper itself looked blank, but she could sense magic woven into its fibers. Gently, she blew a little puff of flame over its surface. Words appeared in sparkling blue ink, written in Sirigosa's flowing, artistic script:

I cannot warn the guards without alerting Talin as well, and I will be far more useful to you if Vyranoth does not suspect me.

If you find this message in time, you must fly to Malygos posthaste. Ellegosa intends to open a little-known passageway from the Chittering Caverns to the Algeth'ar Academy, allowing the Primalists to launch a surprise attack on the blue and bronze dragonflights. I do not know the location of this passageway, though I've heard her mention the "Forgotten Grotto" or "Drake's Grotto" in the past.

I will do what I can to sabotage their efforts. If I can bring the tunnels down upon our heads, I will.

Please, fly quickly. I do not wish to see my flight's legacy destroyed by Vyranoth and her kin. I do not share the same respect Talin has for the Incarnate; I was merely an impressionable young mind, drawn in by the impassioned words of my friends.

—S

"Oh, Sirigosa," Lailastrasza breathed, wondering if the words were true, or if this was another Primalist plot. Perhaps it didn't matter—the blue Aspect should be informed all the same. He could decide what to do with the information, if anything at all.

Stepping from the cell, Lailastrasza carried the note to the blues in the hallway. She extended the note to them, saying, "I found something your Aspect should see."

CHAPTER TWENTY-ONE

MALYGOS HAD BEEN FIGHTING ON THE ALGETH'AR Academy front for almost fifty years, but today was the first day he feared they might not hold Vyranoth and her Primalists at bay.

Under normal circumstances, Malygos and Nozdormu fought together, but Sirigosa's letter had forced the Aspects to change tactics. While Malygos led the bronzes' Temporal Guardians and the blues' Spellscales against Cysanz and his battalions, Nozdormu took his Chronomagi into the academy to defend the two flights from a flanking attack.

For now, Malygos would have to hold the line alone.

The Spell-Weaver lowered his head and narrowed his eyes against Vyranoth's storm. The blizzard swept around the perimeter of the battlefield, held back by a handful of Arcane Wardens. The snow flew with such fury, Malygos could not see the academy's southern spires. Ice coated each one of the academy's floating islands. It was so cold, even the great fires in the braziers shivered.

Vyranoth often brought her blizzards to bear, but today's storm felt particularly fierce.

The Temporal Guardians fought on the front lines, forming a long crescent around the academy's proving grounds. The battlefront was less a *line* than it was a vertical bowl or orb that surrounded the northern islands, preventing the Incarnates from launching an attack from below. Malygos and his blues flew at its heart, providing ranged support. The Spellscales also controlled nearly a hundred arcane elementals that had been glamoured to look like bronzes and blues, which made their forces look far larger than they were.

Under normal circumstances, Malygos had little to fear from the Primalists—Cysanz's Frostscales struggled to take even a talon's length of the academy grounds. But Nozdormu's absence left the Temporal Guardians in uncharacteristic disarray. Malygos's own Spellscales seemed apprehensive, watching the heavy snows with trepidation.

Damn Sirigosa and her ilk! Malygos thought with a shake of his head. They had thrown a well-organized defense into disorder. And when the blue Aspect asked if Sirigosa had been telling the truth in her letter, Nozdormu infuriatingly replied, "Sometimes."

Sometimes? What use was being able to see the future if you couldn't use it with precision? If the letter did not speak true, the Aspects had split their forces and weakened their front line for nothing. If they ignored Sirigosa's warning, they risked being taken unawares. Either way, Vyranoth gained an advantage. It left the Spell-Weaver ill at ease, for he could not guess how the Incarnate would capitalize on it.

To add to Malygos's frustrations, the headteacher of the Algeth'ar Academy, Doragosa, had not been aware of a secret passage into her hallowed halls. She and her resident professors spent the night scouring their grounds for an ingress point; but in the morning, they came to the blue Aspect with empty talons. Like many places in the Broodlands, the Chittering Caverns were riddled with caves and tunnels; there was not time to search them all, and no one seemed to know the location of a "Drake's Grotto." If such a place existed, it was likely a nickname.

To be safe, Malygos had hidden a regiment of Arcane Wardens and constructs in the Chittering Caverns. Nozdormu had taken a position inside the academy, ready to respond with his Chronomagi if Sirigosa's claims were true.

The clouds darkened overhead, turning the light dusky. Malygos sensed a shift in the wind, but before he could react, an enormous bolt of lightning stabbed out of the sky, striking one of the Arcane Wardens on the academy's ramparts. The magic that held Vyranoth's blizzard at the perimeter of the proving grounds weakened, then shattered as the other Wardens lost control of the spell.

The storm swept in with snows so cold, the flakes bit into Malygos's hide like tiny fangs. Ice encrusted his wings. The bronzes on the front lines panicked—though the Spell-Weaver could not see them in these whiteout conditions, the wind carried their snarls, snaps, and pained screams to his ears. He narrowed his eyes against the weather as three bronze dragons fell back, pursued by a Magmatalon who burned so hot, he melted the very storm around him.

"Hold the line!" Malygos shouted, stretching forth his talons and releasing a barrage of arcane missiles at the Primalist. The missiles struck the primal dragon in the chest and wing. With a screech, the Magmatalon fell.

"Vadrugosa!" he called to his flightleader over the howling winds. "Shield me!"

Malygos could barely hear her cry of affirmation, and he certainly could not see her in this storm. Luckily, that meant their enemies couldn't see *him,* either.

A violet-blue bubble enveloped the Spell-Weaver. Flying to the center of the battlefield, he halted in the air and began to channel a supernova. Though he remained alert, he drew upon the arcane energy in the core of his being, the energy in the very world around him. Even the cries on the battlefield turned to whispers, and the howl of wind and snow seemed to fade. His wings crackled with violet-blue sparks as he beat them, faster and harder, until the magic swirled through his veins and rattled against the inside of his skull, desperate to get free.

When he could no longer contain the arcane force, Malygos swept his wings wide and released it into the sky. It exploded out in all directions with a terrible *boom,* pushing Vyranoth's blizzard back and incinerating most of the Primalists' front line on contact, leaving only a hazy vapor in their wake.

Sunlight fell onto the academy's proving grounds, the first touch of warmth Malygos had felt all day. A gentle wind filled his wings, giving him a moment of respite after such a draining spell. He took a deep breath to collect himself, his mana tapped.

The Temporal Guardians trumpeted from the front lines, frantic. Malygos lifted his head. The skies between the academy and the Veiled Ossuary were filled with Primalists, surrounding the blues and bronzes on all sides. Shock drove a painful spike into his chest. By Malygos's rough estimation, there were likely close to a thousand primal dragons in the sky. Vyranoth's Frostscales and Magmatalons had been joined by at least two battalions of Iridikron's Rockfuries, though the Stonescaled did not appear on the battlefield himself.

So, *this* was what the Incarnate had planned. Vyranoth was a clever commander, but she rarely outplayed the Aspects so thoroughly. Exhausted and out of resources, Malygos could not hope to meet such a force on the field, not without Nozdormu's help. He dared not send for the bronze Aspect, not if the Incarnate meant to flank them, too.

Though Malygos could not see her, the Frozenheart's bugle echoed across the battlefield. The ice on the academy's islands shattered, then rose into the air to form massive elementals. The Primalists advanced, darkening the skies with their wings.

On the front line, the flightleader of the Temporal Guardians roared, instructing the bronzes to kick up a storm of sands to slow the Primalists' advance. Great glittering clouds swirled around the Primalists, reducing their speed by half. Meanwhile, Vadrugosa and the other Spellscales rained arcane missiles down upon the ice elementals, culling their numbers.

Still, there were too many enemies on the field to fathom. The bronzes' magic would not last long—a few heartbeats, no more—and Malygos could not send the blues and bronzes to the slaughter. They would not fight another Battle of Emberfall this day.

"Fall back!" Malygos roared. "Spellscales—raise a shield over the academy to cover our retreat!"

The flightleaders trumpeted the order. As the bronzes began to retreat, Vyranoth appeared on the field, swooping to the fore of the vanguard and scattering the bronzes' temporal sands with a burst of wind. At her call, the shattered ice elementals on the platforms re-formed and rose anew.

Aspect and Incarnate locked gazes over the battlefield. Malygos curled his lip, baring fangs. Was Vyranoth so sure of her victory that she would risk appearing on the front lines? Why, Malygos could almost blink to her position and drag her through a portal to the Vault of the Incarnates, just as he had done with Fyrakk. He could end this chapter of the war in one move . . . if he'd only had the mana to do so.

It's a trap, he told himself. Vyranoth could not win at Algeth'ar, so she sought to lure the Spell-Weaver into a very inane mistake. Did she really think him so foolish or desperate enough to risk his own safety?

Still, Malygos could not just turn tail and run, not with the Frozenheart within range. Even in this depleted state, the Spell-Weaver was not without options.

Gritting his teeth, he called upon the last reserves of his strength to manifest two glimmering images of himself. They slid off his scales with a hiss. He sent them charging toward the Incarnate on a roar. Arcane missiles burst from the images' talons, raining down on Vyranoth and her wingleaders.

Vyranoth rolled, dodging the first salvo. Her wingleaders scattered. The second burst of arcane missiles slammed into her left flank as she ducked and wove through her ranks. The Primalists rallied around their Incarnate, but Malygos's images whooshed past them, incorporeal as wind. Vyranoth fled from them.

He stretched forth his forefoot, giving chase. Beyond the glittering tips of his talons, he watched a horde of Rockfuries rush toward him, but he was close, *so* close, to striking Vyranoth down. If he could just damage a wing . . . send her plummeting to the rocks below . . .

"Fall back, Malygos!" someone shrieked.

Just a few more moments—

A great weight slammed into the Spell-Weaver from behind and dragged him back. The Temporal Guardians surged forth, blasting the Rockfuries with superheated sand. His focus shattered, Malygos lost control of his images. He watched them dissipate from the field.

"Do you wish this day to be your last?" Nozdormu snapped, dragging the Spell-Weaver to the safety of the academy's enormous, glittering shield. "This is not the time for heroics—you will not be able to repeat Flamesfall with Vyranoth!"

"Do you think I don't know that?" Malygos exclaimed, shaking himself loose from the bronze Aspect's grip. "I *nearly* had her—a broken wing would have sufficed!"

"The Rockfuries would have fallen upon you first," Nozdormu said with a huff.

Perhaps the Timeless One was right, but Malygos was not about to say as much. With an annoyed rumble, the Spell-Weaver turned back to face the field. Any Spellscale not actively powering the shield launched arcane missiles at the advancing armies, while drakonid repositioned the ballistae to meet the oncoming force. Primal dragons tumbled from the sky, dead before they hit the ground. The Primalist wingleaders called for a halt over the outlying islands, unwilling to risk a siege. At least, not today.

"Did they attack from the caverns?" Malygos asked. "Did Sirigosa's letter speak true?"

"Aye," Nozdormu said. "We defeated their vanguard handily, but most of the ordered defectors escaped. I suspect your Sirigosa was among their number."

"Very well." Malygos sighed, watching Vyranoth lay claim to the academy's outlying islands. In the distance, the blue Aspect could just barely see the sunlight glinting off the Incarnates' icy scales. He could not say for certain, but he thought he saw a cruel smile on the Frozenheart's lips

At least she would not take Algeth'ar Academy that day.

AS NIGHT FELL, NELTHARION joined the other Aspects in Valdrakken. The stars wheeled high above the Seat, indifferent, uncaring, cold. In the distance, the protective barriers around the city shimmered. Beyond them, Neltharion could just make out a little violet bubble around what would have been Algeth'ar Academy.

The day wasn't the disaster it might have been. The academy hadn't fallen, but the Primalists had captured its floating islands. Malygos managed to hold the academy against the Primalist assault, while Nozdormu repelled a flanking maneuver from inside the academy itself. From what Neltharion could gather, Vyranoth intended to pressure the Aspects into a retreat then decimate their armies with a surprise attack.

To support the assault, Iridikron had sent a full battalion of his Rockfuries to the Veiled Ossuary. Their appearance on the battlefield meant two things: One, Vyranoth was growing frustrated with her failure to make headway in Thaldraszus; and two, Malygos and Nozdormu's campaign had been successful enough that the Primalists' campaign required reinforcements from Harrowsdeep.

Iridikron had hoarded his Rockfuries for centuries. The fact that they had taken the field was a concession of sorts, an acknowledgment that even with their superior numbers, the Primalists weren't winning the war.

As Neltharion strode into the council chamber, he found the other Aspects gathered around the campaign map. Two new Rockfury pawns stood at the Veiled Ossuary, while a tiny arcane shield now glittered over the academy. The Aspects nodded their greetings to him but did not stop their conversation.

"I would not consider it a loss," Alexstrasza said to Malygos and Nozdormu. "You managed to halt the Primalist advance while minimizing loss of life—"

"Barely," Malygos replied, tapping his talons on the floor.

"We must celebrate every good thing, no matter how small," the Dragon Queen said with a tender smile. "The Primalists will not fly on Valdrakken this night. And is it true that one of our wayward drakes warned you of the surprise attack?"

"One did, yes," Malygos replied. "Sirigosa."

"I remember her well," Alexstrasza replied. "If her heart can be softened, the hearts of the others may change as well. All is not lost."

Neltharion cleared his throat. "Our enemies would agree with you, Alexstrasza," he said, gesturing to the new pawns on the campaign table. "I would not have thought to see the Rockfuries leave Harrowsdeep, but it appears the Incarnates want for numbers."

"I don't know how we're going to counter them," Nozdormu said, glancing sideways at Malygos. "The blues cannot maintain the shield indefinitely, and our forces are stretched thin."

"I cannot pull any more Arcane Wardens from Vakthros or the archives," Malygos said. "Not without compromising the southern border."

Alexstrasza frowned. "I'm certain that's what the Incarnates want. Ysera, would you be able to dedicate any of your Verdant Preservers to Thaldraszus?"

"Not two battalions' worth, I'm afraid," the green Aspect said. "If we do not defend the plains at our full strength, the Primalists will decimate our herds. The Broodlands would starve."

"And we cannot send any of our forces from the Reach," Neltharion said to Alexstrasza. "We barely control the region as it stands."

"I know," the Dragon Queen said, dropping her gaze to the campaign map. "Our flights have fought bravely, but I fear our campaigns now stand on a talon's point. We must capture Vyranoth, else I fear the scales may tip in the Primalists' favor."

Neltharion and Alexstrasza had been having this conversation often of late—the black and red dragonflights were battered, exhausted, and losing hope. The Frozenheart's glacier continued to expand at a rapid rate. At its current speed of growth, Neltharion thought the glacier would overtake the Reach in fifteen to twenty years.

Removing Vyranoth from the field would stop the glacier and scatter the Primalists to the winds. Though Iridikron would marshal his forces in time, it would give the Broodlands a much-needed reprieve from Vyranoth's unending assault and relentless winter.

"I agree," Neltharion said. "The only question is *how*? What have we not tried?"

Nozdormu sighed. "The Frozenheart learned from Fyrakk's folly. She never takes to the field herself, preferring to lead from far behind the front lines."

"We've tried reaching her with arcane portals, time dilation, illusory armies"—Malygos counted the strategies on his talons—"sandstorms, sand *monsters,* poison, heat waves, stealth attacks, assassination attempts . . . to be frank, my queen, we're running out of ideas."

Not for the first time this century, Neltharion's thoughts turned back to the dracthyr. How would the war have gone, had they been able to take the battlefield beside the five flights? Would the Aspects still be standing here, more than a hundred years after the Battle of Stormsunder Crater, debating how to knock Vyranoth from the sky? Would Iridikron himself already be a memory?

A whisper curled into Neltharion's mind: *You are too weak to defeat her alone.*

With our power, you could capture the Frozenheart.

We can end this war for you.

Even the Stonescaled would bow to our strength.

"We need to draw Vyranoth out," Neltharion said, talking over the voices in his head. "There must be something we haven't tried. She has family in the Frozen Fangs—perhaps we take the whelplings hostage?"

Ysera shook her head. "Given our history, I do not believe it's wise to take any more whelps from the primal dragons."

"On this matter, I agree," Alexstrasza said.

"Then what do you suggest?" Neltharion asked them. "Everything we have tried has failed, and Vyranoth will not fall for a ruse."

The Dragon Queen sat and hugged her wings against her back. She pressed her lips together, considering the campaign map that stretched between them. Very few dragons ever saw Alexstrasza like this—vulnerable and raw, maybe, but never unsure of herself. Though she had grown into her role as queen in recent centuries, Neltharion still saw glimpses of the tenderhearted creature behind her crown of golden horns.

"There is only one thing Vyranoth wants," Alexstrasza said. "*Me.* I will face Vyranoth in talon-to-talon combat. If I lose, my life is forfeit. If she loses, she will submit herself to the Vault of the Incarnates."

Gasps tore through the chamber. Neltharion reared back, shocked the Dragon Queen could even *suggest* such a thing. "Absolutely *not,*" were the first words to leap from the Earth-Warder's mouth. The idea was *preposterous*! There was no denying that Alexstrasza was a capable warrior, but even she would be hard-pressed to defeat Vyranoth in single combat. Even *if* the Frozenheart decided to fight honorably—and Neltharion did not trust the Incarnates to abide by the rules of engagement—the flights could not risk Alexstrasza's life.

"No, sister," Ysera said in a whisper, reaching out and placing a forefoot on one of Alexstrasza's own. Ysera squeezed. "It is far too dangerous, and I cannot bear the thought of losing you."

"I mislike this," Nozdormu said. "Remember what I told you the day the barriers fell: To risk your life is to risk the very survival of the flights."

"Vyranoth will never agree to this," Malygos said, shaking his head. "She will expect treachery."

"I believe she will agree," Alexstrasza replied. "She joined the Incarnates to hold me to account for my actions and the actions of the dragonflights. As Dragon Queen, the responsibility for the five flights begins and ends with me. I must stand to answer for everything that has happened, not only to satisfy Vyranoth's quest for justice, but to prove the goodness of our cause.

"Vyranoth must be stopped," she continued. "I cannot stand behind my defenders any longer, not in good conscience."

Neltharion blew out a breath. He stared at the campaign map, trying to think of something, *anything,* that might spare Alexstrasza from this choice. Outside of armor, there was little the Earth-Warder could do to protect the Dragon Queen in single combat; and as ambitious as he might be, he had no desire to see Alexstrasza fall. The death of any Aspect would utterly shatter a flight; without Tyr, none of them could be replaced. If Alexstrasza lost . . . the war was over.

The chamber fell silent for a moment, each Aspect turning to their own thoughts.

"Alexstrasza speaks wisdom, but we are strongest when we fight together," Ysera said after a long moment, casting her gaze around the chamber. "Thus, I will agree to this plan on one condition—that Alexstrasza fights with a boon from each of our flights. She should not have to face the Frozenheart alone."

Now, *that* was an idea Neltharion could support.

"What do you suggest?" Alexstrasza asked.

"Elementium armor from the forges of the Obsidian Citadel," Neltharion said, already imagining the design—black, gold, and set with gems representing each flight. "I will craft it myself and have the scalesmiths imbue it with the warmth from our forges."

"I will enchant it to resist Vyranoth's frost," Malygos said, looking to the Dragon Queen. "The blue dragonflight will also shield your wings from frost. It's been remarkably effective on the front."

"Yes, precisely," Ysera said, a touch of excitement in her voice. "I should like to imbue her talons with poison, but I doubt that would have much effect on Vyranoth's icy heart. Instead, I will take my golden vines and saturate them with healing magics, which will act as a restorative. It will be as a gentle breath from the Dream—a constant, sweet support."

"Good," the Dragon Queen said, looking to Nozdormu. "What of you, Nozdormu? How might I carry the spirit of your flight into battle with me?"

"Prognostication," Nozdormu said.

Malygos wrinkled his snout and mouthed *what?* at Nozdormu, but the bronze Aspect ignored him and continued on: "The magic is . . . *experimental* at best, but my flight can imbue the Dragon Queen with the Sands of Time from the Temporal Conflux. In theory, the magic should allow her to predict the Frozenheart's attacks and give her more time to react."

"Alexstrasza is not a bronze dragon." Malygos cocked his head. "Will she even be able to manifest or control such magic?"

"She will need my support," Nozdormu said with a shake of his head. "She might otherwise slip into the timeways, and we could lose her."

Ysera and Alexstrasza exchanged a wary glance.

"I'd rather you just lose Vyranoth," Malygos said with a snort.

"If it were possible, I would see to it," Nozdormu said.

"Are we agreed, then?" the Dragon Queen asked, looking to each Aspect in turn. The other Aspects chorused their assent, the fires blazing on their banners.

"Even if I think it madness," Neltharion said. "Aye."

"Very well," the Dragon Queen said. "I shall send envoys to the Veiled Ossuary. Let us put an end to the Frozenheart's reign of terror."

SEVERAL DAYS AFTER THE failed gambit at Algeth'ar Academy, Vyranoth's wingleaders brought her a dragon figurine of never-melting ice. The Frozenheart recognized it immediately—Alexstrasza had gifted it to her centuries ago, and she had smashed it and sent back the shards after Fyrakk had been captured. Now the Dragon Queen had repaired it with gold.

Vyranoth grumbled at the sight of it, thinking that Alexstrasza would invite her to yet *another* parley . . . but this time, the Dragon Queen issued her a challenge: single combat at a time and location of Vyranoth's choosing.

So it had finally come to this—Alexstrasza was desperate enough to face Vyranoth on her own. It was an admittance of sorts, and acknowledgment that the mighty Aspects would soon be unable to continue their campaign against the Primalists. They were losing ground in Thaldraszus and the Reach; not quickly, of course, but Vyranoth was nothing if not patient. Even if she failed to capture the Reach, her glacier would consume it in time.

While Alexstrasza was a formidable opponent, not even she could hope to face Vyranoth on a battlefield of ice; but the Aspects would not risk Alexstrasza's life if they were not certain she would win. Still, perhaps an engagement with the Dragon Queen would be worth the risk.

Vyranoth flew the news to Harrowsdeep herself, knowing the information would be of interest to Iridikron. The Stonescaled loved to turn the Aspects' own stratagems against them. Perhaps he would see the value in accepting such a challenge.

Iridikron received Vyranoth in his war cavern, which lay deep at the heart of Harrowsdeep. Here, the roots of the mountain never stopped rumbling. Magma churned endlessly, lighting the cavern walls. Great lava falls veiled Iridikron's seat of power, which lay at the cavern's far end. Stalactites and dripstones were lit with an eerie, bioluminescent green light. No wind blew this deep, so the air felt stagnant. Heavy.

After checking with Iridikron's wingleaders, Vyranoth landed on the center platform, alone. Iridikron did not keep her waiting long, which was just as well. The oppressive heat in Harrowsdeep threatened to melt the scales off her hide.

"Vyranoth, my old friend," Iridikron said as he landed beside her. He stalked past her, heading for his campaign map. "What brings you to Harrowsdeep this day?"

"News from the front," she said, joining him at the massive stone slab. "Alexstrasza has challenged me to single combat."

Iridikron did not react to that news right away. He turned his head a few degrees, considering Vyranoth. "It's a trap," he said without any affectation.

"The Aspects grow desperate," Vyranoth said. "I believe we should capitalize on their recklessness."

After a long moment, the Stonescaled flicked his gaze down to her feet, then back up to her eyes. "Go on."

"I will take Alexstrasza north, forcing Neltharion to fight at the Reach alone," Vyranoth said, looking down at the stone map before them. She pushed the Dragon Queen's pawn to the Icebound Eye, a massive natural sinkhole in the Frozen Fangs. "With your Rockfuries, I can send Razviik to apply deadly pressure to Malygos and Nozdormu in Thaldraszus, forcing them to fall back to Tyrhold or Valdrakken. This will prompt Neltharion to split his forces and leave the Reach in Levarian's talons—Valdrakken is the greater prize. If it falls, the Broodlands fall. We attack Levarian from the east and west and free Raszageth."

"And Ysera?" the Stonescaled asked, lifting a brow.

"She will come east, too, if Valdrakken burns."

A rumble sounded in the Stonescaled's chest. He considered the map, going still as he mulled Vyranoth's strategy over in his mind. Only the bright, earthy energies on his spine moved.

"You know the Dragon Queen better than I," Iridikron said. "How certain are you that you could best her in one-to-one combat?"

Vyranoth snorted. "I would have killed her at Wyrmrest Temple, had Neltharion not intervened."

"That isn't the story I heard," Iridikron replied. "I confess, Vyranoth, I do not like this strategy. It would be better for us to continue our war of attrition. The Reach will fall in another ten or twenty years, and once we are reunited with Raszageth, Valdrakken will not be far behind."

"Have I not earned this?" Vyranoth said through gritted teeth. "I have asked you for so little, and now I come to you, asking—no, *demanding* that I be given the chance to tear my satisfaction from the Dragon Queen's hide!"

"You *ask* me to put everything we have worked for in jeopardy," Iridikron replied, gesturing to the pawns at Valdrakken. "This fight has always been a personal one for you, but I fear that your hatred for the Dragon Queen may be clouding your judgment."

"No," Vyranoth said, her tone turning to ice. "I see a bold strategy that would allow us to smash through our enemies' defenses, take the Aspects off guard, and bring the Broodlands to its knees. Will you wait for them to come to Harrowsdeep for your head, Iridikron, or will you join me in this offensive and save our kind from their tyranny?"

Iridikron's expression did not change. For a moment, Vyranoth thought he might reject her plan; she knew how loath he was to leave Harrowsdeep undefended.

"Accept the Dragon Queen's challenge, then," Iridikron said. "Let us end this."

CHAPTER TWENTY-TWO

THE DRAGON QUEEN DEPARTED VALDRAKKEN BEFORE dawn, heading to the Icebound Eye with her Ruby Flamebringers and an allied battalion of the finest warriors from the black, blue, green, and bronze flights.

Neltharion did not go to the Seat of the Aspects to bid her goodbye with the others; he'd wished her luck the night before, when they met in the Life-Binder Conservatory after sunset. The Dragon Queen had been calm, resolute; but in private, when their various retainers and majordomos were out of earshot, she confided her fears in him. Alexstrasza was no fool—she knew the morrow might be her last.

Iridikron will take this opportunity to strike, Alexstrasza had said. *You must be prepared to face any challenge he brings, Neltharion. I place the protection of the Broodlands in your very capable talons.*

The Broodlands will not fall tomorrow, Alexstrasza, Neltharion had said. *Nor will you.*

The Dragon Queen had only responded with a determined nod of her head.

Instead, the Earth-Warder spent the night and early morning in frenzied industry, preparing to lead the Earthen Bulwark against Oxoria and Alexstrasza's Heart's Guard against Mithruz. Levarian had flown north to support the Earth-Warder at the front, while Garion had taken the Ironscales to the citadel in the flightcommander's absence. If the green dragonflight was attacked today, Sindragosa would fly west with a host of blues to defend the plains. If the Azure Archives were Iridikron's target, Ysera would come to the blues' aid. Nozdormu and Malygos would hold the front in Thaldraszus.

The Aspects had accounted for every detail. Still, a sense of doom clung to the Earth-Warder like a scale that wouldn't shed. He believed in Alexstrasza. She had led them against Galakrond and hunted with Fyrakk himself—few dragons were as competent as she in battle. But to think the entirety of the war now rested on the Dragon Queen's shoulders sent him into a spiral of nervous energy. Every choice, every sacrifice, every scar might come to naught; for if Alexstrasza did not survive her encounter with Vyranoth, the war would most certainly be lost.

As dawn broke, Neltharion expected Oxoria to trumpet the attack . . . but none came. Gray morning light crept down the mountains' faces, revealing the Primalists' empty camps. Oxoria and her brood had disappeared from their position south of Sunderstorm Crater. Vyranoth's massive glacier lay abandoned— not a single dragon from Mithruz's forces remained. Elegant ice structures—molded to look like sleeping dragons in the moonlight—lay where his scouts expected the Primalists to be.

Furious, Neltharion took wing, flying high above the Reach. How had *hundreds* of dragons disappeared overnight? None of the Shadowscales' sky-watchers had seen so many dragons take flight. Warbringer Rava led the Rockfuries at Algeth'ar Academy alone. Cysanz and the Frostscales had gone north with Vyranoth—he had confirmation they departed from the Veiled Ossuary that morning.

The skies over the Obsidian Citadel were clear, and he had no reports of attacks on the Emerald Gardens or the Azure Archives.

Iridikron was on the move—of this, Neltharion was certain. The Earth-Warder sent his Shadowscales flying in all directions with orders to find the missing Primalist battalions.

The Stonescaled has tricked you, the whispers said. *Fool!*

You are too weak to stop their assault.

The Broodlands will burn for your failures!

Call upon our power, the voices said. *Save your home!*

No, Neltharion said, *if they are not in the skies, nor in the territories surrounding the Broodlands, there is only one place they could have gone.*

The Earth-Warder dropped to the ground outside the War Creche. He stabbed his talons into the earth, listening to the stories the stones told. Long had he guarded the movements of the planet's bones, which were in constant motion, ever shifting, changing, and shaking. He sensed Iridikron deep within the world's crust, exerting an enormous force to . . . what, precisely? Why did the Stonescaled seem to be holding up the very earth?

Neltharion growled, pushing his talons deeper yet. Far below, he sensed a tiny spark of life. Its fast, frenzied movement almost reminded him of insects swarming through a series of underground tunnels, moving south toward Valdrakken . . .

"*No*," Neltharion said with a gasp, his eyes widening.

Iridikron was moving his *armies* underground, holding the mountains over their heads through the sheer force of his elemental might. In a sudden flash of terrible, horrifying clarity, the Earth-Warder realized everything the Stonescaled had done up to this point—the earthquakes, the restless bones of Azeroth, the fissures and aftershocks—hadn't only been to frustrate the flights' work in the Broodlands. The Stonescaled had been picking away at the earth beneath them, expanding existing tunnels to create underground paths into Valdrakken. The shifts had been so subtle, Neltharion had assumed they were natural. No wonder Vyranoth's vanguard had been able to breach Algeth'ar Academy with such ease!

Now Iridikron's armies would march straight into the heart of the Broodlands.

This is your fault! the whispers told him. *You have failed in your duty!* Neltharion shook them from his mind.

Now was not the time for despair, but for *action*. If the Broodlands were lost this day, they would not fall on a whimper but with a roar. Valdrakken would fight while Neltharion still drew breath.

The Earth-Warder leapt into the air, calling for his flightleaders. Levarian would stay in the Reach with his forces—Neltharion dared not leave Raszageth's prison undefended, even if Valdrakken was under attack. He sent messengers to the Obsidian Citadel, commanding Garion and the Ironscales to meet him in the capital and leave the citadel to Vembrion and the Obsidian Guard. Stoltria and her Onyx Reavers would fly to Valdrakken with Neltharion, as would Bojsanz and the Heart's Guard of the red dragonflight.

Neltharion sent his fastest wings to Ysera, Malygos, and Nozdormu, warning them that the enemy was about to attack from underfoot. Additional messengers were sent to the Ruby Life Pools and to the leaders of the Scalesworn in Valdrakken, warning them to prepare for an incoming attack.

Ysera pledged to come at once with her Verdant Preservers. While Nozdormu had gone north with Alexstrasza, his Chronomagi would go south to Tyrhold under Soridormi's command while Malygos held the Rockfuries at the academy.

Neltharion had five companies of dragons at his disposal— the Ironscales, the Onyx Reavers, the red dragonflight's Heart's Guard, the bronzes' Chronomagi, and the greens' Verdant Preservers. All told, he had two Aspects, roughly six hundred dragons, and a thousand Scalesworn. He could not know how many dragons now swarmed under their feet, but he had to assume Iridikron would come in force.

By wing and by talon, the five flights would fight to the last. Valdrakken would not fall that day.

...

ALEXSTRASZA ARRIVED AT THE Icebound Eye at midday. She landed on one of the sinkhole's sharp, icy outcroppings, marveling at its fierce beauty. The Eye dropped more than a hundred wing-lengths into the ground. Tall, mountainous peaks formed a ring around its edge. Fine spears studded its frosted walls, bristling like the gullet of a deep-sea fish. Air currents whirled through the sinkhole, fast enough to dash a full-grown dragon against its glittering teeth.

As the wind blew, a great howl echoed from the depths, sending a shiver through her scales.

The rules of engagement for the day were simple: Alexstrasza and Vyranoth would duel over the Icebound Eye, alone. While their forces would be present to prevent any treachery, interference from an outside party would constitute an immediate loss for the offending side. Both Aspect and Incarnate had agreed to these rules, and yet neither side trusted their opponent to keep them. Perhaps because both sides intended to *break* those rules, should they look close to losing.

Saristrasz and Cristalstrasz alighted on the ledge beside her. A light dusting of golden sand shimmered on their scales, visible only to Alexstrasza's eyes. Nozdormu had imbued her with the Sands of Time before they left Valdrakken, which telegraphed the next movement of any living creature. All the living world shimmered ever-moving.

The bronze Aspect had taken refuge in a nearby cave, providing a stabilizing support for the spell. The bronzes in the skies amplified his reach. *Take care, Alexstrasza,* Nozdormu had said. *You must stay within range of my bronzes, else we may lose control of the spell.*

Given the size of the Icebound Eye, that seemed like a distinct possibility. It would not surprise Alexstrasza to learn the Frozenheart had chosen this location for that very reason—to ensure the Life-Binder would be within sight of her flights, but not within range of magical aid.

The Primalists appeared on the horizon in a shimmer of gold.

"I do not like this," Cristalstrasz said, curling his lip as he gazed into the abyss. "This place gives the Frozenheart a near-endless font of power, my queen. Her abilities will be on par with yours, or nearly so."

Saristrasz shook his head, taking a step back from the ledge. "Please, my queen, do not risk your life like this! Were we to quit this place now, no one would call you a coward."

"I will not turn back." Alexstrasza lifted her head and squared her shoulders. Neltharion's armor gleamed on her chest, warm and steadying. "Though it breaks my heart to fight one I've loved so well, I will show her our might . . . and also our compassion. I go with the strength and hopes of our flights; but should I fall, I expect you to rise and carry the burden of leadership in my stead."

Saristrasz made a choked sound, but the red bobbed his head.

The Frozenheart flew into the center of the Icebound Eye, flanked by one of her wingleaders, Cysanz. The Primalist Frostscales fanned out in the skies above the peaks, forming a crescent along the northern ridge. Alexstrasza's forces did likewise, establishing a perimeter on the sinkhole's southern lip.

"It is time." Alexstrasza launched herself in the air, pausing only briefly to look at her flight. How beautiful they looked with Nozdormu's sands swirling around their wings! They had achieved so much more than she ever dreamed possible; and today, every single hope, every single heart would fly with her. Neltharion's armor shielded her chest, back, and wing-fingers, providing protection and the warmth of home. Ysera's own golden vines adorned her forelegs, infusing Alexstrasza with a constant pulse of healing magic. Malygos had shielded her wings and scales from the frost, allowing her to fly through Vyranoth's fiercest chill.

Alexstrasza's gaze locked with Tyranastrasz's—he gave her a deep nod, almost a bow. The old wyrm hadn't questioned her when she told him of this plan, but rested his forehead on hers and released a quiet sigh. He understood, even if he feared for her life.

"Stay with them, Saristrasz," she said to her majordomo. "Should anything happen to me, you must lead them to safety."

A flicker of grief passed over the majordomo's features, but he made no further protest. He closed his eyes and bowed his head, whispering, "Titans be with you, my queen."

"And with you," she said to him. With a nod to Cristalstrasz, Alexstrasza left the safety of the mountain peaks. They halted ten wing-lengths before Vyranoth and Cysanz, hovering over the great pit. The temperature around Vyranoth plummeted.

Alexstrasza's own life force surged in response—her heart beat a little faster, carrying heat to her muscles.

The Frozenheart's hatred for her ran so much colder than the frigid air around them. Long ago, Alexstrasza had sensed an aching loneliness in Vyranoth, one that left an empty void in her heart. How her vitriol must have festered in her glacier at the Reach, ever fed by Iridikron, who only sought Vyranoth for her power! Her losses fueled her fury, too—her warriors, her fellow Incarnates . . . all the way back to Alexstrasza and the advent of Order magic.

Alexstrasza's first transgression had been sanctioning the removal of primal dragon eggs from the Dragonwilds; but her *second* was abandoning her oldest and dearest friend.

Today, she meant to account for her mistakes.

"Vyranoth," Alexstrasza said by way of greeting, careful not to look at the sands dancing around the Incarnate's form.

"Alexstrasza," Vyranoth replied. Alexstrasza had never heard the Incarnate's voice sound so cold before. The Life-Binder reached for her friend's heart, but she found it encased in ice. Untouchable. Not even the warmth of Alexstrasza's deep love for her oldest friend could break such a barrier.

If she could not melt Vyranoth's enmity, perhaps she could crack it. "Long ago, you wished for peace as much as I did," Alexstrasza said. "Surely you must see the folly of this war by now—"

"The time for words is past," Vyranoth said. "All you do is delay your own demise. I will strike you from the skies this day, though I will take no joy in the act."

"While the Incarnates are mighty, you will still be hard-pressed to meet an Aspect alone on the field," Alexstrasza replied. "Which is why I ask you again, as my oldest friend—let us put aside our differences and work toward a better future for *all* our kind."

"You know I cannot do that," Vyranoth replied, lifting her voice. "After all you and *your kind* have done, how could I ever trust you again? You would drive the Primals into *extinction* if we let you!"

"No. There was room for all in the Broodlands—our holdings, our knowledge, were open to any who sought it, you know that. I would never seek to drive this wedge between our people," Alexstrasza said. "I fight because Raszageth slaughtered mortals and tarasek for fifty summers, because *she* flew on the Reach and murdered my kind for naught but her own amusement. I cannot leave these crimes unanswered, Vyranoth—"

"*Crimes?*" the Incarnate shrieked. "You want to speak of *crimes*, Alexstrasza? Your orders would have had your titan *abominations* take eggs from *my own clutch*! There is nothing you can say that could possibly absolve you of such an act—you, who call yourself *Life-Binder* and who raise our young in your pools! Your drakes had a right to know the *faces of their parents*, but you stole that from them!"

"Perhaps that is so," Alexstrasza said. Then she lifted her voice so that it would ring through the Icebound Eye. "But hear me now: After watching centuries of Primalist cruelty, I do not regret saving those whelps from the wilds. You mourn those eggs, Vyranoth, yet in the same breath you march on the Broodlands to slaughter the drakes they've become. Who then is the *monster*? Ever have I fought to protect life. Ever have I sued for *peace*, but you will not relent. Therefore, I will defend my flights by wing and by talon!"

"No more talk!" Vyranoth roared. Great, gleaming icicles appeared over her back, each one sharp enough to pierce Alexstrasza's armor. The Sands of Time shifted around each shard of ice, highlighting the tip in bright gold.

"Fly, Cristalstrasz," Alexstrasza barked to her flightleader. "Go!"

The flightleader ducked away.

Alexstrasza locked eyes with the Incarnate.

"Long ago, I told you that I was the same as I ever was," Alexstrasza said. "Unchanged, despite the influence of Order magic. Today, that is no longer the case. For too long I sought to please everyone, hoping to preserve the peace; but I have learned that if I am to help my flights fly straight and true, I must have the courage to follow the fires that burn bright in my heart."

Vyranoth growled, bristling her mane.

Lifting her voice, she proclaimed, "I am Alexstrasza, Life-Binder and Queen of the five dragonflights of Azeroth, blessed of Eonar and defender of all living." Her eyes blazed with crimson flames. "And I will not fail in my oaths this day."

WARNING BELLS SOUNDED THROUGH the streets of Valdrakken. As Neltharion's wings darkened the city's spires, a great sandstorm swirled from the Temporal Conflux. Its clouds moved toward the city with unnatural speed, driven by the bronze dragonflight's wings. Green scales shimmered on the southern horizon, and Vakthros and the Azure Archives shot distress beacons into the sky, calling all blue dragons to war.

On the ground, the Scalesworn helped escort civilians to the safety of the Halls of Infusion—they emptied the enclaves, the markets, and the city squares. Drakes were sent to the Ruby Life Pools to help defend the whelps and eggs, while the drakonid positioned ballistae and other artillery on the city walls and landings.

By the time Neltharion arrived at the Seat of the Aspects, he found Garion and the Ironscales waiting for him. The Ironscales were one of the largest battalions in the black dragonflight—or in any flight—boasting nearly two hundred battle-hardened veterans. Each dragon was outfitted in snout-to-tail armor, making them nearly impossible to kill.

"My Aspect!" Garion said, bowing his head as Neltharion landed with the other flightleaders. "What are your orders?"

"The Ironscales will be with me," Neltharion said. "Once we know where the Primalists' egress points will be, we will establish our front line and strike them down as they crawl out of their holes."

Neltharion looked to Bojsanz next. "Surround the Seat of the Aspects with the Heart's Guard—you'll oversee our aerial defenses. Stoltria! Use the Onyx Reavers to provide support to the enclaves as necessary. Egnion and the Shadowscales will relay information on the Primalists' movements, and

Captain Drine and her Scalesworn will provide support from the ground.

"And if the Stonescaled joins the battlefield," the Earth-Warder added coldly, "his life belongs to *me*."

A great *boom* echoed through the city. The Seat of the Aspects trembled. Neltharion looked over his shoulder as the earth cried out and the wards beneath the city buckled.

"They are coming," Neltharion shouted, turning back to the city. He stood on the ledge, puffed up his chest, and spread his wings. His voice rang off the peaks of Thaldraszus as he cried, "Today, the five flights of Azeroth fight as one! Though we may be scattered, we stand together in defense of our beloved home. Strike every Primalist from the sky! Tear them from the earth and rend them asunder! Valdrakken shall not fall, so long as we still live and breathe!"

The skies erupted in a chorus of roars.

The flightleaders barked orders at their companies. Crimson scales flashed as the Heart's Guard surrounded the Seat. In the courtyard below, Captain Drine organized the Scalesworn. Great clouds of bronze sand blotted out the sun. A breeze carried the scent of the Emerald Gardens to his snout—Ysera drew nigh with her company, too.

Even from his perch on the Seat, Neltharion sensed Iridikron's forces rumbling in the depths. A group of them would emerge right under the Seat of the Aspects—a second company felt closer to Scalewatch Caverns. He would send Ysera to engage them.

Neltharion hoped there would not be a third.

The earth jolted, as if the tower's very foundations were under siege. With another great crack, the mountainside at the base of the Seat exploded outward. Giant boulders crashed into the Scalesworn's ranks, slammed into a bridge, and shattered the courtyard fountain. Primalists—Magmatalons and Rockfuries both—poured from the wound in the mountainside. Captain Drine shouted orders at the Scalesworn, and they re-formed their ranks and made a wall of shields. The Primalists surged forward.

Neltharion's blood ran hot. After all these years, he still loved to fight.

"Ironscales, with me!" he cried, pressing his wings to his back and diving off the Seat. The plunge was a breathless one. The Earth-Warder opened his wings at the last second—not to break his fall, but to change his orientation in the air. He crashed into the Primalists in the courtyard, crushing five dragons underfoot and sending a shock wave into the ground. It destabilized the dragons who rushed toward him. Several stumbled. He spun, slamming the heavy, barbed end of his tail into a pack and shattering their bones. Howls of pain stirred his bloodlust. Several half-crushed dragons tried to scramble to safety, but the Scalesworn stepped in, driving their blades between the dragons' scales.

How dare they challenge a dragon Aspect!

How *dare* they think they could take Valdrakken!

"*Insects!*" Neltharion snapped, leaping toward the shattered mountain and tearing the Primalists from its flank.

On the other side of the river, a second fissure opened and spewed more Primalists into the city. Garion fell on them with the Ironscales, not allowing a single dragon to take wing. The Ironscales split as a third fissure opened, then again for the fourth, adjusting their ranks with precision and skill.

Another tremor shook the city, shearing away the earth near Scalewatch Caverns. The violence of the act was so visceral, it rattled Neltharion's bones and teeth. He snarled, flaring his nostrils.

He would tear them all apart for desecrating the earth beneath Valdrakken.

"Garion!" he shouted, crushing a Magmawing's skull under his foot. "Take half your Ironscales and collapse the northern fissures. I will lead the forces here!"

The flightleader gave the black Aspect a nod, then leapt aloft. As Garion shouted orders to his forces, the ground shivered under the Earth-Warder's talons. Before the Aspect could react, the earth shot up and struck him in the chin. His head snapped back. Startled, he stumbled backward, careful not to crush the Scalesworn's line.

A cackle crept out of the fissure's shadows. Two red eyes blazed from within the stone, bright as magma and full of hate. "Neltharion," a female voice said, her scales hissing against stone as she stalked toward him. "How long have I waited to tear the scales from your hide?"

Neltharion narrowed his eyes. "Oxoria," he said with a growl. "There you are."

The Matriarch hissed as she burst from the fissure and into the air. Rocks rained in her wake, bouncing off Neltharion's armor. Oxoria was an ancient wyrm. Her scales petrified into slate-gray stone long ago. Age hadn't dulled her intellect, though, or the sharpness of her talons.

Despite years of fighting her forces on the battlefield, Neltharion had never met her face-to-face. After the fall of the Veiled Ossuary, the Primalists had refused further parley with the Aspects.

"You have caused my brood far too much grief and heartache," Oxoria said, bristling the stony scales around her shoulders. "Your wretched wingleader killed my mate. Too many of my children have fallen at the Reach to you and your titan-magic. Today, I shall take my vengeance for them all!"

Oxoria let out a roar, one infused with so much grief, the earth responded to her call. More fissures cracked open in the bases of the mountains around the Shadowed Pass. Primalists swarmed from the new cracks in the stone. Magmatalons took wing, starting fires in the canyon.

Neltharion bugled twice to the skies, commanding the Reavers to start their first descent.

"If you did not want to lose your brood, Oxoria," Neltharion said with a growl, turning his attention back to the Matriarch, "you never should have flown north to Harrowsdeep."

"I flew north to protect my brood from monsters like *you*," she spat, then dived at Neltharion. He juked to the left, snarling. She hit the ground and spun to face him, digging her claws into the ground for purchase. The flagstones cracked under her weight. He leapt forward, headbutting her with his horns to push her away from the Scalesworn. She stumbled, then snapped at his throat, her rocky fangs screeching against his armor. The metal shuddered under the strength of her bite. He reared back, slashing at her snout with his talons.

Oxoria scrambled back with a snarl. Behind her, the Reavers whistled past, crashing into airborne Primalists. Neltharion stepped aside as a Stormtalon's corpse fell from the sky. Its body burst on impact, splattering them both with gore. With a snarl, Neltharion shook chunks of viscera off his hide and flicked the blood from one wing.

Another corpse tumbled from the skies. Two Reavers dived toward the Matriarch, falling like stars. Oxoria spotted them and leapt off the ledge, plummeting for the Cascades. She was pursued not only by the Reavers, but by the incoming green dragonflight as well. At Ysera's command, a small squad of greens broke away from the company, pursuing the Matriarch up the canyon.

Ysera swooped toward the Earth-Warder and a wing of her greens sped by, dousing Valdrakken's gaping wounds with their poison breath.

"Neltharion!" the green Aspect called, halting and hovering in the air, eyes wide. "Valdrakken is burning! What's happened? Never mind—there's no time. Where can we help?"

"Garion and half the Ironscales are holding the fissures near Scalewatch alone," Neltharion answered. "They could use your assistance."

"We are on our way," the green Aspect replied, then bugled a battle cry to her flight. As she sped north, her Verdant Preservers followed in her wake.

Ysera was right—Valdrakken burned. Magmatalons raced along the canyon, setting everything green and living aflame.

Great columns of black smoke rose into the air, darkening the skies and mixing the bronze dragonflight's golden sand with soot. Black scorch marks marred the city's white stone. The walls glowed with orange light. The broken corpses of ordered dragons, primal dragons, and drakonid littered the streets, each one equal in death.

Neltharion took pride in how few Ironscales were among the fallen, but their forces teetered on the verge of being overwhelmed. More Primalists struggled free of the earth and climbed into the sky, where they were met with the Heart's Guard and the Onyx Reavers.

One by one, Neltharion fought his way to the fissures and collapsed them, superheating the stone with his breath. For every breach he closed, two more appeared. He struck down Primalist after Primalist, tearing wings from shoulder joints, snapping spines, and slitting throats. Still, they came. Relentless. Unstoppable.

The Earth-Warder fought till time tumbled through his talons, till his scales dripped with blood, till he lost track of how many dragons had fallen before him. He fought until every muscle in his body felt heavy as stone itself, and he could no longer hear the screams of the dying. Everything was a haze of violence and death.

The bronzes granted the red, green, and black dragonflights the occasional respite, filling the canyons with sands that aged their enemies so fast, their bodies turned to dust. Sindragosa appeared on her way to support Malygos at the academy, too, coating the mountainsides in ice to stop the fires from reaching the city's center. The Heart's Guard radiated healing light, granting the Ironscales courage and strength as they fought.

Still, Neltharion feared it would not be enough—Iridikron had brought the full strength of Harrowsdeep to Valdrakken. The dragonflights were tiring, their formations loosening, their talons dulled.

As the day grew dark, its embers burning on the horizon, Neltharion spotted Egnion swooping toward him.

"My Aspect!" the Shadowscale called. "You must come at once. Iridikron has been found, and he seeks to destroy the Vault of the Incarnates!"

Neltharion narrowed his eyes. Tired and exhausted as he was, his hatred burned bright enough to sustain him through one final battle. If he could capture or kill Iridikron at the vault, the Primalists' forces would scatter, leaderless. Vyranoth was in the north. Even if she survived her bout with Alexstrasza—which he earnestly hoped she wouldn't—she would be in no condition to lead the Primalists against the city.

With luck, they could strike both Incarnates down on the same day.

"Zerenian, lead them!" Neltharion shouted to the highest-ranking Ironscale on the field. He leapt aloft. "I must go welcome the Stonescaled to Valdrakken."

...

BEFORE THE WORDS *I will not fail in my oaths* were off her lips, a beam of light shot toward Alexstrasza's chest. On instinct, she closed her wings and let herself fall like a stone. One of Vyranoth's icicles whistled overhead, missing the Dragon Queen by a talon-length.

Upon opening her wings, Alexstrasza sensed a golden glow from above. She rolled to her right. Vyranoth plunged past her, drawing an icy fog in her wake. It billowed through the Eye with unnatural speed, filling the sinkhole with a thick mist and blocking out the sun.

Visibility dropped to two or three wing-lengths in any direction. Water droplets collected on Alexstrasza's wing membranes but did not freeze, thanks to the battle-tested strength of Malygos's enchantments. Still, it would be easy for Vyranoth to trick Alexstrasza into impaling herself on the ice. The fog would also make it nigh unto impossible to track Vyranoth, save perhaps by scent.

"Frozen by fear," Vyranoth said with a chuckle. The sinkhole's icy walls reflected the Incarnate's voice, which made it sound as if it came from all directions at once. Alexstrasza thought the sound might be rising, meaning the Incarnate was below her.

A growl nearly escaped Alexstrasza's throat. She swallowed it down, not daring to make a sound. She knew this fight would be dangerous, and that Vyranoth would use every advantage on the field. To survive—no, to *win*—Alexstrasza had to go on the offensive and keep moving. Otherwise, she would be an easy target for Vyranoth's icy spears.

If she could not track the Incarnate by sight or sound, perhaps the cold itself would reveal the Frozenheart's location. The Life-Binder opened her wings and cruised around the Eye's perimeter, gliding silently and searching for a cold front.

The fog made a whorl on Alexstrasza's right. A golden elemental made of shifting sands exploded into sight, followed closely by another creature made from pure ice. Alexstrasza craned her neck and blasted the elemental with ruby flame. It screamed with an unnatural voice—the sound of cracking ice mixed with the shriek of a hawk—then exploded into a shower of razor-sharp shards. Two more golden elementals shimmered from the mist. Alexstrasza beat her wings and whirled in the air, slamming her tail into the first and shattering it utterly. With a roar, she snatched the second and blasted it with fire. It melted in her talons.

A thunderous *crack* echoed overhead. Enormous spears of ice shot across the Eye in a descending spiral, whistling, shrieking, and crashing toward her.

Alexstrasza turned her snout down and dived through the air. She breathed fire as she fell, turning her body into a brilliant crimson comet. The ice evaporated in her wake, hissing. She plummeted through the Eye, searing so hot she blunted the icy spines on the walls. The heat from her body blasted the fog back, revealing a shimmer of sand below.

Golden light shot past Alexstrasza's left ear. The Life-Binder dodged one of Vyranoth's ice lances, then twirled to escape a second.

There! Alexstrasza spotted a flash of golden wing. She dropped onto Vyranoth with a snarl, then sank her flaming talons into the Incarnate's back. Her attack glanced off Vyranoth's icy scales. Growling, the Incarnate twisted, shaking Alexstrasza off.

"I do not wish to harm you, Vyranoth," Alexstrasza said, beating her wings to gain altitude. "Despite our differences . . . despite all the pain we have caused each other, I would *still* prefer peace to violence!"

"There can be no peace until one of us is *dead*," Vyranoth hissed. The Sands of Time shifted left a heartbeat before the Frozenheart did. Alexstrasza followed them, swooping after Vyranoth as the Incarnate tried to take cover in the mists.

Vyranoth's golden apparition banked hard to the right. Alexstrasza shifted her wings and shot after it, narrowly missing the sharp spikes that reared from the fog.

Drawing in a deep, boiling breath, Alexstrasza launched a column of flame at Vyranoth. The Incarnate strafed through the fire, her icy scales sizzling as they melted in the heat. Vyranoth tried to feint away, but Alexstrasza was faster. She folded her wings and slammed into the Incarnate from above, sending Vyranoth careening into the icy spikes along the sinkhole's wall. They exploded as the Incarnate struck them, sending up a dense, glittering cloud of ice.

Vyranoth leapt from the wall, shaking her mane. "You were always a cunning hunter, Alexstrasza," she said, "but even your skills were never this sharp. Who aids you now, Queen of Lies?"

"You fight me, and me alone," Alexstrasza replied. "Perhaps your skills have blunted with age. You move like a glacier, and you need elementals to engage me in combat! Are you too afraid to face me on your own?"

"Hardly!" Vyranoth said, and her golden apparition spread its wings and sprang forward. Alexstrasza dodged left as the Incarnate launched herself off the wall. Before Vyranoth could turn, Alexstrasza spat fire at her flank. Vyranoth's golden apparition dived. Alexstrasza followed it as Vyranoth dropped, too, moving deeper into the shadows of the Icebound Eye.

The ice walls groaned again, flashing a dull gold in the misty air. Another loud *crack* echoed through the sinkhole, louder than close thunder. Alexstrasza halted her descent, hovering in the midst of the Eye. Cautious. Vyranoth disappeared into the shadows below.

The mists shifted on her left. A glittering apparition of an ice elemental charged at Alexstrasza. She dodged. A second golden apparition appeared, then a third, their icy revenants whistling past. She veered and lunged away from them, counting five, then seven, then ten. None tried to attack her in earnest.

"What monstrous power assists you, Alexstrasza?" Vyranoth hissed.

Alexstrasza's heartbeat pounded on her eardrums. One by one, the golden apparitions appeared, forming a ring around the Dragon Queen. What was Vyranoth trying to accomplish with her elementals? Was it just a distraction while she initiated a new, devastating attack? Or was she testing Alexstrasza, searching for an opening?

One of the elementals on Alexstrasza's right side lunged. She swerved away, then dodged the creature who tried to leap on her from behind. Alexstrasza dived, then melted a third attacker in a plume of flame. The Dragon Queen ducked and dodged until Vyranoth's laughter echoed off the Eye's icy walls.

"I think I understand," the Incarnate said, though her voice sounded much closer now.

A glittering apparition of Vyranoth swept toward Alexstrasza. But this time, the apparition's head split into two, showing two potential bite attacks—one to the wing, and the other to the throat. Alexstrasza rolled to the right to avoid taking a hit to the throat, just as Vyranoth exploded into view. The Incarnate slammed into Alexstrasza, knocking the red Aspect off balance. Vyranoth dug her back talons into Alexstrasza's torso, but her talons slipped off the Dragon Queen's armor. With a roar, Vyranoth snapped at Alexstrasza's shoulder, her fangs scoring the scales and tearing a hunk of flesh from the Aspect's hide. Sharp pains stabbed along Alexstrasza's wings and sent a shock of agony down her spine. She shrieked.

"Why didn't you keep your promise to me?" Vyranoth asked, grief suddenly so naked in her voice, so bare. She pulled Alexstrasza closer. "Why was your promise to the keepers so much more important to you?"

"I am queen, Vyranoth," Alexstrasza said through a haze of pain. "It was not order that changed me, but duty. I had to protect my kind—"

"Even as mine paid dearly!" Vyranoth shrieked. "You cast me aside and now seek to destroy the kinship I have found with others—I will not allow it, Alexstrasza! You will not take this from me, too!"

"Vyranoth," Alexstrasza said with a gasp.

The two plummeted through the Eye in a whirlwind of golden sands, icy mist, and crimson fire. Vyranoth hooked her back talons into the gaps in Alexstrasza's armor, driving the red Aspect toward the cavern's walls with dizzying speed. Desperate to get away from Vyranoth—and the pain—Alexstrasza used the strength in her back to flip over. Vyranoth's talons carved deep scores into Alexstrasza's flank as she turned, then caught on the edge of her breastplate. The pain nearly knocked Alexstrasza senseless, but Ysera's vines sent a pulse of healing magic into her body. With a wince, the Dragon Queen drew as much air into her lungs as she could and spat fire in Vyranoth's face.

Together, they slammed into the Eye's cavern wall. Bones shattered within Alexstrasza's body while ice shattered without. One of the spikes tore through her wing membrane, and another glanced off her armor and stabbed into her gut.

With a furious roar, Vyranoth leapt away. In a haze of pain, Alexstrasza slid off the wall and tumbled into the darkness. She fell for a heartbeat; she fell for an eternity.

Alexstrasza struck the Eye's cold floor, and did not move again.

CHAPTER TWENTY-THREE

Neltharion Dived through the Bevy of Bronze dragons and Rockfuries fighting around Tyrhold, incinerating the Primalists before him in an instant. He swooped through their embers and broke through the scrum, emerging in front of the Vault of the Incarnates. He halted in the air. Below, Iridikron stood on the vault's terrace, his back to Neltharion, alone. It wouldn't take long for Neltharion to strike the Stonescaled unawares . . .

A whisper rose in the back of Neltharion's mind: *You cannot defeat Iridikron without us.*

Strike now! urged a second whisper. *End this war in a single stroke.*

The Earth-Warder hesitated. *Tempted.* How easy it would be to call upon those dark powers again and seal Iridikron into the Vault of the Incarnates! With the Stonescaled off the board, the Primalist movement would collapse. Even Vyranoth, with all her impressive strength and strategy, did not have the ability to lead them the way Iridikron could.

And yet Neltharion did not trust those whispers. For all their promises, they seemed predatory, cruel . . . Neltharion did not intend to become their prey.

Iridikron turned. "Neltharion," he said, his affect flat, almost bored. "You're always nipping at my tail, aren't you?" As he moved, large fingers of lava rose from the earth and curled around the vault.

"Only because you are too much a coward to face me and fight." Furious, the Earth-Warder spread his wings wide, ossifying the massive tendrils of lava into unbreakable black rock.

Would the titan-made defenses hold against Iridikron's might?

Neltharion did not wait to find out. Closing his wings, he dived at Iridikron. The Stonescaled lunged left as Neltharion slammed into the terrace. Iridikron spun, whipping the barbed end of his tail toward Neltharion's head. Neltharion ducked. Iridikron's tail whistled over his horns.

You cannot win, a whisper said.

Neltharion sprang forward with a snarl, catching Iridikron off guard.

Call upon our power. Secure victory, said another, louder now.

He raked his talons across Iridikron's stony hide, leaving molten wounds on the Stonescaled's flank. Iridikron roared in fury.

You will not defeat the Stonescaled—

Iridikron pivoted, ramming one of his horns into Neltharion's throat with so much force, he dented Neltharion's armor. The blow left the Earth-Warder gasping, reeling. He stumbled away from Iridikron and tore the armor from his throat.

Not without our power!

Iridikron leapt on Neltharion, snapping at the Earth-Warder's exposed scales. Neltharion shrieked in fury. He pulled the stones up under their feet, using the kinetic force to shove the Stonescaled away. Iridikron went tumbling toward the door of the vault, then slid to a stop with a groan.

That dark power was now at the tips of Neltharion's talons again, calling to him, cajoling him, enticing him. Purple light crept across his scales. It would be so easy to end Iridikron now—it would be so easy to stop centuries of suffering and pain; all it would take was a flick of his forefoot and this war could be over, over, *over*. No more dragons needed to fall. No more lands would be lost. And though Neltharion was the black Aspect and Earth-Warder, he was *tired*. He had been fighting for hours, days, *centuries*.

All he wanted to do was let go and let it end.

ALEXSTRASZA'S CONSCIOUSNESS EBBED BACK, beckoned by Ysera's healing magic. She groaned. Every bone, muscle, and tendon in her body ached. She lay on the rocky floor of the coldest depths of the Icebound Eye. Weak light wafted from the skies above, leaving the pit wreathed in shadow. The scent of her own blood—the only warm thing in this forbidding place—filled her nostrils. Even the heat from Neltharion's armor ebbed, its magic shattered.

In the distance, the red dragons cried out in a chorus, able to sense the Dragon Queen's suffering from afar. Alexstrasza craned her neck, hoping to see them one last time . . . but the shadows at the bottom of the Eye draped themselves over her, thick and impenetrable.

Vyranoth's golden doppelgänger landed a heartbeat before the Incarnate herself, its sands scattering across the Eye's frozen floor. Alexstrasza had fallen out of Nozdormu's reach.

"Well fought, my old friend," the Incarnate said, stepping forward, "but you have lost, and now, your life is forfeit."

As Vyranoth stalked toward her, the Sands of Time shuddered on the floor, shivering with each of the Incarnate's footsteps. Alexstrasza saw a vision of her flights' futures in a flicker of gold: Valdrakken in ruins, its blessed waters polluted, the Oathstones destroyed. Dragons, tortured by the Primalists, their wings torn from their backs, their scales plucked from their hides, their viscera ripped from their still-living bodies; dragons, bound to Iridikron's cruel will; dragons, dead in the Dragonblight outside Wyrmrest Temple, their bodies left for carrion and never burned. Screams—ones Alexstrasza was certain only she could hear—echoed through the Eye in a whirlwind. Alexstrasza felt her heartstrings snap in her chest. A cry escaped her lips.

The sands shimmered again. Her young drakes hushed sobbing whelps in the shadows of the djaradin. Eggs were taken from the Ruby Life Pools and smashed, an end to her kind.

In one final flash, she saw: monsters marching on the world in great number, destruction on a scale she'd never seen before. All fell before their green flame: mortal, tarasek, Primalist. This was the failure of the Aspects' legacy, their charge to protect Azeroth.

In no timeline do the flights survive without you, Nozdormu whispered in her memory. *If you risk your own life, you may risk the lives of us all.*

With a pained gasp, Alexstrasza pushed herself to her feet. Blood welled from her wounds. She couldn't put much weight on her right foreleg or open her left eye. The bones of her left wing were shattered, her armor cracked.

"Still, you fight?" Vyranoth asked, halting a few wing-lengths away.

"I will fight . . . till my last breath," Alexstrasza said through gritted teeth. "I made an oath. Not only to the titans, but to my flights and to all of Azeroth. I will not fail in my duty."

"And yet you cared so little about your promise to me," Vyranoth said with a snarl. "Very well! To the last breath."

Vyranoth leapt at Alexstrasza, using her wings to propel her into the air. Time slowed, but Alexstrasza couldn't tell if it was a trick of Nozdormu's magic or the adrenaline coursing through her veins. Alexstrasza summoned every last ounce of love she had for her flights, letting that crimson fire give her strength. She charged forward, losing herself in the magic, letting it set her heart aflame.

Just as Vyranoth was about to strike, Alexstrasza leapt into her visage, sliding across the ice. Vyranoth sailed over her, whipping the wind around her fragile mortal frame. Alexstrasza pushed herself up with her palm mid-slide, pivoting and turning back into her true form in a blaze of ruby fire.

With a roar, Alexstrasza used the last of her strength to lunge onto Vyranoth's exposed back. She shocked the Incarnate with flame hot enough to vaporize ice, then sank her teeth into Vyranoth's shoulder. Alexstrasza dislocated the Incarnate's wing with a brutal jerk of her head. Vyranoth roared in pain, a sound that shook Alexstrasza to her very core. Growling, she dug her talons into Vyranoth's left shoulder and neck, striking an artery. Blood spurted and sizzled across the Frozenheart's scales.

The Incarnate reared back, throwing Alexstrasza onto the ice. The Life-Binder scrambled to her feet, one wing dragging, expecting a counterassault . . . but one never came.

Vyranoth fell to her knees. Her breath still lifted her broken shoulders, but not for long.

"Vyranoth," Alexstrasza said, though her voice was hoarse with grief and pain. "My oldest friend . . . I am so sorry . . . I am so very sorry."

Vyranoth tried to sob, but it came out as a wheeze.

The frozen fog dispersed. Vyranoth collapsed. Dragons landed all around them, ordered and primal alike, watching. None could interfere until the Frozenheart conceded or died. Tyranastrasz and Cristalstrasz were so close, Alexstrasza could smell them. All she wanted to do was collapse into her consort's side, but she could not concede the ground she stood on.

"Say it, Vyranoth," Alexstrasza said, her voice edged with anguish. "Concede. *Please*. I cannot watch you die."

The Incarnate was silent for several heartbeats, and Alexstrasza thought she was going to watch the Frozenheart breathe her last. But then, quietly, Vyranoth said, "I concede, Alexstrasza . . . The victory . . . belongs to you."

Alexstrasza's sob echoed off the walls. All the stress and strain went out of her body. She collapsed as green and red dragons rushed to her side.

"Do not let Vyranoth die," she said to them. "She will serve her time in the Vault of the Incarnates with the others. But please . . . please save her."

While the reds attended the Life-Binder, the greens breathed a sweet, gentle mist over the Incarnate, putting her into a deep sleep. They worked their healing magics into her neck, stanching the flow of blood. The blues opened portals to Vakthros, preparing to transport the fallen Incarnate.

The blacks and bronzes formed a perimeter around their queen, keeping the Primalists at bay.

Tyranastrasz sat next to her, bumping her snout with his. "I never doubted you, Alexstrasza. I ever only worried for you."

"I know," she said, closing her eyes and breathing deep as the healing magic knitted her flesh and muscle back together. It felt wonderful, just like the warmth of the springtime sun on her scales.

"Much as I would like to celebrate your victory," Tyranastrasz continued, "we had a messenger from Valdrakken not long ago—Iridikron launched a surprise attack on the city in your absence. Nozdormu has already departed. We must return posthaste."

"No . . . No, that cannot be," Alexstrasza said, trying to rise back to her feet. A shock of pain ran down her spine. She winced.

"Rest a moment," one of the reds chirped. "You'll be better soon, my queen, I promise. We need you to remain still—the work on your wing is delicate."

Alexstrasza wasn't sure they had any time, but she wouldn't be much good to Valdrakken if she was still too injured to fight. She acquiesced.

Tyranastrasz growled, a low rumble that started in the depths of his chest. The ancient wyrm stepped in front of Alexstrasza, lowering his head in a warning. Three primal dragons approached them, flanked by a unit of black dragons. The primal dragons paused and tapped their big wing-knuckles to their chest in a salute.

"We mean you no harm," the leader said to Tyranastrasz. "We would have words with the Dragon Queen."

"He speaks the truth," Alexstrasza said. "I sense no ill intent."

With a nod, her consort stepped aside.

The Primalist bowed his head to Alexstrasza. He was an old dragon, one with hoary scales that bore scars from too many battles and horns of pure ice. He fixed his intelligent blue eyes on her.

"I know you," Alexstrasza said. "You are Cysanz, wingleader of Vyranoth's Frostscales. Your legions have struck many of my dragons from the skies. What business do you have with me?"

With a glance at his fellows, Cysanz stepped forward. "I followed Vyranoth, not Iridikron. Without the Frozenheart to temper his hunger, I fear he will drive dragonkind to the brink of extinction for his war. Rava and Oxoria are as fanatical as he; I will not follow them into such a future.

"We will never accept the burden of Order magic," Cysanz continued, "but we will fight you no longer, Queen of the ordered. If you swear to leave my kind in peace—to now honor the promise you made to Vyranoth long ago—we will help you wrest Iridikron from power."

Alexstrasza rose to her feet, muscles still trembling with pain. To find a seed of hope in such a dark place . . . was this a dream? Or was this another one of the Incarnates' plots?

A wing-length away, Cristalstrasz shifted his weight, nervous, but the flightleader said nothing. The other reds looked at Alexstrasza, wide-eyed and confused.

"I sense no deceit in you," Alexstrasza said, cocking her head and narrowing her eyes, as if she could stare into the deepest cockles of his heart. "Still, you must know why I hesitate— Iridikron has ever preyed upon the Aspects' goodwill, and this seems like yet another one of his plots."

Cysanz glanced over his shoulder, watching a team of dragons prepare to move Vyranoth's sleeping form through a nearby portal. The tower of Vakthros glimmered across the portal's mirror-like face.

"You do not need to trust me," Cysanz said, turning back to her. "I do not wish to be a part of your war councils, nor do I seek to be your friend. I only seek the death of a dragon who promised so much and has given so little. Most of my brood died while Iridikron hid in his keep—I will serve him no longer."

Alexstrasza exchanged a look with Tyranastrasz. The old wyrm made no outward sign, but she sensed an aura of skepticism from him. For centuries, the Stonescaled had done everything in his power to undermine the Aspects and their flights. Alexstrasza would never be able to trust anyone who had flown in his ranks . . . but perhaps Cysanz was right. Perhaps she didn't have to trust him to cooperate with him.

"You have my word, not just as Dragon Queen but as Alexstrasza, friend to Vyranoth the Frozenheart," Alexstrasza said, her gaze flicking back to Cysanz. "Help my flights defeat Iridikron, and I will uphold the promise I made so long ago."

THE SKIES RANG WITH screams. The stones of Valdrakken crumbled, and hungry flames devoured everything Neltharion had fought so long and hard to protect. The Stonescaled now stood within several wing-lengths of breaking everything the Aspects had built, of shattering every victory they had won.

Iridikron rose to his feet. Neltharion's scales glowed with violet light.

Call on us, the whispers said.

Do it now!

No, Neltharion told them. *Not like this—*

Finish him!

Neltharion roared in defiance of the whispers, to reject the idea that he was not capable, not powerful, not *exceptional*. He roared till they drowned in a cacophony of sound, until there was nothing left of their lies. And when he finished, the silence stunned him.

"You are alone now," Iridikron said quietly. "Vyranoth will strike Alexstrasza from the skies, and what will you do, once bereft of your queen? There are no more keepers to create a new Aspect—your masters are gone, and you are but a pale shadow of their power!"

"The keepers were never our masters," Neltharion said.

"Is that so?" Iridikron replied, his yellow eyes flashing. "Did you not swear an oath to serve their whims, accepting the collar they put around your neck without question? You are a fool, Neltharion—even after all these years, you still cannot see how they manipulate you!"

"You know nothing of me," Neltharion hissed.

"Hmph," Iridikron replied, baring his fangs and curling to strike. "There are few who understand you as well as *I* do—"

A trumpeting echoed through the skies, interrupting the Stonescaled. A second voice rose out in song, then a third, until the bronzes' voices lifted in a chorus that echoed through the mountains around Tyrhold.

"What is that?" Iridikron asked with a growl.

"A victory trumpet," Neltharion said, blinking fast, confused.

"Are your bronzes so dull-witted as to think you've won?" the Stonescaled asked, lifting his gaze to the heavens. His eyes widened and his stare stretched a thousand wing-lengths long. The citrine energies along his spine faltered.

Neltharion pivoted, then looked up. A massive, anvil-shaped cloud rose over the city, stained pink with the ferocious colors of sunset. Had the fighting gone on so long that the day, too, was dead? Neltharion still sensed the sun hanging over the western horizon, glowering like a red eye through the smoke.

No . . . That was not the light of sunset. Neltharion's heart swelled. His jaw dropped open. That was the crimson light of the red dragonflight's oath, undaunted. Undefeated.

"Alexstrasza," Neltharion whispered, almost in benediction.

In the next heartbeat, the Dragon Queen burst from the clouds. Her scales gleamed with ruby light. The fighting on the field ceased around them as every eye turned heavenward. A hush fell over the city.

"I have captured Vyranoth the Frozenheart!" Alexstrasza roared from high in the skies, and her voice rang off the mountaintops. "Rise up, Valdrakken! Rise up and drive our enemies from our home!"

Alexstrasza's light concentrated in her chest and burned brilliant, just like a miniature star. It exploded outward from her in a ring, rushing through Valdrakken and northern Thaldraszus. As the light washed over Neltharion, he felt himself reinvigorated, his courage refreshed.

"With me!" Alexstrasza called and dived toward the Seat of the Aspects. Dragons—hundreds of dragons—exploded from the clouds, ordered and primal alike.

Those are Frostscales! Neltharion thought with a gasp, watching Vyranoth's battalion accompany a host of reds, greens, blues, blacks, and bronzes. Neltharion did not pretend to know how Alexstrasza had convinced Vyranoth's Frostscales to follow her into battle, but he was awed nonetheless.

"So Vyranoth has fallen," Iridikron said as the Dragon Queen disappeared from sight. "What tricks did you and your comrades employ against my sister, I wonder? Nozdormu was not on the battlefield at Algeth'ar Academy, nor was he in Valdrakken. Did the bronze Aspect go north with your queen?"

Neltharion turned back to the Stonescaled. "Alexstrasza did not need our help to best the Frozenheart. Loathe as you may be to admit it, our power is still greater than yours."

"More lies." Iridikron shifted his gaze from the skies to the Earth-Warder. "We both know Order magic cannot compete with that of the planet's elements—is that why you must rely on dark forces? How long will it be before Alexstrasza sees through your deceptions?"

Neltharion took a step back, drawing his wings up and dropping his chin.

Iridikron chuckled. "Do you think yourself so clever, Neltharion? Perhaps your fellow Aspects cannot see you for what you are, but I can. The day belongs to you and your Dragon Queen. The next will not."

With that, the Stonescaled leapt off the terrace and escaped into the ground below. Neltharion let him run, still seething, as the Primalists trumpeted their retreat.

A whisper slithered into his ear. *Look what your weakness has wrought! Had you the foresight, you could have ended this war.*

This is no victory, said a second. *You have failed.*

Neltharion pushed the voices from his mind, unwilling to listen to their prattle for one more moment. The day was won, and yet all he could feel was a sense of defeat.

CHAPTER TWENTY-FOUR

NOTHING HAD GONE TO PLAN.

Upon returning to Harrowsdeep, Iridikron retreated to his war cavern. He usually felt grounded in its depths, where the lava fell like water and the heat relaxed the stony muscles in his back . . . but the loss of Vyranoth had left him shaken.

With a heavy sigh, Iridikron went to his campaign map. He set Vyranoth's pawn on the Vault of the Incarnates, then moved the Frostscales and Icetalons to the Frozen Fangs. To his surprise, the Frostscales had joined the Aspects at Algeth'ar Academy, helping Malygos chase Warbringer Rava and her forces into the eastern Dragonwilds. Mithruz had fallen in a talon-to-talon battle with Ysera. Oxoria and her shattered brood had barely escaped Valdrakken and had fallen back to Cinderfrost Vale, where they would rest and recuperate before returning to Harrowsdeep.

In a fury, Iridikron slammed one of his wing talons down

on the stone map, cracking it through the center. The pawns rattled, teetering in place.

He should not have put so much faith in Vyranoth! Now she slept beneath a mountain. Half his Rockfuries lay dead in the valleys around Valdrakken. Centuries' worth of careful work on the tectonic plates beneath the Broodlands was *wasted,* and the Primalists had lost their talon-holds in Thaldraszus and the Reach.

Iridikron growled, and the whole of the cavern rumbled with his quiet rage. He had to stand alone against the Aspects now—if he failed, dragonkind would be shackled to the keepers and Order magic forever. He, too, would join his brother and sisters in prisons of stone.

Iridikron would not submit. He would not stop; no, he would find a way to free his allies and destroy the Aspects, no matter the cost. The Earth-Warder would not best him again.

Iridikron was better than Neltharion.

He was better than them *all.*

Without her keepers, Alexstrasza could not raise new Aspects to fight in her name. Iridikron faced no such constraints— even with his losses in Valdrakken, he still commanded hordes of primal dragons, many of whom had only grown stronger from centuries of war. He would teach others the rites and raise up new Incarnates to fight at his side.

If they died trying, so be it.

In the meantime, Iridikron would prepare Harrowsdeep for a siege. The Stonescaled had spent long centuries digging hundreds, if not thousands, of wing-lengths of tunnels . . .

even seasoned wingleaders often found themselves lost in the labyrinth underground.

Now that he was alone, the Aspects would certainly try to push the war out of the Broodlands and back into the Dragonwilds. If they came to Harrowsdeep, perhaps he could weaponize the entirety of the keep against them.

A sweep of wings drew his attention to the front of the platform. He lifted his head, frowning as one of his wingleaders landed before him. "What is it?" he said with a growl.

"Stonescaled," the wingleader said, tapping a talon to his chest. "Warbringer Rava has returned from the front. May I send her—"

"I'll kill him!" a shriek echoed through the caverns. "I will have Cysanz's *head* for this!"

With a sigh, Iridikron gave the wingleader a nod. It mattered not, for Rava rumbled into the war cavern and launched herself into the air, landing on the central platform with a heavy thud.

"I will tear him limb from limb!" Rava said, her stone scales cracked and battered. He had not seen Rava in at least a decade, and it appeared the war had taken its toll. "He betrayed us, Iridikron! He betrayed our kind and our cause, and he killed my wingleaders in front of me!"

"Calm yourself, Rava," Iridikron said, his scales scraping on stone as he turned away from his campaign map. "We will make new plans, find new allies."

"Who?" Rava snapped. "Who is left to us now? Vyranoth's little drakes? Bah!"

"There are still those who hate the Aspects as much as we do," Iridikron said. "Gather your forces to Harrowsdeep. If we cannot beat the Aspects in the air, we shall trap them in stone."

PART SIX

A Hunger in the Deep

After our victories in *Valdrakken* and at the *Icebound Eye*, we pushed the Primalists out of the Broodlands and back into the Dragonwilds. Alexstrasza, Neltharion, and an allied force of red, black, blue, green, and bronze dragons gave chase, while Ysera, Malygos, and I remained behind to defend the Broodlands from invasion. We took no risks, not after we had paid for peace at home with the blood of our flights.

As our forces moved closer to Harrowsdeep, Iridikron's methods became more irregular, almost desperate—the Primalists used ambushes, small skirmishes, feint-and-counterattacks as they retreated, unwilling to risk more conventional battles. The Stonescaled slowed our advance, but he no longer had the numbers to halt it for long.

The Shadowscales reported that Iridikron endeavored to create new Incarnates, but none of the candidates managed to survive the process. Igyniar, one of the Primalists' greatest champions, was felled by an attempt to become the next Incarnate of flame. Vildryc, leader of the fractured Icetalons, suffered the same fate.

For the next few decades, hundreds of primal dragons went to their deaths trying to follow in the Incarnates' footsteps. Perhaps we were lucky that none succeeded . . . though it is more likely that after Vildryc's death, Iridikron could no longer afford to risk his finest on the process. Our forces had won back the territories around Wyrmrest Temple, and the Stonescaled knew Alexstrasza and Neltharion would not stop there.

The Dragon Queen meant to push all the way to Harrowsdeep and tear Iridikron from his lair. As she blazed west across the Dragonwilds, no new allies rallied to the Primalist cause. Even so, we knew the fight at Harrowsdeep would be the deadliest encounter of them all.

I have seen too many horrible battles at that fell mountain: mountain ranges laid low, entire battalions slaughtered by Rockfuries, flightleaders trapped forever in endless labyrinths of stone, volcanic eruptions that set the skies aflame . . . but so long as Iridikron is free, there will be no true peace. We must capture the Stonescaled, even if that means facing the horrors of Harrowsdeep ourselves.

As of today, Alexstrasza stands on the edge of Iridikron's territory. Soon, the rest of the Aspects shall join her.

We shall end this war.

CHAPTER TWENTY-FIVE

IRIDIKRON SPENT DECADES PREPARING TO RECEIVE THE Dragon Queen at Harrowsdeep. The Primalists had slowed her advance, holding Alexstrasza and Neltharion at bay while the Stonescaled made new plans, sought to create new Incarnates, and filled the lightless tunnels and caverns of Harrowsdeep with horrors uncountable. At his command, the thousand halls of his keep would rumble and shift, turning the mountain into an endless, unsolvable maze.

Let the Dragon Queen think she was on the offense! Her confidence would cause her to overlook the dangers Iridikron had crafted in shadow and stone. If she stepped foot inside Harrowsdeep, Iridikron would entomb her under the mountain, just as she had done to Raszageth, Fyrakk, and Vyranoth.

No matter the cost, Iridikron would crush the Aspects to dust, shatter their flights, and wipe Order magic from the world.

He would free the other Incarnates from their prisons, if only to lay Neltharion's work low.

However, to bring his plans to fruition, the Stonescaled needed new allies.

Iridikron found the djaradin chieftainess in a great, yawning cavern deep within the world's crust. Igira the Cruel was a hulking creature, one of the largest of her kind. Fiery markings danced across her indigo skin, and thick scars marbled her flesh. The scent of dragon's blood clung to her unwashed clothing, pungent and rancid. Her battle-axe was notched from biting into the scales of hundreds of red and black dragons.

The giantess sat alone on a rocky promontory, overlooking a lake of magma. She had recently led an allied force into the Scalecracker Peaks, taking advantage of Alexstrasza's and Neltharion's absence in the Waking Shores. After fifteen moons, she suffered a crushing defeat at the talons of the red and black dragonflights, who then chased the djaradin from their ancestral lands.

As Iridikron crept toward her, silent as melting stone, the giantess spoke. "Have you come to fight me, dragon?" Igira made no move. Instead, she watched the great islands of black stone float across the lava. Contemplative.

"I have come to offer you a new challenge. And a chance at vengeance."

The djaradin leader blew a breath out her nose and lifted her chin. Long, matted locks of hair shifted across her broad back. "Would you offer yourself to my axe, dragon?"

"We share a common enemy, you and I," Iridikron said, pausing a few wing-lengths from the giantess. "What if I told you I could deliver to your people not only the Waking Shores, but the five Aspects as well?"

"I would call you a fool," Igira replied. "The Aspects are canny enemies, as you well know, Iridikron the Stonescaled. Have they not beaten you from the skies? Time and time again, I have watched your forces fall to their superior strength!"

Iridikron narrowed his eyes. "You have fared no better against them, Igira the Cruel."

"Then why do you come to me now?" the djaradin said, turning to look at him from the corner of one eye.

"You hate the Aspects perhaps more than I do," Iridikron replied. "You and your kind stand to gain much from their annihilation. We should fight them together."

The djaradin's face remained impassive. She studied him for a long moment, gaze narrow, before turning away. "I would sooner kill you than call you an ally."

"Prove it, then!" Iridikron thumped the ground with his tail, cracking the stone underfoot. A new crevasse formed like a thunderbolt in the rock, racing toward the djaradin leader. Just before it reached her backside, Igira slammed her fist down. The impact shattered a small crater in the stone, halting Iridikron's attack.

The djaradin leapt to her feet and turned. The blade of her battle-axe glowed with bright fire as she charged forward. Iridikron growled and dropped his chin to protect his throat— but otherwise the Stonescaled sank his talons into the rock and stood his ground.

Igira swung her axe in a massive arc, its light searing Iridikron's sight. She slammed the blade into the Stonescaled's neck, where the metal shattered on stone. The blow reverberated through Iridikron's body. He grunted. The broken pieces of Igira's axe clattered to the floor, useless.

The djaradin stumbled back from him, eyes wide. Iridikron thought he saw a tremor roll through her knees, but it might have been a figment of his imagination.

"It will take more than an axe to shatter my hide," Iridikron said.

"Ah, a proper challenge." Igira's lips turned up in a wicked grin, charging at him a second time. "I will kill you with my bare hands, then!"

"Unlikely," Iridikron replied, forcing the ground to buck beneath her. She stumbled and fell to her knees.

The djaradin looked up at him with a snarl.

"Help me kill the Aspects, Igira, and I shall give you the fight you so desire."

She eyed him as she rose to her feet. "If I were to agree to this . . . *alliance*," she said with no small amount of distaste, "what would you ask of me?"

"You have many friends among the djaradin tribes in the Dragonwilds," he said. "Call them to Harrowsdeep."

"Fine," she said, cracking the knuckles of one hand against the palm of the other. "But you will need to bring us your prey quickly, or else we will turn on *you*."

...

TALINSTRASZ SPENT THE NIGHT near Wyrmrest Temple, helping the djaradin lure dragons away from the safety of their flights' patrols. The red would feign injury, pretending to have been struck down by half-giants' spears. Once the target came within range, the djaradin would leap from the shadows, knocking the dragon unconscious. The victims were then chained and transported underground.

The red delivered the dragons to a cavern in the Sawtooth Mountains, conferring quickly with the djaradin huntmaster. All told, Talinstrasz had helped capture twelve dragons in a single night. The huntmaster eyed him curiously, almost hungrily, and Talinstrasz wondered if he would one day be tossed into a cage as well. The red knew Iridikron would never trust him, but perhaps that was just as well—Talinstrasz felt no sense of connection or loyalty to the Stonescaled either.

Talinstrasz fought for Vyranoth, and Vyranoth alone.

Iridikron had ordered Talinstrasz and his comrades to work with the djaradin and capture as many dragons as they could manage. The red approached the task with resolve—he would do anything to help free Vyranoth from the Vault of the Incarnates. She had taken him under her wing, literally and figuratively, and taught him much about the world.

Talinstrasz would not leave her to rot.

As he strode past the sleeping dragons in their chains, a small, hushed voice asked, "Talinstrasz?"

The voice sent a shock of electricity through Talinstrasz's veins—he knew it well. The red closed his eyes, telling himself to leave, to fly away, to *forget*. All that mattered now was freeing Vyranoth from her prison under the mountain.

Against his better judgment, he turned, his tail scraping on the cavern's stone floor.

A red dragon stared at him from a pack of slumbering dragons, her golden eyes pleading. Even cast in shadow, Talinstrasz recognized her face—the high cheekbones; the elegant, four-pronged crown of horns; her large, oval eyes; the sharpness of her snout. A heavy black collar encircled her neck, and three thick chains lashed her to the ground.

His heart stumbled over a beat. "Lailastrasza," he whispered, frozen. "Sister." What had she been doing at Wyrmrest Temple? Last he checked, his sister had chosen to join the Ruby Flamebringers. She should have been thousands of wing-lengths away from here.

Lailastrasza tried to rise to her feet, straining against the taut chains. The light from a nearby torch fell on her confused features. A green drake shifted his weight in the shadows behind her, turning his head to look in their direction. Talinstrasz recognized the green as Atyrannus, one of his sister's oldest and dearest friends.

"What are you doing here?" Lailastrasza said, glancing at a nearby guard. "You . . . Are you working with the *djaradin*? With *dragon-killers*?"

"You won't be harmed, Laila, I swear it," Talinstrasz said, though even he could taste the bitterness of the lie on his lips. "The Aspects fly on Harrowsdeep—you and your fellows will only be used to keep Neltharion from dropping Harrowsdeep on our heads, nothing more."

"Who told you that?" Lailastrasza whispered, tears pooling in her eyes. "Iridikron? Igira the Cruel? You cannot possibly believe that the *djaradin* mean me no harm. I've spent decades fighting them on our borders. They will not spare me."

"They will," Talinstrasz said, ignoring the sharp pain in his chest. He turned away. "I am sorry, sister, but I cannot help you."

"Talinstrasz, please," Lailastrasza said with a sob. The fear and grief in her voice cracked his heart in half, but he kept moving forward, placing one foot in front of the other. "Don't leave us here. The djaradin will kill us! Talinstrasz? Talinstrasz!"

He took flight, allowing her screams to fade away.

CHAPTER TWENTY-SIX

ALEXSTRASZA LANDED ON AN ICY SUMMIT IN THE Sawtooth Mountains, bristling, watching Warbringer Rava and her forces fall back to Harrowsdeep. Iridikron's keep towered over the peaks of every other mountain in the range, a singular, snowcapped behemoth that speared the sky. The sunset turned its tip blood red.

A large valley stretched out below her, looking like a gash in the world's scaly hide.

Neltharion's Earthen Bulwark swept past her in pursuit, chasing the Primalists away from the southern ridge. The Ruby Flamebringers brought up the rear, while the rest of the Aspects' forces halted at the Dragon Queen's signal. This was far enough for tonight—they could use the ridge for protection while they summoned the other Aspects and mustered the remainder of their forces for the siege.

After so many centuries of war, the sight of Harrowsdeep filled Alexstrasza with a mixture of fury and dread. She knew

Iridikron would not come and meet the Aspects on the field. If they wanted to stop him, they would have to descend into the mountain's depths and wrest him out. One Incarnate could not hope to face five Aspects, but Alexstrasza doubted the Stonescaled had been idle all these years.

No doubt Iridikron would try to trap the Aspects under that horrible mountain, just as the Aspects had trapped the other Incarnates in the vault.

Neltharion landed beside her, taking stock of the mountain. "Long have I wanted to set eyes upon Harrowsdeep," he said. "My Shadowscales say the tunnels never stop shifting, turning the keep into an endless, ever-changing labyrinth. We have lost more than one good dragon in those depths."

Alexstrasza let out a measured, steady breath. "I assume you have a plan to deal with the tunnels?"

"I have half a mind to fill Iridikron's warrens with molten stone, or crack the earth and drop the mountain on his head," the Earth-Warder replied, his armor creaking as he gave his wings a pert shake. "But you won't allow that, will you?"

"I must have proof of his capture or death," Alexstrasza said. "I will not risk him escaping, only to bring war to the Broodlands once more with greater force."

"Then we must risk the descent," Neltharion said with a tilt of his head. "Once we're inside, the black dragonflight will keep our path secure . . . though I cannot be sure how effective our stone wards will be in Iridikron's keep."

"Do we know the location of his lair?" Alexstrasza asked, sweeping her gaze over the peaks. "Or does that move as well?"

"As far as we know, it is only the tunnels that move. But no Shadowscale has ever seen the inside of Iridikron's war cavern."

"Very well," she replied. "Let us summon the other Aspects from Valdrakken. Once they arrive, we will call a war council and decide how to deal with the Stonescaled."

Neltharion departed, calling orders for watches to be established and portals to be prepared. Alexstrasza stood on the ridge, alone, till the shadows flooded the spaces between the mountain peaks, unable to look away from Harrowsdeep's cruel peak. How long had she dreamed of this moment? She should feel exultant, triumphant; but the closer Alexstrasza had drawn to Iridikron's lair, the more Vyranoth's final words to Alexstrasza tortured the Dragon Queen.

Why didn't you keep your promise to me? Vyranoth's words echoed in Alexstrasza's memory and gnawed on her heart, leaving a cold emptiness there. *Why was your promise to the keepers so much more important to you?*

Those words still stung. Perhaps not to the side of Alexstrasza who was Dragon Queen, Life-Binder, and red Aspect—that part of her understood why her oath to the titans took precedence, for the safety of Azeroth hung in the balance. But Alexstrasza the dragon, the mother, the sister, the *friend* cried out from the deepest depths of her soul, burdened with the pain and regret of failing her oldest friend. Now all Alexstrasza wanted to do was end this war and bury its horrors under stone, forever. She would not apologize for all that had happened, but she certainly regretted that she might never have the chance to melt Vyranoth's frozen heart. Moreover, she swore not to repeat past mistakes, to listen more and hide less.

A flutter of wings made Alexstrasza turn. Saristrasz alighted behind her, dipping his head. "I am sorry to interrupt you, my queen, but the other Aspects have arrived."

"I will join them at once," Alexstrasza replied, turning away from the mountain as it fell into darkness. Before the sun rose again, the flights would marshal for war.

Saristrasz led Alexstrasza to an aerie that had been hastily hollowed out from the mountainside, expanding on a set of abandoned caves near the southern ridge. Outside, the blues maintained large, glimmering shields. Glowing portals from Vakthros allowed hundreds of fresh wings to join them from the Broodlands. The bronzes wove time enchantments around the camp, preventing the enemy from taking them unawares. The reds organized the drakonid, while the black dragonflight built camps and constructed artillery with the greens.

Alexstrasza swooped into the aerie, carved from gray stone, landing just inside its mouth. The air warmed by several degrees. In a large central chamber, Neltharion and the other Aspects gathered about a stone map that depicted the Dragonwilds with Harrowsdeep at its center. Majordomos and flightleaders filled the cavern, and every head bowed as the Dragon Queen entered. Their scales gleamed with the light thrown from the makeshift braziers.

"To those of you joining us tonight, I bid you welcome," Alexstrasza said, rounding the other Aspects and taking her place at the head of the map. She exchanged a tired smile with

Ysera, then nodded to Malygos and Nozdormu. She looked to Neltharion first as she said, "It has been many years since we have fought on the same front, as one. Tomorrow, we shall bring an end to a conflict that has sought to shatter our flights, raze our homeland, and break our sacred oaths."

Trumpets, calls, and roars accompanied her words. Though grateful for their support, the Dragon Queen lifted a wing, asking for silence.

"Iridikron's forces have been on the run for months now." Alexstrasza turned her gaze to the campaign map below, gesturing to it with a sweep of her talons. She took the pawns for Warbringer Rava and Oxoria and moved them to the keep. "Though the Primalists maintain greater numbers, they will not be able to stand against five Aspects and their flights. Iridikron knows this, which is why I believe the true battle will be fought in the depths of Harrowsdeep."

Alexstrasza set the Stonescaled's pawn on the keep. She swore the stone trembled beneath it.

Malygos made a small humming noise in his throat, thinking. "I worry Iridikron will not be in Harrowsdeep at all. We cannot go inside that mountain, for he may drop it on our heads."

"Harrowsdeep is a trap—of that, I have no doubt." Alexstrasza moved the Aspects' glittering pawns to the southern ridge. "But if we are to put an end to this war, we must capture him."

"I agree with Alexstrasza on this point," Neltharion said. "Iridikron will not leave Harrowsdeep. Crafty as he may be, he believes himself the most capable strategist on the field. Like the others, his arrogance will be his downfall."

The Earth-Warder ran a talon from the Obsidian Citadel to Wyrmrest Temple, saying, "The Primalists' tactics in the Dragonwilds have been irregular, seeking only to hold us at bay. In recent days, we have gained more territory with greater speed. I believe the Stonescaled has finished his preparations to receive us, which is why he has allowed us to approach his keep with such haste."

"Have we any idea of what he might be planning?" Ysera asked, looking to Nozdormu.

The bronze Aspect shook his head. "The warrens of Harrowsdeep are vast and ever moving. 'Tis impossible to know how they will shift. All I can see in the timeways is Iridikron, standing at the heart of the world in a quaking chamber of stone."

"Charming," Malygos replied.

Alexstrasza moved pawns across the map for the dragonflights, as well as their drakonid. "He will not be able to trap us underground. We will establish a portal chamber here"—she tapped the aerie they stood in—"and leave a complement of dragons to defend it."

"That allows the blues to evacuate, but what of the other flights?" Malygos asked, rubbing his chin with a talon. "I can send blues with every company, but we should have contingency plans in place in the event of separation or loss of the mages."

"Can you enchant a stone or a scale that will allow us to return to a predetermined location?" Alexstrasza asked.

"Perhaps," Malygos said, narrowing his eyes and counting their forces on the map. "But I will not be able to make enough for all by the morn. There are more than a thousand dragons with us, not including Cysanz and his Frostscales."

"We won't be taking a thousand dragons into Harrowsdeep," Alexstrasza replied, moving the Aspects' pawns north across the field to the keep. "No more than one hundred will descend into the depths with us."

"You don't intend to take an army into Harrowsdeep?" Malygos asked her, then glanced sideways at Neltharion. "Is that wise?"

The Earth-Warder inclined his head. "We have kept careful count of their numbers. Iridikron will send every dragon to meet us on the field tomorrow, perhaps hoping to exhaust us before we descend into the keep."

"We will use the bulk of our forces to shatter Warbringer Rava's front lines while Cysanz flanks her from the north," Alexstrasza said, moving Cysanz's pawns down from the Frozen Fangs. They scraped along the stone board. "Once the Primalists fall into disarray, the Frostscales will scatter them to the winds. Our flights will secure the outside of the keep, while each Aspect takes a strike force inside."

Ysera shifted her weight, nervous. "That's all very well, but how do we locate the Stonescaled inside an endless maze of subterranean tunnels? That would be a challenging feat even *if* they were not in constant motion."

"We follow the quakes," Neltharion said. "I believe the black dragonflight will be able to triangulate his location based on the seismic waves moving through the cavern's rock."

"This is madness," Malygos said, pressing one of his digits into his temple. "Are you certain you can't bring every scalesmith in your flight and shatter the mountain range entire, Neltharion?"

The Earth-Warder grinned at the idea, but before he could reply, Alexstrasza lifted her voice. "No, we cannot allow him a chance to escape. For the atrocities Iridikron the Stonescaled has inflicted upon dragonkind, he shall take his place in the Vault of the Incarnates. By wing and by talon, I *will* see this done."

The assembled dragons murmured Alexstrasza's final words, which rose in a quiet, determined chorus in the cavern.

"My queen," a voice called out. Alexstrasza lifted her head. Egnion, leader of the Shadowscales, stepped forward. "There was news from Wyrmrest Temple just before this council convened—it may have some relevance to this discussion."

Scales sparkled as everyone turned their heads in Egnion's direction, and the assembly fell silent.

"You have the floor, Egnion," Alexstrasza said, squaring her shoulders.

The flightleader drew a breath. "Over the last few days, more than thirty dragons and drakes have been kidnapped from patrol units around Wyrmrest Temple. My Shadowscales believe the victims are being moved underground to Harrowsdeep by an allied force of djaradin and Primalist sympathizers."

Alexstrasza narrowed her eyes, a flame of fury kindling in her chest. "Iridikron is working with the *djaradin*?" she asked with a hiss. "With *dragon-killers*?"

"What use would the Stonescaled have of prisoners?" Ysera asked, looking to Neltharion, then to Alexstrasza. "Do you think he means to kill them?"

"I am certain Iridikron intends to use them as a shield," Neltharion said, drumming his talons on the floor. "He knows Alexstrasza would never allow the black dragonflight to crush Harrowsdeep if she believes there are prisoners of war inside."

"He is not wrong about that," Alexstrasza said through her teeth. She would not drop Harrowsdeep on Iridikron's head at the cost of innocent lives, not even to win the day. "Can the Shadowscales find where our kin are being held?" She looked from Egnion to Neltharion.

"We will do everything within our power to locate them," the Earth-Warder replied.

"Good," Alexstrasza said, turning to the blue Aspect. "Malygos, can I leave the portal chamber and its defense to you?"

"Of course," he said, dipping his head.

The Dragon Queen blew out a hot breath, considering the board. "Very well, this news informs our strategy, but it does not change it. Prepare for battle—we strike at dawn."

AS THE HOUR GREW late, Alexstrasza lingered in the grand cavern with Neltharion, unable to sleep. She paced back and forth, muttering to herself, while the Earth-Warder lounged beside the war map. He tapped the end of his tail on the floor, the only sign that he was as anxious for the dawn as she. The other Aspects had retired hours ago. Ysera had offered to sprinkle dust from the Dream over Alexstrasza's eyes, but the Dragon Queen declined.

Tonight, a hundred worries picked at her mind like hungry birds—she was not used to facing the unknown on the battlefield. She had always been able to see her enemies' talons and teeth while fighting in the Dragonwilds and in the Reach, but tomorrow she would send her best and bravest into the unknown depths of Harrowsdeep. Not even Neltharion's Shadowscales could say what dangers they would face in those tunnels, nor where the missing members of their flights were hidden in the deep.

Most of all, Alexstrasza worried that she and Neltharion had failed to foresee important elements of the Stonescaled's plans. The Primalists could not hope to stand against the five Aspects, united—and yet Warbringer Rava's forces camped at the mountains' feet and slept as if they would not face the dragonflight's combined wrath on the morrow. Oxoria's brood had disappeared into aeries scattered across the mountains, while Virec, the leader of Iridikron's last company of Rockfuries, had taken the high position on the mountain's subsummit.

The Primalists had two advantages—numbers and the home front. Once Cysanz's Frostscales joined the battle, the Primalists' power would be whittled down.

Iridikron might see his forces as pawns, but Alexstrasza refused to believe he hadn't left the Primalists with a hidden third advantage. *But what?* she wondered. What horrors had the Stonescaled saved for his last stand? Not even Neltharion could guess what awaited them on the morrow.

The Earth Warder rolled Iridikron's pawn between his talons, slowly grinding it down to dust.

"You are going to wear the floor smooth at this rate, my queen," he observed of her pacing. "It is unlike you to worry so."

"I can't help but go over every detail in my mind," Alexstrasza said, stalking past him for the hundredth time. "I think you are right: We will be best served sending the Heart's Guard to the center of the battlefield. They are fresher than the Ironscales and will be better equipped to handle Rava's tactics."

The Dragon Queen paused as the ground rumbled underfoot. With a frown, she turned her head to gauge Neltharion's reaction—the Earth-Warder had his eyes closed, head cocked, listening to the groans of the deep earth. He took a breath, then two, his expression unreadable.

Then he crushed Iridikron's pawn in his talons. Springing to his feet, he said, "Iridikron moves to set off volcanic eruptions under Harrowsdeep and its neighboring peaks—we must wake everyone, *now*! We may be under attack—"

A stony roar shattered the night. Tremors racked the cavern, splitting the floor and nearly sending Alexstrasza sprawling. Neltharion dug his talons into the rock for purchase. The pawns on the campaign table scattered. Braziers wobbled and toppled, and waves of sparks crashed across the ground. Warning bugles filled the air. Together, the two Aspects rushed outside and leapt aloft.

On the other side of the valley, Harrowsdeep coughed great gouts of flame and ash into the skies. Magma crashed down the mountain's flanks, spilling from the gaping wound in its summit. A second peak exploded, then a third; the explosions rocked the air and cast the whole of the battlefield in an eerie orange glow. The light threw the Primalists' forms into silhouette as they locked ranks over the battlefield.

Alexstrasza threw her head back and trumpeted to the sky—a long, commanding note, calling her flights to battle. The sound of her voice filled the valley, a warning and a challenge to the enemies of the Dragon Queen.

The Ironscales were the first to answer her call, having slept in their armor. One hundred and fifty black dragons took to the skies, while Garion carried the Earth-Warder's armor to him.

"We will hold them over the valley," Neltharion said, sliding into his breastplate. "Come as soon as you can."

"A hundred and fifty of you?" Alexstrasza said, wide-eyed. "Against nearly two thousand?"

"I can give you three minutes—five if Nozdormu can slow them down," Neltharion said with a cheeky grin, then trumpeted three short blasts at the Ironscales, who dived toward the mountain and tore hunks of flat rock from its summit. "*Hurry.*"

...

THE DJARADIN HAD DRAGGED Lailastrasza's cage into the depths of Iridikron's keep, wrapping her chains around a thick, unbreakable column of stone. In the low light, Lailastrasza could barely make out the vast cavern around her. Water dripped from the ceiling's rocky fangs, pattering on her scales. The air was moist and smelled of mud and must. The only light came from the djaradin's torches and the large, sickly phosphorescent mushrooms growing in the darkness.

Atyrannus and Rygos were chained nearby, almost close enough to touch. A bronze, Dokkuldormu, was shackled to a wall, along with a red Lailastrasza had known from her work at the Ruby Life Pools, Elistrasza. The others lay unmoving, unconscious. Only Atyrannus watched the shadows with apprehension, trembling.

Before she had been hauled away, Lailastrasza watched the djaradin lead at least twenty other dragons down different corridors. The dragons had disappeared into the shadows with their captors, fighting, trembling, or sobbing.

The djaradin refused to tell the dragons what would become of them. Nor could Lailastrasza guess as to how much time had passed since they had been captured—the growl of her stomach told her it had been at least a day, but without the sun, she couldn't say for sure.

Lailastrasza would never forgive Talinstrasz, not so long as she lived. How could he leave her to *die* in the hands of enemies as nightmarish as the djaradin? He had to know that she and Aymestrasz had led the attack on Scalecracker Keep, delivering a crushing blow to Igira's forces! Why, if one of the djaradin happened to recognize her, they would kill her regardless of the Stonescaled's plans.

A rumble shivered through the floor. Atyrannus lifted his head. "What was that?" he asked.

"Just an earthquake," she said gently.

The words were barely off her lips before the floor jolted so hard, it sent Lailastrasza tumbling head-over-tail into the wall behind them. The whole cavern trembled and groaned. Lailastrasza pressed herself to the ground, looking left and right, while Atyrannus buried his head under her wing. The air filled with the scents of sulfur and smoke. Grit tumbled from the roof in rocky streams. Magma oozed from cracks in the walls. The djaradin shouted orders at one another, their words indecipherable over the mountain's fury.

"What's going on?" Atyrannus shrieked over the earth's frantic cries.

"I-I don't know," Lailastrasza replied. "It might be a volcanic eruption."

"Maybe it's the black dragonflight," he cried. "Maybe they're going to collapse the mountain! Iridikron's down here, right? Maybe they will just kill him and us, too—"

"No, no," she said, shaking her head. "They would *never* do that, not while there are dragons trapped in the mountain."

Atyrannus lifted his head, his breathing shallow. Panicked. "The Aspects might not even know we're gone, Laila—"

A stalactite shook loose and crashed into the ground nearby, startling them both. Lailastrasza turned her face away as shrapnel needled her scales. The green whimpered.

"Someone will have noticed," she told him. "Someone will have told them! We must trust in the Dragon Queen. She knows our names, Atyrannus, she will not abandon us in our darkest hour."

But the keep shook, and shook, and *shook* until Lailastrasza thought Atyrannus might be right—perhaps the mountain would swallow them alive. It was hard to find hope in the confines of her chains, but the red radiated a little ruby light, if only to push back the shadows.

Even if she died this day, she would not die in the darkness. She curled up to make herself as small as possible, trying to take courage. Iridikron's mountain would only rage if the Aspects were on the offensive. Still, hours passed with no respite and the red teetered on the verge of despair.

A glimmer in the darkness drew Lailastrasza's attention to a nearby curtain of flowstone. She lifted her head. The shadows shifted. With a growl, the red pushed to her feet, spreading her toes to give herself more stability as the ground shook.

"Who's there?" she whispered, glancing sideways at the djaradin who kept a lazy watch some twenty wing-lengths away. The half-giants had chained the dragons to large columns of stone . . . but those same rocky features blocked their sightlines, too.

A blue dragon appeared in a sizzle of arcane sparks, watching Lailastrasza with a sharp, intelligent gaze. Lailastrasza caught a gasp in her throat. The blue put a talon to her snout.

"Sirigosa?" the red whispered, feeling a flicker of hope kindle in her chest. "W-what are you doing here?"

"Rescuing you and the other unfortunates from Harrowsdeep," Sirigosa said as she sidled closer. "I can do nothing for the ones who slumber—we will have to hope that the Dragon Queen is successful in her campaign against Iridikron to save them."

"Do you know where my brother is?" Lailastrasza asked. "Is he in the keep, too?"

Sirigosa cocked her head. "Probably, he's been Iridikron's little errand-whelp since the Dragon Queen defeated Vyranoth."

The blue tapped Lailastrasza's collar, then did a little flourish with a talon. The lock slid open. With another furtive glance at the djaradin, Lailastrasza slipped free, relishing her first unrestrained breath.

"That's a useful spell," the red whispered.

Sirigosa made a face. "I know a lot of unsavory spells . . . fortunately, or unfortunately."

By now, Rygos and Atyrannus had awoken. Sirigosa freed them from their collars, too.

Together, they slipped into a shadowy alcove nearby. Sirigosa opened a glowing portal to the Aspects' camp. Rygos and Atyrannus slipped into the portal, thanking the blue, but Lailastrasza hesitated.

"I can't go back, not if Talin is still here," she whispered. "I must see him again, for I may never have another opportunity."

"If you are sure, you may come with me," the blue said. "But you must listen to everything I say—Harrowsdeep is a dangerous place, and I'd rather you not be the death of us both."

"You have my word," the red said.

"Good," Sirigosa replied. "Let us hurry, we have more dragons to free."

AS THE SKIES OVER Harrowsdeep burned, Alexstrasza leapt high in the air. Even with the support of the blue dragonflight, Neltharion and the Ironscales could not hold back the Primalists' onslaught much longer. The front line bowed under the pressure from the Rockfuries.

"Heart's Guard, with me!" Alexstrasza shouted. The battalion answered with a roar, filling the skies with their crimson wings. Below them, Ysera's Verdant Preservers took flight, ready to fall in behind and provide offensive and defensive support to the front lines. Nozdormu's Temporal Guardians had already joined the field, working under the scrums to slow the enemy and protect the red and black dragonflights should an attack come from below. The bronzes' Chronomagi would join the Spellweavers in providing ranged support, while the Onyx Reavers cruised high overhead, ready to drop through clouds of ash and devastate their enemies.

As the Dragon Queen turned to the battlefield, she took a deep, steadying breath, stoking the fires in her chest. Her flights were outnumbered, but not terribly so; no doubt Iridikron had launched a surprise attack to deprive the Aspects of their allies to the north. No matter. Tonight, they would break the Primalists' lines and scatter them across the Dragonwilds.

Bojsanz and Ymistrasza, flightleaders of the Heart's Guard, flanked the Dragon Queen on her right and left sides, respectively. They would serve as her bodyguards while she led the battalion.

"On your signal, my queen," Bojsanz said, giving Alexstrasza a nod.

Alexstrasza bared her fangs. Tendrils of ruby flames curled around her lips. Her blood burned hot, and adrenaline blazed through her veins. She did not love fighting for fighting's sake, the way Fyrakk did, but it still sent a thrill through her every scale.

With a hard beat of her wings, she leapt higher in the air, shouting, "For the Broodlands! For Valdrakken!" A great cheer rose behind her as she trumpeted thrice—two short blasts and one long, warning the Ironscales that the Heart's Guard would perform a dive-and-replace on the Primalists' front lines. A second trumpet echoed over the battlefield, acknowledging Alexstrasza's orders.

The Dragon Queen climbed higher, followed by the Heart's Guard. With an elegant turn in the air, she dived toward the front, whirling to avoid an oncoming volley of lightning. In the next breath, she sped over the Ironscales' heads and rammed into the Primalists' line.

Ymistrasza tucked her wings and slipped beneath The Dragon Queen, spitting fire at two Magmatalons taking aim at the queen. Bojsanz descended on two Stonescales on Alexstrasza's right side, tearing into them. The din of battle became visceral; Alexstrasza felt the bony *crunch* of the Primalists' front line as the Heart's Guard fell upon them.

She sucked in a breath. Crimson flames exploded from her maw in a wide cone, pushing the Primalists back as her reds reestablished the front line. The Ironscales fell back. In the distance, Neltharion shouted, "Flank them from the west! Go!"

The Primalists surged forward, their ranks broken, wild. Alexstrasza rolled sideways to dodge an attack from a Magmatalon, slashing out as she spun. Her talons sliced through the front of his throat. He dropped. Roaring, Bojsanz collided with two Galestrikers above Alexstrasza. Bones cracked. On instinct, Alexstrasza rocketed upward, spiraled, then dropped on her attackers with a snarl, slashing, gouging, and biting. Even with their greater numbers, the Primalists could not hope to best an Aspect.

Alexstrasza took no joy in killing, no matter how proficient she might be at it; she mourned every life that met its end on the battlefield—dragon, drakonid, and tarasek alike. She hated the screams on the wind; she hated how suffering permeated the very air around her; but most of all, *she hated that the only way to stop it was to cause more suffering, more hostility, more pain.*

Stars began to fall from the sky, streaking through the clouds of ash and striking the Primalists. Golden streaks of fire whizzed past Alexstrasza, bright as the noonday sun. Bright bolts of moonfire sliced through the Primalists' scales. Ysera and her Verdant Preservers called upon the heavens' strength to provide offensive support for the Dragon Queen's battalion.

As the black dragons shifted south, Neltharion and the Ironscales managed to catch a regiment of Magmatalons off-guard, surrounding them and striking them down. Spellweavers blinked over companies of Galestrikers and Windweavers, barraging the Primalists with arcane missiles while the bronzes swept past, slowing their enemies' counterattacks. The Onyx Reavers fell from the skies, hitting their targets on the front lines with exacting precision.

To the north, Nozdormu and his Chronomagi formed the rearguard behind Levarian and the Earthen Bulwark. The bronzes' Temporal Guardians fought on the front lines with Levarian, targeting the enemy with time dilation and providing a steady stream of healing for the Aspects' northern flank.

The Dragon Queen stood in awe of them all and what they had wrought—even Vyranoth's legions had not achieved such coordination at the height of their power.

She would not allow her flights to fall this day. They had fought too long, too hard, and with too much heart to fail now.

ALEXSTRASZA TWISTED IN THE air, knocking a pair of Rockfuries away with her tail. Despite the danger, the Primalists came in droves, seeking to overwhelm the front lines with their numbers. The Dragon Queen exuded an aura of ruby light as she fought, imbuing her forces with courage, healing, and strength. Slowly, the flights began to push the Primalists back toward Harrowsdeep. The primal dragons could not stand against the fury of all five flights, especially without the strength of an Incarnate on the battlefield.

Alexstrasza had no doubts that Iridikron monitored the battle, for Harrowsdeep and its surrounding peaks continued to rage. The volcanoes filled the sky with thick, unbreathable ash that blotted out the stars. Even as the battle grew bloodier, the Stonescaled did not join the fray.

Coward! Alexstrasza thought, striking down another one of his Magmatalons.

A chorus of agonized shrieks tore across the mountains— a collective exclamation of grief. Alexstrasza looked west; in a flash of lightning, she saw that Neltharion had Oxoria, the Matriarch, in his talons. With one sharp jerk of his head, he snapped her neck.

Oxoria's children screamed as Neltharion dropped her corpse, diving and swarming the black Aspect. He disappeared in a storm of wings.

"Neltharion!" Alexstrasza cried. The Primalists took advantage of her moment of distraction, surging forward to surround her. With a growl, the Dragon Queen leapt to them, headbutting a Galestriker with her horns. The crack of its skull resonated up her spine. Bojsanz pulled a second primal dragon off her back, while a third hooked its talons in her shoulder armor and tried to stab her in the neck with a wing talon. Alexstrasza rolled to shake the dragon loose, and Ymistrasza snatched it and tore out its throat. The wet gurgle of its shredded windpipe made Alexstrasza's stomach turn.

The Dragon Queen could not see Neltharion through the fury on the front lines—all she heard was the earth-shattering *boom* as another mountain peak exploded, this time along the southwestern ridge. A fountain of fire erupted along their southern flank, shooting massive chunks of rock into the air.

The projectiles tore through the Ironscales' ranks, shattering wings, breaking bones, and knocking nearly twenty dragons out of the sky. The Dragon Queen shrieked as the flames of their lives were doused.

The mountain ridge to Alexstrasza's right shattered next, spitting another volley of stones into the air. Nozdormu was faster, or perhaps he had simply manipulated time—a cloud of shimmering sand swirled through the dragonflights' northern flank, halting the stones' trajectories. With a roar, the Timeless One wove a ribbon of golden light around his talons, then stretched it taut. The stones in the air went sailing back to their mountains, forming their peaks anew. Golden sands glittered along their surfaces to seal them against the Stonescaled's fury.

In the west, Malygos surged to the front line. He set up a series of glimmering arcane shields, defending the weakened Ironscales from the Primalist onslaught. From behind the reds' lines, Ysera ordered her healers to shift south.

Still, the Earth-Warder did not return. Panic flickered in the Dragon Queen's chest, especially when the Onyx Reavers streaked from the sky, plummeting deep in Primalist territory. *How had Neltharion gotten so far behind enemy lines?* Malygos started shouting something about supporting the Reavers, and an entire company of Spellscales blinked away.

"Bojsanz, lead the Guard!" Alexstrasza said. The flightleader nodded, ducking into her place as the Dragon Queen ascended over the battlefield. She took care to stay with Cristalstrasz and the Ruby Flamebringers, but not so far back that she fell into line with Ysera and her greens.

From north to south, the Primalists surged along the front, moving forward in wave after endless wave. The volcanoes continued to spew lava, washing the entire valley in hellish orange-red light. Quakes raced beneath the ridges, shooting additional volleys of stone at the Aspects' flanks. The Dragon Queen considered pushing the front lines higher and out of range of the volcanoes, but the ash fell like scalding black snow at greater elevations. Overhead, the Primalists' Galestrikers whipped the ash into an angry, lightning-laced storm.

Alexstrasza looked southwest. The Earth-Warder fought his way back to the front line, his scales and wings glittering with the Spellscales' shields, his attacks quickened by the Temporal Guardians' time magic. Malygos's arcane bolts struck from the sky. Neltharion slashed with such fury, his talons blazed with the brightness of a forge.

With Neltharion behind enemy lines, the Primalists had redoubled their efforts, trying to break the Ironscales while their Aspect was under siege. A combined host of Magmawings and Rockfuries now assailed the front lines, with more Primalists shifting from the center of the field. Lightning from the Galestrikers rippled through the ash clouds overhead. As the first set of bolts arced through the sky, Malygos lifted one forefoot, protecting the black dragons with a sparkling, domed shield.

In the east, Alexstrasza realized that the Earthen Bulwark no longer rallied around Levarian, but around his second-in-command, Stoltria. Whether Levarian was injured or had fallen, Alexstrasza could not say. The Bulwark had sustained fewer losses than the Ironscales, but even their ranks looked lighter.

The battlefield teetered on a talon's edge—if the southern volcanic eruptions continued, they would ravage Neltharion's battalions. Alexstrasza needed to relieve the black dragonflight and order them to seal the ridges before the mountains claimed more lives.

The Ironscales' line bent inward in the south. Warbringer Rava, Iridikron's favored commander, smashed between the Ironscales and the Heart's Guard, taking advantage of a momentary weakness in their defenses. The Primalists surged into the breach, pushing it wider.

Alexstrasza could not afford to wait. Either she acted decisively, or the Primalists were going to separate the Ironscales from the rest of her forces and flank the Heart's Guard.

"Cristalstrasz!" she called, trumpeting two short blasts and one long to the Ruby Flamebringers. "With me!"

Vermillion scales shimmered overhead as Alexstrasza dived for the Primalist wingleader on the front line. A glittering, golden shield wrapped itself around her as she plummeted— her sister's protective magic—and lunar fire struck Rava's vanguard, smashing through scales and clearing Alexstrasza's way.

The Warbringer snarled as Alexstrasza fell upon her, talons flashing. Her attack glanced off Rava's stony flank. The Warbringer rushed forward, headbutting Alexstrasza in the chest to push the Dragon Queen back and knock her off balance. Alexstrasza's armor caught the brunt of the blow, but the force shoved her into a pair of Ironscales. She recovered in a wingbeat, gaining altitude over the scrum.

All around her, the Ruby Flamebringers fell upon Rava's Rockfuries. Crimson fire twisted around their talons and burst from their maws. They fell into line beside the embattled Ironscales, halting the Primalist onslaught. The Onyx Reavers descended from the ash clouds to defend the flights' wings from above.

"You cannot win, *Dragon Queen*!" Rava shrieked, baring her fangs. "You and your cursed flights will die here on the fields of Harrowsdeep!"

"Do you think I will lose to *you*?" Alexstrasza snapped. "You are not even an *Incarnate*. How can you hope to stand against an Aspect when not even Vyranoth could best me?"

Rava roared, and the volcanoes erupted in concert with her. Rocks rained from the skies. The Primalists on the front lines joined her, until the whole of the valley trembled with the sound of their voices. Beneath the front lines, a glowing crevasse opened on the ground floor, winking open like a massive eye.

"You forget the Stonescaled fights with us," Rava said, gesturing to the rumbling peaks with her wings. "Even now, his power surrounds you on all sides!"

"And yet he is too cowardly to stand beside you," Alexstrasza hissed, setting her talons alight. Using one of Fyrakk's own tactics, Alexstrasza drew a deep breath and unleashed crimson flames upon Rava. She lunged through the fire, crashing into the Primalist. Shrieking, Rava snapped at the Dragon Queen's neck, but Alexstrasza grabbed Rava by the ridges of her head, sank her talons under Rava's jawline, and twisted. The torsion snapped the bones in the Warbringer's neck and shoulders, and her eyes rolled up into her head. Alexstrasza felt the life leave the Primalist's body. Though she took no joy in the act, Alexstrasza was glad to have saved those in the zealot's path.

The Dragon Queen dropped Rava's corpse, watching it crash into the magma that bubbled from the chasm in the ground. A quake raced through the valley floor, making the lava bubble and churn. No doubt Iridikron knew that two of his three wingleaders were dead.

The Rockfuries on the front lines scrambled back as the Dragon Queen turned her gaze on them, tumbling into one another to escape her fury. "Push them back!" Alexstrasza shouted to the Ruby Flamebringers, who surged forward. Drawing a deep breath, she launched herself into the air, then swooped over the Ironscales' front line, breathing her healing flames over their ranks. Ymistrasza flew in her wake, adding a second gout of fire.

As Alexstrasza doubled back, her dread rose. Neltharion was not on the field. The Earth-Warder no longer fought Oxoria's brood behind the Primalists' lines, nor had he returned to lead the Ironscales. Garion still flew at the Ironscales' head, roaring encouragement at the dragons around him.

Has Neltharion fallen? Alexstrasza thought, pulling back behind the Ruby Flamebringers. No, *no*—if an Aspect had been struck from the field, she would have known. A death on that scale would have struck her heart like a javelin, sure and sharp.

Then she spotted the Earth-Warder hovering over one of the volcanoes on their southern flank. Magma spouted on either side of him, silhouetting his dark frame. He reached out one forefoot, issuing a command that shook the mountains to their roots. At first, they exploded with greater fury, shooting geysers of molten lava into the air. Glowing cracks appeared in their stony flanks. The power of their eruptions reverberated through the air and pounded on Alexstrasza's eardrums. Massive slabs of rock sheared from the cliffsides, cascading into the valley below. She thought the mountains themselves might shatter entire.

Alexstrasza's eyes widened. Was this why Neltharion had charged into the fray, alone? Had he sensed that *this* was the final attack that Iridikron held in reserve—an eruption so powerful, it would strike both armies from the skies? Perhaps the Matriarch would have prevented the Earth-Warder from interfering with Iridikron's plans.

Neltharion roared, and the sound matched the volcanoes in its strength and fury. His was the voice of cracking stone and shaking earth, of a rage that burned so hot that it threatened to crack the world in two. He lifted his forefeet and began stretching them apart, as if wrenching the mountain stone from Iridikron's grasp. Even from this distance, Alexstrasza could see him straining, his wings beating wildly, eyes flashing.

One by one, the mountains' bright throats darkened. Their rumblings ceased, and Neltharion disappeared in a cloud of ash. The Dragon Queen released a breath, while the Ironscales cheered and fought on.

Upon seeing the earth bow to Neltharion's command, the Primalists on the western front scattered in terror. Rava's forces in the middle of the field bowed in, bereft of a leader; and in the east, the Rockfuries bled as ribbons of Nozdormu's golden sands danced through their ranks, making time shift and slow for their forces.

The Primalists hung on for another hour, perhaps two, before their remaining wingleader signaled the retreat. As cheers erupted from the ordered on the field, Bojsanz and Garion bugled the advance. The dragonflights would scatter the Primalists to the winds and clear the way to Iridikron's keep.

Alexstrasza watched them run with dispassion, unable to feel even a hint of victory . . . for the horrors of Harrowsdeep still remained.

CHAPTER TWENTY-SEVEN

THE STONES OF HARROWSDEEP NEVER STOPPED MOVING. As Neltharion ventured inside, he sensed hundreds of tunnels in constant motion—shifting, rumbling, quaking, reaching into the deepest depths of the planet's crust. Iridikron would be hiding in that abyss, lying in wait for Neltharion and the other Aspects.

The mountain growled as the Earth-Warder stepped into the keep. Its stones felt outright hostile, unwilling to yield their secrets nor their master's location. The Dragon Queen followed close behind on Neltharion's tail. Alexstrasza paused at his right wing, her gaze roving over the cavern's empty interior. Orange light from the battlefield greased the cavern's maw, highlighting the sharp stalactites inside. Shadows draped most of the interior, hiding its depths from sight.

"Are you sure you must go with me?" Neltharion asked her, softly enough so the others wouldn't hear. "The battle is won—all that remains is to capture Iridikron."

She turned her golden gaze on him. "We are strongest when we work together," she said as the other Aspects joined them. "I will not abandon you at the end."

"Nor will I," Malygos said, wrinkling his snout at the cavern's strong, musky odor. "I won't have you waste the life I just spent so much to save. Crashing into enemy lines, really, Neltharion?"

"It *worked*," Neltharion grumbled.

"Only with the blues' support," Malygos replied with a flick of his tail. "Though I admit, I had half a mind not to save you from your own heroics."

"Ah, but then who would lead you into the depths of Harrowsdeep?" Neltharion asked, selecting a hunk of stone from the ground and superheating it with forge-flame.

Malygos snorted. "Preferably someone *without* a death wish."

Neltharion grinned and levitated the burning stone above his horns, illuminating everything around him in a three-wingspan radius. The other Aspects did likewise—Alexstrasza and Malygos sparked fire, Ysera summoned a pair of lively green wisps, and ribbons of bright golden sand danced around Nozdormu.

Each Aspect had brought their ten best dragons, though Malygos had an extra ten portal-keepers and Neltharion had an entire company of scalesmiths. Once the Aspects had taken the valley, the Earth-Warder had summoned Calcia and her crew from the Obsidian Citadel. The black dragons would reinforce the tunnels with resonant elementium rods, map the

Aspects' progress through the keep, and help Neltharion triangulate the Stonescaled's position.

Egnion and his Shadowscales had gone on ahead, acting as both scouts and the vanguard. Alexstrasza had also tasked them with finding and extricating the thirty-one missing dragons, if they could.

The other dragons followed the Aspects into the cavern, summoning light sources and exchanging nervous glances. They jumped every time the earth shuddered under their feet. Only the black dragonflight appeared at ease, carrying in supplies, constructing makeshift forges, and sending scouting parties. Garion and a combined force of Ironscales and the Earthen Bulwark would stay behind to defend the scalesmiths' camp, as Levarian had fallen in battle.

Neltharion knew he would feel the flightcommander's loss later—for now, he had to focus on keeping a hundred dragons alive while they searched for Iridikron.

Neltharion turned to address the assembly. "Before we begin, does everyone have a portal stone from the blue dragonflight?"

The assembled dragons nodded.

"Good," he said. "If you find yourself trapped in the keep, that may be your only means for escape."

"I hope you have no need of them," Malygos said, "but if you do, the stone will return you to our camps in the south. Each stone has but a single charge—you would be wise not to forget that."

Alexstrasza stepped forward, suffusing the assembly with soft, comforting ruby light. "You each have your orders. Let us form ranks and begin our descent. Be brave! Tonight shall be the last night that Harrowsdeep quakes."

Neltharion and the black dragons took point, leading the company into the lightless depths. As they descended, the Earth-Warder paid careful attention to the warrens below. With each temblor, the rocky strata in Harrowsdeep shifted up or down. Some layers appeared to turn on an axis, though Neltharion wasn't sure how the Stonescaled had achieved such a feat. The tunnels moved in set patterns, sometimes connecting to spacious caverns and passageways, and other times leading to dead ends. The timing and seismic strength of the quakes appeared to be unpredictable, and the largest sections of rock only moved when a massive vibration tore through the mountain.

Their path twisted and turned, heading deeper, until it opened into a gigantic, barbed cavern.

"This place is incredible," Calcia said to Neltharion, craning her neck to take in the sights. Large, phosphorescent green crystal formations burst from the walls, emitting weak light. Bulbous stone columns stretched from ceiling to floor, each one as thick as Neltharion's forearm. The Earth-Warder sensed several paths and tunnels branching from this singular cavern. The realization made him wary.

The scalesmiths spread three points across the ground, sinking their claws into stone to measure the impact and location of the next quake. Mapmakers compared notes, spreading out a parchment to sketch the winding path their company had taken.

"Once the Stonescaled is safely ensconced in the Vault of the Incarnates, I shall want to return and study this place," Calcia continued with a bob of her head. "We might be able to improve upon his methods for our own purposes."

"It's quite rudimentary in its execution," Neltharion replied, sweeping his gaze across the cavern, alert for dangers. He gestured to two nearby Ironscales, commanding them to check the perimeter without a word. "But I agree, Iridikron must have spent centuries designing this keep. He will no more drop it on our heads than we will allow him to fly free."

"I should hope not," Calcia said, rummaging through the tool bag she wore strapped to her chest. "It would be a shame to lose such a marvel."

The Earth-Warder chuckled, charmed by her irrepressible curiosity. They stood in one of the most dangerous locales in Azeroth, and all the scalesmith wanted to know was how it *worked*. "Let us hope it still stands after our confrontation with the Stonescaled, then," he said.

A small quake shivered through the cavern. The dragons behind them shifted when dirt and grit drummed on their scales. Alexstrasza flicked some pebbles off her shoulder, and Nozdormu shook his head from side to side, sending sand flying.

"We wait for the next one!" Calcia called to the scalesmiths. "A larger quake will tell us more."

Neltharion caught the scent of singed hair and stinking flesh. He flared his nostrils and turned his head, but none of the shadows moved.

"No," he said, beckoning to the scalesmiths with his talons. "We take what information we have and continue on—I mislike this place."

The words were barely off his tongue before a djaradin battle cry echoed through the cavern. Ten half-giants leapt from a crevasse in the ceiling, crashing into the ground in front of the Dragon Queen.

Alexstrasza reared, slamming the back of her closed fist into the nearest djaradin and sending him sprawling. As the Dragon Queen's guardians surrounded her, the cavern floor shivered. Craggy, boulder-shaped earth elementals struggled to their feet, their hollow torsos glittering like geodes.

"Stay back! The Dragon Queen is mine," a voice called as heavy footsteps thundered through the cavern. Neltharion whipped around, snarling when he saw the Qalashi chieftainess, Igira, burst from the tunnels astride a massive magmammoth. Flaming markings covered every inch of her chest and limbs, testaments to the dragons she had felled. Her bright-white hair stood in sharp contrast with her cobalt skin. She hefted a massive, bloodstained axe on one shoulder.

Shouts echoed from other tunnels. Djaradin shadows danced along the walls, silhouetted by the flames from their mounts.

"Protect your queen!" Neltharion shouted, sprinting for the djaradin chieftainess as she rode past. The floor jolted, staggering the Earth-Warder. Igira stormed past him. He dug his talons into the stone, hanging on, as a strong quake rolled through the mountain. A crack tore through the floor between Neltharion and the rest of the company. Before he could regain his footing, his section of the cavern shook and rose almost a full wing-length with a violent jerk.

Alexstrasza's section dropped out of sight.

With a shriek, Igira leapt off her mount and into the yawning chasm between the shifting strata of stone, axe brandished over her head. Her magmammoth tripped and tumbled over the edge, screaming.

The two massive stone plates shifted past each other, sealing Neltharion in silence and darkness.

"Alexstrasza," Neltharion said, leaping to his feet. He rushed to the plate, rearing up to place both forefeet on it, but the stone would not heed his commands. "Alexstrasza!"

No one answered him.

Someone drew a shaky breath. Neltharion turned. Calcia stood behind him, staring at the wall of stone, her lower jaw trembling. A scalesmith landed beside her, nudging her with an elbow and asking if she was all right. Calcia gritted her teeth and bobbed her head.

"My Aspect, what are your orders?" an Ironscale asked, approaching Neltharion with a bow.

He swept his gaze over the little party, taking quick stock of their numbers—seven Ironscales, two Earthen Bulwark, and two scalesmiths. It was enough to continue.

"We press on," the Earth-Warder said, striding toward one of the caverns. "I do not doubt the Stonescaled pulled that little maneuver to separate us, but no matter. The Dragon Queen is a capable warrior, and we will travel faster with a lighter party. Come, let us see if we cannot find Iridikron's lair."

...

ALEXSTRASZA SNARLED AS THE djaradin elder leapt over the heads of her personal guard. The half-giantess landed in a crouch, staring up at the Dragon Queen with eyes full of hate. Roars and shouts echoed through the cavern as dragon clashed with djaradin.

"I know you," Alexstrasza said, eyeing the chieftainess. "Igira the Cruel."

"Aye," Igira said with a grin. The half-giantess rose to her feet, running her tongue over her teeth. "You came with fewer dragons than I thought. A pity. My tribe was hoping for more sport."

"You wish for sport?" Alexstrasza said as more djaradin thundered into the cavern. She spread her wings and slammed her forefoot into the ground, setting her scales aflame with ruby light. She dropped her chin as she said, "You have fought naught but drakes—the forces who defeated you at Scalecracker Keep were barely grown. They chased you from your ancestral lands! What hope do you have against an Aspect? You are nothing more than a mite between my scales."

"Ha! Die beneath a sky of stone!" the half-giantess roared, brandishing her axe at the Dragon Queen. The low light gleamed off the blade's wicked edge.

"Unlikely," Alexstrasza said, baring her teeth.

Igira leapt at the Dragon Queen with an ear-shattering battle cry. Alexstrasza juked left, pressing her wings against her back. The chieftainess landed, pivoted on the ball of one foot, then swung her axe at Alexstrasza's head. The blade whistled as it sliced through the air beneath the Aspect's snout.

Before Igira could recover, Alexstrasza charged forward, slamming her head into the chieftainess's flank. Igira staggered back. Alexstrasza pounced, her forefeet connecting with Igira's broad, muscled shoulders. They hit the ground with a grunt and slid several wing-lengths. Alexstrasza's scales rasped against stone.

Igira landed a blow on a tender spot on Alexstrasza's snout, sending bright lights shooting across the red Aspect's vision. The Dragon Queen snapped her head back in surprise. Before Alexstrasza could recover, Igira stabbed a small knife between the red Aspect's toes.

With a pained shriek, Alexstrasza leapt backward. She gave her right forefoot a hard shake, flinging the knife away. Blood spattered over the stone floor.

The elder got to her feet, grinning. Battles raged all around them—with a sweep of his tail, Malygos took the magmammoths out from under five djaradin warriors; Ysera summoned great roots from stone, trapping the half-giants and their mounts; and djaradin screamed as Nozdormu blasted them with a breath of superheated sand. The Aspects' escorts fanned out between them, protecting their flanks and backs.

Igira's axe scraped on stone as she hefted it from the floor. "I have hunted more than just your drakes, *Dragon Queen*," she said with a scoff. "I have felled many dragons from your flights. Now, it is your turn. Soon, I will have your head mounted above my tent—"

A flash of vermillion scales swooped from the shadows overhead, falling upon the chieftainess. A young red slammed Igira into the ground with a snarl, pinning the djaradin between her toes.

"Go, my queen!" the young red said. "We will hold the djaradin at bay!"

"*We?*" the red Aspect said, recognizing the young red. "Lailastrasza, what are you doing here?"

Before Lailastrasza could answer, another half-giantess charged at her, swinging a massive club at the young red's head. With a growl, Lailastrasza caught the club in her teeth and yanked it from the half-giantess's grip. Stepping off Igira, the young red spun and slammed her barbed tail into the other half-giantess's flank, sending the djaradin sprawling.

Igira scrambled to her feet. Before she could strike the young red, Alexstrasza lunged forward, slamming her armored shoulder into Igira's torso. The chieftainess stumbled back with a furious shriek. The Dragon Queen drew a deep breath and held it, allowing the air to feed the fires in her lungs, then released a torrent of crimson flame at the djaradin chieftainess. It wouldn't kill her, no, but it was enough to force her to retreat from Alexstrasza's range.

"Sirigosa freed us from our chains in the keep," Lailastrasza said by way of explanation, speaking so fast that her tongue tripped over the words. "More than twenty fly with us! Let us fight the djaradin, my Aspect—we will not fail you."

"You could never fail me," the red Aspect said as Igira glowered at them. "Very well! I will leave my escort to fight at your side. Titans be with you."

"And with you," the young red said, grinning as she turned back to the chieftainess.

Spreading her wings, Alexstrasza launched herself into the air. "Aspects, with me!" she roared. "We go to end the Stonescaled's reign of terror!"

NELTHARION AND HIS BLACK dragons descended into Harrowsdeep's abyss, following the epicenters of the mountain quakes. The path twisted, the rock shifted; the ground dropped out from under their feet, turning open tunnels into dead ends. A sideways shear of stone could unleash an army of earth elementals upon them. Volcanic vents opened in the floor, spewing magma. They crawled through constricting tunnels, dived off cliffs into the purest darkness, and fought a giant earth elemental that snapped with Iridikron's own power.

Two Ironscales sustained burn wounds from nearly being dragged into a lake of magma by lava worms—Neltharion sent them out via their portal stones. Calcia followed them soon after, her right wing crushed by a falling column of rock.

Still the Earth-Warder pushed on. With every triangulation, the black dragons drew closer to the Stonescaled's lair. This deep in the planet's crust, the earthquakes felt richer, more resonant. No doubt the Incarnate knew Neltharion drew close, for it seemed the entirety of the keep wanted nothing more than to kill them. Injuries claimed Neltharion's companions one by one, forcing the black Aspect to send them back to safety.

By the time Neltharion reached the bowels of Harrowsdeep, he walked alone—which was likely what the Stonescaled wanted. The quakes beckoned him forward, snagging him in the gut like a gravitational force.

You are alone now. The voice rose in the back of his mind, clearer here in the abyss.

All your friends are gone, said another.

You will not be able to win against the Stonescaled on your own, said the third.

Neltharion scoffed, blowing a breath out his nostrils. Had he not led his dragons into the depths? Was *he* not the last one standing, the one who would stride into Iridikron's lair and meet the Incarnate talon-to-talon? An Incarnate could not best an Aspect, not even in the seat of his power. Alexstrasza had proven that much.

The tunnel ended in a smear of amber light. Neltharion stepped into an enormous cavern, one that dwarfed every other chamber in Harrowsdeep. The floor had dropped into an unfathomable abyss, one dark enough to send a shudder through Neltharion's scales. Tall, unbroken pillars of gray basalt lined the walls. Clutches of giant topaz crystals burst from the ceiling. Elemental energies snapped along the crystals' angular tips. The cavern's beauty stole Neltharion's breath away.

Iridikron stood on a large floating island, his back to Neltharion. Massive chunks of rock rotated around the platform at different speeds and orbits, generating the energy for the seismic waves that rocked the mountain.

"Never did I think another dragon would lay eyes upon this place," Iridikron said without turning. He lifted his head. "I suppose it is only fitting that it be you."

Neltharion made no answer. He lowered his head, muscles tensing, expecting an attack.

The Stonescaled wheeled to face the black Aspect, his eyes gleaming with the same elemental energies that blazed in the cavern's crystals. He spread his wings wide, gesturing to the cavern around them. "Tell me, *Earth-Warder,* was it worth it to shackle yourself to the will of the titans?"

"Why would I not take advantage of the power the keepers offered to me?" Neltharion said, looking down his snout at Iridikron.

"That is not what I asked," the Incarnate said. "I asked if their power was worth the *weight* of the oaths they forced upon you."

"My oaths are no burden," Neltharion replied, stalking to the edge of the platform. "*You,* on the other hand, have been nothing but an encumbrance to me for the last five hundred years."

"Still you refuse to give me an answer," the Stonescaled said, cocking his head. "So I suppose that answer must be *no.*"

With a roar, Neltharion leapt into the air, crossing the cavern in one great sweep of his wings. He landed on the central island, bounded once, and collided with Iridikron. Imbuing his talons with fire, Neltharion slashed at the Incarnate's throat, leaving shallow scores in his stony scales.

Iridikron drove his head into Neltharion's chin, then slammed his shoulder into Neltharion's chest, knocking him back. Bright lights burst across the black Aspect's vision.

Neltharion staggered with a gasp, feeling as if the earth pulled at him more than it should.

"You cannot win," Iridikron said. The earth energies crackling along his spine blazed brighter. "Not here, not alone."

"The moment I stepped into this cavern, you had already lost," Neltharion said, charging at the Incarnate.

Iridikron punched a wing talon into the floor. A sharp fin of volcanic rock erupted. Neltharion smashed through it, sending stony shards flying in all directions. He feinted left then slid right, driving his talons into the glowing core in Iridikron's chest. The Incarnate roared, stumbling to the edge of the platform. The whole of the mountain shook with his rage.

Neltharion ignored it, launching himself at the Incarnate. He sank his teeth into Iridikron's wing, yanked it sideways, then jammed two talons into the joint. Snarling, Iridikron wrenched his wing from Neltharion's mouth, leaving his teeth bloody. The Stonescaled sent a shock wave through the floor to knock the black Aspect back. The whole of the cavern shook again. The topaz crystals in the ceiling shattered, their fragments tumbling into the darkness below.

An invisible force yanked Neltharion toward the ground, forcing his left elbow to buckle. He lost his balance, catching himself on his forearm.

You are weak, the whispers said.

In defiance of the voices in his head, Neltharion pushed himself back to his feet. His joints trembled. After centuries as the Earth-Warder, he had grown accustomed to bearing the weight of the world on his back . . . but this force took that burden and increased it exponentially. His bones creaked, threatening to snap. Capillaries burst in the whites of his eyes. Every muscle in his body trembled.

The Stonescaled cocked his head, watching the black Aspect with great interest. "No one is stronger than Azeroth itself," he said softly.

Neltharion could only glare at the Incarnate.

Lies, the whispers said. *We are stronger.*

The stones revolving around the island accelerated. The force bearing down on the Earth-Warder doubled, forcing him to his knees. He gasped, his heartbeat pounding in his skull and on the backs of his eyes, his joints shrieking for relief.

Call upon our power, said one of the whispers, *or you shall die here in the dark.*

The Stonescaled began to circle him slowly. "Despite the power your keepers granted you, even you must bow to the elements."

Call upon us, another whisper said, *or your friends shall perish in these halls.*

"I will break you," Iridikron said. "I will trap your kind within these halls forever, if only to prove to you the folly of order and the impotence of your masters!"

Do it! another voice said. *Do it or you die here, beaten and broken!*

Neltharion would *not* be broken, nor would he lose to one so inferior as Iridikron.

The Earth-Warder unleashed all his physical agony in a roar, squeezing his eyes shut. A terrible, dark power rose within him, blotting out the light in the room. The shadows imbued him with a terrible, world-breaking strength, and his pain slipped away on a whisper.

He opened his eyes and rose to his feet with a snarl, violet light radiating from his scales. It crept over the platform, outlining everything in an eerie, bruised light.

Iridikron backed away from Neltharion, his eyes wide.

"I see you now," the Incarnate said quietly. "So, this is how you bested Raszageth! You called upon this dark power to seal her under stone. This is not titan magic! Does your Dragon Queen know you serve another master?"

"I serve no one," Neltharion said with a growl. As he said those words, a chuckle echoed through the deep places of his mind.

In defiance, the Earth-Warder punched his talons into the platform, sending the shadows to infest the stone. The floating boulders halted on their paths. With a twitch of his talons, he hurled those boulders into the abyss below. As the stones fell, they crashed into the cavern's walls and sent the last quakes through the keep. The remaining topaz stones burst, sparks and pops of yellow fire in the deep darkness.

The weight on Neltharion's back dissipated.

"I should kill you for what you have seen," Neltharion said, stalking toward the Stonescaled, "but I dare not leave a corpse for study. You will sleep along with your allies in the Vault of the Incarnates—Alexstrasza can never know what happened here."

Iridikron snarled as Neltharion drew close, lowering his head to strike. "Do you think you can hide this from her?

Perhaps one day she will find that the greatest threat to our kind was not Primalist or Incarnate, but the very dragon who stood at her right wing!"

Neltharion curled his lip. "I would never betray Alexstrasza."

"You already have," the Stonescaled snapped.

Neltharion leapt on Iridikron, slamming the Incarnate into the ground. With his shadowy strength, he reached into the Stonescaled's chest and took hold of the exposed earth energies there. Neltharion wrenched them sideways, almost as if he meant to tear the Stonescaled's heart from his chest. Iridikron roared in pain, thrashing wildly, but the black Aspect held him firm.

Neltharion lowered his head, his voice no more than a whisper as he said, "To think you believed yourself my *equal*." Iridikron curled his lip, but before the Incarnate could respond, Neltharion sent a shock of shadow into the Incarnate's very core. Indigo light flared in the Stonescaled's chest. It slicked his scales and coughed from the chasm along his spine. Iridikron shrieked as the shadows slipped into his eyes, his back arching, every inch of his body straining.

Then, the Incarnate went limp.

Neltharion kept Iridikron pressed into the floor until the shadows drained from the room. With a shaky breath, the Earth-Warder sank to the ground beside the unconscious Incarnate, trembling.

Harrowsdeep had fallen silent, its quakes broken, its halls unmoving. Still, Iridikron's words echoed in the vast chambers of Neltharion's mind: *Does your Dragon Queen know you serve another master?*

After so many centuries of fighting, the last flames of war died in darkness and silence. Neltharion would bury the truth of the matter here in Harrowsdeep. He made a silent vow that this was the last time he would ever give in to the whispers.

He would bear the burden of truth, alone.

Alexstrasza could never know.

CHAPTER TWENTY-EIGHT

ALEXSTRASZA AND THE OTHER ASPECTS FOUND Neltharion in the lightless depths of Iridikron's keep, surrounded by shadows. The Earth-Warder sat on a platform beside the unconscious Incarnate, his head bowed. He did not look up as the Dragon Queen alighted on the central platform. She ensconced Neltharion in warm ruby light, pushing the shadows away from him. Iridikron lay prone on the floor, still breathing but otherwise still as stone. Neither dragon appeared injured. At least, not physically.

"Neltharion?" she asked softly, approaching with caution as the other Aspects moved to secure the prisoner. "Are you all right?"

The black Aspect shuddered. When he lifted his gaze to Alexstrasza's, the Dragon Queen flinched. Yes, the Earth-Warder appeared to be physically hale . . . but she sensed something broken in him. Stress fractures reached long, spidery fingers into his heart, and Alexstrasza had not the power to peer into their depths. What horrors could have cracked the heart of the Broodlands' most stalwart defender? What terrors could make even the Earth-Warder tremble?

Alexstrasza felt Neltharion's pain as her own—an ache that might be as cavernous and yawning as Harrowsdeep itself. She sat beside him, giving him a gentle nudge with her shoulder.

After a long moment, the Earth-Warder released a deep sigh and leaned into her side.

"I wish you had not come here alone," Alexstrasza said, supporting his weight. Tremors racked Neltharion's muscles, held back by his iron will. "We would have walked into the depths with you."

"I know," Neltharion said, swallowing hard when his voice trembled. When he spoke again, he was steadier. "When the keep's tunnels shifted, I knew I could ill afford to search for you—the best thing I could do was press on."

"You've done admirably, Neltharion," Alexstrasza said softly. The black Aspect's spine stiffened at the praise. "After all these long years, the war is over. Our flights will know peace."

Neltharion closed his eyes. Heartbeats passed before he spoke again.

"It is over," he said, releasing a long, shuddering breath. "It is *over*."

IN THE WEEKS FOLLOWING the Battle of Harrowsdeep, Alexstrasza mourned with her flights. The Aspects had won the war but lost so much—thousands of lives had been snuffed out, and the Broodlands and the Dragonwilds bore the scars of war.

The collective pain of the dragons echoed through the skies, inescapable. Omnipresent. It haunted Alexstrasza's every step and chased her into her dreams. To alleviate the suffering, the Dragon Queen visited the wounded and lifted their spirits. She helped Ysera soothe their lands, coaxed the gardens back to life around Valdrakken, and played with whelps at the Ruby Life Pools. No more eggs would be taken from the nests of primal dragons—this she swore.

Still, the shadow of her flights' trauma never left her, not truly. Nor did the specter of all the mistakes she had made— perhaps they made been mistakes made with the best of intentions, but she had caused harm when she meant to help and had broken a promise to a friend.

No, Alexstrasza hadn't just broken a promise to Vyranoth, she had turned her back on the Incarnate. She had allowed their friendship to wither into apathy, and later, to freeze into hatred.

Alexstrasza would not make the same mistake again.

So the Dragon Queen invited Cysanz and his followers to Wyrmrest Temple, where the dragons discussed the terms of peace. For their war crimes, the Incarnates would remain imprisoned. All hostilities between ordered and primal dragon would cease, and no primal dragon would raise wing or talon against the Broodlands again. Now leaderless, most of the Primalists had already scattered to the winds.

In return, Alexstrasza swore to withdraw from the Dragonwilds and grant those territories to the primal dragons in perpetuity. Furthermore, no primal dragon eggs would be taken from their rightful nests ever again—this was an oath that every Aspect swore, not just Alexstrasza.

In addition, Cysanz asked the Dragon Queen to pardon Talinstrasz and his comrades. Though the other Aspects balked at this request—particularly Neltharion—Alexstrasza granted the pardons, allowing Talinstrasz, Sirigosa, and the other defectors to fly free.

At the end of their parley, Cysanz asked for a moment alone with the Dragon Queen. They met on one of the high terraces, which gave them a breathtaking view of the wild, untamed beauty of northern Kalimdor. The sun shone bright in the skies, making the fresh snow glitter.

"I trust this will be the last time we see each other," the hoary dragon said, extending a small object to Alexstrasza. "So, I wanted to return something to you."

Alexstrasza looked down. There, in Cysanz's talons, was the dragon figurine Alexstrasza had given Vyranoth so many years ago. The unmelting ice caught the light, beautiful and multidimensional. The gold-filled cracks gleamed, adding depth to the ice.

Alexstrasza pressed her lips together, blinking fast. She hadn't expected to see the figurine again.

"I believe one can find beauty in broken things," Cysanz said, setting the figurine down between them. As he stepped back, he said, "I hope you will remember her, Dragon Queen, and that every time you gaze upon this artifact, you will commit yourself to keeping the promise you once made to her . . . and the one you have now made to me."

"I will, I swear it," Alexstrasza said, cradling the figurine in her talons. "Thank you, Cysanz."

The old dragon dipped his head once. "Lead wisely, Alexstrasza. I do not wish to see a war of this like again."

"Nor do I," Alexstrasza said, her throat tight.

In the days after the parley, Alexstrasza flew to every corner of the Broodlands, seeking the dragons hatched from stolen eggs. While many dragons were content with their ordering, more than a few were not . . . and Alexstrasza listened to them all, offering each a sincere apology and a boon from the Dragon Queen herself.

Under Sindragosa's watchful eye, Sirigosa received a private study in the Azure Archives, where the blue was content to spend her days with her snout buried in a book. The twins, Ravia and Obezion, demurred at first . . . but their eyes lit up when Neltharion promised to take them under his wing. Nolizdormu traveled the timeways with the bronze dragonflight's best; Atyrannus wanted to become a guardian of the Dream; and Rygos asked for access to the restricted sections of the archives. The request drew a weighty sigh from Malygos—the young blue was known for his mischief—but the Aspect granted it nonetheless.

Only one request broke Alexstrasza's heart: "I want to see my brother once more," Lailastrasza said. "I must say goodbye."

So, on a clear day, the Dragon Queen flew with Lailastrasza to the Frozen Fangs.

As the Dragon Queen alighted outside Vyranoth's old aerie, she could still smell her friend's scent on the air. Vyranoth's magic imbued the ice underfoot, though its chill lacked its former cruelty or malice. Everywhere Alexstrasza looked, she saw Vyranoth—from the snow trailing off the mountain peaks to the glacier that carved the valley below, the Frozenheart's power infused every talon's length of this place. Alexstrasza's grief swelled, for her friend's spirit still lived on in this place, even if she would never fly through its peaks again.

"Talin?" Lailastrasza called, landing beside the Dragon Queen. The young red took a tentative step toward the aerie's cavernous entrance. "Brother, are you there?"

When no one answered, the young red looked back at Alexstrasza. The Dragon Queen nodded to Lailastrasza—not only had she confirmed that Talinstrasz still called Vyranoth's aerie home, but she had sent a messenger to inform him of their impending visit.

Lailastrasza turned back to the cavern. "Talin, if you don't wish to see me, I understand," she called, loudly enough for her voice to carry. "I only wanted to tell you that no matter what has transpired between us, you will always be my clutch-brother. In time, I hope we can be siblings once more."

Nothing stirred. They waited for several long, heart-rending minutes. When no one answered, Lailastrasza's shoulders slumped. As she returned to the Dragon Queen, Alexstrasza prepared to say something to lift the young red's spirits—perhaps a race back to the Ruby Life Pools, or a favorite meal—but someone said, "Wait."

Lailastrasza halted. Alexstrasza lifted her head, relieved to see a red standing in the shadows of the cavern's maw. Talinstrasz held his head high as he stepped into the sunlight, his gaze fixed on the Dragon Queen. Like the drake who defied her so many years ago, Talinstrasz met the Aspect's gaze with no fear.

"Talin," Lailastrasza said, her scales scraping on the ice as she turned. "You are here!"

"Sister," Talin said, turning his attention to Lailastrasza. "I will invite you in, but your queen must wait outside."

"Oh," Lailastrasza said with a note of hesitation. "But it's so cold!"

"I will be quite all right," Alexstrasza said gently. Then, to Talinstrasz, she said, "My purpose for coming today is twofold: One, to support Lailastrasza and help her realize her dearest wish; and two, to come before you and express my deepest apologies to *you*."

Talinstrasz blinked, almost as if confused.

"I will offer you no excuses; you have doubtless heard them already," the Dragon Queen said. "So, on behalf of the Aspects and the five flights, I come before you to apologize for the theft of your egg and subsequent ordering. I swore an oath to never harm a living creature, but I have caused you irreparable harm and despair. I am sorry, Talinstrasz, and I swear to you this day, the Aspects have ceased this practice now and forevermore."

Alexstrasza bowed before the stunned red, closing her eyes and dipping her head in a shallow bow. Silence rose in the wake of her words, but she embraced it and rose, not expecting to find absolution in this place.

"Vyranoth said . . . she said you would never apologize," Talinstrasz said, stepping forward. He blinked fast, lifting his voice. "She said . . . she said you were so sure you were right!"

When you are convinced of your own righteousness, Vyranoth whispered in her memory, *no act becomes unconscionable.*

"If something lives, it can grow and change," Alexstrasza replied. "I should like to think that includes *Dragon Queens*, too."

The red's lower jaw went slack. He stepped back and sat on the ground, as if struggling to come to terms with this new information.

"If there is aught you would ask of me, Talinstrasz, you may," Alexstrasza said. "I have granted each and every dragon in your cohort a boon."

The red tilted his head, his breath hitching. "I don't suppose you would free Vyranoth, would you?"

"That I cannot do," Alexstrasza replied, giving him a sad smile.

Talinstrasz's wings drooped. He seemed to despair for a moment, casting his gaze to the icy pebbles at his feet. "Then . . . perhaps you could help Lailastrasza and me find our parents, if they still live?"

Lailastrasza's breath caught in her throat. The young red looked up at the Dragon Queen, her golden eyes glittering with hope.

Alexstrasza dipped her head in a nod. "Of course I will help you."

...

ON THE DAY THE flights gathered to seal the Vault of the Incarnates under stone, Alexstrasza descended into the vault's inner sanctum. The three Incarnates entombed in Thaldraszus—Fyrakk, Vyranoth, and Iridikron—each slept inside a great, glowing golden orb. Metal rings rotated along the outside and inside of the cells, trapping the Incarnates in stasis. Nozdormu stood on the center platform, supervising the bronzes and the titan-forged who performed the final inspections.

Alexstrasza alighted on the platform, joining the bronze Aspect as he gazed up at the cells.

"Have you come to say one final goodbye, my queen?" Nozdormu asked, turning. Concern rested heavily on his brow. He, like the other Aspects, knew how heavily the memories of war haunted Alexstrasza's heart.

"Yes," Alexstrasza said, lifting her head to look at Vyranoth. "I would like a moment with her before we seal the vault fully."

"But of course," Nozdormu said. "My flight will finish the final inspections presently."

"Thank you." Alexstrasza turned toward Vyranoth's cell, and almost just to herself, said, "It is strange to think I shall never see her again. I will forever mourn her loss."

Nozdormu tilted his head and considered Vyranoth, his gaze a thousand leagues long. Alexstrasza glanced sideways at him. She could see the sands of time shifting in his eyes, as if he had a vision of some indefinite future event. After her experience in the Icebound Eye, however, the Dragon

Queen knew better than to ask a bronze what they saw in the timeways.

Before she could shake Nozdormu from his vision, the bronze Aspect blinked. He smiled at her and said, "I will wait in the antechamber outside—take whatever time you require."

"Thank you," Alexstrasza said. The bronzes ferried the titan-forged from the vault, leaving Alexstrasza alone with the Incarnates and the shadows that loomed beyond their cells.

Alexstrasza sat before Vyranoth's cell, watching her old friend sleep in a shimmer of golden light. The Frozenheart did not move, nor did she draw breath.

This was goodbye. The last, final goodbye.

Nothing had prepared Alexstrasza for this moment. Of all the wounds her heart now bore, Vyranoth's loss cut the deepest. Alexstrasza had loved Vyranoth with her whole soul—she would treasure the memories they had together. The happy ones, at least.

"Vyranoth," Alexstrasza said, "my oldest and dearest friend, how I wish things had turned out differently between us! How I wish you were still by my side."

She closed her eyes and continued. "But wishing does not change the past—you told me that, once, as we mourned the loss of your mate.

"I will bury the story of this war here, with you. As Aspects, we are united in this decision. I do not want to impose the horrors of this war upon future generations. It will be far better for us to move on, even if it means sealing a part of my heart away, forever.

"To my flights, I will raise my wings in victory . . . but it does not feel like a victory," she said, very softly. "Not without you. I should have been honest with you. I should have *trusted* you with the truth of things . . . A queen must sometimes hide her heart, but a friend never should."

She bowed her head. "This cannot be how our story ends, can it?"

"Alexstrasza," someone said, very quietly. "It is time—we must seal the vault."

Neltharion alighted on the platform behind her. Over the last few weeks, the Earth-Warder had made a full recovery from his ordeal at Harrowsdeep.

Alexstrasza sensed lingering pains upon Neltharion's mind, but who among them did not suffer in the wake of the war? Who among them did not suffer from nightmares and feel the aches in their scars?

The Earth-Warder had never told his fellow Aspects how he had managed to defeat Iridikron in the depths of that hateful mountain—every time Alexstrasza asked him about it, he shook his head. *I will speak about that day in due time,* Neltharion would say. *For now . . . it is best that I bury that memory with the Incarnate himself.*

"Very well," she said to him, spreading her wings and leaping into the air, hovering parallel with her friend's cell.

"Goodbye, dear one," Alexstrasza said, placing one forefoot on the cell. The stone hummed at her touch. She took one last, lingering look at Vyranoth, etching the Frozenheart's features into her memory.

Then Alexstrasza turned and followed Neltharion from the inner sanctum, leaving the Incarnates to sleep in the shadows. They paused at the threshold while Nozdormu wove time enchantments around the inner gate, trapping Iridikron and his hatreds inside forevermore. The Vault of the Incarnates would have three major protections: Nozdormu's temporal enchantments were to seal the inner gate; Malygos would place arcane wards on the titan-made outer door; and Neltharion would bury the vault beneath the earth, laying the Incarnates and their painful legacy to rest. As they stepped into the sunlight outside the Vault of the Incarnates, Alexstrasza lifted her gaze to the heavens. The dragons of the five flights had gathered around the Vault of the Incarnates, their scales shimmering in the sun. A great cheer went up as she and Neltharion emerged and joined Ysera, Malygos, and Nozdormu on the platform. The cheers rang hollow in Alexstrasza's heart—in her mind, there was nothing to celebrate.

"Shall we get on with it, then?" Malygos asked, turning back to the vault door. "I, for one, am ready to put this chapter of our history behind us."

"Yes," Alexstrasza said with a sad smile. "Let us move toward a brighter horizon."

ACKNOWLEDGMENTS

First and foremost: Thank you, dear reader, for taking this journey with us. One of the greatest joys of my career has been to steward characters the Warcraft community has loved (and loathed!) for so long. Though my name appears on the cover, this book is the product of the hard work of many hearts and minds.

To the brilliant, hardworking editorial teams at Blizzard and Random House Worlds—*thank you*. Tom Hoeler, you were an incredible wingman throughout the development of this book. Thank you for working your bronze magic and keeping this project running on time. (Well, *mostly* on time! I'll always be looking for *one more weekend*.)

To Eric Geron, the man who soldiered through that rough first draft with me—the best editors ask the right questions, and so many of yours led to some of the greatest moments in this book. Thank you for your wise guidance, your patience, and your encouragement.

Thank you, Chloe Fraboni, for the magic you cast over the prose in the second draft. I had a delightful time reading through your comments . . . but the one about wine made me laugh out loud. You brought some lovely lines to the book.

To the rest of the Blizzard team—Steve Danuser, Terran Gregory, Damien Jahrsdoerfer, Brianne Messina, Byron Parnell, Corey Peterschmidt, Amber Proue-Thibodeau, Korey Regan, Derek Rosenberg, and everyone else who provided invaluable insights and feedback—thank you. I could not possibly know every hand that touched these drafts, but please know that I saw the indelible mark you left on the work. I am grateful to you.

On my side of the page, I would be remiss if I didn't thank my husband, Bo, who is my constant companion in life and in Azeroth. You cheered me on through every deadline and listened to me work through the troublesome bits aloud. I leapt off a cliff, so sure I would fall . . . but you always believed I would fly. Because of you, I stood beside Queen Alexstrasza. I walked through the shadows of Aberrus with Neltharion and mourned with Vyranoth. The dragons snatched me from the skies until I grew my own wings and flew.

Matt Kirby, you're partially responsible for these shenanigans, too. Thank you for reaching out on that fateful evening and asking if I'd ever played a little game called Diablo—this has been an experience I will never forget.

To the Duck Room—you know who you are, but particularly Stephen, Jayne, Arielle, and Bob—thank you for being such stalwart supporters through this process. I am lucky to be surrounded by such thoughtful, kind, and *forgiving* co-workers. Quack!

To the real-life Lailastrasza, Atyrannus, Rygos, Cristalstrasz, Stahlien, Tahlien, Zorastia, and Timaeustrasz—I am so grateful our shared virtual worlds brought you into my life. Together, we have conquered dragons of all kinds, some real, and some made of pixels . . . but I know how lucky I am to have you at my back. And *speaking* of lucky . . . to my beloved buns, Katoah, Dack, and the rest of our crew, your smiling faces sustained me through countless, relentless long days. I treasure our friendships and the communities we've built together. Much love.

Finally, to all the champions of Azeroth—thank you for making our world so vibrant and alive. Wherever you travel in the world, may the Aspects watch over you.

ABOUT THE AUTHOR

COURTNEY ALAMEDA is a novelist, comic book writer, and lifelong gamer. After almost fifteen years of writing professionally, there are few mediums, genres, and forms Courtney hasn't had the chance to work in, though the novel remains her favorite. She started playing World of Warcraft in 2015 and has been a denizen of Azeroth ever since.

Born and raised in the San Francisco Bay Area, she now resides in the northwestern United States with her husband, one Welsh corgi, two cats, three library rooms, and whatever monsters lurk in the rural darkness around her home.

courtneyalameda.com
Twitter: @courtalameda

WORLD OF WARCRAFT: SHADOWS RISING

By Madeleine Roux

"The Horde is nothing!"

With those infamous words, Sylvanas Windrunner betrayed and abandoned the Horde she vowed to serve. The Dark Lady and her forces now work in the shadows as both the Horde and Alliance race to uncover her next move. Struggling to shoulder the crushing weight of leadership, King Anduin entrusts Alleria Windrunner and High Exarch Turalyon to discover Sylvanas's whereabouts. Meanwhile, the Dark Lady has tasked Nathanos Blightcaller and Sira Moonwarden with a terrifying gambit: to kill the troll loa of death himself, Bwonsamdi.

The Horde now stands at a crossroads. The various factions form a council, leaving the mantle of warchief to rest. But the threats are numerous, and the distrust runs too deep. When the council is derailed by a failed assassination attempt on Talanji—the Zandalari queen and a key ally—Thrall and the rest of the Horde leaders empower the young troll shaman Zekhan with a critical mission to aid Talanji in thwarting the rising threat against her.

As Zekhan and Talanji work to save Bwonsamdi, their journey will be a key turning point in bolstering the Horde against the coming darkness and finding themselves along the way. Failure to save their allies and the trickster god will surely doom them—but through success, they may rediscover what makes the Horde strong.

WORLD OF WARCRAFT: SYLVANAS

By Christie Golden

Ranger-General. Banshee Queen. Warchief.

Sylvanas Windrunner has borne many titles. To some, she is a hero— to others, a villain. But whether in pursuit of justice, vengeance, or something more, Sylvanas has always sought to control her own destiny.

The power to achieve her goals has never been closer as Sylvanas works alongside the Jailer to liberate all Azeroth from the prison of fate. Her final task? Secure the fealty of their prisoner—King Anduin Wrynn.

To succeed, Sylvanas will be forced to reflect on the harrowing path that brought her to the Jailer's side and to reveal her truest self to her greatest rival. Here, Sylvanas's complete story is laid bare: the breaking of the Windrunner family and her rise to ranger-general; her own death at the hands of Arthas and her renewed purpose in founding the Forsaken; the moment she first beheld the Maw and understood the true consequences of what lay beyond the veil of death.

But as her moment of victory draws near, Sylvanas Windrunner will make a choice that may ultimately come to define her. A choice that's hers to make.

For more fantastic fiction, author events,
exclusive excerpts, competitions, limited editions and more

VISIT OUR WEBSITE
titanbooks.com

LIKE US ON FACEBOOK
facebook.com/titanbooks

FOLLOW US ON TWITTER, TIKTOK AND INSTAGRAM
@TitanBooks

EMAIL US
readerfeedback@titanemail.com